INNOCENT DARKNESS

By Edward R. F. Sheehan

FICTION

Kingdom of Illusion
The Governor
Invincible Ignorance

NONFICTION

The Arabs, the Israelis, and Kissinger:
A Secret History of American Policy in the Middle East
Agony in the Garden:
A Stranger in Central America
BENNETT CERF'S TAKE ALONG TREASURY
Leonora Hornblow & Bennett Cerf, eds.
Evelyn Waugh

GREAT TRUE SPY STORIES
Allen Dulles, ed.
Kim Philby

EXPLORING PSYCHOLOGY
Ivan McCollom & Nancy L. Badore, eds.
Conversations with Konrad Lorenz

DRAMA

Kingdoms
American Innocence

INNOCENT DARKNESS

EDWARD R. F. SHEEHAN

VIKING

VIKING
Published by the Penguin Group
Viking Penguin, a division of Penguin Books USA Inc.,
375 Hudson Street, New York, New York 10014, U.S.A.
Penguin Books Ltd, 27 Wrights Lane, London W8 5TZ, England
Penguin Books Australia Ltd, Ringwood, Victoria, Australia
Penguin Books Canada Ltd, 10 Alcorn Avenue, Suite 300,
Toronto, Ontario, Canada M4V 3B2
Penguin Books (N.Z.) Ltd, 182–190 Wairau Road,
Auckland 10, New Zealand

Penguin Books Ltd, Registered Offices:
Harmondsworth, Middlesex, England

First published in 1993 by Viking Penguin,
a division of Penguin Books USA Inc.

1 3 5 7 9 10 8 6 4 2

PUBLISHER'S NOTE

This is a work of fiction. Names, characters, places, and incidents either are the product of the author's imagination or are used fictitiously, and any resemblance to actual persons, living or dead, events, or locales is entirely coincidental.

Grateful acknowledgment is made for permission to reprint excerpts from "Just Across the Rio Grande" by Don Cook and Chick Rains. Copyright © 1986 Cross Keys Publishing Co., Inc./Choskee Bottom Music (ASCAP), a division of Terrace Entertainment Corp. All rights on behalf of Cross Keys administered by Sony Music Publishing, 8 Music Square West, Nashville, TN 37203. Reprinted by permission of the publishers.

The author gratefully acknowledges several ideas on the life of St. Francis of Assisi contained in *Frére François*, Editions du Seuil, 1983, by Julien Green of the Académie Française.

LIBRARY OF CONGRESS CATALOGING IN PUBLICATION DATA
Sheehan, Edward R. F.
Innocent darkness / Edward R. F. Sheehan.
p.   cm.
ISBN 0–670–84779–8
I. Title.
PS3569.H3923I5   1993
813'.54—dc   92–50387

Printed in the United States of America
Set in Sabon
Designed by Francesca Belanger

A.M.D.G.

*For my mother Emilie, for Baldramina,
and for my son, Adonay Edward Sheehan*

Everything was so much simpler in a world still ruled by the innocent darkness of instinct. There is no limit to the trouble caused by the human privilege of reflection. Scarcely has it been exercised it gives rise to more disorder in a single mind than would be needed to tear the universe apart.

HENRI DE LUBAC

AUTHOR'S NOTE

The characters and events in this novel are fictitious. However, during recent time I spent some months in the Rio Grande Valley of Texas and in Mexico, and in many respects my story is true in spirit to what I saw. I have been, I'm afraid, rather too kind in my portrayal of the Mexican police. Occasionally, for convenience, I have rearranged geography slightly and given false names to real places, though I doubt that my contrivances will deceive many residents of that extraordinary region.

PART I

Snow

▼▼▼

Adrian John Northwood loved the snow almost as much as he disliked the modern world on which it fell. When he was a child, his father had taken him to Austria to watch him ski, and in Paris once during a rare blizzard he threw snowballs from the belfry of Notre-Dame at ghostly pedestrians he glimpsed below. He enjoyed the change of seasons around his home, but he preferred winter and the whiteness that covered his lawns. It was snowing, slightly, on the morning that he asked his wife to drive their son to the dentist.

"No," she said.

"Please. I'm late for class."

"Why go? They laugh at you."

"Less than you do."

She was a sensuous woman with dark hair, still recumbent beneath the covers of their bed. The boy, as blond as he, and just turned six, romped in.

"You drive him," she said.

"A child needs his mother at the dentist's."

"A child who prefers his father? You're too fond of him."

The boy hugged his boots, begging him not to leave, but he had no time and dashed to work. When his wife set out for the dentist's, the snow was heavier. She went off a cliff. Her body flew out of the car as it overturned, and she landed so violently on the rocks she died instantly. The boy—their only child—died as uncomfortably in the car. He was decapitated. At the funeral, new snow fell.

Adrian's sorrow at home was compounded by his vexations at The University. He was associate professor in the Academy of Art, but he and the Director tended to quarrel. "Sorry about your wife and son, Northwood," the Director said.

Adrian turned away his etched face, gazing out of the jagged window at the snow. Not only the windows were jagged in the Academy of Art.

Some years before, the Director had announced an international competition to design a new building to house the Academy, but he was unsatisfied with the submissions, so he designed it himself. He wished the building to reflect the disorder and darkness of modern life. It did not bother him that his architecture clashed with the graceful Georgian that surrounded it: such was his purpose.

Thus the place resembled a huge contusion. It rose out of the snow like a vast lump, a heap of cement patched with irregular, opaque windows. Inside, the Academy was a labyrinth of concrete stairwells, steel doors, and cement urns full of black gravel. From various nooks, cement thorns and cactus plants thrust out. "These are the thistles of our age," the Director proudly told awed visitors. Though he went to the Academy often, Adrian never got used to its perils; he kept colliding with cement thorns. No paintings hung in the Academy, only pink mirrors: they softened the scars on the Director's face.

Adrian might eventually have reconciled himself to this environment were it not for the Director's concept of the column. In designing the Academy, the Director had decided to reinvent the column. "The column must cease to be perpendicular," he told his pupils. "It must become horizontal." The result of his reinvention was that the cement columns of the Academy required low ceilings, consumed much of the available space, and resembled wide ham sandwiches. Even after the Academy was built, Adrian continued to quarrel with the Director over his reinvention of the column.

"There are only three kinds of column," Adrian insisted. "Doric, Ionic, and Corinthian."

"You are too classical, Northwood," the Director said.

No sooner had the Director tendered his condolences than he and Adrian resumed their argument about columns. He added, "I wonder whether you could ever be happy here, Northwood. You have no talent."

"I draw well," Adrian protested.

"You draw faithfully," the Director rejoined. "Your pictures are imitations, and you are too devoted to dead tastes. There is no future for the Baroque."

As the Director spoke, Adrian revisited Salzburg, admiring marble fountains. Faintly, a few bars of chamber music, but the Director intruded. "Northwood?"

"Will the Academy ever give me tenure?" Adrian asked.

"No," the Director said. He added a twist: was it only half a joke? "Perhaps, Northwood, you should buy your own academy."

It was thus in the throes of remorse and failure that Adrian resolved to change his life. Though our relations were difficult, he turned to me. "What shall I do?" he asked.

"Where did all this start?" I asked.

"In the snow," said Adrian.

"Why not go south?" I said.

It snowed again on Adrian's last day at home. In his bedroom, he gave a goodbye glance at his marriage bed, then stuffed some painting materials into one bag and some dollars (rather a few) into another. He bade a strained farewell to his mother. When he emerged from the house, the lawns he loved were enveloped in a snowy mist. He got into the old car he had bought for his journey and drove to the cemetery at the far corner of the Park. He paused first at the tomb of his father, remembering happy moments and forgiving him his little fault. And as he shivered in the wind, he knelt at the white graves of his wife and son, crossing himself and trying to pray. Finally he fled and headed south. I should mention that all of this happened as Adrian John Northwood entered his thirty-second year. You will wonder who I am, but I shan't intrude often.

PART II

Amígoland

▼▼▼

2

Adrian drove aimlessly south, uncertain of his destination. He supposed that eventually he might reach Mexico. As he crossed Virginia, the skies turned blue and the sun seemed warmer. But Alabama became a blur, and in Louisiana his eyes could not focus even on the eerie swamps of bayou country. Nor was he sure of what he thought of Texas. At Corpus Christi, he lived in a cheap motel and swam at the public beach, where he was bothered by the jellyfish.

The blobs were everywhere. Children on the beach called them "cabbage heads." They were transparent; their insides were networks of brown tubes, and their heads resembled the ragged stems of cabbages. Adrian avoided them on the beach, but he could not avoid them in the sea. Wherever he swam, he brushed against this floating slime, not just the big slime but the newly born, the shape of golf balls. At night, jellyfish floated through his dreams.

For days, he remained in his motel room and watched television. A satellite dish stood beyond his bathroom window, and he had his choice of fifty channels. The pornographic films all seemed identical. In California, a robot had learned to talk grammatically, improvise words, sentences, and lucid paragraphs. In New York, an actress talked about her new book: "I've finally confronted my fears. In Hollywood, I hated myself. Here, I've fallen in love with me. Now that I'm off cocaine, I get high on my fears. Will I always be alone? Please love my autobiography." *I'll wait for the robot's,* thought Adrian. In Iowa, a couple were married in a laundromat, Duds 'n' Suds. The bride: "We met here. On our honeymoon in Des Moines we'll wash our underwear at Duds 'n' Suds." During the wedding, other customers went on doing their laundry. After the wedding, guests threw detergent instead of rice. Adrian resumed his journey to the south.

In the Rio Grande Valley, the southernmost tip of Texas, as he entered Downsville, the sun vanished, the skies opened, and he was caught in a rainstorm so torrential he feared it might wash away his car. He managed to get off the highway, only to find that the streets were flooded; water was percolating through his floorboards, and his engine protested. He sputtered forward, to drier ground, and found himself on a boulevard lined with palm trees and motels. He decided to spend the night, and slept in the Motel 5½, where he shared his tiny room with cockroaches. In the morning, the sun broiled, Downsville was all wet heat, and he had trouble starting his car.

He drove the machine in fits and jerks to a garage surrounded by a junkyard. He marveled at this immense cemetery of smooth tires and heaped wrecks, beneath a huge red sign, painted on a truck trailer: TRASHED. Mingled with the tires and car wrecks were fragments of rusty machinery, the overturned ends of cement mixers, gears, wheels, bolts, boilers, the size of monsters. A squat Mexican in sunglasses and a white sombrero jumped out of the trailer. "You want somethin'?" he asked.

"Something's wrong with my car," Adrian said. "I think it's the carburetor."

The Mexican lifted the hood. "It's more than the carburetor," he said. "It's the whole car. *Chinga,* look at that engine. You got more rust on your wheels than I got in my junkyard. What happen to your floorboards? This gotta be the first Datsun they ever built."

"I like it," Adrian said.

"It's a shit box."

"That's why I bought it."

"I can't fix this car."

Adrian regarded the junkman in his dirty sombrero. He wondered, Is there something deeper to this stage Mexican than what I see? Could he have anything that resembles a soul? The Mexican crackled some cellophane, offering him a moist tortilla chip. Adrian refused it, fished in his pocket, took out two hundred dollars in small bills. "Here's my deposit. Fix my car by noon?"

"Only two kinds people drive junky cars," the Mexican answered, refusing the money, "dirty poor and dirty rich. Poor, they're Mexicans, illegals mostly. Rich, they're all drug dealers. The Feds are onto them, so they dump their BMWs and drive around in junky cars. You a rich guy?"

"Do I look rich?" Adrian wore scuffed fashion sneakers without socks, faded gray jeans over his tall legs, a torn white T-shirt. The hot wind rippled his profuse blond hair and made the T-shirt cling to his flat stomach.

"You're too good-lookin' to be poor," the Mexican said. "Where you from?"

"The north."

"Where in the north?"

"The north."

Adrian's eye wandered over the junkyard, coming to rest on cars much like his own. The Mexican saw his chance. He said, "You want a good junky car? A junky car that runs? Come on, follow me. See the Volvo? Look at that rust. See that Chevy? Fenders half gone. Look at that Buick! Twenty years old! Falling apart! This is a *vintage* junky car."

"How much?" asked Adrian.

"I get a lotta drug dealers in here," the Mexican said, "so I'm not cheap. *Chinga*, I'll make you special price. Three thousand dollars."

Adrian fished in his pocket, took out four hundred dollars. "I prefer my own junky car," he said. "Fix it."

"It'll cost you."

"Fix it."

"It'll take a week."

"I'll wait."

In the sun, Adrian walked the several miles home to his motel:

it did not occur to him to rent a car. (Was he the only pedestrian in Texas?) At the motel, he realized that he was stuck in Downsville knowing no one and with nothing to do. He showered, changed clothes, fed quarters to machines outside his room for a junk-food lunch, watched television, turned it off and read a book, but the pages swam as despite himself he mourned again for his wife and son. He did eighty push-ups, wrote a letter to his mother, did ninety push-ups, unpacked his painting materials and went out to sketch. His motel stood not far from a boulevard called Boca Chica, so he strolled its length and sketched its wonders.

Beneath a bleak hazy sky, the telephone poles of Boca Chica stretched on as though forever, on a flat asphalt meadow unblemished by trees or sidewalks. Bareheaded beneath the unfocused sun, Adrian crouched on the asphalt and—with charcoal pencil or with pastel chalk, on scraps of white paper—sketched swiftly what he saw: green Dumpsters, gasoline stations, Movieland Video, and Mister Donut. He strode onward, under a stoplight, over railroad tracks, to AUTO ZONE Discount Auto Parts, Brakes Alignments Shocks Hitches Mufflers Air Conditioners, thence to a Service Center, PEP BOYS, with colored statuary of three mechanics in overalls enshrined on a cement pedestal.

The red roof of Pizza Hut resembled a Renaissance cardinal's hat. He came to a shopping mall: pawnshops, National LUBE & TUNE, Academy of Beauty, and soon enough to palaces of fast food—Burger King, Wendy's Old Fashioned Hamburgers, Bandidos Barbecue, Ernie's B-B-Q To Go, Peter Piper Pizza, Church's Chicken, Pick-a-Chick, the gables of Whataburger (OPEN 24 HOURS), which spelled a W, and the ineffable golden arches of McDonald's aspiring above the Dumpsters atop brilliant red poles.

Adrian sketched people too, though he had always had trouble with the human form, and in the shopping mall his tracings of the living ebb and flow lacked movement and suggested scarecrows. Outside Movieland Video, in the parking lots of Mister Donut, Burger King, Whataburger, Peter Piper Pizza, Pick-a-Chick, he was intrigued by the adolescents, or rather by their T-shirts: KICK ASS . . . SPRING BREAK . . . THE KINKS LIVE . . . SSSSSLIPPERY WHEN

WET . . . I BRAKE FOR WEEDS! . . . WHO YOU GONNA SLIME, GHOST-
BUSTERS??? . . . KRAZY KAT KANTINA: FORGET THE TIME, FORGET
THE SALT, FORGET YOUR NAME.

Some adolescents wore earphones, and though the melodies of
their headsets were supposed to be private, the sound seeped out
and Adrian heard rap lyrics and heavy-metal rock. For his own
music, he needed no earphones. He kept an orchestra in his head,
silent much of the time but ever tuned to his subconscious wish,
producing noble melodies with clearer resonance than ever reigned
in the gadget of an adolescent. He played the music backward and
forward, interrupting notes, half notes, quarter notes, to linger over
phrases that especially pleased him. He enjoyed the conversations
between violin and flute in Mozart's first flute quartet, savoring
them as he watched KICK ASS and SSSSSLIPPERY WHEN WET emerge
from Whataburger chewing french-fried potatoes. He played a few
bars from the final movement of the "Linz" Symphony for SPRING
BREAK and brought up the trumpets of Haydn's first movement of
the "Maria Theresia" for THE KINKS LIVE. He shot the verses of
Mozart's *Ave Verum* at the pimpled face of I BRAKE FOR WEEDS!
*Ave verum corpus, natum de Maria virgine . . . Esto nobis prae-
gustatum in mortis examine.*

Mortis made him think of his wife and son. For them he played
Schubert's first piano trio in B flat. How he loved the haunting,
mournful cello. Da-dum-ta-*deee*-dum. Da-dum-ta-ta-ta-*deee*-dum.
No composer could sustain a melody as Schubert could: not even
Mozart. He played the cello passage often; on the road from the
north to Downsville he had played it constantly. Da-dum-ta-*deee*-
dum. Da-dum-ta-ta-ta-*deee*-dum. He could not FORGET THE TIME,
FORGET THE SNOW, FORGET HIS NAME.

He returned to his desolate motel room to eat more junk food
—potato chips, Mars bars, Coca-Cola Classic—and to transform
his sketches into watercolors and some to oils. A bit giddy from
his exposure to the hazy sun, he stayed up all night, painting ma-
niacally until noon. His pride still burned from the Director's accusation that he had no talent, that his pictures were imitations,

too devoted to dead tastes. He was resolved to create something original.

He was ever aware of T. S. Eliot's dictum, "Before you decide to break the rules, it is best to learn them." Adrian knew all the rules, so now he broke them. Turning off his air conditioner (he disliked air-conditioning), he stood in bathing trunks before his easel in the hot monastic room and began his creations, wielding his brush from right to left in fast strokes. For once, he would abandon the Baroque and reproduce the landscape of Boca Chica as his soul perceived it.

He faithfully represented the telephone poles of Boca Chica on the asphalt meadow, then by degrees introduced slight distortions of the gasoline stations and green Dumpsters. Movieland Video and Mister Donut he made only mildly more odd. By the time he had done with Brakes Alignments Shocks, National LUBE & TUNE, Academy of Beauty, and started to address the fast-food palaces, he became outlandish. A demon took possession of his brush, and he turned the crimson roof of Pizza Hut into a true cardinal's hat, tassels dangling. The golden arches of McDonald's became a baldachin above the cardinal's hat, and the gabled W of Whataburger sprouted into wings, hovering above them like a bird of prey. He added T-shirts—KICK ASS, THE KINKS LIVE, SSSSSLIPPERY WHEN WET—floating in the air, and with them earphones, cabbage-head jellyfish, and gray cherubs, all decapitated.

As a Boschian vision of American culture, really it was not bad, or at least I thought so. (Forgive me: I promised not to intrude.) I wished to tell him, "Stop there!" but I remained silent, and even had I spoken he might have ignored me.

When the moist dawn squinted through the drawn curtains of his room, another demon seized him. He had begun his paintings on the right side, but as he approached the left side of his tableaux, more and more he blended his figments of gasoline stations, green Dumpsters, the arches of McDonald's, the gables of Whataburger, T-shirts, jellyfish, with Baroque elegance.

From perfect memory, he interpolated the *Pferdeschwemme,* the marble horse fountain in Salzburg's Sigmundsplatz. The horse pranced on his hind legs, front hooves rising in the air, as though defying gravity and about to gallop into space. He pranced upon a scrolled pedestal, in the midst of a green pond, surrounded by a swirling balustrade. Behind him stood murals of other prancing horses, and in the center a winged horse flying heavenward as beneath him a mere man tumbled from grace. The murals were framed by Grecian pilasters, modified Ionic, surmounted by urns, and in the center atop the Grecian arch sat a naked god and a naked goddess. Adrian heightened the Ionic columns, until finally they dominated his last tableau and soared above the gasoline stations, Mister Donut, Pizza Hut, the arches of McDonald's, the gables of Whataburger, jellyfish, and KICK ASS.

Many critics might have said, "You have mocked Eliot, broken all the rules, and intolerably confused your styles. Your paintings are grotesque." No more grotesque than Adrian's room: by noon it was a shambles of putty rubber, cartridge paper, ragged canvas, oily rags, bottles of turpentine and linseed oil, dippers, palette knives, hog-hair brushes, ox-ear brushes, and tubes of oozing paint. The bare floor and white walls were spattered with vermilion, viridian, Antwerp blue. Adrian's torso was wet with sweat and splashings of rose madder, mars yellow, and burnt umber. He showered, slept for a few hours, then—fed up for now with junk food—returned to Boca Chica, looking for a decent place to eat.

Eventually he chose Whataburger, because it was so cheap. The hamburger left a lump in his stomach. He wandered up and down Boca Chica, burping. The sun set, and as darkness fell the harsh neon illumining the boulevard made him hungry for human company. At the edge of the road, outside Pick-a-Chick, a human chicken waved to passing cars, beckoning them to Pick-a-Chick's parking lot and the delights of that restaurant. Adrian paused to observe this creature.

He was clad from head to foot in a costume of puffy foam plastic: yellow webbed feet, a white floppy tail, a great yellow beak, and a red crest that fluttered in the hot wind. For an instant he lifted the head of his costume open a crack, as though gasping for air. Adrian approached him and said, "Good evening, sir."

"*¿Cómo?*"

Adrian was startled, not because the chicken had replied in Spanish, but because the chicken was a young woman. Through the grille of the great beak he glimpsed her mouth: mauve and sensuous, like his late wife's. Adrian asked, "*¿Qué tal, señorita?*"

She shrank from him, running from the parking lot back to the road, beckoning to passing cars, but he followed her. He said, "Don't be afraid, I have no friends," and he said it in flawless Spanish. (One of various tongues he spoke, and nothing to boast about: his father had told him once, "The stupidest man I ever knew spoke fifty languages.") He asked, "Why are you afraid?"

"Do you work for *la Migra?*" she asked in Spanish.

"*¿La Migra?*"

"Immigration. The police."

"No."

"You do!"

"I don't. I'm from the north. I have no friends."

"Ah. *Entonces quiere dormir conmigo.*" Then you want to sleep with me.

"No. Please. Are you Mexican?"

"Salvadoran. I have a child."

"Where's the child?"

"In El Salvador with my mother. They have to eat."

"How much does Pick-a-Chick pay you?"

"Fifty dollars a week."

"Are you hot inside your chicken suit?"

"*Como pollo frito.*" Like fried chicken.

She was so frightened he left her there, at the edge of the road, but in the evenings that followed he dined at Pick-a-Chick and afterward without fail he spoke to her, exchanging pleasantries in the parking lot. She revealed little of her personal history, but as the nights passed she seemed less fearful, and indeed she had a lovely laugh as she talked of her infant daughter splashing water in a wooden bathtub. He never asked the woman's name, but she was his only friend in Downsville. On the fifth night, he gave her five hundred dollars in cash for her child in El Salvador. On the sixth night, when he approached the human chicken and glanced inside the grille of the great beak, a man was standing there.

"Where's the Salvadoran girl?" Adrian asked in Spanish.

"Immigration pick her up," the man replied in English.

"You're not Salvadoran?"

"Mexican. Legal, and I got card to prove it. You from *la Migra?*"

"No."

"Then f——off."

Adrian returned to his motel, mourning the loss of his friend. From memory he tried to paint her portrait in the chicken suit, but he was ravaged by loneliness and achieved nothing. His room was still a bedlam of oily rags, putty rubber, and his paintings, which he hated. The walls, spattered with rose madder, burnt umber, Antwerp blue, became a suffocating vise. How he missed his little son. His flight from the north he had intended as an act of atonement, but its result was emptiness. His orchestra played, but now he could not modulate the notes, and the sound in his head was deafening. Da-dum-ta-*deee*-dum. He raged about the room, hurling his tableaux and tubes of paint against the walls, sobbing. DA-DUM-TA-*DEEE*-DUM. At home, his mother might have said, "Oh, Adrian, not another *childish* tantrum."

3

Next morning, eager to leave Downsville, he stuffed his pockets with dollars and jogged to the junkyard to retrieve his car. The squat Mexican in sunglasses jumped out of the trailer and said, "*Chinga*, I fix your junky car."

He lifted the hood of Adrian's ancient Datsun. The engine gleamed, brand-new. The floorboards had been replaced and covered with clean blue carpeting. The exterior remained a mess, all dents and peeling paint, but the tires were new and the wheels also, painted brown with sand mixed in to make them seem rusty. Adrian sighed and said, "Not exactly what I had in mind. How much?"

"*Chinga*, you really fool the Feds now."

"Ha-ha!" This perhaps was the first time that Adrian had laughed since the morning of his tragedy, and as he laughed the hot sunshine glanced against his perfect teeth and made them sparkle. "So you still think I'm a drug dealer?"

"Maybe. I know you're a rich guy."

"How?

"Me, I come from shit. Look this junkyard. *Chinga*, I still live in shit. You try and hide it, but I know a rich guy when I see one."

"All right. How much?"

"Four thousand bucks."

Adrian remained amused. (His father: "Only two things, dear child, are more vulgar than having money. The first is boasting of it. The second is fighting over it.") He fished in his pocket and paid the Mexican in cash without complaint.

He returned to Motel 5½ in his counterfeit junky car and left it in the parking lot. He went out walking. He felt more cheerful, more curious about the life of the valley beyond Boca Chica. His instinct told him, Don't leave just yet. Perhaps he hoped to meet another lovely human chicken. As the days passed, beneath the awful sun, he walked or ran many miles over the flat domain of Downsville. Often as he jogged, he paused in farmland or in empty lots to do fifty or sixty push-ups. He wondered, Is this my therapy? One afternoon, seeking a soft-drink machine to satisfy his thirst, he discovered Amigoland.

Amigoland, miles south of Boca Chica, was a vast shopping plaza. Beneath roofs of mock red tile, buildings of ersatz white adobe housed Walgreens, Wal-Mart, Firestone, Payless Shoe Source, on one side of the wide highway, and Weiner's clothing and K mart on the other. As Adrian lingered in a parking lot, sipping his Coca-Cola Classic, slipping his body between countless chromium car bumpers, watching rich Mexicans emerge from the shopping palaces laden with toiletries and video machines, he glimpsed new glories for his bastard art. Ah, how defiantly he would confute this spectacle with his Ionic towers!

Thereafter he ran to Amigoland late each afternoon, a canvas sack flopping against his flank, full of charcoal pencils, pastel chalk, and scraps of white paper. He felt ever more cheerful, grateful that once again he could modulate the notes, half notes, quarter notes, of Mozart and Schubert singing so often inside his head. Before the sun had set, invariably he took his dinner at Amigoland, and invariably at the same place—just inside the atrium at Wyatt Cafeteria. He enjoyed Wyatt's because among the staples along the stainless-steel serving counter he could always find hot corn on the cob; not an evening passed without his feast of corn on the cob. Besides, at his motel the receptionist had handed him some coupons granting him a discount—on a six-dollar dinner he saved sixty cents! After dinner, he wandered through the atrium and the lustrous, air-conditioned corridors of the mall, sketching whatever caught his fancy. People jammed the place, he heard an incessant human din, and the shops were a cornucopia: plastic bathroom scales, silver coffeepots, diamond earrings. From loudspeakers throughout the mall, a woman sang a country song.

> The lights of Laredo
> Dance on the water
> And shine in a young man's eyes
> Who stands on the border
> And dreams of para-dise.

> He's heard crazy stories
> Of how people live
> Over in the Promised Land.
> He heard they eat three meals a day
> Just across the Rio Grande.

Pearl necklaces, Jordache luggage, Cool Touch waffle cookers.

> He's got a wife named Maria
> And a baby named Rose
> And another one to feed on the way—
> Two willing hands that couldn't find work today.
> He stares at the river and curses the future
>   that he cain't understand.
> He knows the child would have the chance
> Just across the Rio Grande.

Electric shavers, exercise machines, charbroil gas grills, Jacquard blouses, Reebok sneakers, sleeping bags, tackle boxes, fishing poles, ten-speed bicycles, electric trains, word processors, cordless telephones, Seiko watches, Minolta cameras, Hawken rifles, navy Colt revolvers, Vidal Sassoon hair curlers, Black & Decker cordless electric screwdrivers, Batman masks, Batman music, Batman videocassettes, Dearfoam's Hush Puppies.

> It's only a river
> That's not so deep or wide

> A boy can throw a stone across
> And reach the other side.
> It's just a muddy water
> Cuttin' through the land
> But a man can make a dream come true
> Just across the Rio Grande.

By now Adrian was in Wal-Mart, sketching the housepaint and glue department. Another cornucopia: Dutch Boy housepaint, Bondex concrete patch, Fashion Fresh ceiling paint, The Fresh Look fast-drying spray enamel, Formby's paint remover, silver spray, gold gilt spray, Rely-On roof cement, Elmer's glue, Krazy Glue, and WilHold. From the corner of his eye he noticed several thin and ragged children, reaching up on the racks to touch the tubes of glue and cans of spray paint and giggling as children do. Are they Mexican boys from the other side? Adrian wondered.

> The lights of Laredo
> Dance on the water
> And shine in a young man's eyes
> Who stands on the border
> And dreams of para-dise.
>
> He's heard crazy stories
> Of how good life is
> Over in the Promised Land.
> And sometimes it seems
> Like God must live
> Just across the Rio Grande.

A uniformed security guard approached the boys, and in a burst of giggling the boys went crazy. They grabbed whatever tubes of glue and cans of spray paint their small brown hands could carry, and dashed away from the guard toward the doors.

> It's only a river
> That's not so deep or wide
> A boy can throw a stone across
> And reach the other side.

By the checkout counters other guards appeared and began to chase the five or six boys up and down the bountiful aisles of Wal-Mart. The boys snatched whatever else they could—candy bars, women's panties, T-shirts—and dashed again toward the doors.

> It's just a muddy water
> Cuttin' through the land
> But a man can make a dream come true
> Just across the Rio Grande.

The guards regrouped between the checkout counters and the main doors; amid much shouting, kicking, punching, crashing of tin cans, they seized five boys. The sixth, a tiny fellow in a filthy T-shirt, FUNKY COLD, managed to escape them and ran out of Wal-Mart.

> Sometimes it seems
> Like God must live
> Just across the Rio Grande.

Adrian followed him. The sun, weirdly umber in the thick heat, lowered westward and blinded Adrian as he chased the child through the flashing bumpers of the parking lot. Why am I chasing him? he wondered. He lost the child. Distressed, he retreated toward Wal-Mart, then decided to explore the high grass of a vacant lot nearby.

In the high grass he found him, crouching, indifferent, and dazed. The urchin had removed his shirt and sprayed his torso with a can of chrome paint. Puffs of silver hovered in the air, enveloping him in mist. Puzzled, Adrian watched the child raise the can to his face, depress the nozzle, and squirt the paint on his lips and nose. Deeply the child inhaled, then twitched in the grass, groaning with pleasure.

How old is he? Adrian wondered. He looked about six or seven but seemed so undernourished, might he not have been older? His black hair was close-cropped, he wore dirty khaki shorts, and he was barefoot. By his side reposed his green T-shirt, FUNKY COLD, the can of paint, and a plastic package of hot dogs. His eyes, when at last he opened them, were a brilliant red. He squinted up at Adrian.

"*¿Trabaja por la Migra?*" You work for Immigration? he asked.

"No. *¿Hijo, cómo te llamas?*" Son, what is your name?

As Adrian moved closer, the child panicked. He snatched the can of paint, T-shirt, hot dogs, and leaped to his feet. Adrian lunged to hold him, but the urchin was elusive. As he brushed by, Adrian caught the foul odor of his breath. The boy ran through the grass, out of the field toward the highway. Adrian might well have overtaken him, but as he emerged from the field his foot hit a rock and he stumbled. He wondered, Why am I chasing him?

The child dashed across the highway, through the parking lot of K mart, past a radio tower in a field of grass, Adrian again in pursuit. Palm trees, railroad tracks, clusters of gray vegetation, flew by: the child disappeared over an embankment. Adrian stumbled downward after him and caught him in high reeds at the river's edge. They wrestled, and in that struggle Adrian was not the master: the urchin was hysterically strong, as though compelled by his chromium trance. "I want to feed you," Adrian gasped. Screaming, the child bit Adrian's bare arm and broke free. Clutching his T-shirt, he ran along the river's edge, tore off his khaki shorts, and, with the clothes clumped atop his head, waded naked to the other shore. He stood there in the sunset, still naked, his ribs protruding from his painted torso, fingering his carrot-shaped phallus indecently and howling at Adrian.

"*¡Puta!*" Whore!

"*Gracias,*" Adrian replied gently across the narrow Rio Grande. "What's your name?"

"*¡A veinte!*" Up yours!

"Where do you live, *hijo?*"

"*¡Safo!*" Get screwed!

"Where's your mother?"

"*¡Me la pelas!*" Kiss my ass!

"*¿Y tus hermanitos y hermanitas?*" Any little brothers and sisters?

"*¡Chinga tu madre!*" F—— your mother!

"I'd rather not."

Again the urchin gestured indecently, then he hopped into his filthy shorts and FUNKY COLD and scrambled upward through the high grass of the opposite shore. "What's your name? Where do you live?" Adrian called after him. The child vanished into Mexico.

Adrian stood miserably in the United States, holding his souvenirs of their encounter, the can of chrome paint and the plastic package of hot dogs. He gazed at the hot dogs. Did I steal his supper? he wondered. He wandered along the twisting river.

The sun had half set, its color transformed from burnt umber to the blazing crimson of the child's eyes. Adrian looked about him, to the Gateway Bridge, where multitudes of feet were shuffling above the river in and out of Mexico, and to the railway bridge not far away, where barriers of barbed wire could not deter a dozen children from entering the United States: they hung suspended by their fingers from the high steel girders, swinging their small bodies with the grace of monkeys and progressing inch by inch toward the Promised Land. As dusk descended, the length of river grew alive with traffic; the evening echoed with barking dogs and contending human voices.

Naked men and boys loitered on the Mexican bank, chattering and laughing as they dumped their pants and underwear into transparent plastic bags. A pregnant woman, fully clothed, waded across the river to the United States, but no sooner had she touched the shore than a pale-green van, U.S. BORDER PATROL, halted on the levee and two agents in olive drab leaped out. The woman crouched in the high grass, but gently they arrested her, sealed her in the van, and drove off. Once the van was out of sight, the naked males began their own migration.

In irregular waves, they swam across the water holding the plastic bags aloft with single hands or clutching them to their heads, shouting vulgar Spanish as they groped for the United States. Upon the shore, they discarded the bags and crouched among the reeds, rubbing themselves with leaves and grass to dry their bodies before they put on their clothes and shoes. They sent a boy up the embankment to reconnoiter, and when he had whistled or shouted

"*¡No hay la Migra!*" they moved en masse upward and over the levee to dash toward Downsville.

Night fell. The human tide increased. Whole families, middle-aged men in straw hats, youths, girls, women bearing bundled infants, were wading fully clothed across the Rio Grande—the Río Bravo, as Mexicans knew it—or seeking rocks between the shores so they might walk. Some carried leather bags or cardboard suitcases, a youth had a bicycle, a girl had a dog, and they babbled in different dialects of Spanish. Adrian wondered, Where are they from? Not all from Mexico. Colombia? Peru? Isn't there a civil war in El Salvador, or is it Nicaragua? Are they Nicaraguans? Salvadorans? Is this where the first world and the third world meet? The night sky was bright, not with the moon or stars but with the reflected lamps of Downsville, of Boca Chica, of Amigoland, of so many malls: and yes, they danced on the water.

Voices muttered, and now they sounded sinister. Men lurked in bushes, behind trees, and in the reflected light, knives glinted. A woman cried out; a child sobbed. A shadow, one hand with a Coca-Cola can, the other with a gun, advanced on Adrian, but his prey was too swift. Adrian fled the shadow over the levee and railway, through the fields of grass, back toward Amigoland—and to Wal-Mart with the urchin's hot dogs and can of paint, to pay for them. "Thanks," the cashier said; she was young, pretty, Mexican-American. "Oh, them chicleros."

"*¿Chicleros?*"

"Chiclet kids, you know? From the other side, you know? They sell chewing gum on the bridge." She rang up Adrian's purchase. "I mean, some do, but we call them all chicleros. They come here—oh, all the time, you know?—to steal."

"I don't want this paint."

"But you just paid for it."

"At least take the hot dogs."

"Wal-Mart don't sell hot dogs."

"I don't want to waste them."

"Try the Red Snapper Deli next door. Have a nice day."

The Red Snapper Deli refused the hot dogs because the plastic wrapper was split. Adrian paid half price, took them to his motel, and fed them to the receptionist's dog. Now as relics of the haunting child he had only the can of paint, the teeth marks on his left forearm, and memory. The wound was superficial and healed quickly, but the memory he could not blur.

For days, he languished in his motel room, at one moment struggling to forget, at the next reliving his encounter with the child: tiny hands reaching up on racks, the chase through the aisles, the crashing of tin cans. Flashing bumpers, silver mist, chrome nostrils, crimson eyes. *¿Trabaja por la Migra?* Fields of grass, the struggle in the reeds, ribs protruding through a silver torso as the sun set. *¡Puta! ¡Safo! ¡Chinga tu madre!* Filthy shorts and FUNKY COLD vanishing into Mexico.

He painted the child's portrait, imagining the first instant when he found him crouching in the grass, dazed and sprayed with paint. As usual his result was no more human than a scarecrow, but did that not somehow suit this child? Starved and addicted, did he not seem a sort of scarecrow? The portrait never satisfied the artist, so he cast it aside. Adrian was left with the can of chrome.

He was tempted to sniff it, to experience the child's trance, but at the last instant lost resolve. Again and again he read the label.

NYBCO
The Original
The Nearest Thing to
CHROME
The Finest Chrome Aluminum Spray Enamel
Made in America
Danger Extremely Flammable
Contents Under Pressure. Vapor Harmful.
Notice. Reports Have Associated Repeated and
Prolonged Occupational Over-Exposure to Solvents with
Permanent Brain & Nervous System Damage.

He decided to paint a portrait of the can. During his first attempts, he firmly traced Ionic columns in the background, but as his tableaux evolved the columns faded and finally disappeared. His definitive oil portrait was of four cans, seen from the nozzled top, the indented bottom, the label side, and the back in its chromium bleakness.

The painting was a catharsis, more self-therapy, and helped Adrian to shake off his languor. (Therapy? He distrusted psychoanalysis, disliked Freud, preferred Jung; several works of Jung's were stuffed in his luggage amid tubes of paint.) He returned to Amigoland in the late afternoons, looking for the child. He saw several gangs of thieving chicleros in Wal-Mart, Walgreens, K mart, even a clash or two with guards, but never the child. Until sunset he walked repeatedly between the railway tracks and the Gateway Bridge along the river's edge, but he could not find the child.

He began to drive his bogus junky car again, to gain time between Motel 5½ and Amigoland. Yet the car was of no use along the river's edge, and he wondered whether to find the child he might not best explore the river far beyond the realm of the Gateway Bridge. He bought a pair of binoculars, and a horse.

He had problems with the horse. After inquiries Adrian found a stable near Los Fresnos pump, miles upriver from Downsville, and a farmer who sold him a five-year-old gelded chestnut named Prince. The asking price seemed reasonable, only three thousand dollars in cash; the farmer agreed (for a handsome price) to stable and feed the horse, but he had no boy to saddle Prince for his new master. Adrian knew rather a lot about riding horses, but he had never had to saddle one.

Since childhood, at Northwood Park, Adrian had ridden nearly every morning, even in rain and snow. His progress from Northwood Hall to the family stables, quite far away, became a ritual for him, for the domestic staff, and for his father. Soon after dawn each day, Adrian the child would emerge from the great entrance of the house in jodhpurs and polished boots, descend the long flight of steps between the balustrades to the gravel drive, where a black limousine waited to drive him to the stables. His father, though often abroad, invariably when he was at home stood behind a mullioned window of an upper floor to observe his elder son's departure.

In his tenderest years, Adrian sensed that this ritual of departure was meant to be a test. When he was eight, at dinner's end one evening, after his mother had withdrawn to write and servants had entered with decanters, his father said distantly, "Beloved child, use your legs. Look at mine, withering. Walk, walk, walk." Thus next morning when Adrian reached the limousine, with the liveried footman holding open a rear door (the chauffeur remained at his post behind the wheel), he resolved to avoid the limousine and to walk to the stables. He sensed also that his father had instructed the staff to insist that he accept transport, so his flight from the servants became a game. They chased him down the gravel path, past the statues and the hedge labyrinth, through the formal gardens, across the vast lawns, into the wood, but already he was swift, and he bounded away from them. When they lay in wait for him by the great doors, he outwitted them again, climbing down drainpipes of that Tudor miniature of Cardinal Wolsey's Hampton Court. And his father watched.

Once outside the servants' grasp, Adrian reveled in his solitary trek of several miles through the woods of Northwood Park toward Northwood Stables. He loved the spring and summer mornings, as he strolled and dashed up and down rocky hills through groves of pine, over wide grassy meadows into leafy reserves of elm and birch, while robins and woodcocks sang in sweet disharmony and the sun rose higher in the new sky, shone unclearly through the mist and sparkled on ponds and streams. But most of all he loved the woods as autumn turned to winter, as the green leaves turned to red and brown and fell from grace and the first snows fell. Were these the happiest moments of his happy childhood? Even in the bitter cold, he tore off his boots and jodhpurs, his jacket, scarf, and undergarments, and plunged naked into icy streams, not so much for the fun of it but that he might boast of his bravery to his withered father.

In winter or summer, whenever he walked out of the wood the stablemaster awaited him at Northwood Stables, alerted by telephone from the great house, for that also was the ritual. All of the equestrian servants assembled for the appearance of the blond child, Master Adrian. Though he never knew it, the stableboys drew straw lots or fought fistfights for the privilege of saddling his horse, and the first groom quarreled with the stablemaster for the right of presenting the reins and holding the stirrup during the ritual of the child's mounting. No women participated in this ceremony, though often the stable wives watched from windows of the barns and marveled as the child galloped off alone on a white steed toward distant ponds and purple hills, sunlight flashing in his golden hair. As the years passed they grew less reverent toward Adrian's dark younger brother, who arrived by limousine and seemed ungainly in the saddle; the stableboys, once he had trotted out of earshot, giggled.

Adrian likewise laughed at his own first efforts to bridle and saddle Prince at the stable near Los Fresnos pump. It was not a light English saddle, as he had always used, but an elaborate Western saddle, as he had seen in cowboy pictures: huge leather flaps, dangling brass rings, a deep seat, a high pommel horn. As he lugged it from the stable wall he sweated beneath its weight. When he reached Prince in the yard outside, he heaved the saddle on backward, with the cantle in front where the pommel should have been and the horn pointing in the wrong direction. As he struggled to turn the saddle around he remembered that first he should water and brush the horse.

He dumped the saddle in the dust, then with a penknife picked out the pebbles and nails from Prince's hoofs. He led him to the water trough, then brushed his mane and tail and tried again to saddle him. Oh, he'd forgotten the blanket, and he returned to the stable to fetch it. On with the blanket: that was easy. Should he have brushed his whole body? He could not remember. Off with the blanket for a body brush. On with the blanket: that was easy. Oh, God, the saddle is sunk in manure. Over to the trough to wash the saddle. He dried it with his handkerchief. On with the saddle: breast cinch in front, obviously! Now the flank cinches, and you connect them with this strap. This strap is frayed; is that buckle rusty? is the buckle broken?

Prince rode well, but after cantering for half an hour he favored a slight limp. Adrian had no mind to demand his money back; he had forged a bond with Prince. Every morning he brought him sugar from Wyatt Cafeteria, not lump sugar (Wyatt's had none), but those small paper packets of granular sugar that people poured into coffee. Prince licked the sugar from his bare hand, slobbering him with froth; Adrian loved it. He smeared sugar on his cheeks and forehead so that Prince could lick his face. He asked, "And how is Your Royal Highness this fine day?"

When they returned from their rides along the river, Prince was thirsty and foamed with sweat. Adrian watered him, unsaddled him, then with a hose washed him down. He washed the legs first, to draw the heat from Prince's body, then lifted his tail and raised the nozzle close to his anus to clean it out. When the washing was done, he dressed Prince down with a water scraper and a curry brush and led him by a rope tether out to pasture. Best therapy yet, he thought as he curried Prince. He whistled. He hummed.

> Sometimes it seems
> Like God must live
> Just across the Rio Grande.

Indeed it did. Upriver and downriver on Prince's back, away from the shopping malls and bridges and the ugliness of Downsville, out in woodland or in vast fields, Adrian found the valley glorious. The river, often narrow, suddenly wide, forever twisting, was gray, green, a muddy brown, a brilliant blue, according to the hour and the sun's whim. Sometimes the shore was nearly flat, but then the river cut through rock, ravines of clay and high grass, before tumbling over stones and rapids toward a delta and the sea.

The vegetation, along the shore and inland into woods and farmland, was as various—shrublike mesquite trees, hugging the land and visible in rows or clumps wherever the eye was cast; sabal palm; cactus, avocado, and black willow. The endless flat farmlands yielded corn, okra, watermelon, sugarcane, rows of tomato plants that reached the horizon; grapefruit, summer squash, and cotton. Much of the earth was ocher red, fallow, awaiting new seed, ditched with canals nourished by the river. Adrian remembered the Nile Valley, where he had met his wife, and hoopoe birds above the ditches.

She never cared to watch birds, but birds had enchanted him since childhood. As his childhood advanced, he had pushed his elderly, shriveled father, bundled in blankets, on a wheelchair through the woods of Northwood Park, watching the birds of winter.

"Look, son, a mew gull."

"Did you see my snowy owl?"

"Wheel me back now. My doctors are waiting with some new medicine."

"You're going to get well, Father."

"Beloved child, beloved child."

Here he sighted green jays, hummingbirds, whistling tree ducks. He brought tubes and brushes in his saddlebags, set up an easel on the river's bank, and painted pictures of ravines, the river's hues, and birds. He added no Ionic towers.

Yet he could not forget the child. The beauty of the river and the company of Prince were not enough: he grew restive and tormented because he could not find the child. His earlier phantoms all returned, and again he could not modulate the music inside his head. Each day on his ride downriver from Los Fresnos pump, he lingered between the railway bridge and the Gateway Bridge, then rode to Amigoland to seek the child. In the parking lot of Wal-Mart, dark Mexican women put down their shopping bags and paused to gaze at this golden figure, bareheaded in shabby clothes, astride a lame horse. Once, he thought, he glimpsed the child.

That happened downriver, in the wild, miles beyond Amigoland near a bird sanctuary. He had tethered Prince to a tree and crouched on the shore, sketching a long-legged whistling duck, when he heard the cries of children from the other side. He raised his binoculars and saw a band of ragged barefoot children assembled in the grass across the river upstream. One held a can of what seemed like silver paint; the others were attacking him to take it away. For an instant, among the contending tiny bodies, FUNKY COLD.

Plastic bags littered the American shore: Adrian tore off all his clothes, shoved them into a bag, and with the bag grasped to his head waded swiftly to the other side. The water was warm, and he felt an oozy sensation as it stroked his loins. In Mexico, he thrust on his pants, dashed barefoot over sharp rocks toward the children. They saw him coming and ran away. He swam back to Texas with bleeding feet.

This episode of the bleeding feet contributed to his growing paranoia, or was it paranoia? For days, he had suspected that whenever he rode along the river's edge, he was being watched. Indeed, more than once, when he raised his binoculars to scan the landscape, he saw a man in the distance with binoculars scanning the landscape. Like jellyfish, it was the kind of image that floated through his nightmares: two men on a flat red field, watching each other with binoculars. On different days, the other man was different men, but always they wore brimmed cowboy hats and uniforms of olive drab. Once, the stranger sat astride a horse, then again inside a green truck, U.S. BORDER PATROL. Aha, *la Migra!*

He kept returning to the wilderness downriver near the bird sanctuary, hoping to see the child. He had tired of sketching birds, so on a brilliant afternoon he tethered Prince to a log and lay down on the shore with his head against it, reading a book. He had brought many books from Northwood Hall, stacked them chaotically in his room, grabbed one on his way out, not caring which. Now he read an essay by Cardinal Newman, on "The Danger of Riches."

". . . love of riches . . . the very possession of riches . . . the very awfulness of riches . . . the idolatrous reliance on riches . . . the deceitfulness of riches . . . the calamity of riches . . . 'When thou makest a dinner or a supper, call not thy friends, nor thy brethren, neither thy kinsmen, nor thy rich neighbours, but call the poor, the maimed, the lame, the blind.' . . ." He began to underline phrases with a stub of charcoal pencil. ". . . 'Sell that ye have and give alms. . . . Woe unto you that are rich! for ye have received your consolation.' . . ." Prince stirred, neighing of a sudden, rising high on his hind legs and tugging on his tether as though to fly away. Adrian put down his book, stood up to stroke the beast, asking, "What's wrong, Royal Highness?"

Birds hovered above the river, diving and screeching. There were some rapids close by: a human body bumped against the rocks, then floated through the reeds and washed half ashore at Adrian's feet. In the muddy water, he crouched over it, looking for signs of life. It had no head.

He pulled the body by the feet onto the sandy shore. It was smartly dressed in Gucci boots and a gray business suit, the suit smeared with blood. A diamond ring sparkled on his right hand; on his left wrist was a golden watch, still ticking. This man was young, Adrian thought, as he opened the jacket and white shirt, running his hand over smooth brown skin. The shoulders and upper torso were elaborately tattooed. At the center of the chest, a sharp instrument had carved a neat inverted cross. Blood seeped from the gray crotch. Oh, God, has he been unsexed? Adrian dared not look.

He propped up the body and gazed at the headless neck. On that snowy morning, when the police had led him to the scene of the tragedy, he had lacked the courage to look into the car at his son's body and severed head, but his cowardice nagged him and he had no such scruples now.

From his career of art, he knew something of anatomy; he peered with fascination at the stump of neck, oozing blood and hacked crudely off, probably (he thought) with a dull knife. The larynx and the thyroid gland had been chopped in half. Horseflies began to buzz above the stump, to feed on the thick bludgeoned muscles, on the wide trachea and esophagus. With his fingers Adrian pushed apart cartilage and the plexus brachialis and squinted down inside the corpse to glimpse the bloody white clavicle where it joined the breastbone in an upright cross. Close above, birds of prey observed him.

A man on horseback galloped down through the high grass, shouting, "Get away from that f——ing body!"

Adrian protested, "Officer, I didn't kill him."

"Stand back!"

In his confusion, Adrian failed to comply and held on to the body. The officer in olive drab leaped off his horse, seized Adrian violently. He threw him to the ground, pinned his arms behind his back, and handcuffed him; Adrian did not resist. He stumbled to his feet, protesting, "I didn't kill him."

"Sir, are you a U.S. citizen?"

"Why did you handcuff me?"

"I'm a federal officer! I gave you an order, sir! Who are you, sir?"

"A U.S. citizen. How dare you handcuff me?"

"For tampering with a corpse, sir!"

"I didn't kill him."

"I know you didn't kill him, sir. I've been tracking this floater for half an hour. I've been tracking *you* goin' on a week! Stand back."

He was a young latino, maybe in his mid twenties, wearing an open-necked, half-sleeved olive shirt with a tin badge and a golden shoulder patch, U.S. BORDER PATROL. Around his neck dangled a pair of binoculars, around his slim waist hung an ammunition belt, a black gun and holster, and a walkie-talkie encased in leather, with the antenna jutting out. He had knocked off his brimmed hat during his encounter with Adrian: it lay tilted in the sand, beside the headless body. His slight mustache was punctiliously trimmed, like his thick dark hair and shaven neck. At the corner of his mouth shone a silver tooth. He unfastened his walkie-talkie, extending the antenna.

"Nine-sixty-six. Six-oh-six."

Static, then a distant voice: "Go ahead, six-oh-six."

"Floater ashore, our side. Please notify authorities."

"Confirm location, six-oh-six."

"Downriver, R.P. forty."

"Informing Downsville F.D. Stand by, six-oh-six."

He fastened the radio to his belt, took a pen and a small notebook from his breast pocket. "Your name, sir?"

"I'm a U.S. citizen," Adrian replied angrily. "I committed no crime, and you're violating my rights. I demand that you remove these handcuffs."

"I want your ID."

"I don't have one."

"What's your name?"

"None of your business."

"You could be Canadian."

"I'm not."

"Why do you hang out on the river?"

"I paint."

"Yeah, I seen your easel. A great cover—for staking out drug runs, sir!"

Adrian kicked open the pages of his book. He said, "Cardinal Newman!"

"Who's Cardinal Newman?"

"A theologian and a poet."

"Jesus!"

"Do drug runners read Cardinal Newman?"

"Jesus!"

"Unshackle me!"

"You won't touch the body, sir?"

"No!"

The officer fumbled for his key ring, removed the handcuffs.

"Thanks. My name's AJ."

"Ay-jay? Ay-jay what?"

"Northwood."

"Northwood? I've heard the name."

"There are many Northwoods."

"I never met one. Where you from?"

"The north."

"Where in the north?"

"The north. What's your name?"

"Rodrigo."

"Rodrigo what?"

"None of your business."

Adrian rubbed his wrists, raised his binoculars to scan the shore of Mexico. Rodrigo asked, "You lookin' for someone?"

"Maybe."

"Who?"

"None of your business."

Eventually, a siren's wail, and across the ocher fields bumped an ambulance, DOWNSVILLE FIRE DEPARTMENT. Two men in white jumped out with a stretcher, scrambled downward through the reeds, and bore away the headless body. Rodrigo spoke to his walkie-talkie.

"Nine-sixty-six. Six-oh-six."

"Go ahead, six-oh-six."

"Floater removed, F.D."

"Resume patrol, six-oh-six."

Yet Rodrigo lingered. Adrian said, "I wonder who decapitated him."

"Traffickers, probably. Tortured him, probably, before they chopped off his head. Drug wars, you know?"

"Which side—U.S. or Mexico?"

"Either one."

"God. And his head . . ."

"Bubbling in some *curandero*'s pot, probably."

"*¿Curandero?*"

"Witch doctor. There's white witchcraft and black witchcraft around here. Like, devil worship? The drug bosses are into it big. Makes them invisible, they think. Oh, f——."

"Something wrong?"

"Lost my top button, I guess when I knocked you down." Rodrigo descended to his hands and knees, scratching in the sand for his button. Adrian laughed and said, "That's a lot of bother for a button."

"You don't understand," Rodrigo fumed, burrowing. "I'm out of uniform. I'm not like them other slobs in the Border Patrol. I'm the best-lookin' guy in the BP, and I'm out of uniform. I hate myself! Out of uniform! Where's that f——ing button?"

Adrian descended to the sand himself, not to search for Rodrigo's button but to do push-ups. Eventually Rodrigo stood up to watch him: "How many can you do?"

"Eighty?"

"Can you do ninety?"

"I'll try."

He did a hundred, paused, and did fifty more. Rodrigo said, "I'm off duty at three. After work, I go to the gym and work out. Want to come, Ay-jay?"

"No."

"It's a nice gym. Compared to you, them other guys will look like fags."

"What do you do there?"

"Run, pump iron, box."

"Boxing's not a sport. Too violent."

"We don't have to box. There's a track outside. I could race you."

"No, thanks."

"Suit yourself!"

Rodrigo retrieved his brimmed hat, mounted his black quarter horse, and rode off. Adrian continued his push-ups, then with his binoculars scanned Mexico again: NO FUNKY COLD. Another failure. Again he glimpsed the headless neck, hacked crudely off, and saw his son's. The music shrieked. DA-DUM-TA-*DEEE*-DUM. DA-DUM-TA-TA-TA-*DEEE*-DUM. He leaped onto Prince and galloped him to the ocher field. Rodrigo rode far in the distance, perhaps out of earshot. Adrian cupped his mouth with his hands and shouted, "Rodrigo?" The horseman did not hear. From the pit of his loneliness, Adrian cried out again. "RODRIGO!"

Rodrigo turned his horse, galloped back toward him.

"Yeah?"

Adrian could not think of anything to say. He shouted, "My wife was killed. My son was decapitated."

"Oh, yeah?"

As I watched these two strong, weak men gallop off together through fields and woods, through groves of mesquite and farms of grapefruit, then along the twisting river under the terrific sun, I grew sad. I knew that, just then, Adrian decided that the environs of this river, for indefinite time, would become his home. Besides: the child. I wished to seize the reins of Prince, to halt Adrian in his blind gallop, to plead with him and say, "Don't do this! Get into your car and flee! If you stay here, you will know moments of joy, very brief, but your heart will be broken again. Do not go to Mexico." That day I told him nothing, because I knew it would do no good, but his adventures at times will be so fearful I shall be reluctant to reveal them.

PART III

Northwood Hall

▼▼▼

4

 letter from Diana Northwood:

. . . and I have rarely, since your childhood, been so angry with
you. You had no right—and with such stealth, before your
departure—to instruct Mr. Burner IV to arrange those half-page
advertisements of my new book in The New York Times and The
New York Review. I suppose you thought that by making them
only half-page you would pacify me because you eschewed your
usual excess, but I was outraged when I saw them.

Will you never understand that I do not write vanity books and
therefore that I resent your meddling? If my publisher will not
spend the money to promote my books, then it is no business of
yours. I have a stable, if small, following of faithful readers who
enjoy my nonfiction and my subtle novels. The moment I saw the
advertisements, I thought, Ah, Adrian is up to his tricks. Ignore
this, and he will embarrass you again; he may even carry out his
threat to buy you a publishing house. *Don't.*

I am displeased with the notices of my book. Simply because I
write about the Renaissance, the reviewers feel they must show off
and prove that they know more about the Medicis than I do. I
cannot *bear* to be compared to Walter Pater, whose research was
sloppy and who knew almost nothing of the period. Some English
pedant, in The New York Review, compared my style to Sir Harold
Acton's—a *worse* insult. Harold Acton could not write English.

And I am angry with you for other reasons. If you wish to pack up, leave Northwood Hall, and live in a squalid motel on the Mexican border, that is your affair—I hardly miss you; we each of us must cope with tragedy by remaining true to character—but you have no right to burden *me* with the statues.

When you have done well I shall be the first to say so, and I do grant that the statue you commissioned of St. Francis for the grove beneath your father's window turned out—despite my initial misgivings—to be lovely. But the statues of Mozart and Schubert, which the sculptors delivered last week, are so ludicrous that I will not allow them, in their present form, to stand with the others in the gallery between the hedge labyrinth and your mock Greek ruins. It is irrelevant to me that Northwood Hall, that every inch of Northwood Park, belong to you; in matters of taste I will not be overruled, and if we continue to disagree I will gladly live elsewhere before I allow your father's legacy to be desecrated.

Why must you insist on making everything heroic? Are you too dull to recognize, as I did long ago, that genius, though conceived in Heaven, invariably dwells on earth in less celestial form? Mozart in his maturity was a short, almost homely man with a nose rather too long for his face, but you instructed the sculptor to make him handsome and six feet tall. I might have reconciled myself to your vulgar mythology were it not for the statue of Schubert that you propose to place at Mozart's side. Schubert was a short, plump man, as myopic as Mozart, yet you have removed his spectacles and turned him into a deity. Were it not for his name on the pedestal I might have mistaken him for Lord Byron. I have instructed the sculptor—the symbolism will disturb you, but art is at stake—to remove Schubert's head and to chisel a new one with blunt features and rimless spectacles. You will have another of your *fabulous* temper tantrums, but I will not be moved.

Your tantrums, over the years, have blemished your radiance and added a churlish crease, however faint, to the lower corners of your mouth. They are rooted in an emotional immaturity for which I am not the least responsible, and which—to this day—I cannot fully understand. I suspect that they may have something to do with your self-indulgent obsession with aesthetics, your obstinate gullibility, and your shocking ignorance of life. In your milder moments you have asked me why everything you have touched has turned to failure. May I suggest again that—leaving your lack of talent entirely aside—you actually believe that, in one way or another, you can go on forever watching birds with your father in Northwood Park? I hear you screaming at me! I take it back! *Please,* let me eat my words! Put it this way: you are convinced that somehow you can live in another century. . . .

▪ ▪ ▪

"What's wrong with living in the eighteenth century?" Adrian raged in his motel room. "You live in the fifteenth!"

Diana had begun the letter in her fine hand, but as the epistle progressed, her strokes grew bolder.

▪ ▪ ▪

. . . and I can imagine the sort of life you lead in Downsville, which by your own account is the most *horrid* place on earth. If I know my Adrian, he is throwing money at every vagabond he meets, but as ever he lacketh charity for his own kin. It is time that you make amends.

You inherited your height, your beauty, and your golden hair from me, but none of my artistic gift. Your brother Pius inherited his smallness, his ungainliness, and his dark looks from your father, but none of his talent for making money. I surmise that Pius is in trouble again—I enclose his sealed letter—otherwise he would not have written to you. His ungainliness and chronic need of money provide you with no excuse to be so *beastly* to your younger brother.

God knows, I have done all I can for Pius; besides, my fortune is minuscule compared to yours. I can understand your exasperation—I have felt it myself—but that is no reason to treat him, as you have for so long, like a chimney sweep. I insist that for once you reply to him graciously, with generosity, and that you remember him in your prayers. At least give him *something.*

As for your other correspondence, it is typical of your absences that letters addressed to you pile up in such enormous quantity I cannot cope with it. I am not forwarding most of the letters because I know that you would not read them. Many are from your Mr. Burner IV, and I assume that they are financial reports. I realize that your father retained Mr. Burner II and Mr. Burner III, but he never trusted them because he knew from experience that all law-yers are scoundrels. I have warned you repeatedly to beware of Burner IV, but blithely you ignore me, and your own interest, as you pursue your fantasies.

I do enclose a sealed letter from The University, because I suppose that you will consider it important.

Cardinal Galsworthy will come to the United States next month on a secret mission for the Holy Father. The President has invited him to pass Saturday night at Camp David, but he has declined because he wishes to spend the weekend here at Northwood Hall alone with me. He will be distressed without you because you were so close to your father. I shall lodge him in your father's apartments near the chapel. I will give him a check for the Holy Father from our joint account No. 3, and of course I shall be generous so that you will not *fuss*.

Finally, will you please *stop* writing to me in German. You use words so obscure that even Goethe would blush. I cannot find my German dictionary, and your own library is so chaotic I dare not enter it. As for your father's: too many ghosts, too many memories of his little fault. If you must show off, write to me in French.

Votre mère,

DIANA DUCHESSE NORTHWOOD

■ ■ ■

The enclosure from Pius Northwood:

■ ■ ■

. . . and I'm really sorry I never made it to the funeral. The fact is, AJ, I couldn't. I was in the middle of my divorce, and I had the kids that weekend, or did Mother tell you? She, I mean my wife, took me royally to the cleaners, and the judge gave her the kids. My lawyer thought the Northwood name would help, but the judge he no budge. Some judge. Some lawyer! (Now I know why you hate New York.) Maybe it didn't happen to your little brother quite the same way, but I feel for you without your wife and kid. Hey, AJ, I've been there! I'm not broke, but between my ex, my alimony, and the vagaries (vicissitudes?) of the stock market, I'm on the brink. I've found a way out, and if you'll give me a little shove I'll be back where I belong. I know you get uptight when I ask, but I guess that goes back to childhood. Mother's been great, but she says her well is dry, and you have all the bucks. I've got a great chance to work into a new venture but I won't say it's a sure thing (even if it is) because I think I said it once before and you got uptight later on. There's this new group, highly respectable, and they're offering me a partnership if I put up a little cash. Ideally I should put up $2 million but I think I can swing it (being cheap, but I never said, hey, how could anybody say, you're cheap, AJ) for a bottom line $1.5. You'll say I burned up my trust funds, but I was hobbled all the way, nothing like you free and clear from day one, and besides payments were tied to my academic performance and I never was a scholar like you, AJ. Sorry, I'm veering close to that touchy subject of primogeniture, item number one with Father, and boy AJ did you clean up by being number one but where does that leave little Pius the ugly duckling? Hey, I know, the breaks. Look, the Northwood name will help me, and you'll say you don't want it but I'll give you a percentage of my earnings for your favorite charity. We'll write that in the contract, AJ. Do you want a contract? Mother says you left home in a junk heap and now you're staying in some crummy motel. How can you live like that, AJ? O.K. you hate the high life but how about a minimum of comfort, laid-back, enjoy? About the new group, very distinguished and respectable, they know your Mr. Burner IV and do deals with him all the time. Get me into this, and I'll never bother you again, just give you your charity dividends when we meet for Christmas at Northwood Hall. I'm reading Mother's new book . . .

▪ ▪ ▪

Adrian read his mother's letter several times, Pius's only once. Where's my checkbook? he wondered. He found it finally in his luggage, buried beneath the works of Jung and some crushed tubes of mars yellow. The checkbook was moist, all smeared with mars yellow, but in the middle he salvaged a clean page and then wondered how much money he should send to his brother. His father: "When fending off a beggar, give but a fourth."

Hmm. Pius's "bottom line" was $1.5 million. Adrian divided that by four and debated whether, to please his mother, he should give Pius $375,000. He wrote the check for $375,000, placed it in an envelope without a word of greeting, sealed the envelope, and addressed it to Pius in upper East Side Manhattan. He sat on his unmade bed gazing at the envelope, reliving his childhood with Pius at Northwood Hall, remembering their quarrels, the fistfights that Adrian always won, and disliking Pius still because his father had.

He rose from the bed, went to the mirror, and regarded his image in repose. "Your tantrums have blemished your radiance and added a churlish crease to the lower corners of your mouth." He thought, She might have mentioned that along with my hot tantrums goes my cold mean streak. He turned away from the mirror, his emotions despite himself wobbling between an incipient tantrum and an ice-cold will to cruelty. With effort, he overruled his rising anger and struggled to be cool.

He picked up his mother's letter and read the relevant paragraphs again. ". . . so *beastly* to your younger brother . . . understand your exasperation . . . reply to him graciously, with generosity . . . remember him in your prayers. At least give him *something*."

As he read the passage for the fifteenth time, he grasped his mother's occult message. She was saying, "Pius also is my son, and it is my duty as his mother to insist that you help him." Yet her train of thought was so subtly constructed that it ended with an escape clause, a devious invitation to ignore his brother's plea for money. ". . . remember him in your prayers . . . *something*."

Adrian returned Diana's letter respectfully to its envelope and filed it in his bureau drawer; he had never thrown away a letter from his mother. He tore up his brother's letter and the envelope with the check and flushed the pieces down the toilet. He thought, I'll remember him in my prayers.

5

Diana's second enclosure, from The University, turned out to be a form letter from Adrian's Tenth Anniversary Class. "We are planning a Special Supplement of *Alumni/Alumnae Quarterly* to honor all our graduates on this great occasion and major milestone along the road of life. Would each proud grad please write an essay of 300 words telling us a little of their life and family, with special emphasis on your accomplishments since graduation ten years—can it be that long?—ago. We'd love to hear from all our grads! N.B. *We reserve the right to severely edit or to entirely ignore all submissions which run over 300 words.*"

Alarmed by the grammar, Adrian nonetheless liked this proposal. His inventory of published essays was not large; here was a chance to communicate something whimsical about himself and his unease in the modern world. Ignoring lunch, he sat down at his cluttered table and, in longhand, on a sheet of foolscap, laboriously began his composition.

■ ■ ■

I was born into a family of great wealth. I never learned in detail how my father—Urban Northwood—made his money. I was young when he died, but shortly before his death I raised the subject. He was taciturn by nature and told me only, "By taking risks."

My mother, Diana Duchesse Northwood, the authoress, was too busy with her writing to inquire into the sources of her husband's fortune and thus was of little help in satisfying my boyish curiosity. I was left to my own devices, but they did not get me far. My exposure to the nature of my father's business was limited to over-hearing muffled telephone conversations behind mahogany doors, to meeting men in dark suits with briefcases who came to call on him at Northwood Hall, and to wondering why he spent so much time abroad.

■ ■ ■

Adrian perused what he had written, disliking it. Was it in proper taste to begin his essay by mentioning money? What he truly wanted was to praise his father, but without mention of his fortune, Urban Northwood lacked identity. Adrian revised his first sentence, deleting "wealth": "I was born into a family of great privilege." He deleted "great": "I was born into a family of privilege." Oh, God, the second sentence ends in "money." He decided to continue writing, to delete when he was finished. He took another tack.

■ ■ ■

I admired my father so, missed him so much after his death, that when my son was born I named him Urban Northwood II. This displeased my wife, who preferred an Italian name, Antonio, pos-sibly because she was half Italian and named Antonia. Her mother was Egyptian. I met her in Cairo, on an archaeological holiday a year after I was graduated from The University. Antonia worked for the United Nations as an interpreter and secretary, and spoke six languages, only one less than I did. The attraction at first was frankly physical. I have never responded to women with wide hips, and when I discovered Antonia standing in a scant costume by a swimming pool, I was grateful and my loins stirred.

She had slim hips and sylphlike legs, skin that was marble-smooth but tinted copper by the sun, a small, carved mouth almost mauve in pigment, rich brown hair, and astonishing green eyes. Her nose was small and straight, tilted slightly to the right. Intellectually she was interesting, absorbed not only by international politics but by art and music, at home in French and in Italian culture, fascinated by Oriental magic—she was slightly superstitious—because she spoke Arabic.

In the evenings when we went out, Antonia's poise enchanted me. She had a way of walking, of holding up her head, of glancing from side to side with her green eyes, that enchanted everyone. On the veranda of the Hotel Semiramis, as she glided through the sultry breezes of the Nile in a cotton dress the color of peach, the eyes of men and of women also followed her until she reached our table. Her stride was not long, but a mixture it seemed of flowing progress and steps that were brisk yet almost delicate. As she walked, she cooled the Nile breeze that struck her face by fluttering a blue fan.

I had known Antonia only a fortnight when, much in love, I proposed marriage. I had not mentioned my fortune, but when eventually I revealed it she refused my proposal. From Cairo I returned to Northwood Hall, and persisted on the telephone.

"Do you want me as a decoration for the Northwood fortune?" Antonia asked.

"You can have your own career," I promised.

Finally from our different directions we flew to Rome, where the Holy See waived the banns and we were married beneath Michelangelo's frescoes in the Pauline Chapel by Augustine Cardinal Galsworthy.

When Antonia arrived with me to reside at Northwood Hall, Diana was rude to her. This upset me—I tend to get upset with my mother—but Antonia spent the next year being nice to Mother. Her policy (she called it that) succeeded. Gradually they grew closer; Antonia lost interest in pursuing her own career and devoted herself to Diana's interest. She did this not out of subservience but in fascination. She envied even Diana's way of walking into a room and by degrees abandoned her short, brisk gait to imitate my mother's longer, nobler stride.

I was not surprised, really. It is enough for a son to admire his mother's elegance—her lithe poise, her mode of dress, her tall, majestic shoulders, her noble head and golden hair enhanced by silver—but the son's view was universal. A fashion magazine, describing Diana in a younger time, called her "the handsomest woman of her generation." The compliment displeased Diana because, like my father, she disliked publicity. She shunned society.

Save for her annual visit to Europe, she remained at Northwood Hall, receiving few friends, sealed for long hours in her vast library, writing.

Since youth, she had thought of little else. She was thirty when Urban Northwood, unmarried, already in middle age, eager for an heir, sought her hand. He said, "I lack grace, but you, Diana, have enough for both of us. We might have beautiful children. Will you marry me?"

"Would you expect me to mix with society?" Diana asked.

"Seldom," he said.

"Would you expect me to entertain?"

"Only now and then."

"You know that nothing could come before my writing?"

"Nothing?"

"There is a matter that must be clear."

"Name it."

"About your fortune."

"I'd give you half of it, Diana."

"I have my own fortune. I want none of yours, and I need your promise that you will not mention it again."

"I promise. How long will you need to consider my proposal?"

"I accept it now."

They were married in Rome, in the Pauline Chapel, by Monsignor Galsworthy. Ten months later, I was born at Northwood Hall. My father admired me; but two years afterward, less pleased with my brother, Pius, he lost interest in siring children. As Pius grew and he gazed at him, he saw a miniature image of himself. "No more ugly ducklings," Father murmured. He withdrew to his apartments in the east wing, and henceforth rarely visited my mother's bed.

Her own apartments, in the west wing, were far from his, separated by scores of corridors and rooms. Except at dinner, they seldom met. They communicated by writing notes that servants carried back and forth on silver trays. The Tudor house, the inner courtyards, the symmetrical gardens, the hedge labyrinth, the stables, the forest, were so extensive that it took me half my childhood to explore them. The house was never completely furnished; whole suites of rooms were sealed, because no one ever lived in them.

My father's apartments were austerely furnished. The paintings on his walls were originals and all bucolic: Constables and Turners, mostly—sunlit lakes, cottages, horses, hay wagons, snowstorms. My mother's apartments were full of artifacts from the Renaissance: rare crucifixes, gilded triptychs, portraits of madonnas, naked pagan deities, landscapes with distant parapets, but all of the paintings were by minor artists because she preferred originals and could not afford the masters.

Though Urban had abandoned Diana's bed, my parents remained cordial; their bond seemed stronger for his absences abroad. At home, they dined beneath the mahogany beams of the great hall, at either end of a long table, shouting to each other over the candelabra, and laughing. Domestics in evening dress served them simple courses with white gloves. Pius and I usually dined earlier, but occasionally I was invited to join my parents, and I sat halfway between them. As my father grew more feeble, I relayed his whispers to my mother.

He died when I was fifteen. It was a wound I was lucky to survive. He left a large benefaction to the Holy See (through Monsignor Galsworthy, by then a cardinal) and some funds in trust for little Pius, but most of his fortune he bequeathed to me. Long before his death, Diana became nearly a recluse, writing.

She wrote as Diana Duchesse Northwood, interpolating her maiden name because she was proud of her French forebears and because she enjoyed the connotation of nobility. In fact, shortly after his marriage, my father had been created a papal duke, and Diana as his consort became the Duchess of Canino. She was welcome at the papal court, but her visits to Rome were brief. Her fictions of intrigue in Roman society were based more on research and imagination that on direct experience. She has written many novels, but they have not done well. The critics have called them too subtle; I have trouble understanding them. Diana is not long-winded like Henry James, but she lacks his gift of breathing drama into a raised eyebrow. Her historical books have done better, particularly her biography of Isabella d'Este, and her masterwork, *Lucrezia*.

She began her biography of Lucrezia Borgia by quoting Giovanni Pontano, a Neapolitan poet:

> *Hic jacet in tumolo, Lucretia nomine sed re*
> *Thais. Alexandri filia, sponsa, nurus.*

> Here lies in her tomb, Lucretia named but
> Thaïs in truth—daughter, wife and daughter
> in marriage of Alexander.

For the next nine hundred pages, Diana disproved that poetaster and destroyed the legend of Lucrezia as a poisoner, murderess, and incestuous madwoman. The chroniclers of the papal court, particularly Burchard and Guicciardini, she exposed as malevolent gossips. Their tales of Lucrezia grappling in bed with her brother Cesare and her father, Pope Alexander VI, were lies. Lucrezia's poison ring, employed supposedly to dispose of tiresome lovers, never existed. On the contrary, Lucrezia was winsome, manipulated, and innocent—the victim mainly of two men, Cesare and Alexander. Feminist critics praised the book lavishly.

Diana herself lacked feminist zeal, at least as it involved this century. She wrote as she pleased, heedless of fashion and advancing her views only after fanatical research. She kept odd hours. Often she wrote all night, retiring at dawn, rising at noon, ringing for her maid, nibbling on dry toast, sipping black tea, reading her correspondence, dictating terse replies to Maude, her elderly secretary, only to begin writing again.

She dressed as she pleased, simply but well. Because Northwood Hall was so cold and drafty, she favored woolen skirts, double cashmere sweaters with the outer sweater draped about her shoulders, and a single string of genuine white pearls. She disliked slacks and pantsuits and would not wear them. Though she was proud of her papal title, she seldom mentioned it, and on those rare occasions when she ventured into society or gave dinners at Northwood Hall, she did not dress like a duchess. Golden bracelets, brilliant rings, diamond tiaras, she regarded as vulgar, like elaborate make-up. She wore black satin, a double string of pearls, and, on her left ear, just below a lock of her golden-silver hair, a tiny sapphire. As time passed, Antonia copied Diana's taste in fashion.

At tea or after dinner, my wife began to take notes of everything that Diana said. My mother did not seem to mind, but eventually asked her why.

"Oh, that was my job at the United Nations"—Antonia laughed—"writing down what people said. Most of them—I mean the diplomats—were crashing bores. Your conversation is so different, Diana. Someday you'll have to write your autobiography, and I thought I might help."

Diana was touched. Maude's advancing years made her increasingly useless as a secretary, and though Diana refused to fire her, she relied on Antonia more and more. As she vanished for those endless hours behind the doors of her library, Antonia vanished with her. The months passed, I saw little of my wife, and I grew angry. At breakfast one morning, I confronted her.

"Why must you spend so much time with Mother?" I shouted.

"She's more interesting than you." Antonia laughed.

As for the nature of their work together, neither at first would confide in me. From fragments of their conversation, I learned that Diana was preparing a panoramic history of the Renaissance. Shrewdly, Diana recognized that I had brought her a pearl, saving her years of research. Ancient Latin and Greek texts she reserved to herself, but Antonia wrote summaries of forgotten sources in French and Italian. Yellowing Arabic texts, bountiful with insights into the origins of the Renaissance, filled a section of the library, but Diana was lost in that idiom, and Antonia's command of Arabic was a godsend. Time turned inside out at Northwood Hall as the two of them receded deeper and deeper into the sixteenth and fifteenth centuries.

At dinner, they spoke French and Italian, hardly a barrier since I had attended a Benedictine school in Normandy and passed part of my holidays in Italy, yet their jokes were all private or subtly aimed at me. Diana could not conceal her low regard for my talent, for my fascination with the late Baroque, and for the drawings and paintings that I created in my library at Northwood Hall or brought home from (The University's) Academy of Art. Gradually Antonia came to share her contempt. On moonlit summer nights, through the open window of my library, facing the formal gardens, I could hear them playing tag among the statues, hide-and-seek in the hedge labyrinth, and laughing.

Are they laughing at me? I wondered. Rarely, Diana would tender teas and luncheons for her New York publisher or scholars of the Renaissance, and Antonia I am sure shone on these occasions, but always I was excluded. In springtime, and once during the autumn, while I was busy at the Academy, Diana sailed to Europe for more research and took Antonia with her. When their opus was finally published—illustrated in brilliant colors, five hundred pages long, and costing much—it sold six hundred copies.

Were any two women ever quite so close? Their friendship was not Sapphic. I knew because, at Northwood Hall, Antonia invariably slept with me. She was delectably soft beneath my touch, yet as smooth as cool marble that warmed soon enough, matching my prolonged lovemaking with her own sensuous cadenzas and delighted when, quite often, her climaxes were simultaneous with mine, though seldom as robust.

My problems with Antonia were never sexual. I revered her intelligence; she scoffed at mine. I prayed that the birth of little Urban might make things better.

Urban II came to us in our mid twenties, three years after our marriage. Until the moment of Antonia's labor, we speculated whether the child would resemble my father, my mother and thus myself, or Antonia. He resembled me, remarkably, not only in his golden hair but in his etched mouth and (may I say so?) in his blue, wistful eyes. I was disappointed in the color of his eyes: I had hoped he might inherit Antonia's startling green. Yet for all of Urban II's fair look, I could not forget that his maternal grandmother was Egyptian and that his veins contained the dark waters of the Nile. From the first day, I called him "my little Arab." Antonia loathed her mother and grew annoyed when I kept it up: ". . . my little Arab . . . my little Arab . . ."

For our next argument, we debated whether little Urban should be circumcised. I favored it, less (I said) for hygiene and because my parents had had the surgery performed on me, but because, as I asked Antonia, "Have you ever heard of an uncircumcised Arab?" She exploded, hurled contempt at me, but I was fed up with her bullying and saw to the surgery of my son. Antonia retreated to Diana's library, where she plunged anew into my mother's work. Thereafter she saw Urban only briefly, in the mornings, refused to nurse him, left his rearing to a governess—and to me. Even my mother devoted more attention to Urban than did Antonia.

I forged with my son a bond so close that it surpassed the affection my father had shown to me. No sooner could he toddle, we haunted the woods of Northwood Park, where I showed him birds.

"Look, son, a woodcock."

"Ba, ba! Ba, ba!"

"Look! Look! Here we go, I'll lift you up! A yellow warbler! A snowy owl?"

"Ba, ba! Ba, ba!"

I carried him through Northwood Park—through meadows, groves of birch, past streams and ponds—until we came to Northwood Stables. The grooms dashed out of the barns, praising Urban's beauty, promising to ride with him as soon as he could mount. When he was four, I dressed my son in tiny jodhpurs and polished boots and lifted him onto his own pony. From the stables we rode together to the graveyard, at the far corner of the Park, to pray at my father's tomb. In my library, I painted my child's portrait a dozen times. As he squirmed in his chair, I hummed to him some tunes of the child Mozart. He hugged me constantly.

In the spring, when Urban was five, my mother and Antonia sailed again to Europe. There—in Rome, I think—they quarreled.

I could never learn the nature of the quarrel, but it was something deep. I suspected that Antonia's contempt had become a habit and that without my presence she turned it on Diana. Possibly she overstepped, making some remark about Diana's talent or my father's little fault to a woman who considered herself a duchess. When they returned from Europe, neither would discuss it, but at dinner Diana was cold, and never again did she allow Antonia inside her library. Shattered, Antonia turned to me. I did not reject her—not in bed—but once outside of bed I retained too many bitter memories and responded with my mother's coolness. In desperation, Antonia turned to her son.

It seemed too late. Little Urban barely knew his mother: whenever she caressed him, he cried. Winter came. The first snows fell, covering the gardens, the hedge labyrinth, the vast lawns, with bleakness. One evening, as I emerged from Urban's room after putting him to bed, I found Antonia in the corridor, dressed in a dark bathrobe, weeping. She had let down her brown hair; the tresses fell behind her shoulders, groping witchlike for her hips. As she followed me into our bedroom, she dried her tears and her mood changed. Shouting, she accused me of poisoning her son against his mother.

I lost control, hurling back accusations of my own, reliving nine years of our bleak marriage, roaring. It was as though I became another person, or two persons, the first suspended from the mahogany beams, observing myself below, possessed by my tantrum. "You ignored him!" I screamed, pounding the bedpost with both my fists. "You refused your milk to him! I'VE RAISED HIM!"

Drained, Antonia seemed to give up. Lying back on her pillow, her face veiled by her long hair, she said quietly, "All right. I won't try any longer. He's your son, not mine."

Silently I climbed into bed beside her, but I could not sleep. She hardly stirred, but in the middle of the night she murmured words in Arabic, a language I never learned. At dawn, it snowed again, a little, and I felt ashamed. Dressing, I remembered that later in the morning Urban had an appointment with the dentist. Ah, I thought, here's Antonia's chance; but when she woke up, gazing at me from beneath the covers of our bed, I sensed that she had reverted to her contempt, and her motherhood indeed had ceased to exist. She shrugged at my suggestion that she drive him to the dentist.

"No," she said.

"Please. I'm late for class."

"Why go? They laugh at you."

"Less than you do."

Our son ran in, circling the bedroom and running out.

"You drive him," she said.

"A child needs his mother at the dentist's."

"A child who prefers his father? You're too fond of him."

By the great doors, Urban hugged my boots, begging me not to leave, but by now I was indifferent to the dentist and dashed to work. What motives changed Antonia's mind? What were her intentions or her half-intentions as she set out for the dentist's when the snow was heavier? On the road, a mile or so beyond the gates of Northwood Park, she drove off a cliff, and died instantly. So did my son, decapitated.

▪ ▪ ▪

At sunset, Adrian put aside his foolscap and prepared to go out on patrol with Rodrigo. Is my essay too long? he debated. It was intended to be whimsical? A bit somber for a college magazine? Marvelous therapy: he enjoyed writing it, and he hadn't finished yet.

I'll edit later, he decided.

He turned on his transistor radio. For an hour each evening, the Evangelical station in Downsville played classical war-horses: today it was Beethoven's Fifth. Outside his motel room, a battered green van screeched up. Rodrigo jumped out. Adrian opened his door. In his holster, Rodrigo carried a new gun; his boots and badge shone. "You look, like, cheerful tonight," Rodrigo said.

"What's this playing?" Adrian quizzed.

"Huh?"

"Beethoven's Fifth Symphony."

"I like country music."

"I quite forgot."

"You comin'?"

PART IV

Níño

▼▼▼

Indeed the two spent much time together: Adrian was happy at last to have a friend in Downsville. So was Rodrigo: like Adrian, he tended to be solitary. He quarreled often with his superiors in the Border Patrol; lately they had removed him from horse patrol, depriving him of the beasts he loved, and reassigned him to a truck. In the truck, on the day shift or at night, Adrian rode with him; off duty, they shared meals at Wyatt Cafeteria and at Whataburger.

Much of their friendship was devoted to harsh physical competition. Not only did they "pump iron" and race each other at the gymnasium; they raced cross-country under the horrid sun and swam at Boca Chica beach through blobs of jellyfish in the Atlantic sea. In these contests they were roughly equal, Rodrigo winning one day, Adrian the next, though Rodrigo, six years Adrian's junior, enjoyed the advantage. When they were done with racing, they rode to the river's edge, in the wild near the bird sanctuary, tethered their horses to mesquite stumps, and Rodrigo taught his friend survival tactics.

What Adrian did not already know of wrestling, judo, karate chops, he learned from Rodrigo. Soon his back was raw from his body being thrown so often to the stony ground. Rodrigo taught him how to tense his muscles, endure beatings, protect his head and genitalia, deflect the blows of drug-crazed thieves, the knives of deranged assassins, and even the assaults of torturers. As Adrian stood bare-chested by the river, Rodrigo rushed downward from the bank with a dull rock, colliding with his torso full force. The game was to avoid falling backward into the water; when Adrian faltered, Rodrigo punished him by rushing at him with two rocks and inflicting terrific blows to his belly, ribs, and ears. What Rodrigo gave he received with grace, standing shirtless by the river and, whenever he stumbled, commanding Adrian to rush at him with two rocks, three rocks, four rocks, until he kept his ground. As the weeks passed, Adrian's body, already hard, became, like Rodrigo's, as resistant as the rocks. He was never ill; he never had been.

And when they were finished with the day's sport, an hour or so before the sun set, they reclined on the sand at a distance from each other and communed in comfortable silence. Sometimes Adrian sketched birds or rose to dabble at his easel, but more often he read his Jung, Goethe, St. Augustine, now and then aloud to Rodrigo.

" '. . . and during my sixteenth year,' " he recited from Augustine's *Confessions,* " 'between Madaura and Carthage, owing to the narrowness of the family fortunes, I did not go to school but lived idly at home with my parents. The thorns of unclean lusts flourished until they towered over my head, and there was no hand to pluck them out. On the contrary my father saw me one day in the public baths, now visibly advancing toward manhood and betraying the teeming signs of adolescence. He rejoiced, indeed, with that drunkenness wherein the world forgets You its Creator and loves Your creation instead of You, that merriment of the unseen wine of a twisted will turned toward baseness.

" 'I rushed headlong on my course, so blindly that amongst the other youths I felt ashamed that my love of vice was less than theirs. I heard them boasting of their exploits, the viler the exploits the louder the boasting, so I set about the same adventures not only for the satisfaction of the vice but for the pleasure of the boasting. I grew in vice through greed for praise. When I lacked the chance to equal others in my vice, I invented feats I had not done, lest I be considered cowardly for my innocence, or contemptible for being chaste. With the basest of companions I strode the streets of Babylon. . . .' "

Rodrigo recited from his own book, indeed his bible (he brought it everywhere), a police manual called *Survival*. " '. . . I like the edge the danger I get a high off it. You're out there in the concrete or cornfield jungle you know the guy you're up against don't care a f—— about you but he knows you got to get him. I like the danger it makes me feel *alive* but I don't jump in danger like a a——hole I'm not gonna give nobody the chance to get even just a little bit of me. Goin' up against danger and comin' out whole because I'm ready *tactically* that's what the rush comes from. My dad used to say there's no new frontiers but there's still one *the street* it's the only place you can be that still has that edge to it . . .' "

"That's *me*!" Rodrigo cried out. " '. . . and use colors to mark your different levels of patrol awareness. Condition White: this is a state of environmental unawareness. Condition Yellow: you are relaxed but alert, cautious but not tense. Condition Orange: this is a state of alarm! Condition Red: what looks bad *is* bad!! Condition Black: panic, frenzy, paralysis. Lights out for you!!!

" '. . . and learn Crisis Rehearsal in your sleep. Watch your own movements in slow motion. Carefully observe where your feet are, what your hands are doing, how your body is postured. When you awake, repeat the scene again and again, gradually speeding it up until it takes place in "real time" and your physical responses are smooth and without interruption. Always imagine yourself responding with calm control. Do not imagine failure or rehearse something the wrong way, or you will reinforce wrong responses!!!' "

Rodrigo paused. "Isn't that *great?*"

"Rules I wish I'd learned," Adrian mumbled, half asleep upon the sand.

" '. . . and on any high-risk call, I will survive because, One, I know the tactics I need, Two, I know the moves I need, Three, I can stay focused . . .' "

Adrian dozed off. When he awoke, it was nearly dark and Rodrigo crouched near him, picking at the silver tooth near the corner of his mouth, sobbing. Off duty he wore a polo shirt, gray jeans, and black fashion boots; in the dusk, his copper skin, neat mustache, and dark hair glistened as he wept more quietly. "What's wrong?" Adrian asked. Rodrigo said, "I bashed a chick last night."

"Where?"

"In bed. I told her, 'This will have to be fast,' but once I came, this dame wanted to talk. I punched her out."

"Badly?"

"A black eye; it barely shows. I hate myself."

Rodrigo needed women: "I make excuses, tell the chicks I'm so busy, because once I come I can't stand the chick and I gotta be alone."

"A common complaint, Rodrigo. It's afflicted me."

"I thought I was special. Why am I disgusted whenever I get laid?"

"Postcoital sadness."

"How do *you* deal with it?"

"You wouldn't care for my method."

"What's your method?"

"Dear Rodrigo, you're so innocent, and . . . I shouldn't like to shock you."

"What's your f——ing method?"

"I'm celibate."

"Oh Jesus why?"

"It's more fun."

"Stop bullshitting!"

"All right: because I choose to be."

"How can I get rid of post—post—"

"Coital."

"—sadness?"

"Stop having coitus."

"I can't! Should I try for more lasting friendships?"

"You'd fail. Happiness comes only in glimpses. The best friendships are fleeting."

"Is that a threat?"

"What do you mean, Rodrigo?"

"Why did you come to the valley?"

"I told you: to atone."

"When you leave, you'll forget me!"

"Dear Rodrigo . . ."

"You'll drop me like a hot brick!"

"Can't you enjoy our friendship *now*?"

"*See?* Like a hot brick! I never knew nobody like you, Ay-jay! How long will you stay?"

The darkness hummed with men and children on the other shore. Adrian raised his binoculars to scan Mexico. He answered, "Until I find the child."

"Then what'll you do—build a hospital around him?"

"What an interesting suggestion."

"You throw money at every bum you meet."

"That's what my mother says."

"I know a rich guy when I see one."

"What were you reciting when I fell asleep?"

"The Ten Commandments of Survival."

"Recite them again."

"Why?"

"They're so musical."

" 'On any high-risk call, I will survive because, One, I know the tactics I need, Two, I know the moves I need, Three, I can stay focused, Four, I can control any problem, Five, I can take each call calmly step by step, Six, I can breathe deeply to control stress, Seven, I can decide not to be afraid, Eight, I can defeat any threat, Nine, I can use deadly force to save my life, Ten, I can survive and keep going even if I am hit.' You won't never find that kid, Ay-jay."

Adrian's next weeks with Rodrigo on his night shift became such a blur of images, fantastic or grotesque, that later when he dreamed of them, or tried to paint them, they were colored green.

Green was the way the world of dark appeared through night-vision goggles. Rodrigo made Adrian wear a bulletproof vest and night-vision goggles when they hunted drug runners. Adrian disliked the stiff vest, but he loved the goggles that allowed him to see through the murk: they magnified ambient light, brightened the world into an eerie green, and inflated fireflies into the size and brilliance of shooting stars. Yet when he took them off, the darker the night and the blinder he became. One evening, as he and Rodrigo crouched in high grass, groaning shadows, bundles upon their heads and backs, waded across the Rio Grande and crept through a meadow toward a thick wood near Dead Man's Curve.

"Nine-sixty-six? Nine-sixty-six?" Rodrigo whispered to his walkie-talkie.

"Nine-sixty-six."

"Six-oh-six."

And on: electronic babble about suspected contraband how many mules stand by computer register repeat? eight sensor hits four-fifty-five Port One R.P. forty-nine request backup repeat? dispatching backup six-oh-six. By now the shadows had advanced halfway through the field toward the wood. Rodrigo abandoned

Adrian behind a bush and dashed away toward the meadow. Enchanted, Adrian watched through his magic spectacles.

The shadows were led in columns by two Mexicans (Adrian guessed), both with assault rifles. The men with great bales upon their backs were "mules," probably poor Central Americans reduced to that peonage in order to survive. For a moment Rodrigo exposed himself, in his bulletproof vest stepping from behind a tree, pointing his revolver with both arms rigidly extended and shouting, "*¡Inmigración! ¡Alto! ¡Tiren las armas!* Halt! Throw down your guns! Hands up!"

The Mexicans raked the tree with bullets, sprayed the meadow wildly, but Rodrigo began a duck walk—a crouching movement that kept his cover, propelled him to and fro in the high grass from bush to bush and tree to tree. A Mexican wore night goggles, but the strap was broken and he held the goggles on with one hand as he shot his bullets with the other and then lost the goggles in the grass. The "mules" huddled behind the gunmen, kneeling, moaning, and crying out to God. Rodrigo was everywhere, crawling on his stomach, duck-walking, hiding his position and withholding fire until he was sure it was time to shoot. The cough of automatic weapons, bullets bouncing from trees and rocks, the smell of gunshot, commingled with the green brilliance of the world and made Adrian marvel at his friend.

How Rodrigo knows his craft! he thought. He is an artist more than I! He heard the voices rushing through Rodrigo's head: Condition Orange Condition Red avoid Condition Black. Watch your movements in slow motion. Where are your feet what are your hands doing? Remember remember respond with cool control I will survive because I stay focused I breathe deeply I am deciding not to be afraid I can defeat any threat I can use deadly force I can survive and keep going even if I am hit! Almost at the river's edge, Rodrigo rose for an instant from the grass and shouted at the backs of the gunmen, "*¡Tiren las armas!*" They whirled toward him, firing stupidly, and he shot them dead in the chests with a bullet each. The "mules" panicked, cast down their burdens, fled howling through the bush toward the river upstream, downstream, and Mexico: Rodrigo let them go. When his backup arrived, those other policemen had only to load the marijuana and the corpses into trucks. Rodrigo said, "Five bullets hit my vest." Adrian removed his goggles, saying, "I can't see."

Rodrigo led him to a truck. They drove to headquarters, where Rodrigo typed a report and the chief agent fussed because Adrian was an unauthorized civilian. He said, "You coulda got killed on that drug bust. You'll never go out on patrol again."

Miserably Adrian returned to his motel, where he relived the drug bust in a green dream. Next morning, from a booth at Amigoland, he rang his attorney on Wall Street, but the beeps seemed an extension of his nightmare, and somehow the words were colored green. A woman answered, "Burner, Burner, Burner & Burner."

"I have a collect call for Mr. Burner from Adrian Northwood."

"*Which* Mr. Burner, operator?"

"Which Mr. Burner, sir?"

"Mr. Burner IV."

"Mr. Burner IV is in a meeting."

"Miss, you must be new there. Mr. Burner will accept my call."

"Will you hold, operator?"

Strauss waltzes played, then a man's voice (contralto, with echoes of an Alabaman drawl) accepted charges and shrieked over a loudspeaker telephone, "AJ!"

"Ah, Burner."

"Where y'all at?"

"Texas. Do I own any newspapers?"

"In Texas?"

"Anywhere."

"Let me peek in my computer, AJ!"

Adrian heard the thud of fingers tapping on a keyboard and resounding over Burner IV's loudspeaker. Burner IV said, "You own partial interest in six community newspapers in California." More tapping. "Correction!" he shrieked. "You did until two months ago!" Burner IV managed Adrian's money, but only once had Adrian stooped to take a meal with him: shared meals were sacramental. Burner IV said, "I sold the shares."

"Why?"

"Dry holes, AJ. It's all in my reports!"

"Can't you buy them back?"

"It may take a while."

"I need a letter now saying that I work for a newspaper."

Fingers tapped. Burner IV said, "Hey, AJ, you own a weekly, the Virgin Islands *Seaweed!*"

"That will do." He instructed his attorney to obtain a letter from *Seaweed* requesting the United States Border Patrol to accredit him as a special correspondent. He added, "I'm running out of cash."

"How much do you want, AJ?"

"Thirty thousand? Make it fifty?"

"Where in Texas are you at?"

"Downsville."

"What's your bank?"

" '. . . the very awfulness of riches . . .' "

"Beg your pardon?"

" '. . . the deceitfulness of riches . . .' "

"How's that?"

" '. . . the calamity of riches . . .' "

"AJ?"

Adrian had no bank in Downsville. He glanced about the mall and saw a sign, BEAN & VALLEY BANK. He said, "Send it to the Bean & Valley Bank."

The money arrived that afternoon, the letter of accreditation on a chartered airplane from the Virgin Islands next morning. At Border Patrol headquarters, Adrian signed a waiver absolving the United States Government of all bond for his safety, and he continued to venture forth in Rodrigo's truck, now as a "newspaper correspondent." He never wrote a word for *Seaweed,* but he did, for his pleasure, more than ever, sketch and paint the river's disorderly pageant of life. The hordes of jobless Mexicans, the swarming refugees from Central America's war and hunger, increased.

8

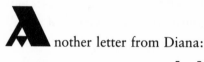 nother letter from Diana:

. . . and it has occurred to me that the letter I sent to you late last
month was perhaps too harsh. Forgive me, Adrian. I was dreadfully
upset by the reviews of my book, and I took it out on you. Above
all, please ignore my preposterous remarks about your talent. You
do have some talent.

My publisher finally has spent a little money of his own and run
small advertisements in Los Angeles and in The New Yorker. He
has asked me to undertake a brief tour to promote the book on
the East Coast and in California, but of course I have refused. I
loathe being asked vapid questions by journalists who have not
even read my books, and I am now too old to appear well on
television. Besides, we have our family canon to avoid publicity at
all costs, and we both do well to observe it. I shan't ever forget
your dear father's epigram "Consort with asps, but never trust a
journalist." When he was offered the embassy to Rome, and then
to the Court of St. James's, I fantasized about the glory, but today
I recognize the wisdom of his refusals, because he would not expose
his family to vulgar curiosity.

Cardinal Galsworthy left on Monday morning after celebrating
Mass in the chapel, his fourth Mass since arriving here on Friday.
Except for several of the servants, I was alone with him in the
chapel, as each of us wished. By special dispensation of the Pope,

he said the holy sacrifice in Latin—in full robes, the alb of precious lace, the golden Roman chasuble that your father gave him—according to the Tridentine rite. Though he knew you would not be here, he said that Northwood Hall seemed half empty without you.

Before the Mass on Friday evening, the Cardinal confessed me. I told him of the cruel letter I had written to you, and through the grille of the confessional, even before he spoke, I could feel his pain. As my penance, he denied me Communion until Sunday morning.

That aside, the visit went very well, and I am still a bit giddy from the Cardinal's presence. At our first dinner, I told him bluntly that I will never forgive the late Pope for having abolished the papal nobility. He said, "I agree, Diana, it's very sad, but we both of us knew it was inevitable. How can we justify dukes and duchesses in the Church of the Poor? There is nothing to be done."

"Your Eminence's logic amazes me," I retorted. "What is contradictory between having the nobility and helping the poor? Urban and I always did."

"Quite true. It is a problem, I suppose, of perception."

"Whose perception?"

"The poor's."

"Nonsense! The poor looked up to the papal nobility. They loved all the incense, the music, the pomp and circumstance. They loved the cardinals in their ermine and long trains, and the dukes in their regalia and white ruffles. They loved the Pope in his tiara, on his portable throne, surrounded by ostrich feathers."

"Dear Diana . . ."

"The poor have always loved a good show, and the Church gave it to them. They depended on Holy Church not just for mystery but for theater, but now you've denied them both. Why did you have to *change* everything?"

The Cardinal sighed. I knew he agreed with me, but out of loyalty to the late Pope, to whom he was close, he remained silent. Though I dared not say so, I continue to attend Mass outside my own chapel more out of constancy than devotion, so much in the Church has changed. Your father and I were the Duke and Duchess of

Canino, a title once held by Lucien Bonaparte. You, Adrian, were created a papal marquis when you were eight, on the day of your Confirmation by Cardinal Galsworthy here at Northwood Hall, but a year later your title was abolished, and your father's, and my own. Do you remember? Do you care?

Whenever we meet, His Eminence is more exquisite with age. His flared nostrils; his full silver hair beneath his crimson zucchetto; the pale skin of his face, stretched tightly on his cheekbones from a lifetime of self-denial: how his image lingers. He was created a cardinal when he was barely forty, but now he is as vigorous in his sixties as he was so long ago, when your father first knew him. He is haunted by the notion that he has a son.

He revealed this on Saturday evening, at dinner in the great hall. He was my only guest. Since my hearing is no longer what it should be, I ignored your father's custom of sitting at either end of the long table and seated the Cardinal in the middle, across from myself. I instructed the servants to leave the courses in their hot tureens and then to withdraw: I served. André had brought up a bottle of our best Barbaresco, though His Eminence barely touched it. I wore my usual black satin with double pearls and covered my bare arms with a blue shawl.

You will recall how your father liked to see cardinals dressed up. Augustine must have remembered, because he came down to dinner in full scarlet. You would have enjoyed his graceful entrance from the stairway, across the corridor, into the great hall, robed in crimson mozzetta and soutane, a lace rochet, buckled shoes. I genuflected to kiss his ring, and we dined by candlelight.

It seems that in his youth, while a seminarian at the Academy of Noble Ecclesiastics, Augustine overdid his studies, his health broke down, and he was told by the rector to take a holiday. Both within the Academy and beyond it, he had no companions, since the clerical discipline of the period discouraged "particular friendships." Augustine boarded the train at Rome and went to Florence, alone.

He took rooms in the Hotel Berchielli, overlooking the River Arno and the Ponte Vecchio. He was miserable because he had been ordered to rest his mind, to abstain from reading, and he hardly knew how otherwise to pass his time. In his black soutane, he visited the churches and the Pitti galleries, took long walks along the Arno, and lunched each afternoon in a trattoria by the river not far from his hotel. Soon he was aware that a dark woman, older than himself, habitually entered the restaurant, sat opposite his table, and gazed at him.

May I say at once that I sympathize with his admirer? If his present appearance is a guide, Augustine in his youth must have been classical. After a week, the woman contrived to leave the restaurant as he did, though like any good seminarian he cast his eyes to the ground and pretended not to notice. Under the hot sun, he strolled along the Arno toward his hotel, fingering his rosary, praying that the woman would not follow him.

He paused by the balustrade, pretending to watch a bird in flight, and glanced behind him. The woman wore sunglasses, and a floral skirt and jacket over her broad hips. She said, "Will you come with me to the seashore?"

"Where?" Augustine stammered.

"Viareggio."

"I can't."

He was relieved that she had spoken to him, and he continued to stammer replies to her entreaties as they walked further along the Arno past his hotel.

"Where do you live?" she asked.

Still holding his rosary, he pointed to his hotel. He feared it might be difficult to pass through the lobby. It was the hour of siesta; the lobby was deserted. "I could hear my heart, hammering." The cassocked youth and the older woman entered the lift unnoticed, ascended to his rooms. When they were done, he asked, "What's your name?"

"Giovanna."

"Are you from Florence?"

"Lucca. I work in Florence, at a flower shop. Will you come with me to Viareggio?"

"I can't."

She put on her clothes and left. Augustine bent over his bed to make it up, and has spent a lifetime of longing ever since. Years after his return to Rome, well into his active priesthood, he became convinced that he and the woman had conceived a son. I asked, "What makes you certain it was a son?"

"He was revealed to me in a dream," the Cardinal said. "I've seen his face in many dreams."

"Does he resemble you?"

"He is an infant child."

"Did you ever break your vows again?"

"No."

Ten years after the event, Augustine hired detectives to find a dark woman named Giovanna from Lucca who had worked in Florence at a flower shop; they searched for five years. After dinner, we strolled in the gardens. In the moonlight, His Eminence admired your mock Greek ruins.

On Monday morning, just before the Cardinal left, I went to my library to get his check. On an impulse I tore it up and wrote another on our joint account, tripling the amount, hoping that this might please you. I told him, "This is in memory of Antonia and little Urban."

His Eminence has written another book, *The Joy of Celibacy*. He gave me an inscribed copy as a parting gift. The style is elegant like Newman's but simpler. He will write to you from Rome.

Since the Cardinal's departure, I have been distraught with loneliness. Except for my writing, I have nothing and no one. In the wood the other evening I saw a piping plover, but without you at my side I felt hollow. I have read your last letter fifty times. You do *write* well. More and more, I sit in the chapel, among the Austrian statues that you so lovingly installed, thinking of you.

Letters—financial reports?—from your Mr. Burner IV continue to arrive here. Don't you think I should forward them?

What do you eat for breakfast in your horrid motel room? Where do you eat dinner besides Wyatt Cafeteria and Whataburger? Have you lost weight? Are you avoiding junk food? I know that you have doubts, but do you go to Mass? *Who* is Rodrigo?

When will you come home? In the wood the other evening I reflected that you are not following the traditional path of remorse. The heartsick mystics of past centuries often lived debauched lives into middle age, before turning to God and atonement. The monastery, the hair shirt, the flagellant's whip, were refuges reserved for later life, but you are still so very young. I kiss your hands.

Ta mère,

Ta mère qui t'aime,

DIANA

O n the day shift, Rodrigo fetched Adrian from his motel at dawn. They drove to Amigoland, where they took their breakfast with Rodrigo's peers before all of them dispersed to their patrols along the Rio Grande. The Border Patrol were an odd sort of army, some of them fair Anglo-Saxons, but most, like Rodrigo, dark young Mexican-Americans who conversed in ungrammatical English and that debased dialect of Spanish, common throughout the valley, "Tex-Mex," muddling Spanish and English so unmusically that Adrian loathed it. These men were good soldiers.

Over their eggs and coffee, they chatted of cars, trucks, of long miles traveled on flat, dusty roads, of country music, professional football, playing squash together, beer commercials, videotapes, television satellite dishes they bought on credit, drug seizures, and of the Border Patrol's poverty. They were hungry stepchildren of the great government of the north.

They were a few dozen men policing scores of miles of river. Their ground sensors mostly did not function, their trucks were bullet-holed, falling apart, their tires had no tread. They petitioned the great government for tires, gasoline, spare parts, but the government paid no heed, so they made do with patches, pieces of wire, and they siphoned gasoline from the tanks of arrested drug traffickers. The government rationed their bullets and to fire them furnished only vintage shotguns and revolvers, so to protect themselves they commandeered the assault weapons of the traffickers or bought their own. From Amigoland, Rodrigo and Adrian drove to the Rio Grande in a rusty truck with an air conditioner that did not cool, a siren that could not sound, police lights that never flashed, as Rodrigo sought illegal vagabonds.

The shore was littered with plastic bags, underwear, and empty wallets. As the sun rose from the flat landscape of Matablancos, the metropolis that loomed on the other bank, and the wet heat began to suck at the armpits, new tides of naked men and boys lined the opposite shore, clutching their plastic bags of clothes, a few of them flogging their soft members and pretending to masturbate, jeering at Rodrigo as he passed. Some aliens waded naked in the middle of the river or near the Texan shore, taunting Rodrigo to come and catch them.

The aliens he caught, in the reeds or running away from the river across the fields toward Downsville, were mostly clothed. Street wisdom told them to dry their bodies in the grass, never to carry luggage, to dress in jeans or Bermuda shorts like Texans, but they could not trick Rodrigo. A stupid alien might cross the river in his underwear, but when he pulled on his trousers the water seeped through and he was betrayed by a wet crotch. Rodrigo pinned his captives against his junky truck, felt their bodies for knives and guns, and locked them in the truck behind a meshed screen; he drove the Mexicans to Gateway Bridge to sign multiplicate bureaucratic forms and then deported them. Laughing, gangs of Mexicans signed their papers of voluntary deportation in the truck, Rodrigo let them out, and they strolled across the bridge to Mexico. Within minutes, they swam back to the United States. Arrested at random, they were driven to the bridge, "processed" yet again, deported to Mexico, and within minutes they swam to the United States.

Mobs of the Mexicans were "river rats" from Matablancos— thieves, murderers, rapists, drunkards, drug addicts, sniffers of glue, men and youths who often combined such tastes and assembled in such numbers in the park near Gateway Bridge that no police force could disperse them, tattooed so grotesquely, some even on their faces, that Adrian wondered, Do they belong to a cult? Many brandished red cans labeled Coca-Cola, though the cans contained not soda pop but glue. The vagrants mashed glue and paint inside the cans and through the holes inhaled the fumes, screaming and raving as the day progressed, but not all Mexicans seized by the Border Patrol were vagrants. Many were jobless youths from deep in Mexico—clear-eyed, robust, some barefoot—squeezed out by the tumid populations of their slums, farms, fishing villages, aspiring toward the rich neighbor of the north in search of wages to feed their families.

Rodrigo did not dump all of his captives on the bridge. Aliens he seized away from the river, in bus stations, in the streets of Downsville, trudging alone or in columns along the hot roads, thumbing rides to escape the valley toward Corpus Christi, San Antonio, Houston, he delivered to Border Patrol headquarters by Route 77, the highway from Downsville to the north—into a cement building, through a steel door with a combination lock, to sit at long tables facing Rodrigo and his fellows, typing out eternal forms, but processing Mexicans was as mechanical and futile at headquarters as it had been on the bridge.

The waves of derelicts, pregnant women, hungry street children, seemed mostly stoic, though some of the glue sniffers—who lived like rabbits beneath the stilts of houses, burrowed in the earth, munched on grass—at times had to be fettered to a bench. Among the Mexican children were flower sellers and chicleros; whenever he could do so quietly Adrian took them to a corner of the great room, where (praying they would not buy glue) he bought bunches of their carnations and boxes of their chewing gum. Once processed, the women were locked in a bare detention room, the males in a much larger room, where they lounged on benches, slept on the floor, or stood about shouting. Eventually they were packed into trucks and driven to the bridge.

Central American captives were not as easy to throw away. Central Americans rarely accepted voluntary deportation and could not be expelled to Mexico. In the lovely idiom of the Border Patrol, Central Americans were not Hondurans, Guatemalans, Salvadorans, or Nicaraguans, but "OTMs"—Other Than Mexicans. Many

OTMs managed to elude the Border Patrol, but unlucky OTMs arrested at the river or throughout the valley became entangled in the metaphysics of the federal bureaucracy. At headquarters, they were read their rights, "*Usted tiene el derecho de permanecer callado* . . . you have the right to remain silent . . . anything you say may be used against you . . . you have the right to consult an attorney . . . ," and then they swam through swamps of paper in circles that bewildered them.

A Border Patrol agent interviewed each OTM, typing at length an I-214 form, an I-217 form, an I-154 form, an I-274 form, an I-770 form, an I-221S form, in sum accusing each refugee of having entered the United States illegally and advising him of his right to appear before a judge to plead against deportation to the country he had fled. Then the refugee was photographed with instant film and fingerprinted, but some OTMs emerged from the scrutiny more comfortably than others. Parents with children were entrusted to the Red Cross, children without parents to orphanages. Men and women who had crossed the Rio Grande alone, couples without children, youths and girls beyond adolescence, were imprisoned.

Rodrigo drove these unfortunates far out into flat land near the sea, to a place, beneath a white water tower, slyly named a Service Processing Center, so dusty and bleak that to Adrian it resembled a concentration camp. It was not a concentration camp; the OTMs (thousands of them) were not gassed or tortured, they were adequately fed, but it seemed dreary on purpose and not quite human. The grounds were vast and treeless, gray earth and grass, encircled twice by barbed wire. Inside the ugly barracks, the OTMs were stripped of their dress, marched naked into communal showers, deloused, then clothed in orange uniforms.

Television cameras monitored their movements, awake or as they slept. In a barrack, scores of orange men and women crowded the linoleum corridors, waiting to be heard by a judge. Through a closed door, his voice droned on, deciding whether this Guatemalan or that Salvadoran deserved political asylum or, more likely, deportation. At pay telephones, OTMs pleaded with their relatives in Miami and Los Angeles to send them money. Through the door a woman wept, "I have no money. I have no friends. I came to this country to work."

Occasionally during day or night Rodrigo was summoned to the north to collect captured aliens, and drove the hundred miles from Downsville to Sarita, where the Border Patrol manned an outpost on Route 77, the last stop on the road out of the valley. Sarita was not a place, only a checkpoint in wild flat cattle country where the agents had a wooden shed. As cars and trucks drove northward, they were halted at the shed and agents politely asked each traveler, "Are you a U.S. citizen?" They waved most on, but they also opened trunks, tapped the sides of doors, climbed inside trailer trucks, seeking aliens and drugs. The agents had a sniffing dog, but as he sniffed one cargo the agents sniffed at others, crouching houndlike over suspicious freight, inhaling the hidden fragrance of cocaine and marijuana with canine skill.

Bundles of cocaine and marijuana were heaped inside the shed, where the agents went serenely about their business amid the bales, pecking at their typewriters, processing handcuffed traffickers and shabby Mexicans and OTMs beneath a sign, SOLO DIOS SABE MI DESTINO. The aliens were caught in fields between Sarita and the sea, creeping northward over cattle trails, now and then triggering seismic sensors that beeped on a computer, hiding in the dry vegetation, refreshing themselves with half-gallon plastic bottles of orange soda pop, playing fox and hounds with the Border Patrol in their shoddy trucks under the sun at noon and the moon at midnight. Inside the shed, they were led down a dark corridor to a windowless cell with a stinking toilet, where often they became so crowded they could not sleep on the floor and had to stand. The Border Patrol fed them sandwiches of baloney and Wonder bread before Rodrigo drove the Mexicans to the river and the OTMs to prison beneath the white water tower by the sea.

Westward of the highway and the shed, converging northward from the border over the endless plain, were the tracks of a freight railway; when a diesel passed, it hauled two hundred cars. After midnight, the train rolled slowly as agents from the shed shone flashlights at the undersides of cars or boarded them and leaped from roof to roof, seeking aliens and drugs.

Men, women, and infant children were sealed in boxcars, crouched in open gravel gondolas, or rode on boards between the wheels. Young men rode bars beneath the axles, squeezed themselves inside the deafening spaces of the diesel engine, or clung to railings on the walls of cars. The agents found some and forced them off, the aliens ran across the landscape, crying out, but the agents caught them and drove them to the shed. These aliens were lucky; others on the trains lost their grasp and were crushed between the wheels, or suffocated when their sealed boxcars were left to idle in the sun.

Yet aliens continued to cross the river and aspire north. The Border Patrol watched all exits from the valley, so the north was not easy to achieve. Trapped inside the valley, alien women worked as maids for pittance wages, and alien men did little better. They worked on farms, harvesting tomatoes and cutting hay, or on the docks of Port Downsville, packing shrimp, for almost nothing. At twilight, as Adrian cruised with Rodrigo near the docks, a thin and tiny youth, strolling on the road in a flannel shirt, shifted his eyes and ran away.

Rodrigo leaped from his truck, chasing the youth toward a tin warehouse. A black bitch and her puppies ran out of the warehouse and howled at Rodrigo as he seized his prey. His prey threw breathless punches, but Rodrigo cast him to the ground and handcuffed him as the dogs snapped. "I'm a refugee!" the boy screamed. "El Salvador! My family was murdered! Look at my back!"

Rodrigo tore off the flannel shirt: near his spine the Salvadoran had two bullet wounds. Handcuffed, he led the Americans and the dogs inside the warehouse, where he had been scraping rust from ship machinery to earn his bread, then up a stairway to a filthy attic too hot for humans or for dogs. The room was strewn with wrappings of potato chips and candy bars. Adrian wondered, Is that his bread? He had no papers. Rodrigo removed the handcuffs and ordered him to pack his things, but his possessions were a pair of socks. The Americans delivered him to headquarters and drove away with a gang of Mexicans to be dumped on the bridge.

At night, the bridge throbbed.

The bridge stood over the Rio Grande on concrete stumps; in the middle was a metal sign that marked the line where Mexico ended and the United States began. It was Friday evening. The lanes were jammed with the cars of bourgeois Mexicans with visas, en route to weekend shopping in the United States. In the opposite direction Mexicans with green cards drove from Texas to their homeland or crossed the bridge on foot. The bridge's sidewalks teemed with Mexicans who crossed beyond the metal sign some footsteps into the United States, until they reached the Customs and could penetrate no farther. These were mostly hungry children, selling chewing gum, flowers, and plastic birds. They harassed pedestrians, and when the pedestrians refused their wares they darted in and out between the cars, rapping on windshields, thrusting their flowers and birds through open windows, beseeching money.

In Texas, the booths of U.S. Customs were bathed in an amber haze, blending with the night beyond and its money changers, pawnshops. Marijuana and heroin, opium and cocaine, flowed across the bridge, but the cars and trucks concealing them were so many and the Customs were so few they seized but little. A sixth sense told the Customs when something was amiss, and they were trained to detect those signs of stress—sweating hands, breathless speech, twitching muscles—that betrayed the smuggler, yet the smugglers took Valium to control their nerves and the cool traffickers were subtle. They favored trucks and vans with large tanks, which they divided into sections, filling some with gasoline and others with cocaine, the cocaine wrapped in chemicals that disguised the smell and confused sniffing dogs.

One evening, Adrian walked to the middle of the bridge, gazing out into the hot night. The twisted river seemed to groan with pain. He heard a woman's distant scream. He knew that up and down the river, families fleeing Central America and beyond were (as always) being robbed, by thieves with knives, machetes, and automatic guns, and perhaps in high grass a woman was being raped as tattooed men pointed revolvers at her children, forcing them to watch.

Suddenly, on the bridge, a gang of twenty, thirty gorgeous women—young, elaborately made up, in strapless dresses and high metal heels, swinging Gucci handbags—rushed from Mexico between the honking cars, down the sloping lanes, past Customs. The agents popped out of their plastic booths, shouting, waving their arms, struggling to arrest them, but the women were too swift and, giggling, most of them escaped into the amber night past the money changers and the pawnshops toward downtown Downsville. Afterward Rodrigo said, "Those weren't women; they were transvestites. They suck c——s and steal cars. They carry slim-jims in their handbags and make seven hundred dollars per car."

"Who pays them?" Adrian marveled.

"The Mexican police."

Often, as such scenes took place, Adrian sketched them on his paper, and afterward, at his motel, very late at night, he transformed them into paintings. Now he had so many paintings that his tiny room could not hold them; he rented other rooms at the motel to house his pictures and the plastic birds, boxes of chewing gum, and bunches of dead carnations that he forgot to throw away. Sometimes as he slept he saw visions of the river on such a scale that when he awoke he put aside his easel as too small and painted the visions on his walls. Cockroaches invaded his oozing tubes of rose madder and Antwerp blue and, crawling across the murals, added their cadenzas. The decorations upset the management, who demanded that Adrian whitewash the walls and then move out. He called Mr. Burner IV.

"AJ!"

"I'm having trouble with my motel."

"What's it called?"

"The 5½."

"Where's it at?"

"Central Boulevard."

"What's it like?"

"A dump."

"Want me to buy it?"

"You'd better."

"Anonymously?"

"Of course."

"What if they balk?"

"Pay them well."

"Should I change the management?"

"Why bother?"

"Any special instructions?"

"Tell them to leave me alone."

After the sale, Adrian rented more and more rooms at Motel 5½, to lodge illegal Mexicans and Central Americans whom he especially pitied. He kept an empty room in reserve for the day he should find the child. Rodrigo knew everything, but—anxious lest he lose Adrian—he looked the other way. Never, perhaps, had Adrian painted so well.

His humans no longer looked like scarecrows—a woman in the rain, tattooed men, flower sellers, a boy in handcuffs, starving street children. His children staring desperately out of boxcars were his most poignant. His drug runs were an eerie green, just as he observed them, and indeed he wore his night goggles as he painted those pictures in the dark.

I am the distinct and singular voice he hears: I told him, "At last, a richness of another kind—your talent."

"Nonsense," said Adrian. "You never gave me any."

"Has it occurred to you as you sketch that you are recording one of the great migrations of history? No one else has bothered! Do you remember the Book of Exodus? 'I have seen the affliction of my people, and I am come down to deliver them . . .' "

" '. . . out of that land unto a good land and a large, unto a land flowing with milk and honey.' You don't exist."

"You're talking to me."

"Am I?"

"These paintings are your best work."

"Better than my marble horses in the Sigmundsplatz?"

 letter from Cardinal Galsworthy:

. . . and I beg your forgiveness for having postponed for many weeks this letter of grateful acknowledgement. The Holy Father's mission kept me in the United States and in Latin America longer than either of us expected, and once I returned to Rome his business took every moment of my time. For in truth I could never have been content with dashing off a few perfunctory lines of thanks, but felt compelled to await this moment of leisure not only to express my gratitude but to share my thoughts. I was touched by your mother's cheque, not least because I knew that the money came from you. I invite you to believe, beloved Adrian, that the Holy See needs and will put to beneficent use your most generous gift in the memory of your wife and son. God can do much with three million dollars . . .

Adrian reflected, Is that all she gave him?

. . . and another portion to reduce the operating deficit of the Holy See. However (and I trust that this might please you), the Pope has told me that he will spend most of the money to ease the famine in Ethiopia. He said to me (I quote him verbatim), "Please send to Adrian, in Our name, Our most paternal, prayerful, and loving benediction. He is one of Our favourite fools."

Let me hasten to explain that his last remark was a private joke. My most recent book, *The Joy of Celibacy,* has been read, to my certain knowledge, by only two souls—the Pope and your dear mother. (Under separate cover I have sent you a copy; will you be the third?) In search of a more glamourous subject, I recently decided to write a memoir of St. Francis of Assisi, first among all of "God's fools." The work will be more a meditation on the life of Francis than a real biography, but the theme is his foolishness for the sake of Heaven. The Holy Father knows this, hence his inclusion of you in the fellowship of Francis is his highest compliment.

Poring over original sources in Assisi and Rome, I have been constantly amused by an irrepressible, divine insanity. You will recall that Francis began his adolescence as a libertine. His companions loved him for his riches and because he sang so well; he was sensual and wildly attractive, a worshipper of beauty, thus no surprise that his youth was debauched, full of wine and fornication. Soon he marched off with a gang of worthless noblemen in a war to conquer Perugia, where he was captured, bound with chains, and flung into a hole in the ground.

For a year, he remained there. Ransomed, he returned to Assisi a cheerful consumptive, still thirsty for pleasure. One day, he met a beggar; for no reason he handed the wretch his silken cloak. He began to have dreams coloured red and golden, and to hear a voice. In the midst of his debauchery he was seized with visions and murmured to his friends, "I shall wed the fairest lady." He lavished alms on every beggar who crossed his path. He ached to return to the ground, finding refuge at last in a cave atop Mount Subasio, where in the darkness he relived his sins and glimpsed himself in Hell.

Eventually, strolling in the velvet countryside of Umbria, he stumbled on a ruined church, where the crucifix spoke to him. Christ said, "Rebuild my Church." He threw off his finery, put on rags, and walked all the way to Rome. In the piazza before St. Peter's, he mingled with beggars, madly envious of beggars, resolving to become a beggar. When he returned to Umbria, a leper—limbs falling off, his face a vast ulcer, stinking to Heaven

—emerged from the forest clanging his bell. Francis ran to him and kissed his mouth.

Next, he robbed the richest cloth merchant in Umbria, his own father, to pay for repairs to the ruined church. As his father raged, hunting him throughout the countryside, Francis hid in a hole he dug behind San Damiano, the ruined church. (I find it enchanting that whenever he faced a crisis Francis sought refuge in a hole.) Finally he returned in rags to Assisi, where he was hit with stones and mud and jeered as a madman.

His father beat him terribly, bound him in chains, then dressed him in new clothes and dragged him to the public square to be judged by the bishop. The clothes were of exquisite colour, silks of the East. Francis tore them off, flung them at his father's feet, and stood naked before Assisi but for a hair shirt. Francis: "Henceforth I have no earthly father. I go naked to meet the Lord." The bishop wrapped him in his cloak. Francis fled to Gubbio through a forest, where the birds flocked about him as he sang. At Gubbio, he found work in a hospice, washing lepers, stanching pus, removing rotten flesh; again he kissed oozing wounds. Still seeking his mission, one day he threw open Scripture and randomly thrust his finger on Matthew: "Take no gold, nor silver, nor copper in your belts, no bag for your journey, nor two tunics, nor sandals, nor a staff." Now indeed he wed the fairest woman—Lady Poverty.

With his marriage, renunciation became the fashion, multitudes followed in his path, and the world changed, or so we should like to think. At least we know with certitude that a man must be crazy to live like Christ. Francis preached to flowers, fish, and birds, who listened and understood him perfectly. Satan attacked him with violent demons, but he saw a Seraph with six wings at the moment that his hands and side received the Stigmata. He went blind. As death approached, again Francis insisted on his hole, on dying "laid down naked upon the naked earth." At dusk, the moment of his death, an exaltation of larks whirled above his cell and sang. I love the sayings of Francis, not that I agree with them fanatically. "The wolf is my brother. Fire is my brother. The moon is my sister. Death is my sister. The enemy is my body. Money is excrement."

But then you know his story, and I dwell upon such moments only because—faintly—they remind me of you. When I was at Northwood Hall recently, your mother talked of your flight of atonement to the Mexican border and insisted that I read your letters. Diana worries for your safety, longs for your return, but at the risk of disloyalty to her I must tell you that I am of another mind.

From your letters I sense that you are compelled by a secret voice. I urge you to listen carefully and to heed its command. Where it will lead you, I know not, but whatever the cost, go there. If at times you are tempted to folly, then do compound the folly and follow the voice, however far. Let us leave aside for now the identity of the voice (we have argued such matters too much at Northwood Hall), because I know from Diana that you still doubt.

Apropos, Adrian, one day you will have to decide what to do with your immense fortune. At Northwood Hall I visited your rooms, almost as bemused as Diana to see the heap of financial reports unopened and your inheritance ignored. Will the voice inevitably speak to you of that also, perhaps sooner than you expect?

Again with gratitude,

In Him,

+ AUGUSTINE

■　■　■

Adrian penned a brief reply, extracted his checkbook from among his tubes of paint, and wrote another check of three million dollars to the Holy See to supplement his mother's in memory of his wife and son. Across the top he scribbled, "Famine/Ethiopia."

It was noon. Rodrigo was at Sarita on drug work; Adrian remained at Motel 5½ and resumed composition of his University Essay. He had added to it at odd moments; his longhand sprawled, the foolscap mounted, and already it exceeded ten thousand words.

■　■　■

. . . nor have I attended Mass since I arrived at the Rio Grande. Cardinal Galsworthy is correct—I doubt the existence of God.

Or at least the deity as he means it. Clearly a mysterious force

animates the universe; we need only common intelligence to catch
its scent. Whether the mystery is a Person, aware of Himself, is
quite another question.

My doubt reverts to childhood. My youth echoed with theological chatter, not only from my tutors at school in France and my
parents at the dining table, but from illustrious divines who called
on us at Northwood Hall. My misgiving came to me oddly.

One evening when I was ten, years before my father died, Cardinal Galsworthy came to us for dinner. My mother, never so lovely
in her black satin and double pearls, withdrew in the middle of
dessert: in those days, not even a Prince of the Church could keep
her from her writing desk. The Cardinal and my father sipped their
port and fell into a heated argument.

My father: "I agree about abortion, but not about birth control.
    Come now, Eminence, the lesser evil."
The Cardinal: "A sophistry. What of the frustrated transmission
    of life? Allow any artifice, allow all. The final contraceptive is
    abortion."
Father: "Nonsense. You've been to Africa and India, seen the
    squalor of overpopulation. If people cannot control themselves,
    they should be forced."
Cardinal: "Forced?"
Father: "To use contraceptives."
Cardinal: "Too many darkies, eh? Just ignore their ancient cul-
    tures? The vast consolations of large families?"
Father: "What's consoling about a starving child?"
Cardinal: "The starving child is loved by God!"
I: "Didn't God the Father practice birth control?"
Cardinal: "Why, child, what do you mean?"
I: "He had only one son."

Awkward silence. I was seated still at the dining table, sipping
a cup of chocolate. My father and the Cardinal sat in armchairs
by the fireplace beneath the beams of the great hall, His Eminence
vested as Father wished in full scarlet and buckled shoes. The young
Cardinal rose, and as he crossed the room past the groping fire, I

admired as my mother did his grace and flared nostrils. I thought, He hates himself for shouting at my father. He came to me, bent down, and kissed my forehead. He laughed and said, "Your son is an original theologian."

From across the room I glimpsed my father's tiny, dark eyes, reflecting the fire's luster and dancing from his medications: I knew at that moment he loved me more than ever. Like him, I loved the Church—still do—for her immense beauty. A religion that can produce St. Francis, the ceiling of the Sistine Chapel, the Requiem of Mozart, must possess a secret very deep.

Until today I am not certain what the secret is. Radiance is one thing, theology something else. Cardinal Galsworthy: "Theology and radiance are the same. No theology, no radiance." Still I stumble. I cannot imagine God with a conscious mind, much less a God who loves. Would a loving God allow children to starve to death, or the decapitation of my son? In Rome some years ago, I denied the intelligence of God again.

The Cardinal: "If God gave you intelligence, why should He deny it to Himself?"
I: "Prove that God gave it to me."
Cardinal: "Prove that He didn't."

I could not, but I cling to doubt. Is my doubt a mere convenience? If God has no mind, the words He uttered were not His, and no need to heed them. I enjoy such riddles because they are so unfashionable, recalling as they do the debates of distant centuries. Besides . . .

11

Now waves of OTMs seemed to overwhelm the valley. Day by day, new droves of Central Americans swam the Rio Grande and invaded Downsville. Alarmed, the government of the north dispatched more men, more rusty trucks, some old helicopters, to reinforce the Border Patrol, but against the flood the show of force seemed futile. When the Patrol arrested a hundred aliens, five hundred followed; the agents caught a few, but the government could barely confine them as its shelters and prisons overflowed. Aliens slept in gutters, in alleys by the white Gothic cathedral, behind the money changers near Gateway Bridge, and when they woke begged for money to feed their children.

Along Central Boulevard stood several abandoned motels, sagging in yellow weeds, without electricity, sanitation, or running water. Aliens moved into them, patching the shattered windows with flattened cardboard boxes and cans of soda pop, cooking gruel of rice and beans over stoves they fashioned from flattened cans, crowding fifteen, twenty adults and children into single rooms, cohabiting with flies, rats, and sickly coughs, defecating into leaky buckets or in the weeds outside, where more aliens with infant children camped without food beneath umbrellas of cardboard against the rain.

Yet when Adrian invaded the motels with Rodrigo, as his friend sought childless aliens to arrest, his keenest sensation was not so much the filth and stench as the sound of slamming doors. Whenever they entered a corridor, it was empty. Aliens scattered in the instant before they came, throwing down their frugal meals, abandoning their stoves of flattened cans, picking up their children and fleeing into fetid rooms, slamming doors and diving out of jagged windows. Once, he glimpsed a child's bare dashing feet before a door slammed. At night, the sound of slamming doors mingled with his dreams of jellyfish, those white transparent blobs, networks of brown tubes with heads that seemed like cabbage stems, floating in and out of rooms, becoming caught in the jambs of doors, oozing free and floating as more doors slammed.

Awake, Adrian thought, Enough of Rodrigo; I can see him at night. He abandoned the Border Patrol, drove his fake junky car to Amigoland, and bought baby food, buckets, mops, medicines, disinfectants, and rat poison. At the motels, he barely knew where to begin. He entered deserted corridors, and as doors slammed he removed jars of baby food and rat poison from cartons and piled them beside the stoves of flattened cans. For his buckets, he had no water. He went out and bought bottled water, then returned to the corridors and began scrubbing them with his disinfectants and a mop. No good; the filth was so profuse it needed first to be swept away. He went out and bought a dozen brooms. When he returned and swept, heads emerged from doorways one by one, and as the minutes passed, hands took up the other brooms and mops, sweeping and mopping in silence with him.

For a week or two, his exertions helped. He swept up heaps of dead rats, and throughout the encampments in the yellow weeds he distributed rice, chocolate, and Pepto-Bismol in such volume that he soothed hunger and the diarrhea of sick infants. Yet the squatters crowded the motels and encampments in such growing numbers, the rats and disease were so willful, he could not keep up. Municipal inspectors arrived one day, bulldozers the next, the sagging motels were knocked down, the weedy encampments depopulated by the police, and the aliens dispersed to the gutters of the city to sleep, defecate, and beg.

Soon afterward he discovered another alien refuge. By the bank of the river, in high grass within sight of Amigoland, not far from where he had wrestled with the child, stood abandoned wooden barracks. Decades ago the U.S. Army had been quartered there to patrol the river and chase bandits back to Mexico, but the buildings had been deserted for so long that the roofs were falling in and the walls gaped with holes. Vegetation groped through ghosts of windows. A rusty fence and barbed wire obstructed the surrounding meadow, though in such disrepair that Adrian drove through them: a rusty sign offered the property for sale. Across the river from the barracks, just beyond the shore of Matablancos, beckoned the Zona Zur, a warren of ramshackle adobe bars and brothels and, faintly visible in the flat distance, the pale turrets of what seemed to be a huge prison.

Bands of Nicaraguan and Salvadoran youths camped in the barracks, unmolested for the moment by the Border Patrol because the Patrol had no place to jail them. Adrian rarely read newspapers, but from the babble of television it seemed to him that Central America was disintegrating; Sandinistas and counterrevolutionaries were casting down their arms in Nicaragua, soldiers and guerrillas were abandoning the battle in El Salvador, and fleeing north. Once across the Rio Grande, they forgot their quarrels in a common struggle to survive. Adrian might have ignored them (didn't guerrillas live off the land?) were they not sheltering women and children.

He wondered, Should I bring them food? He loaded his car with sacks of rice and beans, baby food and bottled water, but at the barracks he was not graciously received. The guerrillas, suspecting a spy for *la Migra,* emerged from the barracks with clubs and knives and told him to disappear.

"At least take the food," he pleaded.

"We can't pay you!" they shouted.

"I'm not here for money."

"Mexican police! raped our women! stole all we had!"

"I hear children crying. Feed them."

"Poisoned food!"

"Good food! I won't leave till you take the food!"

They took it. As he drove off, he thought, They need more than food. He hated his ignorance of how to help them, and again he was bewildered by whatever impulsive steps he took next. At Motel 5½ he picked up a telephone directory and raced through the yellow pages. Hmm. LUMBER . . . NAILS . . . SAWS. No entry for HAMMERS. It did not occur to him to look under HARDWARE. Ah, here's a good one: LAWN MOWERS. Hmm. What am I thinking? Ah, HEALTH SERVICES . . . Through a hole in the barracks he had glimpsed pregnant women: what if they gave birth? MATTRESSES. No entry for BLANKETS. No entry for SHEETS. No entry for ELECTRICITY. Ah, ELECTRICAL CONTRACTORS. No RUNNING WATER. Oh, WATER COMPANIES. Ah, indeed, RAT CONTROL! Where's WATER PUMPS? Here's a good one—GENERATORS, ELECTRIC. Hmm. Where's MEDICAL SUPPLIES?

He began by buying mattresses, but they would not fit into his car, and lacking patience to lash them to the roof, he wondered, Should I buy a truck? He returned to the junkyard, to that great cemetery of smooth tires, overturned cement mixers, and the fat Mexican in sunglasses. "*Chinga,* what kind truck you want?"

"A pickup, I think? With lots of room?"

"Clean truck or junky truck?"

"A junky truck that runs."

"Got one, over there. *Chinga,* she bran'-new, but gimme a day, she look like shit."

"How much?"

"Your drug business it goin' good?"

"It goin' bad."

"Fifteen thousand cash."

As Adrian hauled mattresses, sheets, blankets, bottles of water, and boxes of medicine to the barracks, he gradually gained the guerrillas' confidence. When he brought lumber, hammers, nails, saws, and a power lawn mower, they joined him in his purpose to rebuild the barracks, saw that he knew nothing of carpentry, and taught him how as they took over that task themselves. He replaced kerosene lamps with an electric generator. The guerrillas were a tough lot; as the dozens of men, women, and small children seeking refuge in the barracks grew to scores, the place became an enclave in a mist of violence.

Though they had no guns, the guerrillas patrolled their patch of riverbank at night, beating off thieves and rapists with wooden clubs and saving women and children from evil. Off duty, Rodrigo and a few of his peers in the Border Patrol showed up in jeans and T-shirts and helped with the labor. Rodrigo said, "These OTMs gotta live somewhere. We'll grab them outside the fence." The municipal authorities were less elastic. Adrian asked them to provide the barracks with electricity and water. "Get rid of the rats," they said.

"We got rid of the rats."

"We're coming in with bulldozers."

"You can't!"

"You don't own that property."

Adrian returned to Motel 5½, packed his books and paintings in his truck, and moved into the barracks. At dawn, he ran to the stable near Los Fresnos pump, then rode Prince downriver to a new pasture and a new home in a stall by the barracks that he began to build with his own hands. He thought, Technically it's a crime to shelter the undocumented, and I love that! Should I own this property? He rode Prince to the outer fence and read the rusty sign: THIS PROPERTY FOR SALE OR LEASE APPROX 10 ACRES 542 3876. He cantered Prince across the boulevard to Amigoland, dismounted at an open booth, and telephoned Mr. Burner IV.

Reluctantly. It vexed him mildly that he was so ignorant of finance and that whenever a matter of complexity needed to be arranged he had no recourse but Burner IV. It had not always been thus.

Years earlier, after his graduation from The University and before his marriage to Antonia, he had traveled regularly to New York and tried to manage his inheritance directly. Whenever in Manhattan, he resided at his town house on lower Broadway across from Grace Church Episcopal, at the edge of Greenwich Village.

The house was large, nearly thirty rooms, previously the site of a shabby brownstone that Urban Northwood had intended to restore but then decided to demolish, erecting in its place a more pleasing edifice with a façade that mirrored the spires and cornices, gargoyles and crenellations, of the Gothic temple across the street.

Inside, the house was hardly Gothic. As he deliberated about the décor, in those days soon after wartime before his legs failed him, Urban Northwood went out for a walk. He found himself eventually before a cinema with a film that starred Bette Davis and Claude Rains, two of his favorites. Claude was a famous symphonic conductor, Bette a pianist and his former paramour, now married to Paul Henreid, an impoverished cellist. Claude outacted Bette, if that was possible, entering rooms in flowing capes, creating scenes in French restaurants, with his bare hand crushing champagne glasses in jealous rages. Urban savored his memory of the baroque dialogue.

Claude: "Nothing really matters but music. How dare you suggest that I would use my music as an instrument of revenge?"

Bette: "Do you promise? You won't tell him about us? You wouldn't! You wouldn't!"

Claude: "There is that about you this evening that suggests one of your peculiar moods. Some little secrets can't be kept. Do you believe in premonitions?"

Bette: "So you're afraid of death?"

Claude: "Devilishly."

Bette: "You said you wouldn't tell him. You must promise me again."

Claude: "Would you believe my promise?"

Bette: "You're not going to tell him!"

Claude: "I shall do what I please!"

Bette: "But you're afraid of death?"

Claude: "Devilishly, devilishly."

On the stairway of Claude's mansion, all candlelight and swirling shadow, Bette shot him. Claude (falling, dying): "You little fool. You hysterical little fool." Urban loved the movie, Claude's man-

sion even more. Next day, an underling flew to Hollywood and
bought the interior sketches.

The decorators copied them slavishly, not only the winding staircase, massive chandeliers, marble floors and fireplaces, the Louis
Quinze salon with the brocaded draperies and grand piano, but—
above all—the colors. Or rather, the noncolors. The film had been
photographed in black and white. The house, decreed Urban, must
contain not a hint of color, especially not of gold. The house had
to be all of black and white, with shades of gray and—because the
film shimmered with it—of brilliant silver.

The candelabra, the door handles, the crystal decanters and chandeliers, the baroque mirrors, the wrought-iron balustrade of the
grand staircase, the Ionic columns, Claude's thronelike rococo
chair, in their composition all suggested an incessant dialogue between light and shadow, a blending of illumination and darkness
in clashing tones of silver. In Urban's house, even the paintings—
Venetian lagoons, portraits of Mozart and Schubert—were rein-
vented in shades of silvery black and white.

Adrian disliked the house; he too loved Claude Rains, but without color (even the arrangements of roses were white) he could
barely breathe. In a black limousine he was chauffeured from the
house to the offices of Burner, Burner, Burner & Burner on Wall
Street. The chambers of his attorney he found more suffocating,
located in an old, low building, with high ceilings and thick carpeting, receptionist and secretaries sitting at walnut desks amid
brown leather couches, tapping on noiseless typewriters beneath
oil portraits of defunct Burners on oaken walls, Strauss waltzes
playing, the glazed windows all sealed shut. Whenever he entered
the suite, he began to have a headache, an affliction that grew
worse the longer he was closeted with Burner IV.

Three generations of Burners had represented the Northwood
fortune. In the nineteenth century, Burner IV's great-grandfather
had migrated to New York from Alabama, and his heirs continued
to burnish his memory as a hick. Burner IV never asked "Where
are you?" but "Where're you at?"; he never said "Take care" but
"Take care, hear?"; he had no "ideas," only "*ah*-dees." Burner IV

told prospective clients, "Y'all will deal with gentry, not dudes." Burner IV was born on Long Island, took holidays at his villa in Acapulco, and may never have been to Alabama. The Burners were lawyers only, not brokers or investment bankers, but Urban Northwood had used them as intermediaries because he preferred anonymity and knew what he was doing. During those days when Adrian traveled often to New York, he asked Burner IV, "How did my father make his money?"

"My granddaddy knew."

"But Burner II is dead."

"Yeah."

"Did he leave no records?"

"None about your paw, AJ."

"Must you be so mysterious?"

"Where'd you get that *ah*-dee?"

During their conferences in sealed rooms, Burner IV heaped portfolios before Adrian and enveloped him in stifling detail, delivered in his contralto shriek; he kept interrupting himself to take telephone calls, screeching about deals and money not into a receiver but into his boxlike apparatus and raising his pitch to soprano. The only constant Adrian could grasp was that Urban Northwood never owned a controlling interest in any airline, shipping fleet, block of real estate, and that whenever a corporation lost money he got out.

Adrian took portfolios to the Claude Rains house and studied them, carefully making notes, writing queries in the margins, reading the *Wall Street Journal* for guidance to invest his money. He wrote elaborate instructions to Burner IV, they were duly followed, and he lost money. "Does it matter?" he asked Burner IV. "How could it?" replied Burner IV. "You got so goddamn much." Burner IV could be terse on the telephone when he sensed an impatient client, but in the conference room he was so verbose the meetings dragged on all day. At evening, Adrian returned by taxi to the Village, over the elevated steel highway, under the Brooklyn and Manhattan bridges, and as he brooded on the city lights and remembered Burner IV's blobs of talk he felt an awl stabbing at his brain.

In those days, when Adrian was twenty-two and still lived in the twentieth century, Burner IV's fees for consultation were $250 per hour; today no doubt they had multiplied at least by four. In those days, whenever he opened a bill from Burner IV, he cried out, "OOOH!" "Consultations, $38,753.23. Commissions (Portfolio), $1,763,690.92. Services, $83,294.21. Sundries, $2,115.38. Disbursements, $16,161.32." Once, Adrian invited him to dinner. During dessert he asked, "You're not charging me for the time?" Burner IV sipped his Châteauneuf-du-Pape and said, "Y'mean I should turn off the meter?" He never invited Burner IV to dinner again (God might not exist, but breaking bread was sacramental), and Burner IV never turned off the meter. Burner IV never stole, or rather, he made all of his theft seem legal. He kept scrupulous records, wrote reports into myriad pages, and whenever Adrian questioned an invoice he could justify it to the last decimal.

Adrian persevered, determined to become master of his inheritance. On icy winter mornings he ran up and down lower Broadway in a T-shirt and bathing trunks, then past the overpriced art shops of East Tenth Street to a wooden newsstand at University Place for his *Wall Street Journal*. One morning, he saw a young black woman standing in a doorway opposite, shivering. She wore a plastic jacket and football shoes; by her feet lay a shopping bag: stuffed with her worldly goods? She did not resemble a prostitute or a drug addict, nor did she ask for money. In the mornings that followed, when he glanced at the doorway, she stood there. He was paralyzed, at one instant wishing to offer her food and shelter, at the next too diffident to decide. He did nothing, but took her image to his house.

More snow fell; it grew harshly cold. On a Sunday afternoon, he glanced out of his high window and saw the black woman trudging back and forth before the Gothic doors of Grace Church, gripping her shopping bag, newspapers stuffed into her football shoes. He debated, Should I ask her in? Yet in those days he cared what people thought and would not offend the servants with a pauper in cleats on his marble floors. I'll bring her a blanket. He asked his butler, "Do we have extra blankets?"

"In the closets, sir, locked up."

"Would you get the keys?"

The butler withdrew, then mounted the winding staircase with a ring of keys, each of silver, and led him to a pair of closets, the size of rooms. The first closet had black blankets. The second closet had white blankets. Adrian took a white blanket and went out to the street, where the snow raged. She was gone.

Next day, the Monday morning, he returned to Wall Street to complain to Burner IV about his bills. Burner IV shrieked. Adrian stormed out, walked aimlessly on Wall Street, thinking of the woman in football shoes. On a corner he encountered a classmate from The University, a broker, very young and very rich, whose inheritance was slight beside his own. Adrian blurted out to him the wickedness of Burner IV, but the broker laughed. "How long has Burner represented you?" he asked.

"Forever."

"The devil you know. Better stick with him."

"He steals!"

"They *all* do. Oh, how lawyers are lovely with contracts, with inventing problems where none exist. No problems, no hours, no big bucks. A million dollars to make a contract, written in such a way you'll scream eventually to get out, then five million to get you out. My lawyer would steal half my fortune if I'd let him. The trick is to control the stealing. You might run audits . . ."

"Would it do any good?"

"Not much."

Burner IV survived the audits. It was that, and the image of the woman in football shoes, that mingled oddly to make Adrian indifferent to his fortune. Thereafter he paid less attention to managing his portfolio, his properties, even his bank accounts, and left matters more and more to Burner IV. I have so much, he reasoned. He'll steal anyway. I'd rather not know. Burner IV held his power of attorney, and by that rubric Adrian over time evaded the inconvenience of his riches. Servants forwarded all of his bills to Wall Street, where Burner IV paid them, and paid his own. From the day he stormed out of the office, Adrian never saw Burner IV again, though whenever he needed something they conferred by telephone. He did give Burner IV a strong instruction: "Don't talk so much."

The Claude Rains house he neglected also, dwelling there seldom after he despaired of managing his fortune. Once, he took Antonia to pass a weekend at the house, but the décor frightened her, as did New York, and she returned gladly to seclusion with Diana at Northwood Hall. He never sold the house; he never sold anything. He never dismissed the servants; he never dismissed anybody. A domestic staff of six, including the chauffeur, the butler, and a secretary, remained in residence, awaiting his return, which did not happen. Every day they polished the marble floors, every week the silver; the secretary wrote polite notes to corporations, saying that Mr. Northwood did not read junk mail. Pius hounded him for the house.

"Impossible."

"You never use it, AJ."

"You have a nice apartment."

"It's too small."

"Eight rooms?"

"I'm your brother, AJ!"

"I paid for your wallpaper."

"Hey, at least let me use your house in Paris!"

"*Très impossible.*"

Lately, since he had shunned his great residences and lived in the Rio Grande Valley, Adrian mused from time to time about Burner IV's depredations during his little tasks. How much had he charged to charter the airplane from the Virgin Islands to deliver that letter? To arrange the sale of Motel 5½? For the airplane, $5,000? For the motel, $50,000? More, probably. I have so much he'll steal anyway, I'd rather not know. Now, on the telephone from Amigoland, he told Burner IV to buy the land and barracks by the river.

"What's that number, AJ?"

"Five-one-two, five-four-two, three-eight-seven-six. I'll need electricity, water, a telephone line . . ."

"Means dealin' with city hall. May have to grease some palms."

"I forbid that."

"Would your paw?"

"How *dare* you?"

"I got an *ah*-dee. Runnin' a shelter don't sound easy. How about a lawyer on the spot, somebody who can fix things, open bank accounts, keep books . . . ?"

"Do I need all that?"

"I'll send a guy down."

"Tell him to keep out of my way."

"That's my *ah*-dee."

Avoiding Burner IV's emissary did not turn out to be easy. He was Mr. Ennis, a small minion in rimless eyeglasses and a three-piece suit, as terrified of Adrian as he was of Burner IV, but within days of his presence the shelter had light, water, and a pair of telephones. He asked, "Sir, who is the director here?"

"I suppose I am," Adrian said.

"You'll need an office."

"I don't want one."

"May I suggest, sir, that the legal status of the shelter is tenuous? You'll need records. May I engage a secretary?"

"I suppose so."

"And social workers?"

"Of course."

"Who will sign the checks?"

"You can."

"Thank you, sir. However, may I suggest that we exercise joint signature authority? Mr. Burner is bound to recall me to New York eventually, and to facilitate . . ."

"All right, I'll sign checks."

"How shall I label them?"

"What do you mean?"

"So far as I know, sir, this shelter has no name."

"I'll think of one."

"Meanwhile, the checks . . . may I put your name on the checks?"

"I suppose so!"

"Another detail, sir . . ."

"What's your name?"

"Mr. Ennis, sir, as I said . . ."

Adrian regarded his minion, or rather gazed through him, unable to distinguish him from the queue of retainers who had peopled his boyhood, bowing and groveling as they resented or hated him. Or did they hate? Did they have emotions, inner lives, souls? This lackey was invisible. "Mr. Northwood. Sir?"

"What's your name?"

"Mr. Ennis, sir, as I said . . ."

"Mr. Burner never bothers me with details, Ennis."

"Exactly my instructions, sir. However, with all these pregnant women in the shelter, some of them well advanced, and the hospitals not willing to accept them . . ."

"Can't they give birth in the dispensary?"

"Exactly the detail, sir. May I engage a midwife?"

The shelter mostly ran itself. The refugees flowed in and out, the greater part of them eager to break beyond the ragged fence, to elude the Border Patrol somehow and escape to liberty in the north. The telephones were busy day and night, as aliens implored their relatives in Miami and Los Angeles to send them money. They collected the money at Western Union, then disappeared. The population of the shelter rotated, most aliens lingering a week, a fortnight, a month, but a hard core with no relatives or money or nowhere but these teeming dormitories to lay their heads remained at the barracks and called them home. To protect the refuge from thieves and glue sniffers, a constabulary formed, headed by Baco, a Salvadoran guerrilla, and Octavio, a Nicaraguan guerrilla, both of brutish looks, bullet-scarred, and fanatically devoted to Adrian.

The hard core of aliens cleaned the barracks, ran the kitchen, washed the linen, pressed the transients into such hard service that the place sparkled. Adrian avoided the office and his new secretary, devoting himself to serving meals, mowing lawns, teaching English, scrubbing floors and toilets. He installed showers, a woodworking shop, a billiard table, a soccer field, helping to build them with his blistered hands. He drew up rules, forbidding drugs, alcohol, and guns, and told his guerrillas to enforce them. The guerrillas called him Don Adriano. All the aliens called him Don Adriano. Harshly, he decided to reserve the refuge for Central Americans and that Mexicans—so bountiful with thieves and glue sniffers—must be turned away. He thought, I can't help everybody. The Mexicans have Mexico just over there and must make do with Mexico. Am I too cruel? Can I turn away sick children? Could I turn away the child?

He spent much time in the dispensary. A physician visited once a week, a nurse more often, but otherwise Adrian ran it, learning from the nurse how to apply simple remedies and medications. The ceaseless guerrillas bore bullet wounds all over their bodies; some few were infected and stank with pus; he stanched the pus and dressed the wounds. In Mexico, the aliens had rarely eaten. They had journeyed northward two thousand miles by bus, by hitching rides, and by walking, surviving on berries and soda pop once the Mexican police robbed them of all they owned and dragged young women to cement rooms and raped them. ("Rape me!" mothers cried. "Not my children!") Many suffered from malnutrition, a misfortune that with bread and soup most adults soon overcame; not as easy for the infants. They were feverish, dehydrated, foul with diarrhea. Adrian washed them, swaddled them, fed them water, salt, and gruel. He was fascinated by the act of birth.

Women with child kept turning up, not all of them refugees. Mexican women on the verge of labor or laboring already swam the river now and then to bear their infants in the United States and make them American citizens. In the dispensary Adrian assisted at many births, watching the fat midwife as she poured olive oil on quivering bellies, lubricated distended vulvas between legs spread far apart, thrust her fingers gloved with latex deep into dark vaginas, applied her paper towels to soak up spurts of blood. "*Empuja, empuja,*" the midwife cried. "Push, push."

Late one night, long after lights were out and the shelter slept,

as Adrian painted in his barrack rooms, he heard a woman somewhere moaning and cursing. He went outside; not far from his
door, a young woman in a wet dress lay writhing on the grass. He
grasped her by the armpits and dragged her to the dispensary. Her
bloated stomach heaved; she appeared to be in labor. He lifted her
to the high bed, turned on a fluorescent lamp, debating what to
do next. I must call the midwife she lives in Los Fresnos is there
time? Let me take a look.

She wore a pair of blue fashion eyeglasses, blue shoes with high
heels, and her soaking dress was a mottled yellow. Gently he peeled
the dress from her dark body, and she wore no undergarments. As
he motioned to remove her fashion eyeglasses, in the midst of her
pain she lifted her hand and groaned, gripping the glasses, insisting
that they remain on her face. A trickle of black hair descended
from her navel to the luxuriant patch of pubic hair about her vulva;
beneath the cleavage of her breasts was a bright tattoo of a human
phallus. Oh, God, is she a whore?

He switched on the electronic stethoscope and pressed it to her
womb. The infant's heartbeat was strong and regular, racing just
a little in the throes of the birth struggle. Hello! the heartbeat
thumped. I'm a third world baby! thump-thump. My mom
thump-thump just dropped in thump-thump to have another
third world baby! thump-thump. There are billions of me!
thump-thump third world babies! thump-thump. The woman
rolled, beat her fists upon the bed, screeching. He seized her fists,
wrapped her fingers around the metal bedstead behind her head,
and told her to push. "*Empuja,*" he commanded. "Push, push."

She tried, screaming at one moment, cursing in Tex-Mex at the
next, or both at once. "Oooh! oooh! oooh! *Chinga* f—ck *chile*
c—ck oooh! oooh! *verga* c—ck *huevos* balls oooh! oooh! oooh!"
He put on a pair of latex gloves, pressed her stomach, poured olive
oil on her vulva, inserted his finger into her vagina, tickling it to
coax the muscles. "Oooh! *¡Panocha* c—nt *cachucha* bl—w job
chinga f—ck *chile* c—ck *huevos* balls *burro* c—nt *chisca* bicycle
oooh! oooh! oooh!" He shouted, "*¡Empuja! ¡empuja!* Push! Push!"

She pushed. Her vagina spurted blood, which hit his T-shirt.

"Push!" She pushed. "Oooh! oooh!" Her stomach trembled; he poured more oil, thrust his finger deeper, moved it benevolently back and forth. From her widening vulva more blood erupted, hitting his teeth. He spat it out, but a drop or two clung to his mouth and he tasted the blood, warm and salty. Oh, God, is she hemorrhaging? Hastily he applied his paper towels, blotting up blood, and thus for time suspended she writhed in labor. Oooh! Push! Oooh! Balls! Bicycle!

Finally his probing finger felt a rocklike object inside her vagina. Push! Oooooooh! He bent down, squinted into the vulva, saw the pate of a skull, sprouting tiny black hairs. He poured more oil, tickled the muscles, exhorted her again. *"¡Empuja!"* he shouted. *"Ooooooooh!"* He shouted, *"¡Mujer valiente!* Brave woman! Push! *¡Mas! ¡Mas!* More! More! *¡Empuja!"* Time suspended, the vulva's lips yawned, and the skull emerged, face downward, rotating slightly to either side. For an instant Adrian saw his son's skull, severed from its body: he imagined a machete in his own hand hacking this new head from its body, and he peered at the stump of neck and the larynx and esophagus chopped in half. His hallucination was interrupted by fresh screams. *"¡Huevos!* Balls! Ooooooh! *¡Chisca!* Bicycle!" He prayed, against his will, Lord, not another memory of my son. Let it be a girl.

By the shoulders, he eased the infant from the vulva's grasp and turned it over, delighted with the dimple between her thighs. He glanced at his watch: 4:14 A.M. A blue umbilical cord followed the birth; he cut it at the navel with a pair of scissors, fastening the navel with a wooden clamp. He patted her gently on the back, she whimpered just a bit, and he placed her on the midwife's scale: just under five pounds, yet apparently healthy, breathing well, with her mother's brown skin, brown eyes, and fine, chiseled features. He washed her in oil, wrapped her in linen, and offered her to the mother, who waved her away. He placed her in a plastic cradle, then attended to the afterbirth, pulling the long umbilical cord from the mother's vagina, massaging her stomach and probing inside the vagina until the placenta emerged and he dumped it in the trash can.

He was about to examine the birth canal for tears or ruptures and to wash away the blobs of blood when the woman stirred and stood up, weakly. She slipped her feet into her high blue shoes and gazed at Adrian for a moment, through her fashion eyeglasses, still naked but for the blue shoes and fashion eyeglasses and the tattoo of the phallus beneath her breasts and the streaks of blood about her vulva. From a chair she retrieved her wet dress. She asked, in elegant Spanish, *"¿Podría usar su baño?"* May I use your bathroom?

"Si quiere." If you wish, said Adrian, motioning toward a door. She withdrew behind it, dragging her dress, and locked the door. In a moment he heard what might have been a mop handle smashing glass; by the time he forced the door she had fled through the jagged window. From the window he saw her running in the dark across the grass, clothed again in her yellow dress, toward the river and Mexico.

He returned to the dispensary and the infant in her plastic cradle. She shifted restlessly, crying out. She's thirsty for her mother's milk, he thought. I'll keep her.

He knew something of tending infants from having reared his son. Through the midwife, he engaged a wet nurse to suckle his daughter. Women of the shelter watched her when he was out, but otherwise he kept her cradled in his rooms—cuddling, feeding, changing, bathing her—until she cooed whenever he approached and the bond was deep. He had named his son Urban II after his father. He named his daughter Dianita, little Diana, after his mother.

It hardly annoyed him that Dianita cried in the middle of the night, because so often he was still awake. Painting scenes of the river's life and portraits of ravaged refugees was more vital to him now than ever; his voice told him to put everything on canvas before time ran out. His rooms at the shelter took up much of a barrack not yet restored; the roof leaked and the walls had holes, but he lived with the nuisance because he needed the space for his creations. As his creations grew, so did the shelter, and his renown.

Good souls, drawn by his radiance and by human suffering, appeared from all over the valley, offering food, blankets, and medicine to his refugees as their numbers multiplied. Vaguely, Adrian began to enjoy his luster. He rode Prince to Amigoland surrounded by his guerrillas on foot, as though boasting of a praetorian guard that because of his patronage was beyond arrest. Local children followed in his wake, as fascinated as women were by this blond paragon amid dark rough men.

Angry souls, repelled by his misplaced mercy and fearful of aliens as parasites and thieves, grumbled to one another, then ranted about removing the shelter by legal means or foul. Adrian ignored them until one night a group of men in baseball caps appeared outside the fence with dancing flashlights, shouting obscenities and threats. Next day, from pressure or by coincidence, the Border Patrol, respectful till now of the ragged fence, penetrated the grounds with their rusty trucks, invaded the refuge, and arrested at random a dozen alien men.

Alarmed, Adrian rushed to the gymnasium outside town, looking for Rodrigo. He found him alone in a corner, wearing white fashion sneakers and red trunks, lifting weights. Rodrigo said, "We ain't talkin'."

"Look, Rodrigo . . ."

"We ain't talkin', Ay-jay. It's like I said."

"I forget what you said."

"I called and called the shelter, but they said you was always out, and you never called back. It's like I said. You dropped me like a hot brick."

"I've been so busy."

"Yeah."

"Free for dinner tonight?"

"I'm on patrol. I never knew nobody like you, Ay-jay."

"Why is the Patrol invading my shelter?"

"Policy's changed. Too many OTMs pourin' in, and Washington's p—ssed off. I called to warn you, but it's like I said."

"What can I do about it?"

"Nothin'."

Bored with Rodrigo, Adrian decided to cast him off as he had cast off his brother, Pius. He turned to go, but Rodrigo asked, "You a Catholic, Ay-jay?"

"I'm not sure."

"I'd give you a tip, if we was still friends. . . ."

"Dear Rodrigo, of course we're friends. Forever!"

"There's a shelter upriver, run by the Church. We never go in there."

"Oh?"

"They got a chapel, say Mass on Sunday. How d'you call it— law of sanctuary? We don't never bust a shelter with a chapel."

"An idea! Thanks, Rodrigo."

"I'm free on Friday, Ay-jay. Want to work out?"

"I'll call you."

Adrian knew no priests in Downsville. From Western Union he cabled Rome and Cardinal Galsworthy: RUNNING REFUGEE SHELTER NEED CHAPLAIN AFFECTIONATELY ADRIAN NORTHWOOD. Next day, the Bishop of Downsville rang him up: "I'm sending a priest at noon on Sundays. Where can he say Mass?"

"In the dining hall," said Adrian, "until I build the chapel."

Building the chapel became his next obsession. It was as he created the chapel in an empty ruin of a barrack that he decided to give the shelter a name. Until now it had been known only as *el refugio*—the shelter. It needed a religious name to keep out the Border Patrol, and while he mulled on that he remembered Cardinal Galsworthy's letter. He loved St. Francis and his divine insanity as the Cardinal did, even if the God that Francis worshipped might not exist. He named the shelter Casa San Francisco.

The chapel above all would glorify St. Francis. Adrian would paint the altarpiece. The barrack walls were divided into separate parts by crossing beams: he felt such fragmentation in himself, so he would paint the altarpiece in fragments. He would portray Francis as he flung his silken garments at his father's feet, renouncing his wealth, unclothed but for a hair shirt reaching to his thighs. Francis would be decapitated, his head gazing heavenward and floating in a separate panel above his body. He would have no beard, his hair would be not brown but blond, his eyes would be a wistful blue, and though his body would be the body of a man, his face would be a child's—rather like Adrian's son.

Those days of building and decorating the chapel became Adrian's happiest since his tragedy; serene, almost. He painted the panels in his rooms, even on Sundays while the aliens were at Mass in the dining hall and he could hear them singing distantly.

> *El Espíritu de Dios se mueve,*
>   *se mueve, se mueve,*
> *El Espíritu de Dios se mueve*
>   *dentro de mi corazón.*

> God's spirit stirs,
>   stirs, stirs,
> God's spirit stirs
>   inside my heart.

News on the alien network traveled swiftly, and it was becoming known in lands to the south that the Casa San Francisco was a kindly haven. Hundreds lived there now. He was blithe with his daughter. He was often at her cradle, finding her asleep face down, as she was born and before he discovered her sex. He turned her to marvel at her chiseled, noble face and the blessed happenstance of having her. He said, "I'll have you baptized, Dianita, and I'll name you Northwood too. Beloved daughter, beloved daughter!" *And he said to me, "There are victories beyond art."*

Adrian became intrigued by the tales his soldiers and guerrillas told him of their adventures in Central America's civil wars. Shunning the politics of the twentieth century, he had hardly heard of such wars until he reached the Rio Grande. The soldiers were deserters; the guerrillas had abandoned their insurgencies in disillusion. They gathered about Don Adriano in the dining hall after supper, regaled him with horror stories, and he took the images to bed, where they joined his jellyfish and severed heads.

His dreams were cluttered, a cinema that never stopped. He became a contra, twelve years old, still very blond, in the steep mountains of Nicaragua, roving the countryside in a band of men and boys, trudging to the heart of Nicaragua from Honduras in the north for fifty, sixty days, guns and rockets heavy on his back, across unmerciful terrain, taking shelter in the cold and lofty caves of mountains, living on squirrels and snake meat, roving and running from the Sandinistas constantly, yet finally surprising them in ambush and hacking off their ears and genitalia.

He became a mutilated Sandinista corpse that sprang to life, very young and dark, reliving the myth and romance of the revolutionary struggle, like a cat all claws and stealth, hearkening to the voice of Che Guevara crying from the mountaintop, living on roots and monkey meat, risking mountain leprosy for the holy cause of liberation, and killing counterrevolutionaries by bullets, bayonets, and butchery.

Soon he was a Salvadoran soldier, another peasant boy press-ganged by his government, stepping on a guerrilla land mine, the mine lurking barely beneath the surface of the soil, a piece of plastic garden hose packed with gunpowder, glass, and human excrement, and he examined it in slow motion as it blew his legs off. As suddenly he was a Salvadoran guerrilla, younger and darker still, with missing teeth because guerrillas have no dentists, sleeping on a mountain slope hugging his rifle, with all he owned beside him, living on tortillas when he could steal them, on rabbits when he was lucky, rarely bathing, only in rivers, his body covered with the bites of insects and the scars of wounds, suffering chronic dysentery, diarrhea and blood, worms gnawing incessantly at his bowels; but oh, the macabre idealism of that life! the heroism and ceaseless danger! the saga of sleeping beneath the stars and never being sure he would wake up!

His several soldier and guerrilla selves waged savage war with one another, and he woke up. Today the real soldiers and guerrillas in the Casa San Francisco were done with their mythology that war would make the world a better place, and therefore done with death. In waves these disenchanted killers were crashing on the shore of Texas, seeking the sweetness of life. They were quite prepared to sweat for it—like their camp followers, those dark, thick-hipped women who were their wives and concubines, trailing after them through Mexico with throngs of children. Some of the guerrillas were children.

Adrian was so dazzled by his private cinema that in the mornings he wrote down his serial dreams on the prolix foolscap pages of his University Essay. He lingered over the images of himself—shivering in lofty caves, eating tree roots and monkey meat, risking mountain leprosy and other mutilations—but he asked, "Could I ever truly endure that sort of austere and dangerous life?

"I have taken especially to a child guerrilla—Alejandro, a Salvadoran, of angelic face, thirteen, I think, who lives with us now in the Casa San Francisco. I am tempted to record something of his odyssey, since in his trek from Central America to the Rio Grande he endured so much. . . ."

In El Salvador, in his native province of Morazán, the boy Alejandro had wandered with a cow along a forest path and was kidnapped by guerrillas. The guerrillas ate the cow; Alejandro they forcibly recruited into their war against the government. For months, he fought as a foot soldier in the Revolutionary Army of the People, always scheming to escape his captors. Not easy: they chained him to trees whenever the troops lay down to sleep, and watched him through telescopes of rifles as they waged their insurrection.

The Revolutionary Army of the People held half of Morazán north of a twisting river and bombed-out bridges; the landscape of the guerrilla enclave, hilly, once verdant and mildly prosperous, as the result of the revolt was all desolation. The roads were strewn with bullet shells from automatic rifles, and wherever the eye was cast the humble houses of the peasantry had been gutted once and gutted yet again in battles that never ceased. The government army, forever searching for guerrillas and rarely finding them, put the province to the torch, burning crops of corn and sisal, coffee and cotton, rice and pineapple, and sowing famine. The terrain turned brown and parched as, against the canvas of high escarpments and a necklace of purple mountains far away, fires ravaged the sides of hills, leaving bare patches burned out, skeletons of trees, and ash everywhere.

American helicopters chopped overhead, raining machine-gun bullets; American jet planes followed them, dropping fragmentation bombs that bled the population but could not end the fighting. Then came press-ganged adolescent soldiers, peasants like Alejandro, in American armor-plated trucks and wearing American fatigues, American boots, American water bottles, wielding American rifles, American bullets, American bazookas, American knives, only to be ambushed and slaughtered by guerrillas wielding Kalashnikov automatic rifles and wearing American baseball caps and captured American fatigues, American boots, American water bottles.

Little Alejandro accompanied the guerrillas as they infiltrated government territory and stole into the capital of Morazán after midnight, surprising the great garrison as it slept, slaughtering scores of peasant soldiers with rockets and machine guns, and fleeing back to the revolutionary enclave before the dawn. The guerrillas burned town halls and murdered mayors. They interrupted traffic on the roads, stopping trucks and buses and sometimes shooting passengers. They blew up power lines and in their turn torched crops of sugarcane and coffee. With their mortars, grenades, and cannon, they made their enclave and the space around it a land of refugees, widows, and orphans. Again the government responded with fragmentation bombs on guerrilla redoubts and field hospitals, and some guerrillas bled to death, while the American aircraft returned to bomb the nearby villages where guerrillas lived among the people, razing whatever houses, crops, and schools that happened to stand in the way.

Alejandro normally slept on the ground, shivering upon shards and bullet casings, because that part of El Salvador was so hilly and the nights so cool. His water was rationed, he had no salt, and he was lucky when he was fed cornmeal mush. During pauses between battles he endured confusing lectures by his guerrilla masters about Marx, Engels, Lenin, the doctrines of class warfare, and the dictatorship of the proletariat.

But above all Alejandro and his companion child guerrillas passed their conscious hours planting those plastic land mines, leaving them to lurk in roads and fields just beneath the surface of the soil. The soldiers (or stray peasants) stepped on them, on a blasting cap set off by sulfur mixed with chemicals and sugar, and the mine beneath was tiny—a little piece of plastic garden hose packed with aluminum powder, gunpowder, rocks, glass, and human excrement. Alejandro often witnessed afterward the victims of his mischief—soldiers as young as he was, beardless boys blasted to instant death or left to hobble for a lifetime without feet and legs, sometimes with half their faces gone and their genitals as well.

Soldiers with whole bodies did not treat captured guerrillas kindly; they often slashed their faces, severed their hands and feet, then skinned them alive, ripping away large parts of flesh, exposing bone. Not a fate Alejandro coveted; on a midnight operation with the guerrillas inside a town, Alejandro slipped away from his companions into a churchyard and hid behind the pillars of a tomb. He heard gunfire in the distance, the operation perhaps went badly, and no guerrillas returned in search of him. At last free, he returned by stealth to his village, surprised by what he found.

His father, a poor farmer confused by politics, had been crouching behind the wrong tree when an American fragmentation bomb fell on his sisal field and he bled to death. His mother, in frail health from having borne eleven children and made distraught by the loss of her husband, had succumbed to her mourning and died a week afterward. The guerrillas had killed an older brother. The army had killed a younger brother. His sisters and grandmother had fled to the south, to the capital of the province, to cast themselves upon the mercy of the government and to beg for food and shelter. Alejandro passed a sleepless night in his family's shattered farmhouse, but he knew that the Revolutionary Army of the People would soon return, seeking him. He gazed from a hilltop northeastward to the necklace of purple mountains, and without possessions, without a coin in his pocket, he began walking toward them. Along the road, he stepped over headless bodies. El Salvador is a small place; within several hours, late at night, he crossed furtively into Honduras.

He lived in Honduras and, a little later, farther north in Guatemala, much as he had lived in his country those last months: as a guerrilla, scavenging from the land. He hitched rides in trucks, trudged for days along hot dusty rustic roads, avoided towns and cities, and slept in forests. His nourishment was mostly wild fruit, mangoes, bananas, avocado pears, that he picked from trees. He crept into barnyards and snatched chickens whenever he could, wringing their necks, plucking their feathers deep in forests, thrusting sticks through them and roasting them as he roasted wild rabbits, over crude stoves he built from rocks. As a guerrilla he had eaten monkeys; now when he was lucky he ate snakes. He was always alone, for though he met other guerrillas on their own migrations to the north, he learned from experience to rely on himself and to trust nobody.

Alejandro bathed in rivers, scrubbing his clothes, his whole wardrobe, a torn T-shirt the fading color of khaki, a pair of blue jeans turning white, and black bathing trunks that served as his underwear; he had no socks, but his boots, U.S. Army issue, reposed on the bank caked with mud—little else held them together. He had not seen a mirror in months, but one morning in clear water he caught a reflection of himself: a slight, almost fair-skinned child, with luminous confused brown eyes, profuse locks of light-brown hair, and white teeth still intact. He did not smile at his reflection, but in happier times, when he had smiled, his angelic mouth mingled with his dimples and his laughter and enchanted everyone. His movements somehow had a natural poise, and the shape of his head a noble grace, yet when he gazed at his hairless face and body in the clear water of that river he was troubled.

He was even thinner than he had been with the guerrillas and he ate tortillas and mush, he craved as ever the taste of salt, and though but a single bullet scar blemished his left shoulder, his body was covered with insect bites and ticks that clung. Even now as he bathed, rubbing himself with frond leaves since he had no soap, he felt weakened and dizzy from his dysentery, and again he could not contain the mixture of blood and soft white excrement that oozed from his bowels and defiled the clear water, effacing his childish reflection.

He pressed on, upward through the mountainous terrain of northern Guatemala, on foot, as torrential rains fell and he huddled beneath pine trees for shelter and his body trembled from the cold. This was Mayan country, where earthquakes were a part of life and at intervals the earth steamed; where from the frigid heights the blue volcanoes dropped to plateaus planted with corn and wheat, into squeezed valleys watered by angry streams; then the land ascended to greater heights again in the drizzle and the rolling fog. He ate raw wheat and raw corn on the cob, but by the time he eluded the military patrols and crossed the border into Mexico,

Alejandro's dysentery had become so harsh he fell to the roadside, crying out to God that he could not go on.

In an hour a young priest passed in an old truck, picked him up, and drove him northward through the state of Chiapas toward Villahermosa, opening a leather sack and offering him water and salt, tortillas and hard-boiled eggs, which Alejandro consumed ravenously; offering also to stop at a market and buy him clothes, but Alejandro jumped out of the truck because in his solitude and guerrilla warfare these many months, even kindly strangers wore the horns of devils. He found himself again trudging on a country road, and several days passed before he reached Veracruz on the Gulf of Mexico.

He slept on the muddy beach, begged crusts of bread from picnickers, and prowled in alleys behind restaurants near the sea, groping in garbage cans for rotten vegetables and fish bones. He had broken his little rule of avoiding cities and come to Veracruz because by now he sensed that without medicine he might not survive his dysentery, and for medicine he needed money. Ill and feverish, languidly he begged for money in the mobbed central bus station, retreating to the toilets, crouching under tables of the cafeteria, when the police invaded and, in public view, robbed of all their money the swarms of Central Americans—without papers, without rights—waiting between buses in their flight to the United States. The police roared off in their cars and vans, taking terrified prisoners with them, mostly pretty women, leaving behind children and men, youths and grandmothers, milling about in tears and penniless confusion.

Such scenes confirmed Alejandro in his wisdom of avoiding companions and journeying alone; with his begging money he bought medicine and ate a little better; his dysentery persisted, but it eased. His clothes were rags, in such tatters they did well to hide his nakedness. He began to haunt the great Plaza de Armas—so Andalusian with its sun, palms, and fountains; guitar music, whitewashed arcades, the clashing bells of the cathedral tower—where he stood on the cobblestones with a tin can for coins before him and did his theater.

His theater was mimicry, of two sorts of clowns, conventional buffoons and Evangelical preachers. Since childhood he had observed street Evangelicals in the towns and villages of his homeland, and though he was a Catholic he knew their theater perfectly, for his ear was keen. Scavenging one day in a public dump, he had found a Bible, and no matter his rags, the Bible was prop enough.

Alejandro held the Bible open in his hand, crying out at the top of his lungs, *"¡Mis amigos! ¡Les hablo la palabra de Dios!"* My friends! I bring you the word of God! And He tells us, believe in Our Lord Jesus Christ! And you will be saved and all your house! For this my beloved brothers and sisters believe in God and REPENT, REPENT, REPENT of all your sins! *¡ARREPIENTETE, ARREPIENTETE, ARREPIENTETE de todos tus pecados!* The blood of Christ washes us of every sin and all iniquity *de todo pecado y de toda maldad!* As we know from Matthew Seven, verses seven to eleven!

" 'Pedid, y se os dará; buscad, y hallaréis; llamad, y se os abrirá. Ask, and it shall be given you; seek, and ye shall find; knock, and it shall be opened unto you. For every one that asketh receiveth; and he that seeketh findeth; and to him that knocketh it shall be opened. Or what man is there of you whom if his son ask bread, will he give him a stone? *¿Qué hombre hay de vosotros, que si su hijo le pide pan, le dará una piedra?* Or if he ask a fish, will he give him a serpent? *¿O si le pide un pescado, le dará una serpiente?* If ye then, being evil, know how to give good gifts unto your children, how much more shall your Father which is in Heaven . . . *¿cuánto más vuestro Padre que está en los cielos . . .* '?"

Alejandro shrieked often all to himself, but now and then a knot of people gathered, a few perhaps tossing coins into his tin can. When he had an audience he progressed from preaching into clownish song. For his clowning he had no props—no cane, no funny hat or colored greasepaint—only the mud from his boots that he streaked on his face. He sang a silly song, the kind that singers usually sang to sweethearts but that in his mind he sang to his dead mother. He promised her all she ever wanted: a beautiful house in San Vicente, another in Santa Ana, sandy beaches and grassy meadows, where she would forget every sorrow. He ended each stanza with a WHOOH-WHOOH, a whistle, a wiggle, and a kick. All I'll ever own is yours, little mum, everything in my life, all I have is yours, all I have is yours, mamacita, in my whole life, all I have is yours.

> *Todo lo que tengo es tuyo, mamacita*
> *De mi vida*
> *Todo lo que tengo es tuyo.*
> WHOOH-WHOOH! [Whistle, wiggle, kick]

In his village school he had been happy, a bright student, even learning a little English, for all the warfare in the valleys and the hills. He was the class clown, he loved that, and whenever the children pretended to make a circus they made it around him. Alejandro in the circus: "The girls on this side don't dare to give kisses, but the girls on that side, how they love to s-t-r-e-t-c-h their necks and smooch! WHOOH-WHOOH!" Today in the sunlit Andalusian plaza, Alejandro repeated that sort of nonsense, almost Chaplinesque in his torn T-shirt and jeans gaping at the crotch and knees, his U.S. Army boots much too big, with flapping soles and his toes peeping out. He sang, and as he sang he danced, waving a hand in front, the other behind his hips, swinging his nearly skeletal body and whistling as he kicked his highest kick.

> *Con el chiri viri vi*
> *Con el chiri viri vi*
> *Hay chiri viri viri viri*
> *Hay chiri viri viri viri*
>
> *Con el chiri viri vi*
> *Con el chiri viri vi*
> *Con el chiri viri viri viri*
> BOOM-BOOM-BOOM!

Finally he gathered enough pesos to buy new clothes. He danced along the crowded streets near the great plaza, the coins and small bills bulging in his threadbare pocket, dazzled by the plenty behind plate glass: color television, video machines, German motorcycles, Japanese cameras, Swiss watches, Italian shoes, fashion sneakers, shining suits, Batman masks. He tried to enter several stores, but the guards, alarmed by his appearance and believing him a guttersnipe, chased him to the street. Yet he sensed already from his window-shopping that he could not afford fine clothes. In a street market, he bought used clothes, single pairs of cheap jeans and boots, no socks, another dark bathing suit to serve as underwear, and a red and white T-shirt in English: MARLBORO COUNTRY. With no luggage, he resumed his trek northward.

Walking, begging rides in the rear of open trucks, he proceeded slowly up the Atlantic coast: from Veracruz past Chachalacas through ugly Poza Rica with its oil refinery through Tuxpan past its waterfront of velvet palms, and blinding whiteness, to hideous Tampico with its blue buses and their towering exhaust pipes that filled heaven and the human lungs with black fog. He ran out of money, or rather, with the few pesos that remained to him he bought soda pop along the road, pausing at public garbage dumps to chew on husks. He did not pause to sleep in meadows or in forests, to pluck coconuts from coconut palms along the way and drink the sweet milk, to mimic Evangelicals on street corners or clowns that sang chiri viri vi boom-boom, because as he slept in moving trucks or in the public parks of towns his nightmares or his instinct said that an enchanted destiny awaited him and now he should hurry to the north. He dreamed of a blurred face.

He barely noticed the landscape as he hastened past it, volcanic peaks and crannied shores, timeless pyramids and green lagoons, but as ever he watched for the police. Between Tampico and Aldama, he was trudging on the highway when he saw a barricade ahead. He dove into the bush, crawling to a thicket at a distance from the road, creeping lengthwise through it to avoid the police. Near a cluster of cement buildings the thicket blended with a plum orchard. Peering at the road, he saw some idle buses, passengers standing about, and fat policemen in black uniforms wielding automatic rifles.

The policemen were ripping open luggage, dumping clothes and valuables on the ground, shouting at the Central Americans to empty their pockets of their money and to shut up. In their fright they could not shut up, especially the young women whom the policemen dragged from the road to cement rooms, mothers running after them, screaming "Take me! Not my daughter!" At the cement rooms the policemen slammed shut the metal doors, the mothers pounded on them, or to escape the mothers the police yanked the young women into the plum orchard, where they pinned them against trees, tore off skirts, unzipped trousers, and thrust themselves into reluctant vulvas. Alejandro had never seen rape, not even in his guerrilla war. He waited until dark, then stole out of the orchard, eating a plum.

Throughout the night he continued his northward trudge, imagining murderers and hobgoblins lurking in the brush and, worse, fat policemen in black uniforms pursuing him whenever headlights flashed distantly from behind, and he leaped off the highway into grass. At dawn, a truckdriver picked him up, drove him through La Joya and San Fernando, and at midafternoon dumped him on the outskirts of Matablancos.

He walked forward on Highway 101, past miles of junkyard, wooden shacks tilting in the sandy wind, tin workshops and garages that advertised car repairs, hubcaps, mufflers, owned largely by the police and where their minions altered and repainted luxury automobiles and expensive trucks stolen in the United States. Alejandro could not have known that, but perhaps even his childish eye perceived that Matablancos, after Tampico, before Tampico, was the ugliest place in Mexico, *anus mundi*. He lingered hungrily in a church till dusk, then walked several miles to the Rio Grande. It had taken him two months, nearly two thousand miles, much of that on foot, to reach this river.

He gazed across the river at the United States. A breeze blew, but the night was warm. He crouched in reeds near the railway bridge, opposite the radio tower and Amigoland, grateful to God and dazzled by the lights of Downsville. Not far along the other shore, the Casa San Francisco beckoned, though he did not know its name, in fact had never heard of it—another price he paid for his chosen solitude. He heard Spanish voices, accents of his own El Salvador, the sounds of laughter, squealing children, guitar music, women singing, the clash of cups and dishes as his compatriots ate dinner. The breeze blew from there, and Alejandro thought he sniffed grilled chicken, his favorite food. He felt his harshest pangs of hunger, but his little rule of solitude had brought him this far, he aspired ever northward, and he dared not change now.

Beneath his boot among the reeds was a plastic bag; he removed all his clothes, folded them neatly inside the bag, knotted the bag tightly at the top to be sure no water entered it, and, clutching the bag to his noble head, waded nakedly into the water toward the United States: the plastic bag was his passport and his visa. The river there was rather wide, the current was stronger than he expected (could he have known how many aliens had drowned in crossing?), and weakened by his hunger, he began to lose control.

In the middle of the river he felt his frail body being swept away, rushing toward the concrete stanchions of the railway bridge, and in the whirlpool his head went under once and then again, as he lost his grip and his plastic bag. Water flooded his gurgling throat; with his final strength his thin flailing arms reached out for his clothes, and, just barely, he caught a corner of the bag. Again he went under, clutching the bag, but beneath the water his body hit a jutting rock, arresting his descent. With an arm he hugged the rock, and he raised his head above water. His feet felt other rocks beneath the surface, and wrenchingly he trod on them until he reached the United States, gasping for its air.

The breeze dried his trembling body as he lingered on the shore, before opening the bag and putting on his bathing suit, his jeans and boots, and his MARLBORO COUNTRY T-shirt. He climbed the bank and crawled across a grassy field until he came to K mart. There he placed his back against the wall, peered around the corner into the parking lot, and, seeing no police, proceeded across the parking lot, across the highway, into Amigoland, where he melted into the mob of shoppers and told himself, "I'm free."

Not quite. He was giddy from his hunger. He slept in an alley behind Wal-Mart, but he did not eat that night. By noon next day, he had walked the several miles to Boca Chica, where he scavenged in the green Dumpsters behind Pick-a-Chick and Whataburger for his luncheon, and at night in the Dumpsters of Pizza Hut and Mister Donut for his dinner, but on both occasions in the wet heat the garbage was so profuse with maggots he could swallow but a few mouthfuls. He longed for his snake meat.

In the morning, his dysentery returned, the mixture of blood and mucus so violent as he defecated in an open field that he wished to die. He slept in the field, woke up, and walked on, northward. His destination was Los Angeles because he had a cousin there, though no address, no map, and no notion of the distance. He hitched rides on Route 77; an elderly Mexican woman picked him up, bought him sandwiches at a gasoline station, and warned him to beware of the Border Patrol checkpoint at Sarita. Ten miles before Sarita he walked off the highway and into open range, intending as so many aliens did to tramp around the checkpoint. Yet as he approached it, alone as always, creeping guerrilla-like from bush to bush, he saw the Patrol invade the range in rusty trucks and arrest waves of aliens. His caution and his illness told him, Don't risk it, go back, you won't get through.

Trapped in the valley, he returned to the towns along the river hoping to find work, to escape northward somehow when he had money. However, he felt so feeble he could not look for work, could not join that subproletariat of aliens who toiled on farms, picking grapefruit, harvesting tomatoes, or cutting hay, for almost nothing. Though it rained often, sometimes torrentially, he slept as always in fields and alleys and devoted his energy to finding food. He avoided the Dumpsters behind fast-food palaces, entering the palaces themselves, removing uneaten food from tables before the workers cleaned them off, reaching into plastic barrels for scraps of hamburgers and french-fried potatoes before they were thrown outside and maggots infested them.

Experience taught him to favor Burger King over McDonald's. At McDonald's, when people queued and ordered food, the workers asked them what soft drinks and condiments they wished, and furnished them accordingly from an endless treasure they kept behind the counter. Whenever he could, Alejandro snatched from empty tables abandoned tiny packets of McDonald's Own Ranch Dressing, McDonald's Seasoned Croutons, McDonald's Bacon Bits (Smoke Flavoring Added—100% Real Bacon), McDonald's Oriental Chow Mein Noodles, Keebler's Club Crackers, ketchup, mustard, and mayonnaise. He survived mostly by collecting such condiments in a plastic bag and eating them in the street. Soon, however, his presence became familiar, and he was chased with an empty stomach from one McDonald's to the next.

Burger King was slightly different. There, the Double Whopper Cheeseburgers, the Deluxe Bacon Doubleburgers, the Big Double Chicken Cheeseburgers, were tendered from behind the counter, but the condiments and the Diet Pepsi, 7-UP, Dr Pepper, the salt, sugar, tea, and coffee, were arrayed in a row, all self-service. Alejandro pressed his nose to the window, waiting for those moments when customers were sparse and the workers withdrew from the counter to the kitchen; then he moved. He rushed into Burger King, gathering cups of soda pop and condiments into his plastic bag, and dashed out.

Or he slipped into Burger King when it was mobbed, and nobody noticed as he squeezed into a corner and sat there, praying that someone would offer him a meal. The waiting never filled his stomach, but the ritual gabble improved his English.

The Mexican-American boys and girls by the counter or the drive-in window: "Welcome to Burger King. May I help you, please? We got a Double Whopper Cheese with mayonnaise, lettuce, tomatoes, pickles, an' onions. An' we got cheeseburgers with American cheese or Swiss cheese an' with ketchup an' mustard an' chicken san'wich with lettuce an' mayonnaise. We got Coca-Cola, 7-UP, orange, ice tea, an' coffee right over there. May I help you? For dessert we got apple pie, lemon pie, an' cherry pie. You wannit hot or cold? May I help you? We got salad, chicken salad an' garden salad. In chicken salad we got carrots, lettuce, tomato, an' chicken. Here's your order, sir. Three ninety-two is the change. Thank you, please. Have a nice day. May I help you? Cheeseburger Deluxe? That's double meat, double cheese, pickles, onions, an' ketchup, no mustard. Bacon Double? That's three bacon on top of cheese an' meat, or you wanna Double Bacon Deluxe with onions an' lettuce? That's eight sixty-nine, lady. One thirty-one is the change. Welcome to Burger King. May I help you, please?"

When it rained, Alejandro lived in one Burger King or another until his presence came to the manager's attention and he was kicked out. He favored all-night Burger Kings because he disliked sleeping in alleys, where he had to mingle with glue sniffers. By now his dysentery had so sapped him that his bathing suit and the crotch of his jeans were caked with blood, yet he struggled to remain clean. Often he hid in the men's room, waiting until the place was empty and he could remove his clothes and wash them in the tiny basin. Alejandro was thus scrubbing his wardrobe and his body in the Burger King on Boca Chica boulevard late one evening when Adrian Northwood, alone, entered the restaurant for a snack.

Adrian sat at a corner table sipping a Coca-Cola, munching on a piece of cherry pie, and reading (in the original) Pascal's *Pensées*. ". . . 206. Infinite space means eternal silence, and that frightens me. 207. How many kingdoms know us not! . . . 216. Sudden death alone is feared, hence confessors stay with lords. . . . 228. Objection of atheists: 'But we have no light.' . . . 258. *Unusquisque sibi Deum fungit*. 'He moulds a God like unto himself.' Disgust."

Alejandro emerged from the toilet, wearing his wet clothes, his MARLBORO COUNTRY T-shirt clinging to his sharp ribs. His hair was wild, like his eyes, yet hunger had not made him less angelic. Otherwise the place was empty: across the tables their eyes collided. Alejandro remembered his dream in Mexico of a blurred face, but now the face focused and belonged to Adrian. Adrian saw as clearly: this child resembled little Urban had little Urban lived and grown. He had been struggling with his portrait of Francis of Assisi's floating head, but here was the model. As he gazed at Alejandro, instinctively he glimpsed his history, and he felt—not pity—envy.

The manager stormed from behind the counter, seizing Alejandro by his neck and shouting, "You again! Get the f—— outta here!"

"Leave him alone," Adrian said.

"You know this kid?"

"Quite well."

"Who is he?"

"My son."

Adrian took him by the hand and drove him to the Casa San Francisco. For a fortnight he fed him antibiotics, soft bread, and chicken soup. Gradually little Alejandro grew healthy, cheerful, and a chatterbox, loath to speak Spanish: "May I help you? We got a Double Whopper Cheese with mayonnaise, lettuce, pickles, an' onions. We got Coca-Cola, 7-UP, orange, ice tea, an' coffee right over there. May I help you? For dessert we got apple pie, lemon pie, an' cherry pie. You wannit hot or cold? May I help you? Bacon Double? That's three bacon on top of cheese an' meat, or you wanna Bacon Double Deluxe with onions an' lettuce? Have a nice day. Welcome to Burger King. May I help you?" His vocabulary in English did not much exceed such mimicry, but when he slept he spoke Spanish.

He refused to sleep with the men and boys in the shelter dormitory, so Adrian gave him a cot in his own rooms, but he talked so loudly in his sleep that he woke baby Dianita, and as he relived his adventures with the guerrillas he saw the airplanes dropping fragmentation bombs and the land mines blowing feet and faces off, and his cries became so bloodcurdling they frightened Adrian as well. "*¡Mamá! ¡Mamá! ¡Papá! ¡Papá!*" Adrian told him to sleep thereafter in the dining hall, but by now Alejandro was so attached to Don Adriano he would not obey. He slept in the grass outside his door, hugging a broomstick because there were no rifles in the Casa San Francisco, but he went on crying out. "*¡Mamá! ¡Mamá! ¡Papá! ¡Papá!*"

In the mornings, when he sat for Don Adriano as he painted St. Francis's floating head, Alejandro kept jumping up, touching things—brush handles, tubes of paint, easel frames—and breaking them. Wherever Adrian went, Alejandro dogged his footsteps, popping incessantly out of shadows, asking, "May I help you?" For all his quirks and traumas, Alejandro began to flourish at the Casa San Francisco.

It was well that he had come, since lately Adrian had grown lax in running the refuge, so absorbed was he by his decoration of the chapel. Adrian rarely entered the office where the secretary worked, nor was he sure of what she did, though on the shelter grounds occasionally he bumped into Mr. Ennis in his rimless spectacles and his three-piece suit. "Do you live in Downsville now?" Adrian asked, not that he cared.

"Much of the time," said Mr. Ennis. "The airline connections are problematical, but I try as best I can, at least once per fortnight, to present a personal report to Mr. Burner IV at his office on Wall Street."

"What do you do here?" Adrian asked, not that he cared.

"Why, sir," said Mr. Ennis, "I supervise the administration of the shelter, with particular attention to the protection of your interests. Those are my instructions, sir, from Mr. Burner IV."

At odd moments, unseen hands slipped wads of checks beneath Adrian's door for his signature. Occasionally when he glanced at them the amounts seemed high, but he signed them anyway, with his mind suspended somewhere between Baroque and medieval time, and when he got around to it returned them to the office. Into such languor Alejandro entered, becoming by ceaseless energy the axis of the shelter's life.

He began by being a clown again, by rummaging in the shelter's clothes bank and emerging with whatever funny things he found —a wide-brimmed sombrero with the top bashed in, some baggy checkered pants with shiny red suspenders, a pair of black shoes far too big, and old white gloves with no fingers. From the women in the kitchen he took flour and egg yolk, smearing them on his face; he stuck green peppers into either ear and taped a maraschino cherry to the tip of his nose; from a mesquite tree he fashioned a twisted cane. At meals he hopped on top of tables, regaling adults and children, reliving his triumphs in his homeland doing soft-shoe dances, pratfalls, whistling, kicking, and singing chiri viri vi boom-boom.

He raided the clothes bank often, trying on used jeans and T-shirts until he was better dressed than others and boasted of it. He hounded the new English teacher for private lessons, and with his gift of mimicry made swift progress. He poked about the office, becoming useful to the secretary and in a great black book keeping records of whatever aliens took refuge in the shelter before they groped northward. In a transient population he became a constant, deciding who might use the copier, the telephones, the soccer field, who would get grants from petty cash and who deserved more generous subventions from Don Adriano. Throughout the Casa San Francisco he became the cheerful fixer, the child to see.

He peeked over the secretary's shoulder as she punched the keys of her computer; at night, he turned it on again, by trial and error teaching himself to use it. He was confused at first by the graphs and symbols that flashed across the screen, but he was quick at arithmetic, and as he punched more keys and explored the secrets of the machine he was half able to decipher the sums that looped in and out of multiple accounts.

Puzzled, he telephoned wholesalers in Downsville to check the prices that they charged for their sacks of rice and beans, ground coffee and whole chickens, antibiotics and toilet paper, then he reconciled their statements with invoices he found in a filing cabinet. In the computer he discovered that the bills were paid on checks named "Adrian John Northwood" or on newer checks named "Casa San Francisco, Inc." in various accounts with the Bean & Valley Bank. Yet also in the computer the invoices were inflated, and many thousands of dollars more were flowing from the accounts to a New York bank with an account named "Burner, Burner, Burner & Burner."

Alejandro was a bright child, but even a dull child might have done that addition and subtraction. Much of the money was being sucked from the Casa San Francisco to the mysterious echo Burner Burner Burner Burner in New York City. Late one Friday afternoon, waving bills and computer printouts, Alejandro burst into Adrian's barrack rooms and shouted, *"¡Ellos te dejaran desnudo!"* They're robbing you blind!

The sun was lowering upriver, its beams bouncing off the water through the cracked window of Adrian's studio and bathing half of Alejandro's seraphic face in titian shades of anger. Adrian seized his sketching pad, rapidly drew strokes, and said, "Stand there sideways in the sun."

"Look at the bills for rice and beans! For soap and penicillin! Compare them to the computer sheets! Robbing you blind!"

"Ha-ha! Alejandro, you've such a mobile face."

"¡Ladrónes!" Thieves!

"Ha-ha! Now turn your head just slightly toward the sun."

Finally to quiet him Adrian glanced at the sheets of paper. Burner IV had found new ways to steal: Adrian instantly saw how. With his power of attorney he transfered handsome sums of Adrian's money from accounts in New York to accounts in Downsville, then his minion Mr. Ennis overstated the costs of the Casa San Francisco, awarded the plunder to his master, and how could Adrian complain? He signed the checks. In his reports—which he knew Adrian rarely read—Burner IV would justify his theft with dense allusions to the tax code, the benefits of hidden fees, and other prolix legalisms. I have so much he'll steal anyway; now I know; I'd rather not. He told Alejandro, "Stand less toward the sun." Annoyed that the boy refused, he lunged for him.

Alejandro danced away, forgetting his anger at the thefts and crawling under tables as he taunted Adrian. "May I help you? We got cheeseburger with American cheese or Swiss cheese with ketchup an' mustard an' with lettuce an' mayonnaise. We got apple pie! Lemon pie! Cherry pie? You wannit hot or cold?" He poked his head from beneath another table as he asked, "May I help you? We got salad, chicken salad an' garden salad. In chicken salad we got carrots, lettuce, tomato, an' chicken!" He sprang from shadows, still eluding Adrian's grasp. "May I help you? That's eight sixty-nine, sir. One thirty-one is your change. Have a nice day! Welcome to Burger King. May I help you?"

Laughing against his wish, Adrian chased him outside, over the gravel paths between the shelter barracks to the meadow, where Alejandro resumed his dance, whistling, kicking, dashing through the grass from tree to tree, challenging Don Adriano to come and get him as he waved a hand in front, the other behind his hips, singing Con el chiri viri vi, con el chiri viri viri viri boom-boom-boom. He ran through the ragged fence, onto other people's property, to a wooden tower whose construction was not finished as it aspired still skyward. A crude ladder leaned against the scaffolding, and in his frenzy the boy began to climb it. Adrian shouted, "Don't go up there!"

The boy ignored him and in the twilight clambered up the ladder toward an unfinished platform near the top, Adrian in pursuit. Hastening upward, Adrian thought, Come, let us make a city and a tower, the top whereof may reach to Heaven. From that height as night fell Adrian saw Amigoland twinkle and the river crawl with aliens; the air keened. When he reached the platform Alejandro's mood had changed: he crouched quietly by the ladder, impatient for Adrian's presence. A man sat on the platform's edge, swinging his legs in space and smoking a cigarette that glowed in the dusk. He wore a pair of dusty boots and dark overalls but no shirt. Around his neck hung a pair of battered binoculars, and on his head was a visored cap, TOM'S MACHINE TOOLS.

"Oh!" said Adrian. "We're sorry!" He took Alejandro's hand to lead him down.

"You Ay-jay Northwood?" the man asked.

"I'm afraid so."

"God damn almighty."

"Goodbye."

"I been watchin' your place."

"Is this your tower?"

"Me and some buddies is buildin' it."

"I've noticed."

"This your kid?"

"One of them."

"Another goddamn mouth to feed!"

"Have you some legitimate objection?"

"Oh my, don't we talk fancy?"

"Farewell."

"Hold on there, buddy. Figure as we should talk? I got a barbecue goin' tomorrow night."

"Vamos, Alejandro."

"Like you to meet my friends."

"Impossible."

"Drive north Route 4 to Boca Chica, go east on 4. Up a ways you'll see Lone Star Trailers? Across from the laundromat's my trailer? How 'bout seven?"

"Out of the question."

"Name's Jody. Jody Corn? Don't bring the kid."

▲▲▲
13
▼▼▼

Next evening, Adrian entrusted Dianita to her wet nurse and, curious to learn more about the tower, drove his truck inland past Boca Chica to the Lone Star Trailer Park. In a dirt yard by some mobile homes he found Jody Corn, bare-chested, potbellied, wearing oily dungarees and a wide straw hat. Jody waved a can of beer and cried at Adrian, "Good buddy!" Fireflies danced; an outboard motor lay disassembled in the weeds. On an overturned boat two dark unshaven Mexicans sat drinking beer, and though it was Saturday night they seemed more sober than Jody did.

"Ah, your friends?" asked Adrian as he shook their hands.

"My neighbors," said Jody. "My friends'll be along."

Jody was as young as Adrian, with a smooth face, a sandy mustache, and an anchor tattooed to his left shoulder, which suggested military service. He popped open a can of beer, put the can in a holder of foam plastic, and handed it to his guest. He said, "I'll get you p—ssed tonight."

"One or two will do," said Adrian. "I run, you see, and beer slows me down." He felt uncomfortable as he spoke: he did better in Spanish than in English communing with the poor. His can holder said, TOM'S MACHINE TOOLS. Adrian continued, "I gather that you sell machine tools? Where's Tom?"

"Tom'll be along, and I ain't got no job," Jody said, " 'cept the cause and building that tower. My wife works in Conoco on Route 4?"

"Pumping gasoline?"

"It's self-service! She works the cash register! Sells candy bars and hamburgers? God damn almighty, Ay-jay, where you been all your life?"

A young woman, pretty and well-groomed, emerged from a trailer with a pan of meat, followed by two scrubbed girls with pink ribbons on their pigtails, the children bearing utensils and paper plates. They put them on a table near the grill, then hugged their father. He said, "This is Dolly. Jennie and Bette-Sue, my little girls?"

The children frolicked with the father, and Adrian regarded the wife, as blond as himself. Perhaps inadvertently, as she arranged the table she brushed her body against his buttocks, and for an instant his loins flared. He asked, "Are you from Texas, Mrs. Corn?"

"Arkansas. We used to live there."

"But you prefer Texas?"

"My parents didn't like Jody's style." She turned to her husband. "Jody, I'm tired of being kept waiting by Tom and his gang."

"They'll be along."

"The girls are hungry, and we're going to eat. Ready for your spareribs, Mr. Northwood?"

"I'm starved."

"Will you help Jody with the spareribs while I'm in the kitchen? Mashed potatoes?"

"I'd rather not."

"Do you prefer corn on the cob?"

"Oh, thank you!"

She withdrew to the trailer with her daughters. Jody said, "Dolly's quiet, but she thinks like me. She don't want our little girls growin' up in no People's Republic of Texas?"

"Are there communists in Texas?"

"Half of them's hidin' in your shelter."

Jody began to rant, neglecting the spareribs and bombarding Adrian with disconnected accusations as he guzzled beer.

"Red Chinese . . . subversives . . . tuberculosis . . . terrorists . . .

coyotes them goddamn smugglers your f——ing A! . . . You a communist, Ay-jay? . . . communist guerrillas . . . settin' up a communist state in the Rio Grande Valley your f——ing A! We gotta dig a f——ing ditch! Build a f——ing wall! Call in the f——ing army! Every fifty feet put f——ing soldiers there! They're gonna set up a communist state and make the valley secede from Texas. We're takin' you to court! Me and Tom is goin' before a federal judge we're gonna close your place down! I ain't no god-damn radical? KKK and skinheads I hate 'em they're comin' unless peaceful folk like me and Tom close you down! You're infecting the valley with socialism, tuberculosis, hepatitis, and AIDS. You're turnin' the valley into another third world shithouse. Violence is possible any day? The f——ing border's wide open? Espionage, agents, terrorists, opportunists, drug traffickers! You got guns and drugs passin' through your place! I know the rules in your safe house the alien has to be hungry and need a place to flop. You're a magnet for every hungry bum from south of the border! You're suckin' up our resources we ain't got no more money no medicine no schools we can call our own? It's a goddamn national security problem! Anti-American movements! Subversive forces workin' in the name of God, politics, or humanitarian concerns! Do-gooders like you, good buddy! We're bein' invaded! Ain't that right, Pepe?"

"Ri-i-ght," the Mexican said.

"Ain't that right, Lupe?"

"Ri-i-ght," the Mexican said.

"Why don't you visit the shelter," Adrian asked, "to see that we have no guns, no drugs, and no communists?"

"Hold on, good buddy! I don't wanna catch AIDS! There's no screenin' for terrorists! No screenin' for AIDS! No screenin' for Red Chinese! The terrorists are flopped down in your place and all over the valley. The open border! They're out of control! The border's out of control! They're floppin' down with their blankets, shit, cardboard shanties, paper bags, and garbage? The smell? You'll have crosses burnin' in front of your place if you don't clear out! Watch out, me and Tom and my buddies, we're comin' in

with bulldozers. You're throwin' shit out the window? You and
your do-gooders, good buddy! I been roughed up by coyotes and
drug dealers right by the river. Ain't that right, Pepe?"

"Ri-i-ght," said Pepe.

"Ri-i-ght," said Lupe.

"Lowest form of humanity. Them coyotes will do anything for
money. They take money from them scum, then drive 'em around
back roads, tell 'em they got around the Border Patrol, tell 'em
they're in Houston, then dump 'em right back here outside of
Downsville. You're workin' hand in glove with them coyotes to
ship the terrorists out. I seen you in your truck truckin' them out!
Whadda you think we built that f——ing tower for? Them coyotes
hang out at your gate, pick up the terrorists and drive 'em north?
They tell 'em, 'Wanna ride to Houston?' The scum is spreading,
good buddy, all over the United States. You want another beer?
Why don't you want another beer? I messed with them coyotes
outside your place, and they almost killed me. You know them
taxis outside your place? They run coyotes, terrorists, and drugs I
check on 'em every day. Whadda you teach in your place? Liberation theology? You a Catholic, Ay-jay? Your Church is teachin'
communism. The Klan come down here in the seventies, burned a
few crosses, shot a few wetbacks, our problems went way down,
good buddy! There's liberation theology, filth, motherf——ing shit,
scum, coyotes, total corruption right over the river there in Mexico!
You heard what goes on in Mexico? Them coyotes keep them
Central Americans hostages, they get 'em from the police the police
sell them terrorists and kids to coyotes they keep 'em hostages, the
police work with the coyotes and the scum from Central America
they gotta wire their families in Miami or wherever for ransom
money? You ever go by Western Union, Ay-jay, you ever see them
coyotes hangin' out by Western Union waitin' for their ransom
money? Tomorrow me and Tom we're goin' over to Matablancos
to check on subversive literature. Them terrorists is all indoctri-
nated they tell 'em what to say. They sell maps to your place, good
buddy! I check license numbers outside your place write 'em down

those terrorists and coyotes beat up on me almost killed me. You
don't believe me, Ay-jay? You speak Spanish, Ay-jay? ¡A veinte!
Up yours! Right, Pepe?"

"Up yours," said Pepe.

"Up yours," said Lupe.

"You got Uzis and AK-forty-sevens in your place! I seen 'em,
Ay-jay. You a rich guy? People says you're a goddamn rich guy. I
saw them Uzis and AKs in your truck. Dig a f——ing ditch! Build
a f——ing wall! Call in the f——ing army! Class B misdemeanor
petty thefts twenty dollars, a hundred dollars, two hundred
dollars—them scum kids comin' over from Mexico stealin' jewelry,
cassettes, T-shirts, baseball caps, but you know what them coyotes
got that hang out at Western Union? You ever been to Western
Union, Ay-jay? Corner Saint Charles and Eighth, Levee and Ninth?
They got thousands they wait till the scum come out with all their
money from Miami, then they promise to drive 'em to Houston
and they drive 'em down a alley and rob 'em to their socks! Them
smart coyotes they know when the Border Patrol changes shifts,
they send a big bunch of a——hole Nicaraguans across the river
right into the Border Patrol's f——ing arms, then they know the
Border Patrol will be tied up all night with chickenshit paperwork
then they cross with their own scum and they rob and rape and
steal and smuggle drugs? Used to be three, four million worth
cocaine crossed the river every year now it's quarter or half a billion
in two months I talked with the DEA. The smugglers got boys on
rubber rafts and rubber tubes right in the middle of the f——ing
Rio Grande. They're dockin' right in your alien sanctuary, good
buddy? The other day I was watchin' with my binoculars from the
tower I saw a pregnant woman wade across the river naked as a
worm with the umbilical cord and the f——ing baby's foot danglin'
from her p—ssy? Tom's got a videocamera, we're gettin' arrivals
and departures smugglin' operation terrorists coyotes we're gettin'
it all. Your f——ing A! I seen the Border Patrol arrest fifty scum
outside your fence another fifty got through the fence and the
Border Patrol won't stop 'em because you got a chapel? We're
gonna find a lawyer we're goin' to court and we're gonna knock

you on your ass, good buddy? Your terrorists are destabilizing our society they're a welfare burden and those coyotes? Dig a f——ing ditch, build a f——ing wall, call in the f——ing army!"

Dolly came out of the trailer with her daughters, bearing tureens of mashed potato and steaming corn. She said, "Jody, you haven't even lit the charcoal for the spareribs. Where's Tom?"

"Go inside and get that book," said Jody.

"What book?"

"The book I got in the bathroom."

"Mr. Northwood wants to eat."

"Go get the f——ing book."

She retreated to the trailer, returned with a pamphlet. Jody said, "Oh, this beautiful book! Look here, good buddy?"

Dolly protested, "The girls want to eat."

Adrian flipped through the pamphlet, "Satan's Own Work: Liberation Theology," published by the Christian Antiterrorist Crusade. ". . . liberation theologians see the world of the future as a communist utopia created by the revolution . . . 'liberating the oppressed' . . . 'class warfare in the name of Christ' . . . 'the oppressed person rejects the oppressive consciousness which dwells within him, becomes aware of his oppression and commits himself to the transformation of the poor' . . . 'only socialism can enable us to break the shackles of oppression' . . . high churchmen mouthing the Marxist line . . . maps of Mexico with Texas, New Mexico, and Arizona annexed to Mexico under the hammer and the sickle and 'The People's Republic of Mexico' . . . Cuba . . . revolutionary propaganda . . . violent revolution . . . secret police . . . the U.S. border is the principal focus of attack . . . destabilization of the border is the first step, but the ultimate goal is to destroy the United States . . . the patron saint whose theories they embrace and whose terrorism they endorse and practice is Leon Trotsky . . . Maoists . . . Comintern . . . guerrilla warfare within the United States . . . thereafter the subversive elements who are working to destabilize the border with massive illegal immigration inspired by the Marxist-Leninist revolutionary subversive government of Cuba plan to spread the revolutionary abscess from Central America upward through Mexico through Texas, New Mexico, and Arizona toward Oklahoma, Kansas, and Illinois toward the Canadian border and eventually through Manitoba and Saskatchewan to the Arctic Circle . . ."

Jody asked, "Ain't that *great?* I told Dolly many times, if somethin' was to happen to me so many people hate me I get packages from Michigan or Idaho we don't know a f——ing soul there we don't know nobody. If somethin' was to happen to me it's inevitable and you don't hurt people's pocketbooks asked my wife to carry on. My mission is awful strange moved back and forth twice to Arkansas but I was drawn here? The situation down here which you know what it is? Stand here and fight not for me but not just my children's children but all children? I'm not no goddamn member of the KKK no skinheads I'm just anybody with common sense. Our forefathers!"

Dolly had forgotten the salt and butter. Adrian chewed ravenously on the unseasoned corn.

"Those communists and terrorists and you ask me violence put it this way two kids starving and there's no way you feed 'em you would go out and do somethin' wouldn't you. Don't matter if you got no shoes you feed the kid what happens when you got a million people? Want me be f——ing honest with you? There's a communistic plot to take over the Catholic Church and then they go from there the whole United States and adiós good buddy! Adiós ain't that right, Pepe?"

"Adi-o-o-s," said Pepe.

"Adi-o-o-s," said Lupe.

"It's the total destruction of the U.S. Constitution! P——ss your ass off. I go down to the newspaper I write letters all the time they don't print them they printed one letter how a paper can control a town they cut my letter to shit those communists? Thank God I got my wife my little girls? I been stakin' out your place till four in the mornin'? I been attacked outside your place but I confiscated some subversive communist literature? Your f——ing A! Don't you love this book? Every time I take a shit I read this book."

"May I use your bathroom?" Adrian asked.

"End of the corridor by the kitchen," Mrs. Corn said.

Adrian withdrew to the trailer, one of those dwellings that resembled railroad boxcars and arrived on wheels but once planted in the weeds remained there. The living room was chaotic, all oily machine parts scattered on the carpet with no pictures on the walls, only mirrors and American flags and newspaper clippings about aliens and Cuba and the Ku Klux Klan. The furniture was of cheap striped wood, like paper; plastic, probably. The trailer had no air-conditioning, and despite a fan that rustled the heaps of newspaper, the air was stifling. The kitchen, evidently Mrs. Corn's space, was clean, like the bathroom, full of lotions and hair curlers arranged primly. Adrian had hardly tasted his beer and could barely urinate, but as he heard Jody raving in the yard and Mrs. Corn asking "Where's Tom?" he panicked.

In the living room, away from the yard, was an open window; he climbed through it. "Dig a f——ing ditch, build a f——ing wall, call in the f——ing army!" His truck was in the street within view of the yard, but as Jody screamed and Mrs. Corn complained "How you carry on," Adrian crept around to the far side, released the gears, and with effort pushed the truck over the flat asphalt and the speed bumps until he was out of earshot. He jumped in, turned on the motor, and fled.

As he drove home, it vexed him that some of Jody's rantings were so true. Indeed they were a pox, those coyotes, those smugglers of human contraband, those grizzled men who lingered by the fence of the Casa San Francisco in their trucks and taxis, or even infiltrated the shelter posing as poor refugees, promising to deliver aliens to Houston, sometimes doing so but too often cheating them of all they owned.

Adrian carried on. The tower continued to be built.

The harassment followed a strange rhythm. For days, even for a fortnight, no one mounted the tower to spy on the shelter and to imagine a nest of terrorists. Then the men would return, a few, half a dozen, a dozen, drinking beer on the platform, gazing through binoculars, calling out more obscenities and threats through bullhorns. At night occasionally, they poured gasoline on the meadow near the shelter fence, held torches to the grass, and started brushfires. Adrian rushed out with aliens to beat the ground with sticks; twice he had to call the fire department.

Once, as he fought a fire, he glimpsed Jody Corn through the smoke in his cap and overalls, and he thought he saw a man with a shaven head. Fearful for the shelter's future, dauntlessly he pursued the decoration of the chapel and clung more than ever to Dianita and Alejandro. "Beloved son! Beloved daughter!"

▲▲▲
14
▼▼▼

letter from Diana:
■ ■ ■

. . . and how dare you name a whore's daughter after me? I am not moved by her sordid birth, by your valor as a midwife, nor least of all by your bizarre sense of mercy in deciding to raise the waif as your own child. When finally will you stop compensating for the death of little Urban? And in Heaven's name as your guilt mellows and the child matures what will you do with her? I shan't permit you to give her the Northwood name. Where will she live? Not at Northwood Hall; not near my apartments. *Who* is Alejandro?

I implore you to consider the direction of your life. It is all quite well to help the poor, live with the poor, share the sorrows of the poor (as you put it), or (as I would put it) to waste a trivial fraction of your fortune on another flight of self-indulgence. If you are that intent on assuaging the agony of mankind, then you would do better to channel your charity through agencies that deal less romantically and more effectively with human misery. You will protest that you have contributed amply to the charities of the Holy See and that your Mr. Burner IV has standing orders to contribute to a list of noble causes. I will urge you again to take charge of your fortune and to focus your attention on misery that exists within miles of your home, here in the north. The more you write of your Casa San Francisco, the more attached you seem to it, the more protracted your absence grows, and the farther is your heart from Northwood Hall.

I need you here. A number of decisions must be made, and since Northwood Hall is yours, only you can make them. We must do something about the stables. My arthritis now forbids me to mount, and save for your pleasure the grooms, stableboys, and all those horses serve no purpose. I glanced the other day at the salary list; the waste is embarrassing. Yes, the equestrian staff were devoted to your father, but the horses are no longer bred for competition, much of the staff are elderly, barely able to mount themselves, and they should be pensioned off. I dare not take this decision by myself; you refuse to fire anyone, I am loath to risk another of your tantrums, and what I have said of the stables is even truer of the household staff. At least the stableboys can pitch manure; whenever I emerge from my library, the butlers and maids hover in the shadows, saying nothing but by their silence beseeching me for something to occupy their time. I am at my wit's end about two of our retainers particularly.

Maude's arthritis is so advanced she can no longer type; she is becoming deaf and incontinent. The other day as I tried to dictate, she excused herself in midsentence and hobbled toward the lavatory, but her bowels opened on the Isfahan carpet. She wept hysterically as I cleaned the mess up, unwilling to mortify her by summoning a maid. I am reduced to typing for myself; if I engage another secretary it will kill her.

André has lately been too feeble to climb the stairs from the wine cellar. If ever a servant was superfluous it is that steward. Six thousand bottles of vintage French and Italian wine, cognacs as well that no guest will ever taste, yet if I sip more than a quarter of a glass at dinner it leaves me drowsy and I cannot write of an evening; you protest that wine upsets your stomach and slows your running, yet you refuse to share the cellar with your brother Pius. Last week, André had another heart attack, but as with Maude it will kill him if I send him from this house. Your father was fond of him. I am engaging a nurse and installing him under an oxygen tent in his own infirmary in the south wing, where he will have much sunlight and eventually will die in peace. I trust that you will sanction this arrangement.

Maude is my only company. My writing is going badly. On some days I cannot write at all but linger as ever in the chapel, rereading your exquisite and maddening letters *malgré moi*. I have abandoned one novel to begin writing another, which I shall probably abandon. I cannot bear any longer to read my own books. There are parts of my biographies of Lucrezia and of Isabella d'Este that I still half admire, but the style is too elaborate and the books are much too long. I was enraged at the critics for misunderstanding my novels, but now I am as philistine as they were because I resent my sophistries and find the endings so elusive they seem pointless.

As a child you asked me once why I wrote books. In this at least I am constant, for I would tell you today what I told you then: to achieve immortality. The promise of Holy Church that the reward for the struggles and virtue of my life will be eternal communion with God in Heaven is not enough; I must leave behind something imperishable on earth. The notion that in five hundred or even in a thousand years some questing soul will enter a library, happen on a book of mine, pick it up, turn the pages, then sit down, read it, and be ennobled by it has always been my vital inspiration. No, now I am not even sure of that. More and more as I touch pen to paper I glance across my library to a gilded mirror, glimpsing what I am: an aging widow in an empty house, abandoned by her children, surrounded by senile servants, writing literate drivel that will die with her.

Enough of self-pity; it is cathartic to say it and to you, Adrian. Often as I brooded in the chapel or here in my library I have been tempted to call you on the telephone, or even to end my seclusion in Northwood Hall and to fly to you on the edge of Mexico, but I have not done either, nor shall I, because it is not in my character as the counterpart is not in yours. Better the sweet anguish of separation, of not seeing each other for so long, of communing only by pen and paper as we would have done were we living in your eighteenth century or in my fifteenth. It suits us more than ever that we are a recusant family.

Yesterday I received an hysterical and semiliterate letter from Pius announcing that unless he receives $1 million within thirty days he will be forced into bankruptcy. He is bitter that you did not acknowledge his last appeal; I am in a ghastly dilemma. I feel guilty that my previous request to resolve the matter was perhaps ambiguous, so let me be clearer now.

Apparently whenever you consider your brother's plight you become paralyzed. If for whatever reasons of diffidence or contempt your hand cannot sign a check, let mine. I would not dream of touching our joint account No. 3 unless I were certain you would approve. Transfer $200,000 to the account; when I receive the bank notice I will see it as a sign of your acquiescence, add $50,000 of my own, and send the sum in my name with an ultimatum to your brother that this money must be the last. Besides, the scandal of his bankruptcy might reach the newspapers. Do this, not for Pius, but for me. Maude is having another crisis and I must go.

Votre mère,

DIANA

■ ■ ■

Adrian read the letter many times, chewing and digesting each phrase. ". . . as your guilt mellows and the child matures what will you do with her?" He strode to Dianita's crib; she lay on her back gripping a pink rattle; when she saw him she cooed. Are her features as noble as I fancied? he wondered. When he lifted her, perhaps for the first time his nostrils recoiled at her smell. As he changed her diapers and oiled her he said, "Dianita Northwood, Dianita Northwood . . ."

He looked through his cracked window and saw Alejandro on the gravel, dressed in a new T-shirt, CHICAGO BULLS, barking orders at aliens, then amusing them with song and dance. Adrian sat at a table, and on a scrap of sketching paper scribbled a note.

Ennis,

Tell Burner IV transfer $250,000 to Northwood Hall acct
3 held jointly w. my mother.

AJN

He went to the door and called Alejandro, who bounded to him,
like a mountain panther. "Don Adriano!"

"Take this to the office for Mr. Ennis." He handed him the note,
wondering, Should my brother suffer as this child did?

"Don Adriano?"

"Give me that."

He took the note back, threw it away, and thought, Won't bankruptcy do him good?

15

Next day, by messenger, Adrian received a note handwritten on blue stationery:

> Mr. Northwood,
>   Would you come to me tomorrow at my ranch, past Bean fifty miles from you off Route 77. Please arrive by 7 a.m., before the heat. I knew your father.
>   Cordially,
>   MRS. SEBASTIAN BEAN

Adrian knew that Mrs. Bean owned the Bean & Valley Bank and much of the Rio Grande Valley. He rose before dawn, pulled on his jeans and boots, donned a T-shirt and an old safari hat, drove his truck northward in the night, and turned into the gate of Bean Ranch as the sun rose. From a corral yonder a woman in boots and jodhpurs trotted toward him riding a thoroughbred sorrel, a riderless sorrel tethered to a rein beside her. Beneath a cowboy hat the woman's hair was colored silver, her face though aging was stately, and Adrian remarked that she rather resembled his mother. She asked, "Do you ride?" Adrian nodded, and mounted the other horse. He asked, "How big is the ranch?" She said, "Three hundred thousand acres," and they cantered toward open country.

The land was flat, so utterly flat that it seemed to extend infinitely into space and make the roundness of the earth a fiction. They rode for at least an hour through scrub, no living soul in sight, only parched grass, mesquite tree, and cactus plant. Eventually the flatness grew more verdant as windmills sucked water from beneath the soil and red cows and spotted bulls grazed behind enclosures. In the woods of ebony and live oak, beyond them in green and arid fields, the animal kingdom reigned; owls, hawks, and wild geese; bobcats, turkeys, and mockingbirds; anteaters, partridge, and white-tailed deer.

They paused by a windmill to water their horses. Mrs. Bean said, "Look, Mr. Northwood, the antelope—a blue buck, very rare. I imported the herd from Burma—a birthday gift for my late husband." Adrian found Mrs. Bean more interesting; as he glanced at her slightly prunelike countenance, he guessed that like his mother she had been a beauty once, and like Diana had foregone cosmetic surgery, something of a pity, as daylight lacked charity and the sun rose ferociously in the hazy sky. He asked, "How do the cattle survive this heat?" She said, "Oh, this is cool. By noon, it will be one hundred ten. The cattle lie down beneath the shade. They graze at night, under the moon, so bright it seems like day." He said, "I like your beautiful simplicity." She answered, "You're charming, Mr. Northwood."

They rode onward, past neat white cottages and Mexican tenant farmers hauling stacks of hay with tractors as big as ships; then they entered a new wood, whose willow trees and cactus were mingled for another hour with the stumpy rigs of oil wells, until they reached an endless wall of pink brick. "Bean Park," said Mrs. Bean, but they had to ride an hour yet before they saw palm trees, duck ponds, and a vast velvet lawn around a great Victorian house, all white and wooden, embraced by arcaded porches and sur-mounted by a gabled tower. Mexican men dashed out of stables to take the horses; the lady led her guest inside.

Adrian entered a haze of damask and mahogany. The walls were half red damask, wainscoted to the floor. Mahogany fireplaces with rococo carvings stood in every room, but the house had no marble and few rugs. The stairway and the floors were of simple polished wood, yet the golden draperies were elaborate, like the First Empire furniture studded with ormolu. The paintings were a disappointment, expensive copies of heroic Davids and Ingres, vain princesses and pinched statesmen, originals of the American southwest, Indians on horseback, cowboys herding buffalo on the range, and, among the paintings, jutting from a wall, a stuffed head of a blue antelope with wide horns. The mixture jarred Adrian, and his eyes said so. Mrs. Bean answered, "Perhaps you'll like the library."

He did. It was an immense room with fifty thousand books that rose two stories high, the upper shelves reachable by ladders and a mezzanine. Instantly a shelf with first editions caught Adrian's eye; with childish delight he cast away his safari hat and bounded to it. He ran his finger reverently across the oiled leather bindings, Coleridge and Shelley, Keats and Gray, and was about to open a volume by Lord Byron, not his favorite poet, when he noticed something better. Open on a table were two huge volumes: he leaped to them to turn the yellowed pages, eager for his favorite definitions in Dr. Johnson's dictionary, laughing and calling them out to Mrs. Bean.

" 'BLISTER: A pustule formed by raising the cuticle from the cutis, and filled with serious blood.' Ha-ha! 'CANT: A corrupt dialect used by beggars and vagabonds.' Ha-ha! 'CULLY: A man deceived or imposed upon; as by sharpers or a strumpet.' Ha-ha! 'NETWORK: Anything reticulated or decussated, at equal distances, with interstices between the intersections.' Ha-ha! Ha-ha!"

Mrs. Bean smiled. Adrian felt almost giddy from his exposure to the sun. He continued: "A duchess told him, 'Dr. Johnson, I am so delighted that your dictionary has no unchaste words.' Said Dr. Johnson, 'Madam, how do you know? Did you look for them?' Ha-ha!"

"I love my library," said Mrs. Bean. "I was dyslexic as a child."

"Did you hear of the dyslexic theologian who doubted the existence of Dog? Ha-ha! Ha-ha!"

"You're charming," Mrs. Bean said. "Do sit down." She motioned Adrian onto a long sofa with lyre ends, then sat far from him at its other corner. Her accent blended a very slight twang with a very slight British affectation; Adrian had been told that she owned a house in London. A Mexican woman in maid's costume entered the library bearing a silver tray laden with confections and glasses of lemonade. Unconsciously Adrian reverted to Northwood Hall and his persona of lord, reaching for a lemonade and waving away the sweets without glancing at the servant. He said, "It's been so long since I talked to someone who reads books."

"No doubt," said Mrs. Bean. "However, I did not invite you here to discuss literature."

Adrian sighed. "You knew my father?"

"Not well. Or, should I say, not for long? I did business with him."

"When?"

"Oh, I was still quite young, and so was he, sort of. It was after the war, and Texas was having a boom. Some friends and I formed a conglomerate in Houston—real estate, oil drilling, the first shopping malls, that sort of thing—but we needed heaps of capital."

"And my father provided the capital?"

"Some of it. He came to Houston quite often with his attorney—"

"Mr. Burner II?"

"Yes, now that you remind me. Rather an unpleasant person, I thought. Shady."

"Mr. Burner or my father?"

"Mr. Burner." Adrian smiled. Mrs. Bean continued: "Like you, your father could be charming. He did not always seem quite lucid. He complained of pain in his legs, and sometimes he seemed heavily medicated. He could become very foggy whenever we pressed him about specific sums of cash, but possibly that was his way of negotiating. Eventually he agreed to invest one hundred million dollars, for an inordinate share of the profits. He gave us thirty million, with the contractual promise that the balance would arrive presently, and we went ahead. He kept delaying the delivery of the balance, and the more we pressed him, the more he promised. Finally he sent twenty million, and the more we pressed him for the rest, the more he promised.

"Suddenly his Mr. Burner II showed up in Houston and announced that your father was withdrawing his entire investment and his earnings. When we refused, he stood there in the board-room, screaming at us about loopholes in the agreement and threat-ening to drag us into court. For compelling reasons, we decided not to fight your father. He took his fifty million and another thirty million, leaving us high and dry. Ghastly."

Adrian flared. "Are you suggesting that my father was dis-honest?"

Mrs. Bean rose, walked to Dr. Johnson's dictionary. She said, "When you read to me, you mentioned 'cully' and 'strumpet' and 'sharpers.' Let us see how Dr. Johnson defines 'sharper.'" With her speckled hands she rustled through the second volume, bent over it holding a magnifier. "Ah," she said. "'SHARPER: A tricking fellow; a petty thief; a rascal.'" Gripping the magnifying glass, she turned to Adrian. "I could hardly call Urban Northwood a petty thief, nor shall I go so far in your presence as to call him a rascal. He was a tricking fellow."

"May I take another lemonade?"

"Oh, do help yourself."

"How did my father first make his money?"

"*You* don't know? Neither do I! There were various theories, conjectures, dark rumors, nothing we could be sure of. He told us that he inherited money, but his origins were as murky as his methods, and we never believed him. Some people said he made his first fortune before the war, manufacturing pencils in Budapest, others that he dealt in munitions before the war, during the war, after the—"

"I don't believe that!"

"Then I shan't mention the—the even darker speculations. Let me say simply that from my experience your father was a dark, elusive, mischievous little man. My heavens, you're good-looking. Such a noble bearing. Such bone structure." With her mottled hands she touched his fair and sunburned face. "You did not get those looks from your father."

"From my mother."

"I'm rather sure I'd prefer her to your father. The newspapers call me the richest woman in Texas, but I have reason to be certain,

Adrian Northwood, that my fortune is less than half the size of yours."

Adrian pretended to yawn. Mrs. Bean opened a drawer, removed a pair of binoculars. She asked, "Would you follow me, Adrian Northwood?" She led him up a flight of stairs to the library's mezzanine, then through a door and up a winding wooden staircase to the top of her gabled tower.

The summit was enclosed in glass; the sun had dissolved the morning's haze and as noon approached shone brilliantly in a blue sky. Mrs. Bean lifted her binoculars, scanned the horizon, grimaced, and handed them to Adrian as she sat down on a bench. From that height Adrian did not need binoculars to gaze eastward across the rangeland to sandy beaches and the distant sea. Miles from him, between the tower and the sea, dark clusters of men and women, some of them bearing infants, walked northward across Mrs. Bean's land, their plastic bottles of orange soda pop flashing in the sun. Aliens, thought Adrian, headed toward Sarita and Houston. Will the Border Patrol catch them? He lowered the binoculars and glanced at Mrs. Bean. Her eyes met his and said, I hope so.

"Ah, that's why you asked me here?" Adrian replied.

"What other motive could I have had?"

"It's hardly my fault that aliens trespass on your ranch."

"But you're helping them to invade the country."

"I'm feeding a few hungry mouths!"

"Haven't you hunger in the north?"

"You sound like my mother."

"Do you want a list of my charities?"

"No," said Adrian.

"There is hardly a hospital or an orphanage in the valley that I have not endowed."

"I'm moved."

"Do sit down."

"I'll stand."

"Shall I ring for more lemonade?"

"Not thirsty."

"Why are you so terse?"

"My father was."

"Why must a young man so handsome and rich as you be mixed up with such scum?"

Adrian gazed out of the tower to the trickle of trudging aliens and beyond them to the dazzling sea. He said, "Scum? Have you any idea, madam, of the change in my life since I came to this valley and discovered this scum? I used to live as you do, in luxury. Like you, I gave money to the poor, but I never mingled with them. I hadn't the faintest notion of what it felt like to descend to my hands and knees, to scrub filthy floors, to clean up the leavings of the poor. I'd never dressed their wounds or fed their starving young. I'd never reached inside their wombs and drawn their unborn children toward the light.

"My mother tells me that as I mingle with the poor I am playing a game with my great fortune, and compensating for the failure and tragedy of my life in a fugue of remorse and self-pity. May I confess something? My mother may be right. I may be here not so much to help others as to help myself. Isn't all human motivation mixed? What difference do my cloudy and imperfect motives make so long as the poor eat? I saw a terrible human need—multitudes of sick and starving people pouring over the border—so I responded as I could.

"Now you intrude upon my life to echo my mother's misgivings and to suggest that my father's fortune was illegitimate. Oh, God, could that be so? Must I also feel remorse for that? I hate this century! I hate the greedy culture of the north! I tried to live in New York City, but every time I opened a door a man already rich stood there with his hand stuck out. I grew up as you did in the culture of the rich, and it bores me to the marrow of my bones. I'm in this valley to share the drama of the poor. Oh, yes, I'm quite selfish, for I find the poor far more interesting than the rich. Nothing among the rich I've ever seen can compare with the struggles and excitement of the poor. The poor are more interesting than the rich! I envy the poor! Have I been voluble enough?"

Mrs. Bean said, "You're overwrought. Has it never occurred to you, the harm you're doing? This valley is being overwhelmed. Our society is being destroyed. All these sick and dirty people pouring in, bearing disease, contagion, and drugs. I am a devout Presbyterian, but there is a limit to Christian charity, and we must spend our charity on the poor among us who have the right to be here. Your shelter is notorious even two thousand miles south. Those riffraff and subversives in Central America hear of your bizarre compassion and arrive on the Rio Grande with maps and arrows pointing to your shelter. I've seen the maps, Mr. Northwood! Your shelter is a magnet for all the riffraff, subversives, for all that scum south of the border."

"You're welcome to visit the shelter, Mrs. Bean, to see for yourself—"

"Oh, I'd never risk contracting some horrid disease. I've no wish to meet all those subversives and terrorists. May I suggest a reasonable solution, Adrian Northwood? Your property abuts a piece of mine; I could have bought it, never did, and how I regret that now. I wish to buy your shelter."

"To close it?"

"Within a fortnight. I shan't be unchristian to the sick."

"Not for sale!"

"You're shouting at me, Mr. Northwood. It's a nest of terrorists."

"You sound like Jody Corn!"

"Jody's a bit crude."

"How on earth do you know Jody?"

"Everybody knows Jody."

"Who's financing his tower?"

"Will you stop shouting? You're like your father now and not a gentleman. The tower is on my property. I loathe those fires. I told Jody and Tom that I will not have violence. If you persist, there is bound to be violence."

"Who's financing his tower?"

"I am. I'm pressing the federal government to put your aliens in detention."

"The federal government has no place for them."

"I have influence in Washington, so we shall see about that. Meanwhile, I may take you to court."

"I thought Jody was taking me to court."

"Jody talks. I have the best attorneys in Texas. However much time and money it may take, I shan't rest until I close the Casa San Francisco. Whatever the means, this invasion must be stopped. If I have my way, we'll dig a ditch, build a wall, call in the army. . . ."

16

Soon Mrs. Bean and several of her rich friends filed suit in federal court, contending that the Casa San Francisco was not a true religious sanctuary and endangered the public safety. Mr. Burner IV sent in "hired guns," expensive attorneys from Houston, who promised Adrian that they would challenge the suit with endless briefs and motions, so entangling it in legalisms that the complaint might never be resolved. It comforted Adrian occasionally —it did now—to seek refuge behind the shield and power of his fortune. He assured himself that the lawsuit was a trifle, and lived more than ever in a kingdom of his own, illumined by his music, books, and painting. In the mail, he received a new book. Aha, he thought aloud, at last, something *important*!

By roundabout routes from Rome, via ocean ship and Motel 5½, it was his copy of Cardinal Galsworthy's *The Joy of Celibacy*. He halted his decoration of the chapel, summoned Alejandro to care for Dianita, and, gripping the gift, ran out to the riverbank. Resting his back against a mesquite trunk, he read the book with curiosity and fascination.

It was the kind of unorthodox tome that no New York publisher would ever touch. It had been printed on expensive paper in Naples by an obscure house, the typesetter evidently so ignorant of English that the text was marred with misspellings. Adrian remembered Cardinal Galsworthy's remark that the book had been read only

by Diana and the Pope. Diana had compared the style to Newman's, but as Adrian turned the pages he suspected that at most
his mother had merely glanced at them, and it amused him to think
that the Cardinal's audience was confined to the Pope and now
himself. The work owed little to Newman, far more to the author's
namesake St. Augustine and to Blaise Pascal, and it evoked often
enough the erotic imagery of St. John of the Cross.

The narrative was uneven, lurching between the confessional
style of St. Augustine (personal revelations of surprising candor)
and austere propositions in the manner of Pascal's *Pensées* (some
few fully developed, others left dangling mysteriously), but the
theme throughout was coherent: celibacy as an adventure.

Adrian was stimulated and confused by the Pascal-like propositions:

■ ■ ■

... 23. Thus the ennobling struggle.
   24. The struggle for its own sake: a drama of beauty.
   25. St. Augustine on beauty: "I was in love with those lower
       beauties. I was sinking into the very depths and I said to
       my friends, 'Do we love anything but beauty? What then
       is beautiful? and what is beauty? What delights and allures
       us in all we love? Nothing in them could allure us but
       grace and beauty.' "
       Expand.
   26. Celibacy was never intended to be easy.
   27. The danger of narcissism in the struggle to maintain per-
       fect celibacy. Explain.
   28. The love imagery of John of the Cross.

> *Descubre tu presencia,*
> *Y máteme tu vista y hermosura;*
> *Mira que la dolencia*
> *De amor, que no se cura*
> *Sino con la presencia y la figura.*
>
> Reveal your image clearly,
> And kill me with the beauty you discover;

> For pains that come so dearly
> From love, cannot recover
> But through the presence of the lover.

Explain that the images are misleading if we consider them an ode to carnal love. Superior mystical love cannot start until carnal love slumbers.

29. Lucifer. Bearer of light. What sort of light? His light is darkness? Light = darkness. Symbiosis of light and lust: develop. Ceaseless pushing toward light and lust. The paradox of Lucifer: insofar as he conveys light, does he retain an element of goodness? Classical theology says "no." *Ergo,* no.

30. Connect Proposition 29 above to a fragment of Pascal's Proposition 372: "*For I strive only to know my nothingness.*" Connect that with his Proposition 379: "It is not good to have too much liberty." Connect that with a fragment of his Proposition 453: "From lust men have extracted excellent rules of policy, morality, and justice."

31. Lust is such a waste of time! . . .

■ ■ ■

Eventually Cardinal Galsworthy told the story he had so painfully revealed to Diana at Northwood Hall—of his youthful encounter with a dark older woman in Florence and his notion that he had fathered a son. Yet in the book (possibly to avoid embarrassing the Pontiff) he did not explicitly confess his breach of chastity and suggested that the encounter, the orgasm, and the conception all happened (involuntarily) in a dream.

By this device of dreams, his son's imagined infant face haunted a whole section of the book, and the Cardinal could repeatedly confess his anguish that his vocation to celibacy forbade him children of his flesh. "Of all the crosses that chastity lays on us, this is heaviest. The burden is stranger for its mood of emptiness, of weightlessness, of loss. Remember Proposition 26: Celibacy was never intended to be easy."

Adrian loved the Cardinal's last chapter:

■ ■ ■

. . . and as I gaze backward over my years before, I wonder often what the rigours of chastity have done to my flesh. You have heard the phrase "a priestly face." How has the struggle touched my face? (That is not where the war was waged.) As I glance at the mirror, may I seek any signs of ennoblement? A lovely woman once touched my face. She said, "Chastity has raised your cheekbones and stretched the skin. You have the faint pallor of parchment." She said nothing of ennoblement. If I seek evidence of my joy, it cannot be in any looking glass.

I will confess to you that I have long enjoyed the company of lovely women. Rome is hardly a puritan place, and cardinals as princes are expected to mix in society. As a youth I was terrified of women, but as I matured in years and advanced in the government of the Church I grew more relaxed in their presence and more pleased by their attentions. It did not strain my intellect to discover that beautiful women were attracted to priests not for their sensuality but precisely for their chastity. Male chastity seemed to them not merely a curiosity but in priests a mystery they wished to fathom, and—in rare cases—to conquer.

I will go further and confess that as I rose higher in Holy Church and into the Sacred College I contrived to place myself in the company of lovely women to see whether I could survive the risk and challenge to my chastity. At soirées in Rome and Paris I practised in several languages the art of diffident charm. If I liked a dinner partner, in the morning I might send to her a bottle of Lacrima Christi or a book of mystical verse. Unkindly tongues began to call me an *abbé de salon*. I was not content with nuns as secretaries. More than once, I engaged a young woman who was not under vows and not especially religious. I am mournful in particular about one of my secretaries.

She was Heide, an Austrian of the mountainous Tyrol who had come down to Rome in pursuit of her beloved, a Neapolitan rake who had impregnated her in Bolzano and abandoned her to her tears. I met her through the Sisters of the Good Shepherd, favourites of mine and beneficiaries of my meagre charity, in whose house she had sought refuge as she awaited her accouchement.

Heide was twenty-two, brown-haired, with a fair but ruddy Alpine colour, and, being Tyrolese, fluent in Italian. Upon the birth of her daughter I baptised the child; since Heide had no means I ignored the censure of Canon Law against priestly proximity to young women and gave her a minor post as a typist in my secretariat. When we passed in the corridors often our eyes met; in Heide's I glimpsed more than gratitude.

She had a delightful, low-pitched laugh. I asked her, "Darling Heide, what are the little things in life that give you pleasure?"

She said, "I love the opera and ice cream, Your Eminence."

I bought her tickets for the opera and sent ice cream to her room at the House of the Good Shepherd, where she lived with her child. Soon enough she managed to remain at work, as I did, after my other staff had gone home. I should have recalled the Church's ancient rule of "avoiding the occasions of sin," but I was too taken with my conceit of confirming my celibacy by exposing it to risk.

One evening, as I dictated to her, she broke down, and between her tears she told me, "I've fallen deeply in love."

"With whom?" I asked.

"With you," she said.

As though in a dream I watched myself rise from a chair, walk deliberately to her, and grasp her lovely head against my breast. I had been a cardinal for some years, but still I had not reached fifty, and the warmth of her was more than my resistance could sustain.

I drew back, full of remorse for having led her on, and said, "Tomorrow."

I walked across St. Peter's Square to my residence near the Tiber, where I repaired at once to my chapel, struggling to pray and wondering what I might do. Later that evening, as I lay in bed, I was tempted achingly to throw away my cardinalate and to flee with Heide. My conscience and my motives were miserably confused. I thought I loved Heide, but in different ways I loved my cardinalate as much, and I hoped that I still loved Christ. Long before Heide, I had loved my celibacy as I loved my priesthood. Poets speak of "delicious anguish," but the taste of mine was dust and ashes. Could I imagine myself in any life but my cardinalhood?

And what of Heide? In my pity for myself, what mercy had I for her? I had told her, "Tomorrow." That kind of tomorrow never came. Next day I remained at my residence, and the day after that I left on a journey long planned, to the Far East, on a secret mission for the Pope. From Tokyo I wrote to my Undersecretary, instructing him to remove Heide from my premises and to find her decent work and lodgings elsewhere in Italy but far from Rome.

Since Heide, my celibacy has not ceased to be an adventure.

Differently.

The more I devote my mind and body to remaining chaste, the more conscious I become of beauty.

Celibacy blossoms. Lust is barren.

What sex coarsens, celibacy refines; what sex is blind to, celibacy sees; what sex dulls, celibacy hones to sharpness. Celibacy is a drug that more than any beverage of the psyche magnifies the power of the senses to perceive. It heightens colour, the melodies of music, the shape of faces. Its terrible detachment propels the soul upward from the flesh toward realms of joy where all things float. . . .

■　■　■

In his rooms Adrian wrote at once to Cardinal Galsworthy on a clean piece of paper. ". . . and I do admire your mysticism. Maybe, in lieu of condoms, in plain brown wrappers, your book should be distributed to American high school students. . . ." He wrote another note on a dirty piece of paper.

> Ennis,
>   More rednecks around tower lately & I'm afraid of fires; engage professional security guards to patrol fence. I loathe the publicity fr. federal ct. & keep "media" away fr. me. Tell B. IV he's stealing fr. me far too much & there must be a limit to his greed.
>
> AJN

Then Adrian changed Dianita's diapers and carried her in his arms about the Casa San Francisco as he made his evening rounds. Guatemalan women followed him like servants; the shelter resembled Northwood Hall insofar as pairs of hands were ever waiting should he wish to hand her away (as he had little Urban II) in order to attend to a task. Recently (almost as though to mock his mother and Mrs. Bean) he had assumed a new task.

After midnight, Adrian strode barefoot to the river, bearing a burlap sack over his shoulder. He shed his clothes, shoved them with his burlap sack into any plastic bag that lay discarded on the shore, and balancing his freight upon his head swam naked to Mexico. Over his wet body he pulled on his jeans and T-shirt and, still barefoot, walked upward in the moonlight past garbage dumps, abandoned cars sunken in weeds, tilting wooden houses built on stilts, until he came to the Zona Zur.

The Zona Zur was an old brothel quarter, renowned for its stabbings, closed by the police and boarded up, in its center a fountain of pink marble, chipping away. It abounded in the crumbling heraldry of love: cement slabs and adobe walls with graffiti of red lips and hearts pierced with arrows. Rubble littered the streets, adorned still with wrought-iron benches painted white, primly enduring in gardens of ragweed that grew through cobblestones. Bars once convulsive with life, the Lipstick Lounge, Hot Banana, Pink Pussy, stood deserted in the moonlight.

At the end of the main street stood a high adobe building that still flourished as a brothel—many of its clients were policemen—before the Zona Zur blended again into tilting, sagging shacks built on stilts and cement blocks. Adrian passed the brothel's busy entrance and laid down his burden in the shadows, sitting on a cement block as he opened his burlap sack. It contained a kettle, a camper's stove, plastic cups and bottles of water, packets of instant soup powder, and small loaves of bread.

Adrian filled his kettle, placed it on his stove to boil the water, and—amid the babble of male and female voices blaring from the brothel yonder—sat patiently on his cement block in the filthy street by the tilting shacks, whistling now and then as though to make his presence known, waiting.

One by one, children (boys, mostly, but little girls as well) emerged from beneath houses on low stilts and cement blocks, from abandoned bars and brothels boarded up, from huge hollow cement building blocks and abandoned trailers teetering on oil drums, and silently approached Adrian. These children, most of them barely into adolescence and many much younger, were glue sniffers.

They had no parents; their fathers were faceless men who out of habit had thrust themselves into anonymous vulvas, paid the fee or none at all, and fled; their mothers, most of them, had borne too many children by different fathers to feed them all or even to keep count. The children were of the breed that Adrian had met in Amigoland, who crossed the river regularly to stretch their little hands upward on the racks of Wal-Mart, to snatch the tubes of glue and cans of spray paint and giggle as children do.

They lived here near the river in the Zona Zur, squeezed between the earth and shacks that stood on stilts or inside abandoned brothels or hollow building blocks, for nourishment burrowing in the earth, munching like rabbits on grass that grew beneath the houses or on candy bars they stole from Wal-Mart. They had no parents, but they did not live utterly without love. They had each other; when they were done with stealing and sniffing glue and paint, they lay down to sleep beneath the houses or in the building blocks with their arms entwined, hugging one another.

They had no mothers, they had no fathers, but they had Adrian, and though they mumbled between themselves they rarely thanked him, hardly seemed to notice him as he served each of them hot soup and loaves of bread.

"Ah, Carlos," he said. *"¿Más sopa?"* More soup? "Enrique! *¿Más pan?"* Another piece of bread? "Marta! My little princess! Dip the bread in your soup!"

They nodded now and then and remained silent. He never lectured them, never tried to talk to them of their addiction: it would do no good. One cannot converse with zombies. Worse, Adrian thought of his son, for in their special way glue sniffers, also, were decapitated. All of these children were sick, some very sick, not simply undernourished but consumptive and brain-damaged. When they walked their movements were jerky and their heads and bodies twitched. Their hands, torsos, nostrils, were smeared with the leavings of Krazy Glue, roof cement, concrete patch, paint remover, turpentine, chrome spray, silver spray, gold spray, and their eyes were always red. Their bodies reeked of lice, yet some of their T-shirts (just stolen?) seemed new: I LUV MADONNA . . . MADONNA WANTS MY BODY . . . I MAKE IT WITH MADONNA . . . but they could not read.

Each night as he served bread and soup Adrian fancied that among the children he might meet the child.

No FUNKY COLD.

When they had sipped a little of their soup and nibbled on their bread (many had no appetite; the delicious trance of glue dispelled the pangs of hunger), like wound-up little toys the children jerked and twitched their way back to their habitations beneath the floors of houses, and Adrian gathered his stove and kettle in his sack, preparing to go home. More and more at that hour, long after midnight, in the brothel nearby, whores ascended to the roof and leaned over the balustrade, watching Adrian. Tonight they cried, *"¡Ven acá arriba!"* Come up here!

"¿Quién, yo?" Who, me? asked Adrian, looking upward, pointing to himself.

"¡Sí, tu!"

He recalled the Cardinal's statute about avoiding the occasions of sin. He answered, *"¿Por qué no?"* Why not?

He entered the brothel, like a rat's labyrinth with low ceilings and a moldy smell and dirty white adobe walls that sagged. The corridors were as warped, meandering this moment, straight the next, leading to murky alcoves and a lumpy staircase that twisted skyward in odd directions to one level and then another. Before a curtained alcove on an upper floor, young lean men and older obese men, half naked, belts and pistols around their waists, queued impatiently to be satisfied. The whore in there must be the prettiest, thought Adrian. He heard mariachi music, guitars and rattles, trumpets and concertinas, drifting from the roof.

He felt his bare feet scuffing and his sack of metals jangling against his shoulder as he mounted the misshapen staircase to the roof. Beneath the moon the brothel seemed more pleasant. The flat roof abounded with pots of flowers. The girls seemed to live on that vast roof, each inhabiting her own cabaña, curtains in her window and by her doorstep a pot of flowers. When Adrian appeared, the women rushed to him from the balustrades and the doors of their cabañas, touching his locks with their painted fingers, admiring his fairness and fondling his body.

The women wore short, tight dresses, sheer black or brilliant red, tinsel earrings and green eye shadow, white boots or spiked blue shoes. At the bar, a youth served beer and played mariachi records. Adrian put down his burlap sack, sat on a stool, and, having no money, asked for a glass of water. A whore, skeletal and almost old, with bleached hair that stood up straight and resembled straw, sat beside him and seized his crotch. She had purple fingernails inches long; they dug into his phallus through his jeans and started to unzip his fly. He thought, Sex with a scarecrow? and eluding the grasp of other whores, he leaped to the dance floor. There, to the rhythm of mariachi guitars and drums, distracting the women with the graceful movements of his bare feet, he danced alone.

These whores were coarse, most no longer young, one or two were hags, but as he danced in his chaste isolation, swaying his hips, twirling, advancing, retreating, swinging side to side, a beautiful woman ascended to the roof, smoking. Shunning jewelry or make-up, she wore low heels, a white blouse, and a denim skirt. She had a snub nose, auburn hair, and slim hips: Adrian thought of beloved vintage movies and Susan Hayward. Her skin, still smooth and ruddy, had no doubt been exquisite but was congealing faintly into a mask of contempt. Ah, thought Adrian, she must be the whore from down below, the favorite of the armed policemen.

Her cigarette was a stub of marijuana, and as she approached Adrian on the dance floor her green eyes swam and she seemed as high as the mountains of the moon. She tossed away her stub and knelt before him, languidly cupping her nailless hands about his flanks.

"*Eres si feo.*" You're so ugly, she said.

Adrian: "*Sí.*"

"*¿Quieres cachucha?*"—a ribald offer, in Tex-Mex, of oral sex.

"*¿Cuál es tu nombre?*" What's your name?

"Susana."

"*¡Nombre lindo!*" Nice name!

But he danced away from her, and when in her drugged trance Susana understood his diffidence, she drifted to the bar and leaned her back against it. She noticed his gunnysack and opened it, rattling the metals and removing leftover packets. She asked, "What's this?"

"Soup," said Adrian, still dancing. "Would you like a cup?"

"I'd love one."

She led him, bearing his sack, to her cabaña, neatly kept, a wayside shrine. In a niche stood a statue of the Holy Virgin of Guadalupe, standing on a cloud in a golden radiance, surrounded by Susana's votive candles, flickering in red glass. On the wall nearby beneath glass hung a dark painting of Christ's hands, only His hands, gripping His cross.

On her own Primus stove, Susana boiled the water for the instant minestrone, and Adrian sat beside her on her bed as she sipped it. They hardly spoke. She asked him, "*¿Eres del otro lado?*" Are you from the other side? Mexicans of the border never mentioned the United States, only "the other side." Nor did she ask his name, calling him only "*tu, el feo*"—ugly you—or just Feo—Ugly.

Thenceforth Adrian returned to the police brothel often, in the wee hours after he had fed the glue children, to visit Susana in her cabaña and to share with her a cup of soup. He allowed her to run her smooth hands through his fair hair, and always he hugged her warmly, but otherwise he felt like Mahatma Gandhi, who took beautiful women into his bed and did not touch them in order to test his chastity.

At the lower levels of the brothel, amid the moldy odor and warped corridors, or as he passed them on the lumpy stairway, Adrian became ever more familiar with the faces of the police. They smiled at first, flashing gold and silver teeth, but in time they seemed less friendly. One night a fat policeman asked for his identification. "I don't have it with me," Adrian said. "You're in Mexico illegally," the policeman answered, but perhaps because officially the brothel did not exist, he said no more; he was one of Susana's lovers.

Adrian mounted to Susana's cabaña for their session of soup and silence, but within minutes half a dozen policemen in various states of nakedness, all with belts and pistols dangling, knocked angrily on her door, kicked it in, complaining that she spent too much time with the blond gringo and demanding her favors. Sighing, setting aside her instant minestrone and lighting a stub of marijuana, she withdrew from her sanctuary and followed the policemen downstairs, leaving Adrian alone.

Or rather, one of the men lingered, browsing about the cabaña, picking up Susana's things, fingering as though with reverence the Holy Virgin of Guadalupe and Christ's hands and crying "Oooh!" when he touched a flickering votive glass and it burned him. Adrian remained seated on Susana's bed, watching this creature.

His appearance was comic and mildly grotesque. Thrust down to his eyebrows was a blue baseball cap, emblazoned in white, SSDD (SAME SHIT—DIFFERENT DAY). His bare torso was tattooed with hearts, a snake, and a spiderweb on either shoulder. He wore filthy black trousers and was barefoot. When he removed his cap to run a hand through his bushy hair, dark like his goatee, Adrian surmised that in age he might be almost thirty. Either side of his forehead, only very faintly, was tattooed with an inverted cross. Adrian asked, "Are you a policeman?"

"No," the man said, "*pero son todos mis compañeros.*" But they're all my pals. "*¡Soy pescador!*" I'm a fisherman!

"Where do you fish?"

"In a swamp. No fish, no money. I make windshield wipers. What do you do?"

"I try to paint."

"I love pictures! What's your name?"

Adrian smiled. "Susana calls me Feo."

"But you're not ugly."

"What's yours?"

"Lázaro."

"What do your inverted crosses mean?"

Lázaro giggled. He said, "I'm religious, like Susana. She never brought a guy up here before. Do you f—— her every night?"

"I'm far too fond of her. . . ."

"Want a joint?"

"Some other time?"

"Will you buy me a beer?"

"I have no money."

At the bar, Lázaro begged a bottle of beer on credit and shared it with Adrian in separate glasses. Like all Mexicans, he squeezed lemon juice into his beer. Adrian wondered, Will I despair of Mexico? He had already despaired of Lázaro, who took a Mickey Mouse watch from the pocket of his foul pants and uttered blasphemous lamentations over the broken strap. "It's a good watch," he assured Adrian. "Waterproof. Look!" He dropped the watch into his glass of beer, then retrieved it, still ticking. He said, *Tu dices pintor pero pareces como rico.* You say you're a painter, but you look like a rich guy.

Adrian ran away from him, descending to the dance floor to do push-ups: "One-two-three-four." The turrets of the prison yonder came suddenly ablaze with light, and the rat-tat-tat of automatic guns reported through the wet air. Adrian wondered what it might be like inside that great penitentiary. He glanced up at Lázaro. "A riot," said Lázaro. "Or an escape? A bad place." He giggled again. "I've been there."

Susana returned from her exertions on the lower floors. She had a swollen eye. She lifted her marijuana stub to take a puff, and the flimsy paper stuck to the blood of her bruised lip. For an instant her eyes met Adrian's, but as though with indifference, she looked away. Policemen followed her. From their glances Adrian knew that it was time to take up his gunnysack and go. His burden clanked against his shoulder as Lázaro pursued him down the lumpy stairs, asking, "Will you give me your shirt?" Adrian tore off his T-shirt, threw it in Lázaro's face, thought better, and snatched it back. He emerged into the night, debating whether he should ever come again to the police brothel.

He returned to the tilting shacks on stilts to look beneath them for the child, then inside the hollow cement building blocks and the trailers teetering on oil drums and the abandoned bars and brothels: no FUNKY COLD. On the riverbank, he cupped his hands around his mouth and cried toward Mexico in darkness, "¡NIÑO, NIÑO!" CHILD, CHILD! He lingered there for several minutes, looking everywhere about and waiting for an answer: nothing. He swam back to the United States and ran to his barrack rooms in the Casa San Francisco, where he turned on a lamp and found Alejandro sleeping in a cot, with tiny Dianita dozing in his arms.

He thought, Why aren't they enough? and though it was nearly dawn he resisted sleep. He took up Goethe's *Faust,* which lately as a little game he had been committing to his memory. THE LORD: Know you Faust, my servant? MEPHISTOPHELES: Lord, indeed I do, that servant strange and fervent. *Fürwahr! er dient Euch auf besondre Weise.* From food of earth he doth refrain. *Nicht irdisch ist des Toren Trank noch Speise.* His fever drives him to a lofty plane. In madness . . .

He fell asleep at his cluttered table, bent over, his head against the musty pages of his Goethe, and his dream resumed. His constant jellyfish floated languidly in space, tattooed with spiderwebs and faint inverted crosses. He descended to the lower floors, parted the curtains of an alcove, and found a fat policeman possessing Susana. He tore her from the policeman's grasp and kissed her bleeding lip. She said, "Feo, my soup is cold." Mrs. Corn came in, brushed her body against his flanks, and said, "He prefers my mashed potato."

In his dream I made no appearance (I am not Mephistopheles),
but I did speak. (Is it time you knew that I narrate his thoughts,
his dreams, every word you read?) I asked, "Why is the child so
important?"
    He answered, "After my son, he was the first."
    I protested, "For your own sake, stay out of Mexico."
    He laughed at me and said, "You're a dream inside my dream.
Mexico also is a mystery."

The rising sun woke him, magnified through his cracked window,
burning his face. Alejandro and Dianita slept on; he did not disturb
them. Ignoring breakfast, he left the shelter and ran five miles along
the levee, then mounted Prince and cantered him upriver to the
wilderness. When he returned to his barrack, Alejandro was playing
on the grass with Dianita. He hugged them both and went inside
to resume his painting, but first he scribbled another note, and
Alejandro brought it to the office.

    Ennis,
        Media people keep showing up here. Urban N: "Consort w.
    asps but never trust a journalist." If you can't keep them away
    fr. me I'll tell B. IV to dismiss you.

                                         AJN

Until late afternoon he worked on his sacred panels; he felt like
the atheist Matisse decorating the chapel at Vence. He was half
satisfied with his Stations of the Cross, but he struggled more than
ever with the head of St. Francis: he could not achieve the effect
he sought of childishness and wisdom. A commotion outside his
door.
    Through the window he saw Mr. Ennis, in his spectacles and
suit, remonstrating with a woman and a man with a television
camera, KQYQ. The man had his camera running; the two were
resisting Ennis's entreaties to leave. Adrian went out to confront
them.
    "Shut off that camera!"

"Oh!" the woman exclaimed as the man filmed him. "Are you Mr. Northwood?"

"Shut off that camera!"

Ennis: "I beg you, sir, to accept my regrets for this crass intrusion. I have been trying—"

Adrian: "Go back to the office, Ennis."

Woman: "A two-minute interview, Mr. Northwood? Yesterday in federal court—"

Adrian wrested the camera from the man's grip, tore out the film, and handed back the camera. The woman seemed intimidated too, possibly by Adrian's wild appearance: his hair and bare torso were splotched with viridian and burnt sienna. She said, "I'm sorry. I didn't mean to intrude. My boss insisted." She turned to the cameraman: "Get lost, José."

José ran beneath the weight of his equipment toward the fence. She said, "You must be real strong, Mr. Northwood. José's a big guy."

"Here's your film."

"Keep it. I'm Vicki. Vicki Rice?"

Adrian regarded her. She wore tight black slacks, a white blouse wrinkled by the heat, and blue shoes that reminded him of the whores' shoes in the police brothel, though her spiked heels sank and vanished in the path of gravel where she stood. She was pretty in a way, with a boyish haircut of dull blond, slim almost to anorexia, and though she was easily thirty, her light make-up could not conceal the childish acne that kissed her cheekbones. Reciprocally she seemed more pleased than Adrian by what she saw. She asked, "Could we—someday, I mean—have lunch?"

"I eat potato chips for lunch."

"Dinner, then?"

"When?"

"Now?"

Adrian for months had lived monastically; he sensed intrigue. He asked, "No interview, Miss Rice?"

"Vicki. Promise."

"I'll have to shower."

She followed him into his rooms; watched as he pulled clean clothes and linen out of closets, then withdrew to the bathroom. The bathroom door was shattered, and he was half visible as he disrobed. Paintings were stacked opposite the door; Miss Rice pretended to take an interest, fingering through them, holding them up, glancing at Adrian as he showered. He did not bother to draw the curtain, and when he emerged from his ablution he felt flattered by her prurience, standing nude within her line of sight, whistling, humming, turning this way or another, as leisurely he toweled his body. Omitting his shorts, he vested his nakedness with a pair of gray jeans and a white shirt and came out of the bathroom laughing. Miss Rice leaned against his paintings, humming as he had done. He asked, "Shall we?"

They emerged into twilight, walked to the fence and her white BMW, and she drove over the railroad bridge toward Mexico. "I don't have my passport," said Adrian. "They won't ask for it," said she, nor did they. She parked at Mortelo's, an expensive place; they sat on the patio, enclosed in glass, where they ordered shrimp and lamb chops. From a trolley a man served drinks; Adrian sipped beer; Miss Rice ordered margaritas. Adrian, who hardly drank, watched with curiosity as the Mexican chilled the glass in a gourd of ice, mixed gold tequila with Triple Sec and lemon juice, and smeared salt around the rim of the wet glass. "Too much tequila," complained Miss Rice after several tastes, handing the mixture back; the man mixed another. "Too much lemon juice," she told him after drinking most of that. "Too much salt." She asked Adrian, "How old are you?"

"My mother thinks I'm three."

"I went to Lake Tahoe last month on vacation with my mother. I'd say you're twenty-five?"

"Thirty-one."

"So am I. You don't look it."

"Neither do you."

"You mean my acne?"

"It makes you younger, Miss Rice."

"Vicki. Does it? Can I call you Adrian?"

"How about AJ?"

"Is your family filthy rich?"

"My brother's bankrupt."

"Do they all look like you?"

"I don't care for my looks."

"You're kidding. Do you care for mine, AJ?"

"On television you must be smashing."

"Then why do I go on vacations with my mother?"

"You've never been married?"

"No. And you, AJ?"

"I'm not married."

"Oh, God, those blue eyes, that wistful face. You're too fine to be a hunk. Do you write poetry?"

"Not well."

"Who's your favorite poet?"

"Who's yours?"

"Oscar Wilde!"

"A better dramatist than poet?"

"Oh, I adore his 'Ballad of Reeding Goal.' "

"I beg your pardon?"

"The Ballad of Reeding Goal."

"Ah, of course. 'In Reed-ing goal by Reed-ing town, There is a pit of shame . . .' "

"That's it!"

" 'And in it lies a wretched man, Eaten by teeth of flame . . .' "

"I *adore* it!"

" 'No need to waste the foolish tear, Or heave the windy sigh, The man had killed the thing he loved, And so he had to die. . . .' "

Adrian had no money; Miss Rice paid for dinner. She drove back to Texas and along the river to a golf course. Turning off her headlights, beneath the moon she bumped the BMW onto a fairway, where she parked in shadow by a mesquite tree and began to kiss Adrian on the mouth.

———

He remembered France, where in his adolescence he had learned to make love. On weekends he escaped his Benedictine school in Normandy, a rocky priory on the English Channel beneath a winged statue of St. Michael, and took the train to the Gare St-Lazare , whence he walked down the boulevard Haussmann toward a notorious quarter called Strasbourg St-Denis (Straz-boor San-*nee!*). His father had recently died, there were no restraints on his inheritance, and he had all the francs he might ever wish in order to indulge his fancies, still childish though hardly innocent.

He never came with a companion, tending to be solitary anyway and needing no schoolboys to share his games. Along the boulevard Sébastopol and in the squeezed doorways of the rue du Caire, the passage Lemoine, the rue Notre-Dame-de-Nazareth, he solicited agreeable women, the closer to his own age, the more agreeable.

He learned early in lovemaking that he liked to take his time, to linger over his partner's body during languid afternoons and evenings in frugal rented rooms, to savor her various mounds and nooks for hours before he ejaculated. He hated women who told him, *"Dépêche-toi"*—Hurry up. He threw hundred-franc notes in their faces and took flight, but he paid patient girls handsomely. He never used condoms, un-Catholic and (worse) unaesthetic, just as he disliked long fingernails digging into his flesh and favored slim hips even then. When at last he was ready to ejaculate and achieved the final friction of his phallus against the woman's damp moss, he felt not so much a thrill as immense comfort. It seemed to him that his body was in space, floating.

In adolescence, no sadness after sex. He slept alone in his large house on the avenue Foch, amidst his inherited Watteau drawings, Sèvres porcelain, inlaid boulle tables. In the corridor outside his bedroom, as though keeping watch, was a bust of Apollo, the bust and its pedestal of bright Fouquet faience. In that dwelling, Adrian had no dreams.

Tonight, on the Downsville golf course, as he embraced Miss Rice in her BMW, two battered trucks of the Border Patrol invaded the course and chased aliens across fairways as flat as ponds. Some of the aliens were women, or were they transvestites? One of the trucks had a working searchlight, and, dancing, the light chased men in strapless dresses and metal heels, until agents caught a few of the false women as others ran free through moonlit groves of trees.

In the BMW, all red leather and phosphorescent dials, Miss Rice was struggling to seduce Adrian; his jeans were open and his genitalia were exposed, but the gearshift between their seats was an inconvenience. She opened her door and, grabbing a seat pillow, tumbled supine on the grass. As he scrambled after her and she removed her blouse and black slacks and placed the pillow below her buttocks, preparing to receive him, he remarked that her body was not anorexic but ivory and svelte. He had not possessed a woman since Antonia's demise; such seed as he had lost he had discharged in sleep, dreaming of his dead wife. As he hovered above Miss Rice on his bare knees, his emotions clashed.

He craved the vast comfort, but his fear of sadness in its wake, his mourning for his wife and son, his pride in his chastity as atonement, distant quaint notions of right and wrong, a faint repugnance as Miss Rice reached upward and clutched his back with sharp nails, for a moment made him hesitate. Chastity was meant for the old and ugly; it amused him that it might be meant for youth and beauty. As ever, he was in thrall to cloudy motivations. More strangely, even as he felt a terror of remaining chaste, already he felt his body afloat in space. Consort with asps, but never trust a journalist. His tumid phallus touched her slim thighs, an inch from her vulva and damp moss.

Suddenly he stood and, pulling up his jeans, ran across the fairway, as the Border Patrol's dancing searchlight followed him.

Next morning, he felt guilty, and decided to give Miss Rice a gift. A painting, perhaps? At the barracks she had seemed more pleased by his peep show than by his art, and he mused that one of his own pictures might be unsuitable. He visited the art shops of Downsville, but even for high sums he found nothing but offal. Lately he had instructed the staff at Northwood Hall to send him hundreds of his books; they crowded his barrack rooms on shelves he improvised with planks and bricks; when he returned in the small hours from feeding the glue children he read them until his lids closed. Now as he ran his finger across the bindings, he happened upon a volume that he thought might edify Miss Rice.

It was an art book, *Salzburg,* with a brief text in German and full of watercolors and pencil drawings by an obscure painter called Hans Liska. Adrian had browsed one youthful summer in a secondhand bookshop in Salzburg's Getreidegasse; his eye was drawn by the pretty scenes of the Mirabell Gardens, the onion-domed chapel of the Mozartplatz, urn-crowned balustrades, equestrian fountains, and he bought the book for a few schillings. He could not, of course, part with his own copy, but now no other gift would do for Miss Rice. He wrote a word to Mr. Ennis.

. . . & was published Munich by Verlag F Bruckmann KG Graphische Kunstanstalten 1960. If B. IV can't find it NYC tell him try Munich old shops Salzburg Linz Vienna etc. I want book my hand within 3 days.

AJN

Mr. Burner IV was delighted by this assignment. Immediately from his London branch a subaltern was dispatched to Munich and, finding the publisher defunct, flew to Austria. In Salzburg, he failed, but not in Linz. By charter aircraft, the book reached Adrian before his deadline. For time, services, sundries, and disbursements Burner IV charged Adrian's account $69,046.23. Adrian left the book at KQYQ-TV with an inscription.

Miss Rice,
    Sorry about the other night, but I wished you to know that I'm fond of you. Please accept this little book as a memorial of my affection. Yours,

A.J. NORTHWOOD

Miss Rice wrote no reply. A week later, on his evening rounds, he saw her in an apron, serving supper to refugees in the shelter cafeteria. She said, "Thanks for the book. I adore Dutch art."

"Still chasing a story?" Adrian asked.

"I've been fired by KQYQ," she said.

"Why?"

"I wasn't pushy enough."

"What will you do?"

"I don't know."

"Why are you here?"

"It's a way to be near you."

"We won't have sex."

"I was afraid we wouldn't."

"You can help out here whenever you wish, Miss Rice. With the children, the women, whatever you think needs doing. I'll pay you well."

"I won't accept a salary. I won't be here forever."

"Neither will I. I learned that—in a dream—last night."

"When will I see you?"

"At night, like this, in the cafeteria. You might lend a hand as I decorate the chapel. See Alejandro holding little Dianita over there? We could go on picnics together now and then."

"Will you ever hug me, AJ?"

"Here, I'll hug you now, Miss Rice."

At Amigoland, days thence, Adrian ran into Rodrigo, alone, off duty, clad splendidly in fashion jeans, black boots, a cowboy hat. He said, "We ain't talkin', Ay-jay."

Said Adrian, "I agree we shouldn't. I've ignored you and I'm contemptible."

"Yeah."

"Dear Rodrigo, you look so blue."

"I seen your bare ass on the golf course the other night."

"Ha! Was that you with the searchlight?"

"Yeah. You was f——ing that TV chick."

"But I didn't—"

"I hear she's hangin' out at your place. You f——ing her every night?"

"No. Listen—"

"An' you said celibacy was more fun."

They stood in the parking lot outside Wal-Mart; bourgeois Mexicans poured from the shopping palaces, pushing wire-mesh carts heaped with microwave ovens, fishing poles, word processors, cordless telephones, cordless vacuum cleaners, Japanese cameras, videocassettes, Jordache luggage. From ubiquitous loudspeakers, the relentless hymn.

> The lights of Laredo
> Dance on the water
> And shine in a young man's eyes
> Who stands on the border
> And dreams of para-dise.

Adrian asked, "Why are you so blue?"

"My truck got stolen," Rodrigo said.

"That junk heap?"

"Not my B.P. truck. My own truck! Last month, I bought me a new truck. Mother, what a cool truck!"

In erotic detail, Rodrigo relived his truck: a GMC Syclone pickup with four-wheel drive, four-wheel antilock brakes, turbochargers, 280 horsepower, 4200 rpm! Deep upholstered bucket seats! Body color crimson red! "This is a f——ing *sport* truck! Cooler than a f——ing Firebird! Quick-stomp the pedal and feel more f——ing force than a f——ing linebacker! We're talkin' zero to sixty mph in four seconds flat, Ay-jay!"

> He's heard crazy stories
> Of how good life is
> Over in the Promised Land.
> And sometimes it seems
> Like God must live
> Just across the Rio Grande.

To compound his loss, Rodrigo was changing apartments, and in the truck's open rear he had left much of his body-building equipment: his 21st Century Gym Machine, with its triceps push-downs, inner-outer thigh kicks, and abdominal crunch; his eleven-speed self-motivating stationary bike, programmed to simulate the ascent of mountains; cardboard boxes full of Muscle Mix non-steroidal anabolic pills, testosterone-rich Mexican sarsaparilla in convenient capsule form, Victory Nutrition for the Next Century bio-chromium capsules with gamma oryzanol, a Train Your Brain IM-1 Brainwave Synchronizer in a computerized audiovisual unit with headphones and mauve-tinted glasses to induce relaxation, enhance motivation, and build muscle; not to mention half a dozen dumbbells and various inspirational videocassettes.

> Sometimes it seems
> Like God must live
> Just across the Rio Grande.

"How much did you pay for the truck?" Adrian asked.

"Almost thirty thou! On time, forty-eight months?"

"I'll buy you a new one, Rodrigo."

"Jesus, Ay-jay, I got my pride."

"Any idea who stole the truck?"

"Yeah, some fag transvestite."

"How do you know?"

"Because one of the guys was over in Matablancos the other day and he seen the chief of the judicial police drivin' my truck around! With all my gym gear still in back! He runs that f——ing gang!"

Adrian glimpsed a transvestite car thief, caked with rouge and eye shadow, then a pair of them, one high on marijuana, the other on hormone injections blossoming in female breasts. They lurked one night in the parking lot of Rodrigo's building on Boca Chica or Central Boulevard or wherever it was he lived, coveting his new truck and the seven hundred dollars the Mexican police would pay them when they delivered the prize. Once no one was about, they approached the truck, glanced furtively around them, removed their slim-jims from their Gucci handbags, forced open the cabin, and with swift expertise tampered with the ignition until it turned. Shrieking laughter, they zoomed the truck beneath palm trees and neon signs down International Boulevard past the pawnshops and money changers in the amber haze to Gateway Bridge and into Mexico, where a policeman told them, *Buenas noches, señoritas,* what have we here? Adrian wondered, When they age, do they have mastectomies?

By now Adrian and Rodrigo had walked from the parking lot, across the highway and a meadow to the river's edge. Rodrigo had his arm around Adrian's neck, pretending to strangle him but hugging Ay-jay in his special way and barely able to hide his happiness for having regained the company of his friend. It was late afternoon, but anticipating nightfall along the bend of river, bands of unclad aliens were already wading into Texas; Rodrigo, off duty, shrugged. Adrian's eye in its relentless quest darted in all directions, and Rodrigo said, "You won't never find him, Ay-jay."

Adrian asked, "Do you still have the keys to your truck?"

"Here in my pocket."

Adrian broke free of Rodrigo's grip and fairly danced in the downing sun. He cried, "Then sweet Mother of God, Rodrigo, what are we waiting for? Let's go over to Mexico and steal back your truck!"

"I'm a *federal officer,* Ay-jay. My boss hates my guts, I hate his guts. If I got in a shoot-out with the Mexican fuzz I'd lose my f——ing job. No way!"

They dined together at Wyatt Cafeteria, where they munched on corn on the cob and Adrian continued to plead for the countertheft and Rodrigo continued to resist. They parted in discord, though again good friends. The injustice of the stolen truck gnawed at Adrian, just as he was dazzled by fantasies of adventure in aspiring to steal it back. His father: "Take risks, child, take risks." He hounded Rodrigo on the telephone.

Rodrigo answered, "You got no idea of the danger, Ay-jay. You remember Condition Red? This here idea is Condition Black—like, bonkers. I'd have no backup, no *tactical control.*"

"Couldn't we at least go over and look around," asked Adrian, "before we grab the truck?"

"Jesus, will you stop jerkin' off? You got a goofy streak, Ay-jay."

"Sorry I mentioned it. See you, Rodrigo."

"When?"

"I'll call you."

Adrian hung up. At dawn, in a sombrero and dark glasses, Rodrigo was on his doorstep: "Let's move."

They walked over the railway bridge past Mexican customs, then westward along the river on Calle Hidalgo, then south for several blocks to Calle González and the cement headquarters of the judicial police. It was still early, the police parking lot was empty, and Rodrigo was happy for the time he had to reconnoiter. High buildings stood along that block of Calle González; the Americans mounted to a flat roof, where with his binoculars Rodrigo crouched and studied entrances, exits, every foot of the terrain below.

Not until noon did a new crimson truck turn a corner from Calle 16 onto Calle González and screech into the police parking lot, the rear of the pickup still laden with Rodrigo's gymnastic equipment. It puzzled Adrian that a thief should display such telling evidence, but when the driver emerged from the cabin he understood: the man was a slob.

As he lingered in the parking lot talking and gesturing to other policemen, Adrian borrowed the binoculars and watched him: a tall slovenly fat man in a white sombrero, sunglasses, and a sleeveless leather jacket. Suddenly he opened the door of the crimson truck; out jumped a barking police dog, which the man restrained with a rusty chain while he gestured and shouted as though threatening the other policemen. Adrian mused, Ah, I know him, I think, from the police brothel. Finally the men went inside with the dog.

"Do we move?" Adrian asked.

"We wait till they eat," Rodrigo said.

With the binoculars, Adrian scanned the horizon. To the south he saw the the Plaza Mayor and the spires of the cathedral, beyond them the miles of junkyard where stolen cars and trucks were stripped and repainted. To the north, less than a mile thence, he saw the serpentine river, Amigoland, and his own Casa San Francisco, where women and children were romping on the grass. Immediately below him, next door to the judicial police, was the great penitentiary; in the yard hundreds of prisoners milled in the sunshine, most of them doing nothing, while some scrubbed laundry in cement troughs and hung it up to dry.

A high window embellished the headquarters of the *Policía Judicial*. As policemen came and went, the fat *jefe* sat at a messy desk, signing papers and patting his dog's head. Behind him on the wall hung a collection of guns. Adrian said, "God's mother, so many guns."

"Yeah," said Rodrigo. "You name it, they got it. Uzis, nine-millimeter automatic pistols, AR-fifteen automatic rifles, AK-forty-seven assault rifles—you name it, they got it. They love dum-dum bullets, use 'em on everybody. You know dum-dums, in the metal jackets with the hollow points, Ay-jay? Don't explode till it's in your gut, then rips your guts out? Still want to steal my truck, Ay-jay?"

Near the penitentiary was the Maxi Cafeteria; through the glasses Adrian watched as in the kitchen women fried the dough of enchiladas in oil and red sauce, fashioned tacos by filling tortillas with onions, peppers, tomatoes, and chopped meat. Presently boys in white shirts and black trousers filed out of the cafeteria holding aloft dull metal trays heaped with tacos, enchiladas, fried chicken, white rice, red beans, pastries, and bottles of beer. They entered police headquarters, where they placed the trays on metal desks and wooden chairs, and the *jefe* and his underlings began to devour the food.

Rodrigo said, "Let's move."

The Americans descended to the street, crossed to the wall opposite, and approached the open portals of the parking lot. "Walk in casual," Rodrigo murmured to his friend, but once inside, anxious to be invisible, he crouched behind a car, and Adrian did likewise. The red truck was parked beyond the *jefe*'s window, near the end of the lot, nothing changed except the license plate, now

Mexican. Rodrigo began a duck walk behind parked cars, beneath the *jefe*'s window, Adrian aping his crouching movement, keeping his head down and inside it Rodrigo's rules racing: Condition Yellow you are relaxed but alert cautious but not tense avoid Condition Orange state of alarm! watch your movements in slow motion where are your feet what are your hands doing? Rodrigo reached into his pocket, withdrew his key ring, opened the cabin, crawled inside, opened the other door, and Adrian joined him. Suddenly Rodrigo was erect in the driver's seat, inserting his key, turning the ignition, and grunting, "Let's move."

He reversed the truck slowly, hoping to avoid attention, then straightened the wheels and at minimal speed began to roll forward out of the lot. A dog howled, hurling his paws at the headquarters window, and beside him stood the *jefe* with a taco in his hand and an enchilada halfway inside his face. The truck passed him on Adrian's side, and the *jefe* saw Adrian as clearly as Adrian saw the *jefe* and his men as they drew their guns. Rodrigo stepped on the pedal (zero to sixty mph in four seconds flat, Ay-jay), and they careened out of the lot, Rodrigo shouting, "We move!"

He turned right onto Calle González, then screeched immediately left the wrong way onto Calle 15, missing oncoming cars by millimeters, but at once they heard the wail of sirens, and when Adrian glanced back he saw a police van and a pair of cruisers in pursuit. Rodrigo redoubled, conjuring in reverse all his skill in police tactics, outwitting radio calls and roadblocks by zigzagging in crazy patterns, down Calle Bravo, turning left the wrong way again on Calle 10, then westward on Calle Bustamente, then northward on Calle 12 until they came to Calle Hidalgo and the railroad tracks that ran beside it.

Rodrigo drove straight ahead across Calle Hidalgo and at full speed hit the railroad tracks head-on: the truck leaped into the air, and some of his cardboard boxes and body-building gear went flying out. On the other side of the tracks he drove the truck, still upright but tilting dangerously on the embankment, around a northward bend toward the river and the railway bridge. The police at the bridge were waiting for him, though in the few minutes since his escape from Calle González they had scarcely time to block the bridge with a single cruiser flanked by a pair of flimsy wooden barriers. When they saw the truck they started shooting.

Just before the bridge a bullet flew through Rodrigo's open window, kissed his skull, and fled through the roof with souvenirs of his hair and blood. Stunned, his head fell toward the dashboard as he said, "Holy f——." Adrian grabbed the wheel, steered it blindly through a wooden barrier, and stepped on Rodrigo's foot stepping on the pedal. Condition Red remember remember cool control stay focused breathe deeply defeat any threat decide not to be afraid avoid Condition Black. The bullets continued to pursue them as the truck bumped wildly over the rails and paving of the bridge, but what remained of Rodrigo's jutting gymnastic machinery deflected further carnage. Halfway across the bridge, Adrian glimpsed a sign, UNITED STATES OF AMERICA. At the booths, Rodrigo's friends in Customs greeted him as a hero, nor did he need a hospital, since Adrian himself attended to his superficial wound in the dispensary of the Casa San Francisco.

Thenceforth in his gratitude Rodrigo devoted himself to Adrian. After work and the gymnasium, he screeched up in his crimson truck and lavished his time in civilian dress on the Casa San Francisco, organizing sports, cooking, serving meals, and helping to refashion the barrack that would be the chapel. As his reward, perhaps once a week, Adrian gave him a hug. Rodrigo liked Miss Rice, though he vied with her in his exertions to please Adrian.

"I never knew nobody like Ay-jay," he told her.

"Life is so uncomplicated without sex," she answered.

"Tough, though?"

"At night . . ."

"Yeah . . ."

"You're . . . really rather cute, Rodrigo."

"Hey, so are you, Miss Rice."

"Vicki."

The flow of refugees had subsided lately but it waxed and waned; Adrian continued to feed hundreds of homeless aliens a day. Jody

Corn and his companions continued to harass the shelter with obscenities and brush fires, but the guards contained them; in federal court Mr. Burner IV's hired guns continued to wage guerrilla warfare against Mrs. Sebastian Bean's attorneys, at vast cost. It seemed to Adrian that in the lupine world he had created an enclave of lambs.

More and more, he felt joy. One Sunday afternoon, he decreed a picnic, on the mowed grass between his barrack and the river, for Miss Rice, Rodrigo, Alejandro, and little Dianita. Alejandro was growing, speaking better English; Dianita was sprouting raven hair, though she could not yet say "Papá." They were all, more and more, his family. From her wicker basket on a plaid blanket Miss Rice produced roast chicken, hard-boiled eggs, and tomatoes the color of blood. After luncheon, as Dianita dozed on the blanket, amid much laughter Miss Rice played tag football with Adrian, Rodrigo, and Alejandro. Rodrigo paused to show Alejandro how to punt the football, but Alejandro kicked it clumsily. Adrian watched the ball ascend in space, eclipse the sun, and descend into reeds toward the river. He ran there to fetch it.

The football bounced from a jutting rock, and as it did so an urchin rose out of the reeds lifting his fingers toward the sky as though to catch it—but the football glanced off his hands and he crouched again among the reeds, gripping a plastic bag of filthy clothes and a little girl whose dress was smeared with blood. The urchin's shirt said FUNKY COLD: the child.

17

During the days that followed, Adrian learned in little pieces why for so many months he had not found him.

The child had returned to Reynuestro, a horrid border town rather far upriver, to see his sister. His home was a single room, a shack on the city limits by an automobile cemetery and a garbage dump, where fourteen people slept. The child's mother, possibly a prostitute in retirement as addicted to glue as he was, or paint or alcohol or all together, apparently could no longer cope with life, so her children coped as they could.

Several of the children, large and small, survived reasonably, having swum the river yonder to work on farms in Texas, or they swam the river to steal in Texas, or they stole in Reynuestro or sold their bodies in Matablancos. Or they stayed at home to scavenge for hubcaps in the car cemetery they sold to junk dealers, and for food in the garbage dump they brought home and ate. Even now the child was loath to tell Adrian his name, so Adrian called him Niño—Child. Niño said, "*Mi hermanita se llama Eva.*" My little sister's name is Eva.

Eva (aged six or seven? Niño nine or ten?) was the sickest of the children. The others were merely undernourished, ill from scabies and diarrhea, annoyed by lice and ringworm, but Eva was consumptive. Even in the fog of his addiction and away from home, Niño fretted over her. In Downsville and Matablancos, when he had stolen enough hubcaps and T-shirts and had a little money (without money his mother would not let him in the house), he hitched rides back to Reynuestro and found Eva coughing blood.

Niño made a bargain with his mother: she took all his money, he took Eva and fled from that house.

Thereafter he led her from one hospital to the next, begging a bed and treatment. At the public health center in Reynuestro the nurses gave her two aspirins and told Niño to take her home, not so much because the nurses were cruel but because the bureaucrats who ran such clinics stole all the medicines and sold them. At private clinics, because the children had no money they could not get beyond the doors. At the *Hospital General* in Matablancos, the doctors accepted Eva for a night, but in the morning they said they had no bed or medicine and told Niño to take her home. In the Zona Zur, where Niño dragged Eva when he went to look for glue, the glue children pointed across the river toward the Casa San Francisco.

Adrian decided not to place Eva in a clinic. He had her X-rayed at a hospital and made a clinic of his dispensary.

Ennis,

Would you hurry up w. that equipment? These Downsville doctors seem competent but I can't accept their prognosis. Tell B. IV engage best pulmonary man NYC & I want him here tomw.

AJN

Eva lay in bed attached to intravenous tubes, attended by a nurse, slipping in and out of sleep. Antibiotics and nourishment had softened her cough, though she still drooled blood. Adrian thought, In another life she might have been a lovely little thing, but look at her. Arms like toothpicks, black hair turning orange at the roots, brown skin splotched with pink, an ulcer on her lip, is that white gown the cleanest thing she ever wore? In the next room, Niño was not doing much better. Miss Rice and Alejandro had strapped him into bed, forcing him to taste some soup as he twitched through involuntary withdrawal. The nurse came in and said, "X-ray his brain—it will be full of holes."

Late next afternoon, a Dr. Dudley flew in from New York. Dr.

Dudley wore a lush Vandyke goatee, but when he held Eva's X-rays to a fluorescent lamp the gray hairs grew suddenly translucent, revealing that he had no chin. He said, "Wow. I've been in practice for thirty years, but this takes the cake. Look at those lungs."

There ensued an incantation that in its antiseptic swiftness Adrian did not totally grasp. ". . . rapidly progressive pneumonic forms, exudative in character . . . cavity formation accompanied by obstinate eventually permanent scar tissue . . . semiliquid substances containing tubercle bacilli dripping into the bronchial tree and aspirated in contiguous bronchi . . . bronchogenic . . . hyperbronchogenic . . . particular perils to a young child occasioned by invasion of the bloodstream with ensuant miliary tuberculosis or meningitis . . . hemoptysis . . . pus-filled phlegm . . .

"She has no defenses. She is undernourished, apathetic, and feverish, and she can barely breathe. Evidently she has been slipping in and out of coma for some days or weeks, and the paramount danger at present is that even with antibiotics and intravenous nutrition she will regress into a coma from which she may not wake. As to incremental complications . . .

". . . kidneys, lymph nodes, intestinal network . . . lesions . . . tuberculous abscesses . . . tuberculous meningitis, a frequent complication of miliary tuberculosis, the disease in its most virulent manifestation, and look here . . ."

Dr. Dudley droned on. Adrian had stocked the dispensary with enough antibiotics—hain, rifampicin, antiestreptolicin—to treat fifty consumptives, but Dr. Dudley used them sparingly. Instead, during the next days and nights he focused on Eva's nutrition, not only feeding her intravenously in meager doses but hand-spooning her solutions of water, sugar, salt, and baby food. "With luck, I'll save her," he predicted. Yet as hard as he tried, he could not stop the hemorrhaging of her lungs and intestines. At increasing intervals she coughed up blood.

"Why don't you give her more antibiotics?" Adrian asked.

"Will you stop looking over my shoulder?" Dr. Dudley objected, again holding Eva's X-rays to the fluorescent light.

"I insist that Eva survive."

"She has a chance."

"Why don't you perform surgery?"

"Surgery would kill her."

"I've all this plasma. A blood transfusion?"

"I gave her a transfusion. More transfusions would make no difference."

"Do you know what you're doing?"

"Will you stop staring at my chin?"

Adrian slept fitfully on a cot in the dispensary, as Dr. Dudley did. Now Eva entered and emerged from coma, each coma a little longer. When she seemed lucid Miss Rice or Rodrigo brought Niño to her, and though he never spoke, he hugged and kissed her. Once, almost inaudibly, when Niño hugged her, just before she regressed into coma, she moaned and mentioned her mother. On the sixth day after Adrian found her with Niño in the reeds, just before dawn, Eva died.

Bitterly, loudly, Adrian told Dr. Dudley, "You didn't save her. You're the leading lung specialist in the country, and you failed."

"Eva didn't die of tuberculosis, Mr. Northwood," said Dr. Dudley. "She died of starvation."

A stirring in the corner, and they looked to the doorway, where Niño stood gazing at his sister's corpse. He twitched stoically, clad in a white hospital gown that reached to his knees but even in its fullness could not conceal his skeletal protruding ribs. Adrian telephoned the Bishop of Downsville, who did not complain of being roused from bed and straightaway sent a young priest.

There, in the dispensary, the priest put on a white chasuble and celebrated the Mass of the Angels over the body of Eva, unembalmed in a maple box. Adrian and Niño, Miss Rice and Rodrigo and Alejandro, interred Eva outside beneath the mowed lawn and a wooden cross mounted with an icon of the Holy Virgin of Guadalupe as the sun rose higher in the hazy sky and the priest intoned Spanish prayers. Adrian crossed himself and added, in remembered Latin, "*Requiem aeternam dona ei, Domine, et lux perpetua luceat ei, requiescat in pace.*" Dr. Dudley did not remain for the rites, but as soon as he witnessed the death certificate took a taxi to the airport and returned to his rich practice in New York City.

Adrian lodged Niño in his rooms, to watch and care for him, the child clinging to his plastic bag of filthy clothes as though he could never part with those possessions now that his sister was dead. Niño's body twitched, and his head with the holes and dead cells inside went on jerking, but within days of Adrian's ministrations of soup and bread he began to gain a little weight. He rarely spoke.

After the child had lived with Adrian for a week, he seemed to accept his routine, and especially he seemed to enjoy watching him as he worked on Francis of Assisi's floating head. For hours Niño sat there silently, in a wooden armchair, clad in clean new jeans and T-shirt, staring at the mutations of the decapitated saint. Adrian sensed a supernatural bond between Niño, born into squalor, and little Urban II, born as crown prince of the Northwood fortune, the motive no doubt for his devotion to the child, but though the mystery enchanted him he could not grasp it. He reflected, I'll never return to Northwood Hall.

Alejandro slept in a separate room, as always holding Dianita in his arms, but Adrian kept Niño in the cot next to his own. Late one night, Adrian half woke up as he heard Niño stirring, then twitching and moaning beneath his bed. In his half sleep Adrian paid no heed as Niño rummaged through the plastic bag of clothes, but vaguely he began to pay attention when he heard the barrack door squeak open and slam shut. He hurried to the window. By the light of the security lamps he saw the child, barefoot but otherwise fully clothed, clasping his bag, standing on his sister's grave, kissing the Holy Virgin of Guadalupe and hugging the wooden cross. Then with his bag he ran away, not to the river but toward Amigoland.

No moon shone that night; Adrian jumped into his jeans, grabbed the night-vision goggles he wore when he painted in the dark, and ran to the stable, where in moments he bridled Prince and leaped on his bare back. As he galloped toward Amigoland wearing the magic spectacles, the night was bright with eerie green again, fireflies resumed the size and brilliance of shooting stars, and in the meadow by the highway he saw the distant running child. From afar, when Niño heard the thud of Prince's hooves he turned and dashed toward the river, but the horse was too fast.

Niño now had his back against the girders of the radio tower, as though resigned to capture, yet as Adrian approached, the child drew a can from within the garments of his plastic bag and sprayed his face with paint, enveloping himself in mist that through his glasses Adrian saw as phosphorescent silver. In slow motion Niño's head and body twitched, and as the mist lowered like a veil, his ecstatic features became sharply clear and his eyes glowed like green coals.

Prince brushed past a mesquite tree; a low branch caught the edge of Adrian's spectacles and tore them off, turning him instantly blind. He reined in his horse; as he blinked in the darkness, struggling to see, he heard the child's feet running through grass toward the river.

He cried out, "Son, come back to life!" Dismounting, he let go of Prince's reins and knelt in the grass, blind and dazed, knowing finally that he had lost the child forever.

PART V

Lázaro

▼▼▼

18

Adrian's University Essay, composed in hasty fragments over many months, began to resemble a tome, a heap of foolscap stuffed into a drawer, painful evidence to the author that it would never be published. He went on writing it.

■　■　■

. . . and should I give away my fortune? Would I have to give up Northwood Hall? To failure must I add the flaw of cowardice? I can glimpse my hand signing away my fortune, but could I ever relinquish Northwood Hall? I am distraught to blackness by the death of little Eva and the disappearance of the child. What is happening to me? At The University, I loved the pedants' phrase, "to turn logic on its head." Have I grown too fond of turning logic on its head? More than Pascal (if that is possible), I hate the world. I hate modern culture. I hate all secular wisdom. More than Pascal (if that is possible), I wish to leave the world. Before, I found my refuge from this horrid world—from its politics, its culture, the media!—in history, in literature, in music, but my logic of escape no longer works. Now from memory, since I cannot find the *Pensées* amidst my junk: "227. *Order by dialogues.* What ought I to do? I see only darkness everywhere. Shall I believe I am nothing? shall I believe I am God? 'All things change and succeed each other.' You are mistaken; there is . . . 228. Atheists protest, 'But we have no light.' *Objection des athées: 'Mais nous n'avons nulle lumière.'* "

Par exemple!

It is as if to spite my saner self I intend to compound my follies.
(Three in the morning, I cannot sleep, and from the river I can
hear the hum of migrants, thieves, and traffickers.) Against my will,
I have become more reckless, playing bolder games with danger.
What is happening to me? God may not exist: I am certain that
the Devil does. Those troops of Satan, the Mexican police . . .

■ ■ ■

After the feat of stealing back Rodrigo's truck, Adrian dared not
return to the Zona Zur for fear of encountering the chief of the
judicial police. The *jefe,* frequenting the brothel near the habitations
of the glue children, might not greet Adrian kindly as he served
his bread and soup. Besides, in his sorrow for Eva and the child,
Adrian could no longer bear to witness the self-destruction of the
glue children. He hired a Mexican caterer, wondering whether the
caterer would be as zealous in feeding the children as he was in
demanding money. And yet Adrian stumbled into new adventures
with the Mexican police.

At the Casa San Francisco, aliens complained to him of friends and
kinsmen from Central and South America being held for ransom
in Matablancos. Slave traffic, the sale of refugees for mounting
sums, was beginning to rival cocaine traffic as the border's growth
industry.

Migrants from the deeper tropics arrived in Matablancos at the
bus station, where the municipal police, the immigration police,
the judicial police, intercepted and robbed them. Aliens who eluded
the police at the bus station or shunned the depot altogether
crowded into mean hotels nearby—the Azteca, El Dorado, the
Motel Marco Polo—where they met furtively with taxi drivers and
other smugglers who promised for immense fees to transport them
across the river and thence to Houston, Dallas, or Corpus Christi.
The police raided the hotels or arrested refugees in the streets,
packed them into vans, drove them to dens throughout the city,
and—for fifty dollars a head—sold them to traffickers.

The traffickers locked the migrants, adults and children, into tiny
hot rooms with the windows boarded up, where they lived on soda

pop and beans served once a day among piles of their excrement. The migrants wrote telegrams to relatives in Texas, Florida, and California, imploring transfers of cash to Western Union Downsville payable to the traffickers; the price of liberty per captive was five hundred dollars. Hostages who could not produce ransom were put to work for no pay building luxurious houses in Matablancos or were recommitted to the care of the police.

Ennis,
   Bring me $15,000 cash before 8 tonight.
                                                        AJN

Adrian paid such ransoms through intermediaries, receiving live bodies in exchange, which he cleaned and fed in the Casa San Francisco. The arrangement worked until the traffickers grew greedy and took the ransoms but kept the bodies. He decided on countermeasures, to be undertaken after midnight.

Before going out, he went into Alejandro's room. Alejandro slept as usual hugging baby Dianita, whose dark curls reposed against his childish breast. How he admired their noble heads. He wondered, Does she love Alejandro more than she loves me? Is she my daughter? Is he my son? Must I risk making them orphans again?

He had recruited half a dozen of his guerrillas for a raid in Calle Bustamente, but given his horror of knives and guns, he armed them only with baseball bats. Beneath a moonless sky the band descended to the river, waded across with plastic bags aloft, then dressed and penetrated Matablancos over railroad tracks and Calle Hidalgo. They had only three blocks south to walk to Calle Bustamente, part of Rodrigo's escape route when he retrieved his truck and not far from the penitentiary and the judicial police. It was four in the morning, and the street slept.

Adrian's target was a tilting wooden house of two stories that stood beyond an alley and a yard strewn with garbage. The house was silent, except for a sealed moan or two of a woman or a child. With his guerrillas arranged stealthily behind him, Adrian mounted the sagging porch and gazed through cracks in the door. He saw a lamp burning, beside it a burly man asleep in a stuffed chair. An empty whiskey bottle protruded between his thighs. On the wall behind him hung an automatic rifle and a printed sign, NO SE VENDE CERVEZA SIN COMIDA. No beer if you don't eat. Partially visible was a game table, *futbolito,* that contraption of rods and figurines that players flipped at little balls, pretending to play soccer. It took two for *futbolito,* suggesting that elsewhere in the house the goon had a companion. The door was secured by a broomstick.

Adrian huddled with his guerrillas. They favored a frontal assault, battering swiftly through the door with their bats and body weight before the goon emerged from his dream. Adrian feared that he would shoot and yearned to be more subtle. Why not lure the goon outside with a sound, so rare, so eerie, that he could not resist its siren? Adrian placed his mouth against the door and, in rasping whispers, chanted Faust's first conjuring of Mephistopheles.

> *Erst zu begegnen dem Tiere,*
> *Brauch ich den Spruch der Viere.*

In his whiskey dream the goon dozed on. Adrian sang louder.

> *Salamander soll glühen,*
> *Undene sich winden.*

The goon stirred, rubbing his eyes, glancing about.

> *Sylphe verschwinden,*
> *Kobold sich mühen.*

He got up, in his stupor gazing at the door, then stumbled to the wall. With his Kalashnikov, he advanced toward Adrian, now silent. He removed the broomstick, opened the door, and stuck his head out. Baco, the Salvadoran guerrilla, with a thud brought down his baseball bat on the back of the goon's skull.

They dragged his unconscious body inside, took his keys, and crept upstairs. Adrian was sad that Octavio, the Nicaraguan guerrilla, now wielded the Kalashnikov, but Octavio's foresight served them well. Another goon, in blue pajamas, walked sleepily barefoot

down the corridor, fumbling to load a cartridge clip into an automatic pistol. Octavio filled his legs with bullets.

Instantly the band opened locked doors along the squeezed corridors of the house, recoiling at the stench, releasing two dozen
men, women, small children, who came popping out of the rooms
dimly, terrified, the women fluttering their arms, like dark butterflies bursting from cocoons.

The gunfire no doubt had raised the neighborhood, and for
liberty haste was paramount. Downstairs, as he ripped out the
telephone, Adrian gazed at the supine, unconscious goon, dressed
as the *jefe* had been in a sleeveless leather jacket and slovenly
enough to be his twin. Adrian relived the moment when he saw
the *jefe* at the window with the enchilada in his face, and marveled
at the likeness: *was* this goon his twin? On the floor the goon
groaned, then stared at Adrian. Baco raised his bat again to restore
him to his dream, but Adrian intervened.

"Lock him in a stinking room," he said, and led the hostages to
the garbage-strewn yard, through a labyrinth of alleys behind the
house, running down them zigzag to elude the police. They heard
sirens on Calle Bustamente, saw flashing lights, and kept running.

They halted in an alley near Calle 13, huddling, crouching,
women hushing their young, a mother stifling her infant's whimper
with a trembling hand. Squad cars cruised on Calle Hidalgo. The
police for a moment out of sight, Octavio ran across Hidalgo to
the railroad tracks and along the line of boxcars until he forced
open a door. He waved his white baseball bat, beckoning to them.
Adrian sent the hostages across Hidalgo in groups of three until
within quarter of an hour all hostages and guerrillas were shut
inside the boxcar. Soon they heard voices near the tracks, but the
police had no dogs and could not find them. The fugitives waited
in darkness for another hour, then descended to the river. Minutes
before first light, on inner tubes, Adrian and his guerrillas floated
the hostages to liberty.

Evenings later, nearly at sunset, Adrian was running on the river's
edge when a commotion broke out on the railway bridge. A shirtless

man sat high on the Mexican side of the girders, drinking from a bottle, shouting obscenities, and hurling beer cans at cars and pedestrians beneath. Policemen in dark blue were on the bridge, commanding him to come down. He threw his bottle at them, harmlessly. They drew their guns. He leaped from his perch into the river.

He swam upstream, but they jumped to the Mexican shore and chased him. A policeman aimed his pistol, a burst of smoke, and the man went under, in little bubbles of blood. Adrian dove in, grabbed him as he sank, and heaved him to the United States.

As he writhed on the shore, screaming, his right forearm spurted blood. The bullet had ripped through the forearm, emerged from the wrist, and as it said *adiós* removed the fingernail. In haste Adrian took off his T-shirt, tore it into strips, and tied a tourniquet above the elbow. Several policemen watched from the other shore, and though they respected the convention not to shoot into the United States, they called across with mounting anger, "We want him back!"

Adrian wondered, What branch of the police? Dark blue, the river, therefore the naval police? In Mexico, so many police, such an armory of guns; naval police, municipal police, judicial police, federal police, immigration police, highway police, narcotics police: did the list end? It amused him to torment whatever branch of the Mexican police; he ignored their howls as he draped the man over his shoulder, and they watched as he carried him away toward the Casa San Francisco. Not until later, in the dispensary, when the creature was dry and sedated and a physician dressed his wounds, did Adrian recognize the Mexican.

Mother of God, he thought, is this Lázaro, from the police brothel? The goatee was gone, but there were the tattoos of hearts and spiderwebs on his torso and, when he emerged from his sedation and brushed back his bushy hair, the faint inverted crosses at the extremities of his forehead. He sat up on the dispensary couch, with cloudy eyes regarded Adrian, and asked, "*¿Por qué tu lanzastes la camiseta en mi cara?*" Why did you throw your T-shirt in my face? Dimly Adrian recalled his flight from the brothel—when Lázaro chased him down the lumpy stairs, begging for his shirt, he flung it at him and retrieved it. Now the Border Patrol was on the telephone: "The naval police are demanding that bum back." Adrian: "I'm keeping him."

Adrian's grant of sanctuary was not wholly humanitarian. For the chapel he had begun to paint a panel of St. Michael Archangel, and he needed a model for Lucifer. He started the figure of St. Michael from images in his head, memories of the winged statue hovering above his school on the rocky coast of Normandy, but as his sketches progressed the archangel had no face. He propped a mirror up beside his easel, glanced at it as his hand raced across the canvas, and gave the saint his own fair hair, blue eyes, and wistful mouth, the body floating in a white robe but without the conceit of wings. Lucifer's image was less easy to achieve. Adrian stood the mirror on the floor, descended to his back, and writhed as Satan had when St. Michael thrust his avenging spear, banishing him from Heaven, but the mime would not do. Nor were any of his guerrillas he tried as models nearly sinister enough. Lázaro was a godsend.

Adrian told him, "We'll need your goatee—will you grow it back?" For days he kept Lázaro supine on the studio floor, writhing as he had at the river's edge, waving his left arm and his bandaged right arm and kicking up his bare feet. The painting was almost a photograph of Lázaro's foul black pants and elaborate torso, tattooed with hearts, a snake, and the blue spiderweb on either shoulder. He heightened the inverted crosses on Lázaro's forehead, tinting them red, thus suitably Satanic. The total effect, as St. Michael descended in space and thrust his lance at Lucifer, began to satisfy the artist.

The artist! Laymen who lacked Adrian's high culture could not quite grasp that artists choose models for their appearance, not for their charm. Adrian's friends found Lázaro's presence disturbing. Miss Rice said, "He's horrid and he smells." Rodrigo: "He's a river rat. Kick his ass out." Alejandro: "In El Salvador, we shot such garbage." Even Mr. Ennis shed his normal circumlocution: "Why, sir, he could be dangerous." Whenever she saw Lázaro, baby Dianita cried. Lázaro swore oaths that he would never take another drink, never again touch marijuana, though he would not renounce his maddening habit of dropping his strapless Mickey Mouse watch into Adrian's Coca-Cola. "Listen, Don Adriano, it still ticks!" Lázaro spent most of his time in Adrian's studio, which he madly loved.

He browsed, forever picking up and fingering Adrian's possessions, his books, his brushes, foolscap, letters, photographs of Diana, Antonia, and Urban II, but above all his paintings. At first he seemed to favor Adrian's earlier creations, the watercolors and oil canvases of the food palaces of Boca Chica. For hours he sat on a wooden stool, shuffling through the bizarre impressions of Pizza Hut, Burger King, Pick-a-Chick, the gables of Whataburger, the ineffable golden arches of McDonald's, commingled with T-shirts, jellyfish, decapitated cherubs, and Ionic columns.

"These paintings are so *beautiful*," Lázaro said.

"Junk," said Adrian.

"I wish I'd painted them."

This seemed too sensitive a thought from a mere river rat. Adrian asked, "Have you ever painted?"

Lázaro fell silent, gazing out of the studio over the river. Finally he said, "I'm a fisherman. I make windshield wipers."

In the days that followed he doted as well on Adrian's paintings of the valley—woodland and vast fields, the river often narrow, suddenly wide, forever twisting, gray, green, a muddy brown, a brilliant blue, according to the hour and the sun's whim; shrublike mesquite trees hugging the land into indefinite perspective; sabal palm, cactus, and black willow; endless flat farmlands of corn, tomato plant, and cotton; fallow earth, ocher red, ditched with canals nourished by the river; green jays, hummingbirds, and whistling tree ducks. "*Hermoso, hermoso*"—beautiful, beautiful— Lázaro kept mumbling. He marveled at the woman in the rain, the men tattooed much like himself, the flower sellers, the starving street urchins, the boy in handcuffs, the children staring out of boxcars, and all of the desperate eyes.

"These children selling flowers," he said, on the verge of tears, "and the children on the trains. So true, so true. Is there another man on earth like you, Don Adriano? You're . . . beautiful."

And he loved Adrian's Stations of the Cross. These were recent creations. Adrian had worked on them for many weeks, suffering over each detail, mustering refugees from the shelter to pose as models and act out the parts. Jesus is condemned to death. He receives His cross. He falls for the first time beneath His cross. Simon of Cyrene takes up His cross. Veronica wipes His face. He falls for the second and the third time beneath His cross. He is stripped of His garments. He is nailed to the cross. . . .

But Adrian set his Via Dolorosa in present time, inspired by an image from a nightmare and making Christ Hispanic, dressed in blue jeans. His mother was a Salvadoran war widow, Simon of Cyrene a Nicaraguan peasant, Veronica and the other women of Jerusalem shriveled wives from the Guatemalan highlands and the slums of Tegucigalpa. Roman soldiers were Mexican police, bearing not lances but automatic guns. Christ was crucified in shredded jeans. A plastic bag with His other clothes leaned on the foot of the cross. Calvary was the bank of the Rio Grande.

Lázaro continued to baffle Adrian. To test him, Adrian left little piles of cash lying about, but Lázaro did not touch them. He avoided eye contact, but such was Mexican culture. He spent mornings staring at the Stations of the Cross.

Yet the central painting of the chapel would be the altarpiece, and that belonged as ever to Francis of Assisi. Never had Adrian worked so hard or for so long on a single portrait. His body of St. Francis he considered a success: lithe and mobile as his youthful hands flung his silken garments at his father's feet, Francis unclad but for the hair shirt that gnawed at his flesh and touched his thighs, all that in sublime renunciation of his riches. It was the head of Francis, to be separated from his body by a wooden beam, the head a fragment unto itself and floating in space, that Adrian found hardest to finish—as he was at pains to record on the foolscap pages of his University Essay.

■ ■ ■

. . . and in a hundred variations of the face I could not combine childishness and wisdom. It occurred to me at last that what I wished to convey together was innocence and darkness. Innocence was grace without pain; my models were the memory of my son and the angelic countenance of Alejandro. Darkness was knowledge of the world and the terrible suffering of self-denial that St. Francis imposed upon himself.

Finally, desperate for success, I reached into my own youth. In Umbria as an adolescent, I had climbed the Sabine Mountains to the abbey of Subiaco, where I saw a fresco, the only surviving portrait of Francis painted during his medieval lifetime. His face was divided vertically into two distinct parts. The first half was youthful, smiling, insouciant, full of illusion about the goodness of the world, and the eye seemed dazzled by the beauty of creation it beheld. In the other half the eye was sunken, turned inward; the countenance was shadowy and disenchanted. Yet oddly the whole suggested supernatural joy.

Thus for my own head of St. Francis I abandoned my attempt to blend innocence and darkness, and vertically divided his countenance into disparate halves. The first half is of a child, faintly out of focus, in age somewhere from five to twelve, fair like myself and little Urban, angelic like Alejandro, happy for the gift of life, and utterly untouched by experience, sadness, or lust. The other half is much older, sharply in focus, with a brown beard turning gray, the mouth turned downward, the flesh ravaged from the struggle with its own corruption, yet in its deep socket this eye of Francis is hopeful. Like the child's, it is blue and gazes heavenward. . . .

■ ■ ■

In his gazes Lázaro seemed to admire the finished altarpiece more than the artist did. He helped Adrian to carry the paintings from his studio to the chapel. Adrian had experimented with painting scenes on wood; unsatisfied with the results, he painted everything on canvas for mounting on the walls between the beams, but that he would do in the days ahead, before the chapel was consecrated.

With the paintings done, Lázaro's presence in the Casa San Francisco became an inconvenience. Adrian intended that as his wounds healed he would steal quietly back into Mexico, but Lázaro lingered. He slept in the men's dormitory but continued to enter Adrian's rooms without knocking, to shuffle through his rustic and Boca Chica paintings as though through decks of cards. He no longer touched Adrian's books.

He had his own books, leftovers from the shelter library, pulp cartoon novels devoted to passion and horror. He sat on Adrian's chairs or stretched out on his bed, brooding on naked breasts and bloody knives and snakes and vampires and green gorillas and corpses hanging from trees and rabid dogs in graveyards baying at the moon.

As he brooded, Lázaro munched on apples and bananas, leaving the remains beneath the chairs or on Adrian's bed. He was dressed as when he had arrived, in filthy black trousers, shirtless and barefoot. Adrian asked, "Will you *please* pull up your pants? You frighten Dianita with your pubic hair."

"Will you buy me a belt?" Lázaro demanded.

"You can take a belt from the clothes bank—and shirts and shoes and clean trousers."

"I won't wear old clothes."

"*I* wear old clothes."

"*¿Por qué tu lanzastes la camiseta en mi cara?*" Why did you throw your T-shirt in my face?

"I'm sorry! When are you leaving?"

"What's your hurry, Don Adriano? Look, my watch still ticks."

"Will you take it out of my Coca-Cola?"

At night, Lázaro began to disappear, slipping into Downsville and Market Square, where he mingled with other river rats, borrowed money, and resumed his drinking. At the weekend he returned just after dawn, apparently very drunk, leading a donkey.

"Where did you get that donkey?" Adrian demanded.

"I'm trying to remember," said Lázaro.

"You can't keep him here."

"He can room with Prince."

"You have three days to get out."

Lázaro got out that night, very late, as the Casa San Francisco slept, and took his donkey. In the morning, Adrian found a note tacked to the door of the chapel.

Muy estimado Don Adriano,

Yo regresé a México pero quién sabe donde? Quizás la próxima vez tu no lanzarás la camiseta en mi cara.

Tu compañero,

LÁZARO

I've gone back to Mexico but who knows where? Maybe next time you won't throw your T-shirt in my face. Your pal (!). With the letter, Adrian suffered two shocks. The first was that Lázaro could write. The second was the change in the chapel.

The paintings were gone—all of the Stations of the Cross, the canvases untacked and carefully removed from their wooden frames; and more. Strangely, Lázaro had left behind the painting of St. Michael Archangel and himself as Lucifer, and the body of St. Francis as it flung the precious garments at his father's feet. The head, its blue eyes gazing heavenward, had vanished, and with that discovery Adrian knew that decapitation had become a constant of his life.

In his grief he fled to his studio, where he shuffled through his secular paintings and found several missing. Though he did not admire his impressions of Boca Chica and his bucolic pictures, he knew that some were better than others: with uncanny judgment, Lázaro had stolen the best, not least the flower sellers and the children in boxcars with their hopeless eyes. Lázaro had stolen no money, not that Adrian cared.

He could not call on the Mexican police; from his experience in Mexico he assumed that if he hired private detectives they would endlessly demand money and do nothing. Instantly he decided to seek Lázaro in Mexico himself, and to stay there until he recovered his pictures.

He scribbled notes to Mr. Ennis and Miss Rice, appointing them guardians of the Casa San Francisco, then in a whirlwind he gathered clothes and money for his journey. As he did so he paid the price of his luxurious childhood, when the hands of servants always hovered in the shadows to clean up his disorder. His rooms were chaotic; he could find neither his suitcases nor his passport. He thought, I'll go there without them, and stuffed some belongings into a plastic bag, debating whether to include a letter from Diana.

■ ■ ■

. . . and despite the oxygen tent, André has died. I spend much of my time attending to Maude, now totally bedridden. If you don't come home to manage Northwood Hall and your inheritance, I shall take matters into my own hands and begin to reduce the domestic staff. Your brother Pius is on the verge of penury, but in your obstinate cruelty you will not help him. *Who* is Lázaro? . . .

■ ■ ■

He cast it aside. In his commotion, Alejandro and Dianita rose from sleep. He kissed them both and told Alejandro, "Take good care of her." Alejandro protested, "You can't! you can't!" Miss Rice walked in: the news of Adrian's departure so disturbed her that she flew to the office and telephoned Rodrigo and Mr. Ennis to come running, as Adrian sought again without success to find his passport.

With Dianita in Alejandro's arms, the group pursued Adrian from his rooms to the river's edge, imploring him not to go. Adrian glanced back at the tower, where a man in overalls watched through binoculars. Mr. Ennis said, "May I, sir, with all respect, suggest that your venture would benefit from additional reflection?"

Adrian removed his shoes and clothes, shoving them into his plastic bag. Naked came I out of my mother's womb and naked shall I return thither. As he disrobed, other thoughts raced through him, which made no sense: Am I chasing Lázaro for my pictures or do I have a deeper reason do I envy his poverty or his nothingness did I pity FUNKY COLD for his addiction or crave his nothingness for I strive only to know my nothingness? He said, "I haven't much money with me, Ennis. I'll call you."

The morning sun rose in the hot, wet sky. Rodrigo rushed at Adrian, trying to pin him to the earth, but he had taught his friend too well. Adrian broke free, leaping from Rodrigo's grasp into the river, where he stood facing them with the blue water to his waist to hide his nakedness. Mr. Ennis fussed with his glasses, wiping them, groping for words that he could not find. Dianita, confused, reached out for her father, then sucked her thumb. Alejandro and Miss Rice wept. Rodrigo, still earthbound, punched a rock.

But by now Adrian Northwood was in the middle of the Rio Grande, gripping his possessions to his head, swimming to Mexico.

PART VI

Staírways

▼▼▼

Adrian walked past the abandoned cars and garbage dumps to the Zona Zur and the police brothel. That early in the day, as he climbed the misshapen stairway to the roof, he saw no policemen, and the brothel slept. Susana, however, was awake, burnishing the icons in her cabaña, demure beneath her comely auburn hair, and sober. She said languidly, "Ah, Feo. Did you bring me soup?"

Adrian held up his empty hands; she seemed disappointed, even cool. He asked, "Have you seen Lázaro?"

"He was here last night," she said, "down below—with a donkey." And yes, he had many paintings, neatly rolled in newspaper and packed in burlap sacks on the beast's back. He had unraveled some and shown them proudly to Susana.

Adrian said, "He stole them from me."

"Lázaro said *he* painted them."

"Mother of God, my pictures!"

"Yours, Feo? I didn't care for them."

"Where did he go?"

"I . . . I don't know."

"Where does he live?"

"I'm . . . not sure."

"Will he be here tonight?"

"I doubt it, Feo. The police want him."

"I may be back tonight."

"Bring soup."

As he ran to the bus station to deposit his belongings, Adrian probed his brain for inklings and remembered a remark of Lázaro's; from the bus station he ran to an industrial park, seeking a factory that made windshield wipers.

Thousands of factories stretched westward along the border from the Atlantic to the Pacific sea, the creations of American industry happy to help Mexico by polluting her water and paying her laborers a few dollars a day. Adrian raced along miles of fence, past vast lawns and clipped palm trees and futuristic buildings of aluminum and plastic. Running, he wondered, Is money of mine invested in this park? Do I own any factories between here and California?

He ran through a fence and an amber doorway, into an immense tin shed and a fluorescent haze, where hundreds of young women and adolescents were arranged in long rows, assembling windshield wipers. Blue machinery chopped out rods that flashed like silver; little hands in plastic gloves, so diaphanous they resembled condoms, fluttered above benches inserting strips of rubber into metal ruts. Adrian hastened along the assembly line, showing a photograph of Lázaro he had consulted as he painted Lucifer. He asked the drudges, "Do you know this man?"

Eventually he found himself in the office of the managing director, well-groomed, wearing a turquoise shirt, the sort of bourgeois Mexican Adrian had so often seen leaving Amigoland laden with video machines and expensive cheese. The director said, "Who could forget Lázaro?"

"Does he work here?" asked Adrian.

"He did, when he wasn't stoned. A good worker—that's why I kept him. Very exact. Bored crazy on the assembly line. I used him to repair machinery. I had an odd feeling about Lázaro."

"Odd?"

"That maybe, in his childhood, he was meant for nicer things."

"And you fired him?"

"No, he stopped coming to work."

"Where does he live?"

The Mexican consulted a computer. "Flores Faustino, Lázaro. Calle Córdoba, 29B." He added, "That's south of town, off National Highway 101, not a nice neighborhood."

Adrian took a taxi to Highway 101, but the driver refused to approach Lázaro's address. Adrian walked down the highway, asking strangers for directions to Calle Córdoba. "In there," they said, pointing past sheds and concrete buildings painted green. Jutting from the wood and concrete, flapping in the wind, were rusty signs, TALLER DE MOFLES Y REPARACION DE RADIADORES. Muffler Shop and Radiator Repair. Adrian walked beyond them, into a treeless barrio of unpaved dusty roads, junkyards, shacks, dirty children, garbage heaps, and more muffler shops.

Finally, in the parching sun, he found Lázaro's shack, not even a shack but a jerry-built attachment to a tumbling house. It had no lock, and when Adrian pushed in the door he saw why. There was nothing to steal—only a cement floor, a torn mattress, a backless chair, and bits of dirty laundry. Stuck to a yellow mirror on the wall was a snapshot of Susana, smiling, standing before the sea and a fuzzy place, possibly a fishing village? The room was suffocating. The remains of apples and bananas lay about, so shriveled that the flies ignored them. Lázaro surely had not returned here with his donkey or the paintings?

Adrian withdrew to the street, wondering where to turn next. He wandered through the neighborhood, asking children and old women whether they had seen Lázaro. "Not for weeks," they answered, shrugging. He found himself on Calle Marco, then on Avenida Patriotismo, full of muffler shops and grease pits and axles in weeds and smooth rubber tires. Near a grease pit, men were covering hubcaps and windows with newspaper and spraying new cars with fresh colors. Several new cars and trucks with Texas license plates filed down Avenida Patriotismo, followed by a pair of squad cars marked POLICIA JUDICIAL.

Youths drove the cars and trucks, effeminate youths with jewelry and long fingernails but otherwise dressed as men. "In daylight I'm a man," a transvestite had told Adrian in Downsville. The half-men descended from their Buicks and BMWs, their Ford and Isuzu pickups, leaving the keys inside the vehicles and standing by a grease pit until the policemen joined them. The judicial police wore civilian dress, bearing their pistols without holsters inside their belts, the black handles jutting out. Distracted for a moment, Adrian paused and watched as the policemen handed rolls of dollars to the youths and the youths carefully counted the money. A policeman noticed fair Adrian standing in the road, and walked over to him.

"*¿Sus papeles, señor?*" Your papers, sir?

"I forgot them," Adrian said.

A new red truck drove up. The *jefe* jumped out, in his sleeveless leather jacket but without his dog.

"Good afternoon," he said cordially in English as he thrust his fist into Adrian's face.

20

The judicial police handcuffed Adrian and beat him harshly about the head as they drove him away. His lip began to swell from the *jefe*'s first blow, but when he raised his hands to touch the wound the *jefe*'s men hit him with their pistol butts and forced him to lie with his face on the floor of the squad car. They kept hitting and kicking him as they dragged him from a parking lot, past a high window, into the cement building on Calle González, past the arsenal of automatic guns that hung on the wall, down a gloomy corridor with black doors, into a cement room.

He kept repeating, "I demand to see the American consul . . . the American consul . . . American consul . . . ," but removing his handcuffs and rattling their keys, they laughed at him. Children were sprawled about the bare floor of that great room. At the far end was a pair of cells, packed with youths and men. Rusty bars creaked open, he was hurled into a cell, and his captors withdrew, laughing.

Dazed by his blows, Adrian blinked and found himself in a space, no bigger than his bedroom closet at Northwood Hall, with two dozen dark men and boys, from their looks and smell the offal of Matablancos—pickpockets, car thieves, glue sniffers, murderers? They crowded about his body and gazed at his blond head; at once he knew that to survive he must defend his space. In the crush he placed his back against the corner between the rusty bars and the cement wall, pointed to the floor and shouted, "*¡Mi espacio!*" My space! They crowded him all the more, but he thrust his hands and feet at them with karate chops, and they backed away by half inches.

At the far end of the cell, sunlight streamed through bars and a broken window; from beyond that came cries of other prisoners, in an open yard of the great penitentiary. "Give us your clothes!" they shouted. "Give us your shoes! Give us your money!" Blobs of wet human excrement flew through the broken window, hitting the walls and ceiling and some of Adrian's cellmates in the face. Thus did it fly for minutes, fifteen minutes, half an hour, as with howls of desperation the weaker of the youths and men stripped to their undergarments and passed their shoes and clothes through the window to their tormentors. "More shirts! More shoes! No money? More shit!" Adrian remained in his space by the door of the cell, clad fully in his blue T-shirt, faded gray jeans, scuffed white sneakers, and ready with his hands to defend his decency, but throughout the atrocity as the waste flew his soul was elsewhere.

Da-dum-ta-*deee*-dum. Da-dum-ta-ta-ta-*deee*-dum. How he loved the haunting, mournful cello. He played the music backward and forward, interrupting notes, half notes, quarter notes, to linger over phrases that especially pleased him. Da-dum-ta-*deee*-dum. Da-dum-ta-ta-ta-*deee*-dum. No composer could sustain a melody as Schubert could: not even Mozart.

He read and reread various beloved passages of Mozart's letters. "Vienna, 9 June 1781. *Mon Très Cher Père!* Well, Count Arco has made a fine mess of things! So that is the way to persuade people and attract them! To refuse petitions from born stupidity, not to say a word to your master from lack of courage and love of toad-yism, to keep a fellow dangling for four weeks, and finally, when he is obliged to present the petition in person, instead of *at least* granting him admittance, to throw him out of the room and give him a kick on his behind—that is the Count, who, according to your last letter, has my interest so much at heart—and that is the court where I ought to go on serving! The scene took place in the antechamber. . . ."

Behind the broken window, as the sun set, the hurlers of excrement withdrew, and in the great room beyond the cell's bars the black door opened, admitting a mob of distraught women bearing food. These were the mothers of prisoners, of the dozens of children huddled outside the cells on the cement floor. With shrill lamentations the women embraced their young, feeding them tortillas and fried bananas, cursing the guards who stood about and shrieking denials that their children picked pockets or stole cars. Other women assembled at the bars, passing tacos and soda pop to the men and boys inside the cells. Adrian had not eaten all day; not a soul offered him a crust of food; yet his bowels stirred and he longed to urinate. He dared not cede his space, so he ignored the foul bucket at the other corner of the cell. At midnight, a guard fetched him.

The guard refused his plea to use the toilet, leading him down the corridor through another black door into another cement room, where the huge *jefe* sat in his sunglasses and sleeveless leather jacket beneath fluorescent light at a steel table. "Good evening," said the *jefe* in his cordial English.

"I demand to see the American consul," said Adrian.

"Do you have identification?" asked the *jefe* in Spanish.

"My passport's in Downsville."

"How inconvenient. Are you sure you're North American? *Podrías ser sueco.*" You could be Swedish.

The *jefe* rose from his table, walked toward a door. "You don't need a consul." He laughed. "I've called your friends."

Two men entered: an officer of the naval police and, in civilian dress, the *jefe*'s twin. Vaguely now Adrian remembered all three men as clients of the police brothel. The naval person smiled and said, "*Buenas noches.* You were naughty to take Lázaro from us." The twin touched his skull and said, "*Buenas noches.* And tonight, no baseball bat? Machine gun! My pal . . ."

"Slave trafficker," replied Adrian softly.

The goon moved toward Adrian, but the *jefe* restrained him. The *jefe* said, "Oh my, you speak good Spanish. Where did you learn your Spanish?"

"In Spain," said Adrian.

"And with such a good accent. Why must a cultured man consort with whores?"

"I am not a client of the brothel. I visited the neighborhood to feed the children."

"Of course. I saw you once, serving bread and soup! Susana, then, was an exception?"

"Susana and I did not have sex."

"That's what *Susana* says. And yet . . . she must have found you very special." From his belt he removed his black revolver, aimed it at Adrian's face: "Take off all your clothes."

Adrian disrobed, then crouched on the cement to conceal his loins. The *jefe* snatched his jeans, searched the pockets. He said, "Two hundred thirty dollars? That won't do." He put the money in his desk. "What's this key for?"

"My locker at the bus station."

"Is that your residence?"

"I live in Downsville."

"Where in Downsville?"

Adrian hesitated. "Motel 5½."

"He's lying," said the naval person. "He runs the Casa San Francisco, and he's filthy rich."

"*Is* he?" the *jefe* marveled. "What's your name?"

"Northwood."

He scribbled notes. "Nort-wud? How do you spell it?"

"N-o-r-t-h-w-o-o-d."

"Nort-wud. First name?"

"I demand to see the American consul."

"Profession?"

"I paint."

"Ah, a rich *painter*!"

The *jefe* tossed Adrian's key to his twin, with a glance dismissing from the room that goon and the naval person. Within moments, boys in black trousers filed in, bearing metal trays laden with food, spreading the feast primly across the *jefe*'s desk. "Will you forgive me, Mister Nort-wud? Time for my dinner." He sipped red wine, munched on enchiladas, then upon various round and bloody tournedos, wrapped in bacon nearly raw, the meat more bloody as he added sauce. "Tabasco sauce! How I love Tabasco, Mister Nort-wud!" Before he finished, his twin returned, bearing Adrian's plastic bag, followed by a pair of other goons.

The *jefe* placed the bag before Adrian on the cement floor, crouched over it, removing his possessions one by one. "So. Laundry. Dirty laundry? T-shirts. Trousers. Dirty sneakers? Is this your wardrobe? Not very promising. Ah, some books! Blaise Pascal? Johann Wolfgang Goethe? C. G. Hung?"

"Jung."

"Thank you for educating me, Mister Nort-wud. I am—you are convinced of this—an ignorant policeman. Will you stop covering yourself? I've seen private parts before, and men with more to hide! Oh my. Money?"

He withdrew a brown envelope, counted the contents. ". . . fifteen hundred . . . eighteen hundred . . . two thousand . . . two thousand forty-seven dollars." The *jefe* rose, locked the money in his desk: "Not bad, Mister Nort-wud, but can't we do better?" He crouched again over Adrian's possessions. "Oh my. What's this?"

He withdrew a shiny bag—red, white, and blue, emblazoned with a single star and DON'T MESS WITH TEXAS—bound by elastic; he removed the band and looked inside. "Oh dear. What's this little plastic pouch—not so little, really!—of pure white powder? For your bath, sir? Talcum powder?"

Adrian: "It's not mine."

"But it must be yours. It's here among your things! Have you a sweet tooth? Could it be sugar? Let me taste it."

The *jefe* thrust his nail through the plastic, licked his finger: "Not sweet. May I confide in you? I feared it might be cocaine." He bounced the bag from palm to palm. "Nearly half a kilo, I should guess. How lucky for you, dear Mister Nort-wud, that it's not cocaine. It's . . . heroin."

The *jefe* stood; in the bright fluorescent light he removed his sunglasses, replaced them with a sparkling pair of spectacles tinted green, and Adrian glimpsed his tiny black eyes. "I'll need a signed confession, of course. Immediately."

Adrian: "No."

"You sound quite serious. Really, I'm rather pleased. The sentence in Mexico for possession of such a quantity of heroin is less than the sentence for cocaine—a mere twenty years. I have seventy-two hours to obtain your signed confession, sir, and within that limitation I am in no hurry. Since you have lived in Spain, I assume that you know something of Spanish history, as do I, sir, in rich detail. Does that surprise you, Mister Nort-wud? You, sir, even naked, are so evidently a man of culture. Why, you read Goethe, and C. G. Hung! Does it astonish you that a policeman such as I might—secretly, of course—look to vistas beyond my goons? When not eating, drinking, visiting the brothel, interrogating criminals, sir, I read history!"

The *jefe*'s voice, low and almost musical, rose gradually in resonance, echoing against the cement walls. In his boots he paced the floor, turning now and again to point a dark finger and hurl a phrase at Adrian's head.

"Let me refresh your memory—but surely you know this—of Spanish law. Do you remember Joseph Bonaparte, Napoleon's older brother? Not one of the brighter Bonapartes. In 1806, Napoleon made Joseph king of Naples. In 1808, he created him king of Spain. Though he never bothered to learn Spanish, obediently His Majesty King Joseph introduced to Spain the Napoleonic Code, and from the Kingdom of Spain it spread to Mexico before we won our independence. That lovely code remains with us, not least as it applies to criminals such as . . . yourself. A prisoner is guilty until proven innocent. The burden of proof—in your case, that this heroin was not in your possession—rests on your shoulders, not on mine. For seventy-two hours you will have no right to an attorney, and you shall see no consul, since you lack identity. Nonpersons, Mister Nort-wud, have no rights. In seventy-two hours, I shall conduct you to a magistrate, who for the next year or two will investigate your crime before you are sentenced to twenty years of service in—don't you love the terminology?—our Center for Social Readaptation. I should personally like to witness, my dear Mister Nort-wud, your social readaptation. Your situation—I invite you to believe me, sir—is grave. It is a matter of supreme indifference to me whether you should choose to confess your trafficking of heroin tonight, tomorrow, or the day following, but may I assure you that before your audience with the magistrate I shall have your confession? I enjoy my work. I am, in my work —may I boast a little?—famous throughout Mexico for my attention to detail. Oh my, look at this bottle! This Tabasco sauce is nearly finished! I have more. Do you share my passion for Tabasco sauce, Mister Nort-wud? May I venture, sir, that by various methods of persuasion . . ."

Da-dum-ta-*deee*-dum. Da-dum-ta-ta-ta-*deee*-dum. As the *jefe* ranted, Adrian was elsewhere. "*Mon Très Cher Père!* . . . I have written three memoranda, which I have handed in five times; and each time they have been thrown back at me. I have carefully preserved them, and whosoever wishes to read them may do so and convince himself that they do not contain the slightest personal remark. How easy it would have been to persuade me to remain! By kindness, but not by insolence! I sent a message to Count Arco saying *that I have nothing more to say to him. . . .*" (Mozart's italics.) The *jefe* once again was speaking musically, his voice vaguely penetrating the cloud of Adrian's detachment, something about avoiding the inconvenience of a Mexican penitentiary, something about money, furtive subventions to the naval police, to the investigating magistrate, to the goons, to himself, to all whomsoever in Mexico with reason to dislike Adrian: money, large sums of money, very large sums of money.

Adrian: "No."

The *jefe* stopped pacing, approached him, and sighed. "You make me sad. I wished to spare you considerable discomfort."

He gestured to the goons, who yanked Adrian to his feet and bound his hands behind his back, not with handcuffs but by joining his thumbs with thin, sharp wire. The *jefe* strode to a steel cabinet, from which he removed a bottle of mineral water, a bottle of Tabasco sauce, a jar of dry chili, and a transparent plastic bag. He moved toward Adrian, said "Oh my," then, as though with an afterthought, returned to the cabinet and took out a long cylindrical metal object. He asked, "Do you know what this is, Mister Nort-wud?"

"*Una chicharra*," said Adrian. A cattle prod.

"Ah, such a command of Spanish," the *jefe* rejoiced, touching the prod to Adrian's stomach. "Runs on batteries. Leaves no marks."

You will remember that long ago, when I first tried to warn Adrian Northwood to avoid Mexico, I confided to you that at times his adventures would become so fearful I would be reluctant to reveal them. I think that now, as the unpleasantness takes place, I should remain loyal to that reticence.

You do have the right to know certain general procedures. In their harsher interrogations the Mexican police are accustomed to begin by placing a plastic bag over the prisoner's head, tightening it at the neck, holding it thus until the victim cannot breathe, and the anvil pounding from his chest toward his brain becomes so unbearable he thinks he is going mad. For subsequent steps preferences vary, but the jefe *enjoys combining the discomfort of the plastic bag with the lubricants of mineral water and Tabasco sauce. He likes to pour the water, the sauce, and dry chili powder into the bag, shake it well, secure it to the subject's head, and—for long minutes—watch as the criminal writhes at his feet. And often he lays the bag aside, smiling as his goons turn the victim upside down and he administers the mineral water and Tabasco sauce into the nostrils and eyes directly.*

There, I have done my duty! If you must know more, then I leave you in the dark corridor outside the jefe's *chamber, and from the thumps and Adrian's muffled screams your imagination may provide the pictures. . . .*

From the goons Adrian has received many rough punches, but so far he has absorbed them well. His running, his push-ups, his resilience when Rodrigo rushed at him with rocks, have made of his body a hard shield. As the blows rain down he tenses his muscles to resist them, and though with his hands bound behind his back he cannot shield his head, whenever possible he freezes in a fetal position to protect his ribs and genitalia. Condition Red remember remember cool control stay focused breathe deeply you can defeat any threat you can decide not to be afraid avoid Condition Black! The *jefe* interrogates.

"How often did you f—— our dear Susana?"

"I didn't."

"What were you doing in her cabaña?"

"Drinking soup."

The goons, not quite as flabby as the *jefe*, nonetheless tire easily of administering their discipline, and when they pause they drink cold beer. Adrian welcomes these intermissions. "*Mon Très Cher Père!* . . . In view of the original *cause* of my leaving (which you know too well), no father would dream of being angry with his son; on the contrary, he would be angry if his son *had not left*. Good God! *He* knows that my sole aim is to help you and to help us all. Must I repeat a hundred times that I can be of more use to you here in Vienna than in Salzburg? I implore you, dearest, most beloved Father . . ." The discipline resumes, not least as the *jefe* applies his electric cattle prod to Adrian's genitalia. . . .

Adrian is stubborn, but his cries grow sharper. A goon strides down the corridor gripping a rusty chain and the *jefe*'s police dog. The *jefe* employs the beast mostly to frighten people: he knows that afterward rich victims sometimes complain in high places and that fangs that penetrate the flesh leave marks. Adrian cannot know of the *jefe*'s benign intentions, and—when the black door opens and he sees the dog—his bowels empty on the cement.

▲▲▲
21
▼▼▼

Yet he did not yield. The *jefe*'s torture continued for another three days, each session more elaborate than the last, yet Adrian did not yield. When not in the *jefe*'s presence, he was dragged back to the great cement room with the children on the floor and the pair of packed cells. Amid the ordure of Matablancos he was forced to use the foul bucket at the far corner of his cell, but despite his weakness from the beatings his reserves of strength enabled him to defend his space in the corner between the rusty bars and the cement wall. Since he had no money he could buy no food or drink, but when the mothers flooded in he appealed to their mercy and managed to survive on scraps of tortilla and greasy meat such as princes might toss to hounds.

Each afternoon, prisoners on the other side of the broken window resumed their ritual of crying "Clothes! shoes! money!" and of hurling blobs of wet excrement, but still as he thrust his hands and feet at all intruders into his space he remained clothed. Sleeping was less easy; with no room among his stinking cellmates to lie on the floor, he leaned against his patch of wall and tried to sleep standing up, but his wounds and bruises throbbed and for his sanity he resumed reading the letters.

"*Mon Très Cher Père!* . . . I implore you, dearest, most beloved Father, for the future to spare me such letters. I entreat you to do so, for they only disturb my mind and vex my heart and spirit;

and I, who must now keep on composing, need a cheerful mind and a tranquil disposition. The Emperor is not here, nor is Count Rosenberg. . . ." A guard came to conduct Adrian back to the *jefe*. ". . . Count Rosenberg has commissioned Schröder (the eminent actor) to look around for a good libretto and to give it to me to compose. . . ." In the *jefe*'s chamber, the *jefe* showed Adrian a document, neatly typed, composed in elegant Spanish.

"Your confession," the *jefe* said.

Adrian: "No."

The goons were summoned; the beatings resumed. ". . . For the Archbishop's concert I composed a sonata for myself, a rondo for Brunnetti and one for Ceccarelli. . . ." Now the plastic hood. ". . . At each concert I played twice, and the last time when the concert was over I went on improvising variations. . . ." Now the Tabasco sauce. ". . . Well, if he does not want me, that is exactly what I wish. Instead of taking my petition or procuring me an audience or advising me to send in the document later or persuading me to let the matter lie and to consider things more carefully— *enfin*, whatever he wanted—Count Arco hurls me out of the room and gives me a kick on the behind. . . ." Now the cattle prod. ". . . Well, that means in our language that Salzburg is no longer the place for me, except to give me a favorable opportunity of returning the Count's kick. One of these days I shall write to the Count and tell him *what he may confidently expect from me*. . . ." (Adrian's italics.) By now the law's Napoleonic seventy-two hours were expiring, the judge waited in his court, and the *jefe* needed a signature.

Adrian: "No."

Soon he lay on the cement, knocked out. The *jefe* took up a pen, poised to sign "Nortwud" in his own hand, then remembered that he had failed to press Nortwud for his Christian name. What Christian names did North Americans have? Jack, Billy, Bob? Bob would do. He signed the confession "Bob Nortwud," retrieved the pouch of heroin from his desk, and commanded a goon to empty a bucket of ice water onto Nortwud's face. The goons dressed Adrian; the *jefe* followed as they bore him with his arms about their shoulders down murky corridors and flights of stairs into the presence of the magistrate.

Mistily Adrian emerged from his reverie, enough to recognize that now he was handcuffed and in some sort of courtroom, a basement chamber, all cement, with tiny windows near the ceiling that admitted no sunlight, only the sounds of prisoners in the yard shouting, "Clothes! shoes! money!" An elderly man with an old-fashioned hearing aid, wires dangling, sat at a dark wooden desk on a dais beneath a judicial seal, a portrait of Mexico's president, and a dirty flag, the green, white, and red of the Mexican Republic. In whispers, the *jefe* and a more elegant man, in a pin-striped business suit—the state prosecutor?—huddled before the dais, but the magistrate kept asking, "*¿Cómo?* . . . *¿Cómo?* . . . *¿Cómo?*" What? What? What?

Both magistrate and prosecutor glanced at Adrian's confession, neither making a fuss about the forged signature, for though they must have recognized the *jefe*'s handwriting, evidently they were as anxious as he was to be bribed. The *jefe* handed the magistrate the pouch of heroin, but the old man recoiled in seeming horror. Finally he regarded Adrian and said, "The charges against you are very serious."

"I'm innocent," Adrian said.

"*¿Cómo?*"

"Innocent."

"*¿Cómo?*"

"I'M INNOCENT."

"Not according to the evidence, Señor Nortwud, nor according to the testimony of the judicial police. Mexican laws are meticulous and stringent. Your case, furthermore, is compounded because you have entered Mexico without identification and you are therefore, Señor Nortwud, present in our sovereign republic illegally. Do you have an attorney?"

"No."

"*¿Cómo?*"

"NO."

"You needn't shout at me, Señor Nortwud. I shall appoint an attorney, in due course, who will undertake to represent your defense. He will need funds, of course, for various . . . fees. Can you pay him?"

"THE *JEFE* STOLE ALL MY MONEY."

"You will forgive me, Señor Nortwud, but I didn't hear you. No matter, may I in any case suggest that you exert yourself for contingencies of personal finance? Meanwhile, I hereby order you remanded to the Center for Social Readaptation, Matablancos, pending this court's investigation of the charges pressed by the state."

A goon handed Adrian his plastic bag of clothes (minus, he soon discovered, his best T-shirts) and led him, still handcuffed, out of the courtroom and the realm of the judicial police into the street. The sun shone brilliantly; Adrian rejoiced in the sunshine on his bruised face and in his ephemeral sensation of freedom among the pedestrians and motorists of the hectic street, even as he glanced upward at the beckoning turrets of the penitentiary and the guards in blue uniforms fingering automatic guns. From the Maxi Cafeteria the boys in white shirts and black trousers filed up Calle González, holding aloft their ritual trays heaped with enchiladas, fried chicken, and bottles of beer for the *jefe*'s luncheon. Adrian felt pangs of hunger, wondering when he would eat decently again and how much time might pass before he regained his liberty, if indeed he would.

He was led to the warden's office just outside the prison's gate, or rather to the warden's antechamber, another cement room, where women sat at steel desks so tiny that for space to shuffle papers they tilted their typewriters upright. Adrian was shoved down a row of headless women behind teetering typewriters until his goon found a free typist, a youngish auburn woman who— very slightly—resembled Susana. She seemed kindly; when she finished asking myriad questions and typing teeming documents, she allowed Adrian to use her telephone. He called the American consulate. "The consul is in a meeting, sir." Finally he was connected to a vice-consul.

"Toole here."

"My name is Northwood, Mr. Toole. A. J. Northwood."

"Northwood? Where have I heard the name? How can I help you, Mr. Northwood?"

"I'm a U.S. citizen and I'm in jail."

"Where?"

"I was with the judicial police, Calle González. I'm about to enter the, ah, Center for Social Readaptation."

"How long have you been detained?"

"Nearly four days."

"Oh, Jesus! Those goddamn Mexicans are supposed to inform the consulate within twenty-four hours! What's the charge?"

"Heroin possession. I'm innocent."

"How have they treated you?"

"Badly. I'm innocent."

"You may well be innocent, Mr. Northwood. I've yet to meet a heroin trafficker who told me he was guilty."

"I left my passport in Downsville."

"You'd better get it back."

"Can you bring me a new one?"

"I can bring you an application."

"When will I see you?"

"This is a two-man post, Mr. Northwood, and we're over-whelmed. In our consular district alone, hundreds of Americans are in jail, most of them for smuggling drugs."

"When will I see you?"

"A week, maybe. Ten days . . ."

"What can you do to get me out?"

"Nothing."

"Mother of God."

"Do you have money, Mr. Northwood?"

"The police stole it."

"You'd better find some more, and I mean a lot. Anyone you want me to call?"

Adrian hesitated. He could not countenance the thought of Diana's anguish were she to learn where he was or of the wounds that the police had inflicted on his body. At the Casa San Francisco, the news of his misadventure would cause Alejandro and Miss Rice incalculable sorrow, and it would rip Rodrigo apart. He knew that liberty could be his within an hour if he called Mr. Ennis and paid off the *jefe* and his cabal, yet such bribery offended not simply his sense of justice but his deepest notions of decorum. More deeply still—he hardly thought of this—he was on a pilgrimage of atonement, and wherever his atonement led him he must follow. "Mr. Northwood? Anyone I should call?"

"No," Adrian said.

He hung up. At the iron gate, all bars and chains, the goon removed his handcuffs and the guards pushed Adrian into the milling bodies of the penitentiary. At once he received some shocks. The first was that the jail had been built for two hundred guests but today it contained more than a thousand. The next was that the warden and his guards did not mingle with the guests but left the internal government of the prison to *coordinadóres,* trusties. The final shock was that thenceforth Adrian would be at the mercy of those criminals.

They shunned him at first. He was at a loss for where to turn, for a friendly voice to tell him where to place his sack of clothes, where to shower, and where to sleep. It was early afternoon. The space of open air and sickly trees between the cellblocks was thronged with men and random women. At a long cement trough, young men in baseball caps scrubbed laundry in stagnant water. With nothing else to do, Adrian emptied his sack of clothes into the trough, and though he had no soap he struggled as best he could to scrub the stains of blood and excrement from his underwear and shirts. That done, he wrung them out and hung them up on string hard by the whitewashed wall, allowing the sun to do its work as warily he watched, now and again practicing karate chops in pantomime to broadcast his prowess and protect not just his laundry but his person. Several muscular and tattooed men—trusties?—stood by and smiled as he gathered his moist laundry and returned it to his bag.

At dinnertime, he followed a mob of prisoners into a jammed

refectory, where his meal turned out to be a tortilla and a bowl of tepid water garnished with sprinklings of cornmeal and red beans. Other prisoners ate better—tacos and enchiladas, salads and cupcakes—but from their badinage he knew that the food was from their families or had been bought with money. For the first time in his life, Adrian was without money. He had sometimes wondered what it might be like were he truly poor, to wake one day without a penny in his pocket, to subsist at the very edge of life, to be forced to beg simply to survive. Now he began to learn.

As though half mad with hunger, he drained his tin bowl of its watery soup, then rose and, holding up the bowl, roamed among the tin tables of the refectory, begging scraps of food. Most prisoners laughed at him, one or two kicked him in the seat of his pants, but a few dropped scraps of onion, pepper, and dough into his tin bowl. Adrian returned to his place, where with his bare hands he shoved the leavings into his mouth.

After dinner, he sought out inmates who had tossed him food and sold them his cheap Chinese wristwatch and half his clothes —not least his favorite torn T-shirt, a gift from Rodrigo, LET'S ALL PUMP IRON—for a meager several thousand pesos so that he might eat tomorrow. After tomorrow, how would he eat? As he stood helplessly in the yard, a tattooed trusty beckoned him to enter the cellblocks. The trusty led him down a yellow corridor, beyond some bars into a large room tiered with scores of bunks.

"This is cellblock Number 3," the trusty said. "Do you want a bunk?"

"Where else would I sleep?" asked Adrian, puzzled.

The trusty laughed. "There's a ninety-dollar cleaning fee. Payable weekly. The bunk will cost you two hundred twenty-five dollars. Payable weekly. Both in advance."

"*No tengo dinero.*" I have no money.

"*El jefe dice eres un muy rico.*" The chief says you're a rich guy. "No money? Sleep on the floor. The Committee will receive you in the soccer yard tomorrow morning at ten o'clock."

He left Adrian alone in the room. Presently two hundred men jammed into the room, sixty or so filled up the bunks, the bars slammed shut, and the lights went out. With the other bedless men Adrian reclined fetally on the floor, his diminished sack of clothes his pillow, but he did not stay there long. Rats half the size of poodles scampered from the walls, nibbling on crusts of food inmates had let fall from their bunks, and on Adrian's toes. He leaped to his feet, kicking the rodents away, and passed the remainder of the night leaning sleepless against a wall, counting the rats, intrigued against his will by the weird rhythms of their running feet.

At daylight, when the barred doors clicked open, Adrian hurried to the yard, where at the canteen he bought a banana and an orange for his breakfast. The banana cost him the equivalent in pesos of one dollar, the orange nearly three dollars, or most of the money from the sale of his clothes. At ten o'clock he walked over to the soccer field, all dust and litter, for his meeting with the Committee.

The Committee were present, but otherwise engaged and not quite ready to receive him. The several men stood beyond the rusty soccer posts at the end of the yard, their hands sheathed in plastic gloves, holding metal buckets, hurling blobs of wet excrement through the broken windows of the cells in the dominion of the judicial police. "Give us your clothes! Give us your shoes! Give us your money!" Amid muffled shouts and sobs, shirts and jeans, shoes and underwear and coins and paper money, flew through the windows into the yard like flocks of frenzied geese. Eventually the Committee noticed Adrian standing there; laden with their morning's treasure, they turned to him, smiling.

They pushed him from the soccer yard through a rusty metal door, down a narrow cement tunnel, into a windowless cement room. "Our office, Señor Nortwud," a trusty said, unlocking a metal cabinet. He took out a bottle of something amber, a sack of something brown, and a pouch of something white. "What's your pleasure, Señor Nortwud—whiskey, marijuana, cocaine? Or all three?"

Adrian said nothing. The trusty said, "Try some," dipping his finger into white powder, thrusting specks of cocaine into Adrian's nose, but Adrian retched and sneezed it out. Another trusty produced a hand grenade, a long piece of string attached to the pin, placed the grenade around Adrian's neck, and led him like a hound around the room. He said, "Bark, Nortwud. Bark, bark, bark." Nortwud would not bark. They demanded money. He remained silent. There ensued the sort of discipline that he had endured at the hands of the *jefe*—a suffocating plastic bag over his head, generous doses of mineral water and dry chili powder in his nostrils, a cattle prod to his genitalia, until he blacked out. When he regained lucidity, for good measure he was made to kneel naked with his face against the cement wall as the Committee beat him with sticks across his kidneys, his legs, and the soles of his feet.

He repeated, "*No tengo dinero.*"

"But you'll get money. You'll get lots of money."

Adrian said nothing.

"A pity, Nortwud. Until you change your mind, we've reserved a special place for you. *Se llama 'cielo.'* We call it 'heaven.' It's where we keep people, not gentlemen like ourselves, but—unpleasant people? Enjoy it, Nortwud! It will cost you two thousand dollars to descend from heaven."

He was allowed to dress, to take up his sack of clothes, but his feet already were so swollen that he could not pull on his sneakers. Escorted by the full Committee, he was brought out of the windowless office into sunlight, thence inside a tower with a winding metal stairway painted a brilliant blue. Painfully he mounted the blue staircase on his bleeding feet, staining it perhaps with driblets of his blood. The level at the top was as circular as the stairway —cells of various sizes, some empty, others packed with shouting men, facing one another in a gloomy orb. Adrian was sealed in a cell by himself, narrow enough that when he reached out his arms, his palms were flat against the cement walls, yet not quite long enough that he might lie down. The sole embellishment was a plastic bucket, evidently intended for his sanitation. The ceiling, however, was lofty. At the far wall, a slit opened to cloudless sky: by standing tiptoe Adrian could glance out and glimpse the world.

There, not a mile distant, flowed the violet, snakelike river; he could see the flashing chromium bumpers flowing to and from Amigoland; and the green mowed grass that encircled the barracks of his Casa San Francisco. Maybe he imagined this, but so wretched was his loneliness he was certain that even so far removed he saw a man playing football—passing it, kicking it—with a boy. Rodrigo and Alejandro? Dear Rodrigo! Dear Alejandro! Where was dear Miss Rice? Dearest Dianita! How he missed his quarrels with his mother. How he yearned for a letter or a book from Cardinal Galsworthy.

For much of his life, he had lived at arm's length from most of his acquaintances and his few friends. Such distance, he had fancied, suited his temperament. Yet now, even as he ached for friends, he asked himself whether his isolation in this cage had not been inexorably predestined. He asked aloud, "Did fate blindly lead me here, or do I deserve this? Is this—somehow—all my fault?"

Facing his cell, by the chipped banister of the blue stairway, sat Baltazar, the custodian of heaven, a man of theological ugliness, dressed in black denim, his forehead totally tattooed with miniature blue crosses and inverted crosses. Cross, inverted cross; cross, inverted cross; cross, inverted cross. In a great metal cage, he kept a dozen white mice. He fed them well, constantly dropping to his darlings scraps of yellow cheese and uncooked red meat.

Toward Adrian he was less bountiful, faithfully serving him three tortillas and two bowls of thin soup a day, a tin dish of dark beans now and again, a glass of water if he begged enough for it, but nothing else. Or nothing else until in his frantic hunger Adrian sold to Baltazar the remainder of his clothes, retaining only a pair of jeans, two T-shirts, two pairs of shorts, his sneakers, no socks. With the pesos bit by bit Adrian bought from Baltazar some bars of chocolate, a box of crackers, and such morsels of yellow cheese as the fat white mice did not seem to want, determined to ration these provisions to his greedy stomach over the everlastingness of a week.

Adrian slept in his cement cage sometimes crouching, sometimes half standing up. He was allowed out of the cage only on odd-numbered days, and then merely to empty his sanitation bucket because the other inhabitants of heaven objected with such vehemence to the smell. He was not allowed to wash his body. After five days, he was taken down the blue stairway to the windowless office of the Committee, where he was beaten again, but he did not relent: "I have no money."

In the evenings after their supper young men from all over the penitentiary gathered on the steps of the blue stairway, removing their shirts and often their trousers to submit themselves to Baltazar's exotic art. Baltazar tattooed them. Tattooing, so long the source of much infection throughout Mexico, now lay outside the law; thus only in prisons was the art preserved. Convicts bore the decorations on their torsos, legs, buttocks, and their foreheads as signs of honor and of manhood, attracting women of rough tastes who likened them to aphrodisiacs. The stairway was dim by that hour; Adrian from his cage could not see all, but it seemed to him that laboriously Baltazar punctured the skin of his eager victims with an arsenal of fine needles, injecting, rubbing in inks of red and blue in complex patterns, bizarre designs of spiderwebs, hearts pierced with knives and lances dripping blood, snakes with men's and women's heads, and crosses, inverted crosses, crosses, inverted crosses.

Adrian thought, This is an Aztec Mass. From his Jung he knew that such rites originated in the deepest regions of the soul; from an immeasurable richness of images which millions of years of human life had hoarded all together; indeed that such compulsions reposed not just in the darkness of the collective psyche but in instincts born before humanity existed—in apes, hyenas, snakes, mollusks, and even in the first amoeba. Eventually primitives adored the moon and sun; Christians worshipped the Triune God; some moderns worshipped Satan.

Since Adrian lived spiritually in the eighteenth century—and had so rarely read newspapers or watched television—he was unaware that dwelling with him in the Center for Social Readaptation were a cult of Satanists; as the days passed he realized that they were locked in cells to either side of his. From fragments of their conversation, and whispers of Baltazar, he learned slowly of their sacraments.

They had begun, apparently, by slaughtering horses. Giddy on peyote cactus and cocaine, at midnight they had roamed the countryside along the river in stolen pickup trucks, invading remote stables or seizing horses that grazed beneath the moon, strangling them with barbed wire, slicing their throats from ear to ear, then hanging them by their heads from the limbs of trees.

From such minor sacraments they moved with awe to human sacrifice, again at midnight invading farmhouses, snatching old peasants and adolescent goatherds from their beds, carving out their beating hearts, chopping off their heads and limbs and private parts, hurling the pieces with carrots and turnips into pots and making stews and eating them.

Adrian, once or twice, as he was allowed to leave his cell to dump his sanitation bucket, only glimpsed a face or two of his Satanic neighbors, but as he languished crouching in his cage he heard their voices constantly. The Satanists were not themselves goatherds or children of the slums. From their Castilian Spanish, their flutelike accents, they were all—it seemed to Adrian—children of the university. They chanted mythic rituals that chilled his blood and terrified him the more because he could not see them. Baltazar saw them. Seated on the banister, facing the cells, his hands rarely ceasing to drop snacks to his white mice, he followed the ceremonies with fascination. Every movement of the rites seemed to enlarge the inverted crosses on his face, as he mouthed exotic blasphemies beneath his breath, or—carried away—shouted them aloud.

The Satanists seemed very rich. Often throughout the day the boys in black trousers from the Maxi Cafeteria climbed the blue stairway with trays of steaming food; the Satanists used Adrian's hands to pass dishes back and forth between their cells, inviting him to share their nourishment. In his hunger Adrian had been more and more the victim of hallucinations, fantasizing of grilled chicken, lamb chops, corn on the cob corn on the cob corn on the cob, but he feared his neighbors morbidly and dared not taste the food that their hands had touched. He had reason.

They insisted also that he pass from cell to cell eerie things— herbs, ointments, dry branches, human hair, melted candles, cigar butts, bottles of amber potions, amulets, gold beads, pieces of peyote cactus, and chicken heads. They chattered incessantly of Oshun, the voodoo god of money, sex, and power, and boasted to Baltazar—he seemed to believe them—that when they ate their stew of vegetables and human parts they had become bulletproof and invisible. Between the cells they passed through Adrian's hands strange writing on scraps of paper, horizontal arrows crossed by vertical arrows, arrows in the shape of *X*'s, spiders and crescent moons whose extremities were arrows, snakes whose tails were arrows and snakes whose heads were pierced with arrows, all intermingled with the names of animals—horses, goats, ducks, roosters, rabbits, bats—and sums of pesos and of dollars that suggested sales of cocaine and heroin since the sums were so very high. ". . . *corazón de gallo . . . corazón de chivo . . . corazón de gato . . . una piedra imán . . . ajo hembra . . . un anzuelo"* . . . rooster's heart . . . he-goat's heart . . . cat's heart . . . a charmed stone . . . female garlic . . . a fishhook . . .

Soon Adrian refused to pass further Satanic charms or hieroglyphics. The Satanists resumed their mythic chants, howling through the bars and walls obscenities, blasphemies, and curses at Adrian's head. Sobbing, he hurled himself against his far wall, standing tiptoe to his tiny window to see the sky, crying out to his beloved friends and little daughter across the river as though praying that their arms might reach across to embrace him and protect him. "O Jesus!" he cried also. "O Holy Virgin of Guadalupe! O Mother of God! Mother of God! Deliver me! deliver me!"

Deliverance came. Not before he was taken downstairs again to the office of the Committee and badly beaten, yet he said, "No money." Possibly in despair from his willfulness, his captors decided on different arrangements. Next evening, a dog climbed the blue stairway and after him the *jefe*. As the dog bared his fangs and beat his paws against the bars, the *jefe* asked, "How do you like heaven?"

Adrian turned his back on him, lifting his shirt to show his wounds. The *jefe* answered, "You don't deserve heaven. Now we'll try hell."

22

At daylight, Adrian's hands and feet were chained, he was packed into a van with other men and driven seventy miles upriver to the Center for Social Readaptation at Reynuestro. On the way, it rained, a little.

The penitentiary at Reynuestro had been built for two hundred guests; today it housed . . . twelve hundred? Like the penitentiary at Matablancos, within its painted concrete walls, a sickly mauve, trusties governed it. From the instant he was hauled inside, Adrian knew that he had entered a madhouse.

Oddly, the lunacy of the place at first favored his health. The trusties were so many of them aloft on clouds of marijuana and cocaine that either they were unaware, or had forgotten, they were supposed to torture him. Moreover, he was not locked in a cage, or even in a cellblock with hundreds of men. There was no more room for men or rats in the cellblocks; new guests were accommodated in the open courtyard, once a place for playing games but now of necessity a teeming dormitory. At the end of the courtyard, he found a wooden crate. He knocked an end out. Thereafter he slept inside and made the crate his home. Otherwise he could walk about, stretch his legs; he had the liberty of the prison, and soon he knew its every nook.

The place was a dreamlike kingdom of opulence and squalor. Prisoners (drug traffickers) with much money occupied private rooms, equipped with air conditioners, cable television, and private baths, video machines, facsimile machines, and mobile telephones; they lived amid their own furniture and Persian rugs, indulging their luxurious tastes in food, women, and black-label whiskey by ordering them à la carte from their henchmen in the world outside. On weekend evenings, the director of the penitentiary penetrated the inner walls of trusties with expensive whores and a mariachi orchestra and joined his wealthy guests in noisy parties. Their revelry blared throughout the prison until daybreak as they danced and sang, laughed and fornicated, ate and drank and sniffed cocaine.

Arrangements for the poorer inmates were less elaborate, though even the poor needed considerable money to survive. The walls and floors of the communal showers oozed with mossy slime, crawling with cockroaches and lice; Adrian showered twice a day, though he had no soap. He had no food. Or rather, every crust of bread he ate, he begged. He learned, and very quickly, to live by his wits.

Desperate for money, he began by selling the remainder of his clothes, including his sneakers and the ragged underwear on his loins. Within two days, he was barefoot and down to the single torn T-shirt on his back and the threadbare jeans that covered his nakedness. He rapped on every door of rich prisoners, offering to clean their rooms, but there was a surfeit of such sweepers, and they turned him away. He persevered, offering to scrub floors and toilets for payment in food, finding a client here, another down the corridor, proving by his industry that he excelled at scrubbing. He even earned a little money. Within a week he was eating not well but more often, and becoming rich enough to buy two pieces of underwear, an old pair of shoes, and an extra T-shirt, TOUR OF THE WORLD.

It began to rain more heavily. The courtyard-dormitory had no drainage; within a day or two the open space became a dirty pond. Water reached the blankets of the prisoners' cots, then covered them; Adrian moved his meager things from the inside of his wooden crate and during downpours slept on top of it. With sunshine, when the floods receded, and though he ached still from his beatings at Matablancos, he reflected: My body is resilient, but most of the men and women here are weaker and worse off. How may I help them?

From the communal showers, the mossy slime crept down a little hill, down a narrow crooked lane with tiny rooms whose entrances were nylon curtains that stirred in the wind, and from the lane, beneath the curtains, the moss invaded the cubicles themselves. The poorer addicts of cocaine and heroin lived in the moss behind the curtains, most of them men, some of them women, the women sitting at the men's feet as the men sniffed or smoked cocaine or thrust green needles into their arms, legs, and necks. Adrian pitied them and thought: They are beyond help.

He was of greater service in the women's dormitories, where the inmates slept on mattresses without sheets in bunks stacked like squeezed bookshelves, or on the floor. The trusties and their rich friends pressed all younger women into whoredom, a sport that Adrian could hardly stop, but he comforted the women in other ways.

Nominally the prison was served by a physician; Adrian never saw him. Officially the infirmary was stocked with antibiotics, but the director and the trusties intercepted them and sold them for cash. Adrian asked himself, Isn't most of the third world governed like this penitentiary? He drew on his experience in the dispensary of the Casa San Francisco and struggled to repair the women's health. He hounded the rich inmates, all but falling to his knees to beg for money to buy antibiotics, disinfectants, and rat poison. To be rid of him they gave him handouts; on his hands and knees, he helped the women to scrub and disinfect their dormitories; with medicine, he eased the dysentery of some women, and with solutions of salt, sugar, and gruel he arrested the diarrhea and dehydration of the hungry infants born to them in that place. Women were with child; he delivered children. Without a stethoscope, he put his ear to wombs. Hello! the heartbeats thumped. I'm another third world baby! thump-thump! *"¡Empuja!"* Adrian commanded—"Push! Push!"—as dazzled as before by the feat of birth. For the consumptive women, he could do nothing.

As the weeks passed, Adrian's presence in the penitentiary became a consolation to many inmates, men and women. Some asked him, "¿*Eres norteamericano?*" Are you North American? He replied invariably, "*No soy nada*"—I'm nothing—and he half meant it. In the evenings, as he sat upon his wooden crate at the end of the courtyard, scores of prisoners approached him for a hug.

For the men whom the police had beaten so badly they could no longer walk, he could do nothing. Now and again beaten prisoners died in jail, not only Mexicans but North Americans accused of trafficking drugs, who languished too long in the penitentiary without money for food or medicine. Adrian feared this fate for one of his new gringo friends, Freddy, perhaps nineteen, a youth with raven eyes who must have been hardy when he was whole.

Freddy was of the valley; one evening he drove across the river into Reynuestro, looking for a little fun. In a bar he found a pretty girl and took her to a motel room. As he reposed in her arms, the narcotics police raided the motel, broke down his door, and accused him of smuggling cocaine. "They drove me to a baseball field, Ay-jay. It was real dark, and at third base a big cop tore off my pants and raped my butt. At headquarters, they beat and tortured me for three days. I mean, my lower back was shattered? Want to see me walk, Ay-jay?"

Freddy was seated in the infirmary on a folding chair, with a wooden cane between his legs. He rose and walked, but his body was so bent that his back went parallel with the ceiling and he seemed to mime a feeble gnome as he tapped his cane on the cement. Though in unceasing pain, he shunned comfort from cocaine or heroin, which encouraged Adrian to hope that he might be innocent. Adrian had no balm for Freddy beyond his general benediction. Punctually each evening at eight o'clock, the gnomish youth emerged from the infirmary, and—bent over, tapping his cane—crossed the courtyard, awash with criminals and mud puddles. Patiently he awaited his turn, hoisted himself to Adrian's crate, and received a hug.

Adrian's popularity with the poorer inmates did not endear him to the trusties, nor indeed to the *jefe,* who appeared one day at the penitentiary, enraged to learn that he had not been tortured. By gracious leave of the director, the *jefe* was permitted to be present as, that afternoon, in another cement room, down the crooked lane from the communal showers and the habitations of slimy moss, Adrian was rendered to his new tormentors.

The cattle prod was lost or broken, but what the goons lacked in machinery they remedied with zeal. Two of the goons were so high on "crack" cocaine they seemed uncertain of where they were, and thus in their confusion they bounced Adrian off the walls. The *jefe* said, "The wire on your thumbs is much too loose, Mister Nort-wud. Let me be nice and tighten it. Recently, sir, I completed some research in Downsville. Not only did you pay those high gratuities for our guests; it is common knowledge that you have spent princely sums on other projects of philanthropy and culture. *There* we are, neat and tight! You will be charged, dear Mister Nort-wud, an accommodation fee of fifty thousand dollars, which includes my personal assurance that you will not be disciplined further. When we have disposed of that matter, we may discuss others. . . ."

Adrian's mouth was dry weeds, but with will he summoned moisture from his throat and spat on the *jefe*'s boots. For the discourtesy the goons bashed him as he had never been bashed before and hurled him with such vigor to the floor that he felt even sharper stabs of pain in his ribs, ears, arms, and back. A goon with heavy boots jumped with such prolonged devotion on his bare toes that they bled and began to swell. A plastic hood was produced, filled now not with Tabasco sauce but with snowy quicklime, yet before it could be cowled on his head (did he think it was cocaine? was he more terrified of cocaine than of quicklime?), Adrian fainted. When he revived he heard the *jefe* say, "No, enough." The *jefe* sighed! He said, "*El Hoyo*"—the Hole.

¿*El Hoyo?* Adrian as usual had been disrobed for his torture, and he remained so as he was borne by goons more deeply down the twisted lane, the *jefe* following, to a mossy cellar that on different levels kept descending until the steps ended at a grate. The grate was lifted, and, naked, he was thrown into the Hole. The Hole was narrow, but long enough, and Adrian rejoiced that he could lie down. He looked up to see the *jefe* standing dimly on the grate, in his white sombrero and sleeveless leather jacket, tossing a little key from palm to palm, not laughing but with a puzzled gaze that suggested pity. The *jefe* lingered, then climbed the steps—sighing—his boots soft against the moss, leaving Adrian alone.

How long did he remain there? Days, a week, a fortnight? He lost his sense of time and sooner or later could not care. He had no bed, only his mossy floor, and not room enough to stand. For moments (in the morning?), the sun streamed through an opening above and touched his grate, but otherwise he lived in murk or total darkness. Later (in the afternoon?), the grate creaked open and he was handed down a bottle of water, a tortilla, and a cup of mush, so rancid it made him retch, but he ate it anyway for strength. Later (in the night?), it grew cold in that deep earth, and his body shivered, but he was too wise to beg for a blanket. Hunger, thirst, and cold were the luxuries of his living tomb.

The inconveniences were spiders, so annoyed he had disturbed their webs that they crawled across him, stinging now and then. The grate kept out the rats, but he heard their feet above his head and wrenched his body to avoid their droppings. As he lay supine, his swollen toes touched the wooden bucket he used to relieve his bowels, but one day (one night?), the grate creaked open and a hand reached down to remove the bucket, neglecting to bring it back. Heroically for time suspended he contained himself, cohabiting thereafter with his feces, sad enough when they were solid, more unpleasant when his dysentery started. Lying naked, with his back on moss, diarrhea, mucus, blood, he entered another sphere.

He floated.

Over the centuries witnesses have established that in the ecstasy of prayer certain saints have risen from the ground and floated. Generally such mystics—St. Alphonsus Liguori, St. Joseph of Cupertino—rose gently a foot or two into the air as they communed with God. St. Teresa of Ávila was observed during levitation. She explained in her autobiography that the marvel happened when her soul lost all feeling, became unconscious of the world, and she

awoke in the bosom of God. St. Francis of Assisi was seen in a
forest by several of his friars conversing with Christ and suspended
in air "enveloped by a shining cloud." In the Hole, Adrian did not
achieve that kind of physical levitation, but the effect on him of
his deep wish was much the same: he floated.

". . . and do not be anxious, most beloved Father, about the
welfare of my soul. I am as liable to sin as any young man, but
for my own consolation I could wish that all were as free from sin
as I. Probably you believe things of me of which I am not guilty.
My chief fault is that—*judging by appearances*—I do not act always as I should. It is not true that I boasted of eating meat on all
days of fast; but I did say that I did not scruple to do so or consider
it a sin, for I take fasting to mean abstaining, that is, eating less
than usual. I attend Mass every Sunday and every Holy Day and,
if I can manage it, on weekdays also, and that you know, my Father.
The only association that I had with the person of ill repute was
at the ball, and I talked to her long before I knew what she was,
and solely because I wanted to be sure of having a partner for the
contredanse. Well, I must close, or I shall miss the post. Farewell,
dearest, most beloved Father! I kiss your hands a thousand times
and embrace my dear sister most cordially and am ever your most
obedient son, WOLFGANG AMADÈ MOZART."

Hovering in space, Adrian devoured time, nontime in the eighteenth century. He visited Salzburg, browsing in bookstores on the
Getreidegasse; wandering under a brilliant sun through the Mirabell Gardens, admiring urn-crowned balustrades; in the Mozartplatz onion-shaped domes; in the Sigmundsplatz his favorite horse
fountain, Ionic pilasters, the Grecian arch.

Sleepless, he devoted all of nontime to pondering—each in its
turn, in wide scope and in miniature detail—such creations of the
world as he loved. Selectively he played the symphonies of Haydn,
beginning at number forty-eight with the "Maria Theresia" and
onward through nearly another sixty to "La Reine" and the "Ox-
ford" and the "Miracle" and the "Military" and the "Clock" to
the final movement of the "London." He played all the symphonies
of Mozart from the first movement of the Twenty-ninth through

the "Linz" and the Fortieth to the end of the "Jupiter," though he
dwelt so long on the first movement of the Twenty-ninth, the final
movement of the "Linz," the first movement of the Fortieth, the
first movement of the "Jupiter," interrupting so many notes, half
notes, quarter notes, allowing finally the crescendos to soar so
loudly, that he had to raise his palms to his ears to avoid going
deaf. Then he reverted to his Schubert of the mournful cello. Da-
dum-ta-*deee*-dum. Da-dum-ta-ta-ta-*deee*-dum. Others might tire of
that melody; it might at length grate on their ears; Adrian never
tired of it. Da-dum-ta-*deee*-dum. Da-dum-ta-ta-ta-*deee*-dum. He
played it for three days? seven nights? ten thousandfold?

He shut off Schubert and saw books. The pages turned before
his eyes. He shouted out the lines. MEPHISTOPHELES: *Deine Schritte
durchs Leben nehmen, So will ich mich gern bequemen, Dein zu
sein, auf der Stelle. Ich bich dein Geselle.* I'm not the grandest
fellow or the best, But should you act at my behest, Join with me,
and make a common quest, I'm much at your disposal. Consider
my proposal: I'll make a pact with you. . . . FAUST: *Und was soll
ich dagegen dir erfüllen?* And what return am I to make? PASCAL:
233. *Que gagerez-vous?* What will you wager? *Oui; mais il faut
parier.* Yes; but you must wager. *Cela n'est pas volontaire: vous
êtes embarqué.* It is not optional: you are embarked. *Lequel
prendrez-vous donc? Voyons.* Which will you choose, then? Let's
see. *Puisqu'il faut choisir, voyons ce qui vous intéresse le moins.*
Since you must choose, let us see which interests you least. *Vous
avez deux choses à perdre: le vrai et le bien; et deux choses à
engager: votre raison et votre volonté, votre connaissance et votre
béatitude; et votre nature a deux choses à fuir: l'erreur et la misère.*
You have two things to lose: the true and the good; and two things
to wager: your reason and your will, your knowledge and your
happiness; and your nature has two things to shun: error and
misery. . . .

He had memorized only fragments of Dante, and those neither
from Purgatory nor Heaven but only from the first part, Hell. Yet
the fragments he knew he saw as lucidly on floating scraps of paper

as he had his Goethe and Pascal. In the deep, at the top of his lungs, he screamed them out.

> *Ma ficca li occhi a valle, ché s'approccia*
> *la riviera del sangue in la qual bolle*
> *qual che per vïolenza in altrui noccia.*

More quietly, after each triplet he paused, improvising a loose translation.

> But fix thy gaze below, and see nigh
> The river runs of blood, and steeped therein
> All men by brutish act made others sigh.

> *Oh cieca cupidigia e ira folle,*
> *che sí ci sproni ne la vita corta,*
> *e ne l'etterna poi sí mal c'immolle!*

> O greed so blind, O foolish sin
> That goads us to such evil ere we die
> And drowns us, everlasting, in chagrin! . . .

He resumed the composition of his University Essay, his impatient hand racing across the white foolscap, though with unusual worry about punctuation. When he finished a paragraph, he revised it carefully, tinkering with the commas, dashes, colons, semicolons, until he thought, This drives me mad.

▪ ▪ ▪

. . . and although my father built Northwood Hall long before my birth, until his death he continued to embellish it. Cardinal Wolsey's Hampton Court contained over a thousand rooms; Urban Northwood never aspired to that scale, scores of rooms would do, but with Wolsey as his inspiration he did create an oddly lovely rose-red castle of towers and chimneys, of courtyards and galleries, in gardens and woods that I miss terribly. Like Wolsey he was obsessed to leave behind a monument of himself, and intent to pile bricks and timber until the effect was grand enough to please him.

Throughout he maintained a style of almost pure Tudor; not for him the incongruous accretions of Henry VIII and (much later) of Sir Christopher Wren on Wolsey's original palace. Urban took particular care with glazed and mullioned windows, selecting the glass himself and hovering over the artisans as they poured the lead and fashioned the windows on successive floors. The house had several galleries, ambulatory spaces with long porticoes, halls with high windows on either side, looking to woods or symmetrical gardens.

Urban was no less painstaking with the gardens, supervising the terracing, the planting of the maze hedges, the erection of Greek statues and balustrades with great urns, making certain of the fulfillment of line and spacious concept. All was symmetry, the gardens neat and formal, the broad paths of gravel extending to the forest the lines of the house and the beds of brilliant flowers. Nothing could clash against the color of brick and timber. All must be congruent with the house—itself so symmetrical, chimneys cut of molded brick, gatehouses graced with toothy turrets and bay windows and, like the rest of the mansion, varying in color according to the light of day from faint red to purple-umber. The inside was as symmetrical: a succession of courts built on an axial line of arches that led to the various apartments.

The common rooms were sparely but finely furnished, with Isfahan and Damascene carpets, ewers, goblets, and candelabra of silver but none of gold; and Gobelin tapestries, old and rare, embroidered with fleurs-de-lis, but none of silk. Unlike Wolsey, Urban favored neither gold nor silk, no doubt agreeing with my mother that gold and silk were showy and therefore vulgar. Some walls he covered with red linen damask, but his favorite color he took from Wolsey—byse, a fierce light blue. The walls, the draperies, the very air, glowed with byse, as did my boyhood and as do my memories now of Northwood Hall.

You will remember that earlier I mentioned the simplicity of my father's rooms—the few appointments, the bucolic paintings on his walls, the Constables and Turners of sunlit lakes, hay wagons, snowstorms. Yet like Wolsey's, Urban's apartments were the largest and remotest in the house, reachable only by passing through various galleries and courtyards, and all the paintings hung on walls of lustrous byse. Like Wolsey fleeing the burdens of his office, Urban Northwood craved privacy and achieved it by withdrawing behind inner moats. I was alone with my father when he died.

As death approached, his rooms had been crowded. Cardinal Galsworthy, distraught by a cable from my mother, had rushed from Rome to his bedside. No governors, senators, or university professors attended Urban's final hours (Diana would not allow them in the house), but his bedchamber was mobbed by his little family, his physicians, his nurses, his mournful domestics, his gardeners, his grooms, his stableboys, a number of priests, monsignori, bishops, and (despite my mother's misgivings) several of his mysterious business associates, those men in dark suits.

Cardinal Galsworthy—vested to please Urban in his scarlet mozzetta and biretta, French lace and buckled shoes—administered the last rites in Latin. He was assisted by the bishops in their purple as they tendered the holy oils and a ciborium with the Blessed Sacrament. Behind them the priests and monsignori held aloft a silver crucifix, a thurible with burning incense, and a silver bucket with a sprinkler of holy water. Other priests held candles. As the rest of us knelt, we heard a choir singing the *Ave Verum* in the chapel. The room was a blazing forest of beeswax candles.

The Cardinal's prayers took very long, exhausting the dying man as his eyes danced. When it was time for Urban to confess, a bishop handed His Eminence a purple stole, and the Cardinal placed his ear against my father's mouth. The rest of us drew back, but it was not necessary to leave the bedchamber, it was so vast. The mob of us withdrew to the corners; I gazed at the byse walls, the color—I supposed—of the walls of Heaven.

After the confession, the Cardinal prayed against the power of the Devil, then dipped his thumb in holy oil and anointed Urban's eyes, ears, nose, lips, hands, and feet, invoking God's pardon for whatever sins he had committed by his senses. When he had received Communion, Urban lifted his feeble hand, waving everyone out but me. My mother in her mantilla and my brother Pius in his blue suit; the physicians and domestics and men in dark; the Cardinal in his scarlet, the bishops in their purple, the priests with their blazing candles—all bowed to Urban and in a whispering of robes backed out, leaving behind a stench of incense and burning wax. It was like the death of a French king.

I was alone with my father. His strength was ebbing, yet with all of it he held up his withered arms to embrace me. He could barely speak, but I knew his mind and as I watched his mouth I deciphered what he wished to say—something about a gift for Diana that so far she had refused.

"A publishing house, Father?" I asked.

He nodded.

"I'll try, Father. Mother has her own mind."

He sighed. I watched his mouth: "Avoid my little fault."

"I must."

He clutched at his sheets, drawing them aside and exposing his bare legs. They were atrophied from pain and lack of use, brown and hairy like a monkey's, full of little punctures from his medications. With his eyes he begged me for an injection. The nurses had neatly arranged his medicines on the night table, beside them the needles and syringes steeped in alcohol, but I refused. Instead, I kissed his face. He said, and very clearly, "Scratch my foot." I did, and he died.

With my thumb I closed the lids of his small, dark eyes; I covered his body with the white sheets and, my mind vacant, remained alone with the corpse for a quarter of an hour. When I withdrew to the antechamber and the waiting crowd, I noticed something odd.

The Duc de Saint-Simon has told us that hardly an instant after the death of Louis XIV, the entire court in their gowns and periwigs stampeded like a herd of cattle through the corridors of Versailles to the apartments of the dauphin, now Louis XV. Something faintly akin to that happened to me. Everyone, even Cardinal Galsworthy and my mother, gazed at me strangely. Throughout Northwood Hall, among the maids and footmen and lingering bishops, I sensed a mood of embarrassed deference. I could hardly enter a room but everyone stood up: I was no longer merely the dauphin.

Next morning, in our vaulted chapel, beneath the painting of St. Michael Archangel banishing Lucifer from Heaven, we said the funeral Mass. The choir, with a chamber orchestra, sang the Introit and the Dies Irae from Mozart's *Requiem*. Cardinal Galsworthy officiated, wearing not the white vestments of the new ritual but a black Roman chasuble and (by dispensation of the Pope) reciting the old liturgy in Latin. *Sed libera nos a malo*. But deliver us from evil. *A porta inferi*. From the gate of Hell. We interred my father only miles thence, in our own cemetery at the corner of Northwood Park, beneath a simple gray headstone. *Requiem aeternam dona ei, Domine. Et lux perpetua luceat ei. Requiescat in pace*. We did not publish an obituary until a fortnight after the burial.

We were in greater haste over Urban's will. Out of deference to Cardinal Galsworthy, anxious to return to Rome, within a few days of the interment the family gathered in mourning dress at the long table of the great hall to hear Mr. Burner III read the testament. (Burner II had long since deceased; Burner IV was still in law school.) At her insistence, Urban left nothing to my mother, as though his riches were so suspect Diana would not touch them. The will was an insult to my brother Pius—barely one million dollars in trust funds to the ugly duckling. Little Pius cried, "It's not fair!" As Burner III read out the bequest to the Holy See— fifty million dollars—the Cardinal's fine eyes narrowed. Possibly he and the Pope had expected more.

The balance, as you know, was bequeathed to me, with no regency for my mother and no other restrictions. With my boyish lack of tact, I asked Burner III, "How much am I worth?"

"Hard to say, Master Adrian," Burner III answered. "Your father's holdings were so vast, and we have hardly begun our inventory. It may be months before we know the total. Millions, tens of millions, keep turning up."

It was morning; sunlight flared through the mullioned windows. From a distant room beyond a courtyard came the laughter of servants. At the door other domestics, in white gloves, entered with silver trays, bearing pots of coffee, glasses of milk, bowls of butter, baskets of French bread, and tureens of fresh strawberries. I was fifteen years old. . . .

■ ■ ■

In that paragraph, Adrian's sphere dissolved, he ceased to float, and with a thump he lay again in his diarrhea, mucus, and blood. He felt his hunger. He wondered, Have they forgotten me? Will they leave me here forever?

Days (?) passed. They left him there, in his growing dread.

In the darkness he saw a descending flashlight, then heard a key turning in the grate. Two men reached down, retching from the smell, and lifted him from the Hole. He could not walk. They assisted him up the steps to the communal showers, where they helped him to wash the filth from his body. They handed him his clothes, freshly laundered, and fed him a plate of rice and beans. They said, "You have a visitor."

Ah, thought Adrian. At last. The American consul.

They took him to a clean room with metal chairs and a conference table. The visitor was Mexican.

"Señor Nort-wud? I am *Licenciado* Héctor Acosta Casanova, your attorney. Appointed by the court at Matablancos. At your service, Señor Nort-wud."

Licenciado Acosta Casanova was elderly; he wore a gray wig, a white mustache, and a merciful, wet smile. He said, "Oh, look at you, Señor Nort-wud. Are you a ghost? I saw you once, with the judicial police. What has happened to you? Shocking, shocking. Let me see. I know the director. I shall speak to the director. Yes, yes. *¡Hoy mismo!* This very day! Yes, yes. I shall protest personally to the director. Shocking, shocking. Are you a ghost?"

Adrian wasn't sure. His bowels rumbled from his dysentery, and even as he sat his knees wobbled. A man as fair as he did not need to shave often, but he had not shaved at all since his captivity because razors cost money. Now he had a beard, and his hair nearly touched his shoulders. He wondered, Have I lost half my weight? He asked, "What do you want?"

"I want to help you, Señor Nort-wud."

"I don't care whether I live or die."

"*I* care very much."

The lawyer's voice was high-pitched, like Burner IV's, yet soothing. Adrian replied, "Leave me alone, Don Héctor or whatever they call you. You're probably as corrupt as they are."

Don Héctor laughed. "If you mean that Mexican justice is corrupt, I agree with you, Señor Nort-wud. I will go much further and insist that all of Mexico is corrupt. Yes, yes. Let me tell you something. Corruption is the Mexican vodka. Every Mexican— well, nearly every Mexican—wants to drink it until he's drunk. Every politician is expected to grow rich in office, and he does. Every businessman is expected to cheat his workers, gouge his customers, defraud the tax collector, and he does. The trade unions and the civil service are extortion machines. I hardly know a clerk who does not steal from his boss, or a doctor who does not traffic in penicillin intended for the poor. Shocking. The police are a Mafia. Lawyers . . ."

"But you, Don Héctor, are the exception?"

"I do my best, Señor Nort-wud. Yes. You're here for heroin?"

"I'm innocent."

"I'm sure you are. How did the *jefe* incriminate you?"

"He had a bag of something."

"Sugar, probably, or talcum powder—though when it serves his purpose he uses real merchandise. A frightful man. The accusation will be difficult to disprove."

"I have no money, Don Héctor."

"I have been informed otherwise, Señor Nort-wud."

"Does it matter, since you're so honest?"

"Were it not for my children, I would defend you for nothing. My own fees will be most reasonable."

"What do you mean?"

"I'm worried for your health, Señor Nort-wud. Look at you. If you remain here much longer, you will indeed be dead. Shocking. Yes. In a few minutes, I shall make vigorous representations to the director. I'm confident I can guarantee that for three days—as the arrangements are worked out—you will not be mistreated further."

"No."

"You cannot be serious, Señor Nort-wud, nor can I carry on my conscience the burden of your continued torture. Here is my card. You may call me in Matablancos at any hour. Yes. I am always at your service."

Adrian tore up the card, tossed away the pieces. He shouted, "How well do you know the *jefe*?"

"My number is Matablancos two–three four six oh. May I suggest that you carry it in your head? Two–three four six oh. Yes. The *jefe*—can you imagine my shame?—is my nephew."

Don Héctor walked out. Adrian limped to the foul toilet, where again he emptied his bowels. It was dusk, beginning to rain, as he emerged from the mossy slime and rejoined the prison populace in the courtyard.

The poorest inmates rushed to him, rejoicing in his liberation from the Hole, voicing shock at his appearance, and begging him for hugs. "Don Adriano! . . . You've returned from the dead! Don Adriano! Don Adriano!" As he moved amidst his flock, embracing people, for a few moments he was happy. He felt . . . love: it was his new fortune.

The inmates' voices, festive when they started, turned to mutterings and anger as the word flew on wings throughout that place and more and more prisoners swarmed into the courtyard. "Don Adriano! . . . Don Adriano!" These were the young women whose infants he had delivered and nursed to health, and the older women after them, hurtling from their squeezed dormitories; the cripples from their barren infirmary, which was as rife with rats and cock- roaches; even the rich drug traffickers from their private air-conditioned rooms—all outraged by his ghostliness and screaming to touch him. Bodies jostled him; hands tore away pieces of his T-shirt and clawed at his flesh, eager for bits of it and drawing drops of his blood. "Don Adriano! . . . Back from the dead!"

From the roof the director of the penitentiary and Don Héctor at his side watched the mood of the prisoners as it rose toward riot, thrusting upward at their worried faces as the guards in their turrets loaded clips and belts of bullets into automatic guns. Beneath in the center of the courtyard, where the mob had hoisted him above its head, Don Adriano also saw the danger and struggled to arrest it, shouting, *"¡Calma! ¡Calma!"* and kissing outstretched hands. The courtyard throbbed. The guards aimed their guns.

The skies opened, releasing such a torrent of rain that the riot stopped. Adrian retreated to his wooden crate and crawled inside. Even in the downpour he heard the tap-tap-tap of an approaching cane. He raised his head outside the crate. "Freddy?"

He got out of the crate, leaning down to kiss the crippled youth. Freddy seemed more bent than before. The torrent lessened. Freddy looked up at Adrian's wasted face. He said, "Oh, Jesus, Ay-jay."

"I have no money, Freddy, and I'm too feeble to scrub floors. Could you beg a little, so I can eat?"

"Here's three bucks, Ay-jay. I'll beg some more."

"And some diarrhea medicine?"

"Sure."

"How's your pain, Freddy?"

"Killing me."

"Dear Freddy . . ."

"Can I have another kiss, Ay-jay?"

Adrian slept in his crate that night and throughout most of the morning. In the afternoon, he ate some bread and soup with Freddy's money. He returned to the crate and brooded on his riddle.

Never had he been thrust so close to the core of evil. Twice, during his trance in the Hole, he saw the back of Satan's head—covered with eyes, snakes crawling out of them. Now he confronted a choice that seemed as vile.

If he surrendered to their extortion, then the *jefe* and the magistrate and Don Héctor and the other malefactors would be encouraged to inflict their atrocities on endless victims after him, and he would help to entrench evil. Yet if he did not soon win his freedom, they would drain his life from him. They might smash his spine, and he would hobble thereafter down the path of life with his body bent like Freddy's and his back parallel to heaven.

He groped for justifications to pay the extortion. Classical theories of the lesser evil, elaborate syllogisms about good effects juxtaposed with bad effects, raced through him. What would Pascal have done? He thought, If I pay them money, and they want a lot, I will be guilty of terrible cowardice. *Oui; mais il faut parier.* Yes, but you must wager. Would I ever forgive myself? *Il faut choisir!* You must choose! Ah! he mused, would my cowardice be less odious if I paid them for more than my own liberty? What if I ransomed a few of the unfortunates in this madhouse? What if I ransomed Freddy? No, I cannot justify it.

He dozed off, still undecided.

Nor could he decide during the next two days. Freddy's diarrhea medicine did not work. He could not arrest his discharge of mucus and blood. On the third day he thought, Tomorrow they will resume the torture, then return me to the Hole. They jumped on my toes and they will jump on my hands and I will never paint again. In the evening, from a trafficker's telephone, he called Matablancos 2-3460. A machine answered. "This is the office of Licenciado Héctor Acosta Casanova. I am always at your service. Yes. Please leave a message when you hear the beep."

Beep.

Adrian: "Nort-wud here. Call Downsville five four six–oh two nine two and speak to Señor Ennis. E-n-n-i-s. Tell him to meet you tomorrow morning and to come to me in the afternoon. Emphasize secrecy."

Late next afternoon, a trusty led Adrian to the prison roof, reserved usually for the director and rich prisoners. It had a patio, deck chairs, and a bar. At a table with a beach umbrella sat Mr. Ennis. He said, "Sir? Oh, dear."

"Ah," said Adrian, "such a lovely view."

"Mr. Northwood? Is it you?"

"The river . . . The United States . . . How are my son and daughter at the Casa San Francisco?"

"Everyone is well, sir. However—"

"You look so sporty, Ennis."

"I . . . I'm trying tropical colors."

"I miss your three-piece suit. Oh, look. The stretch limousine in the parking lot? Must be the director's."

"No, sir, it's mine."

"Who's the young woman talking to your chauffeur?"

"My interpreter."

"She's pretty."

"Thank you, sir."

Adrian understood, and tried to imagine this lickspittle in the act of love. He asked, "You told nobody I was here?"

"Only Mr. Burner, sir."

"No one else must ever know."

"Here's your passport, sir."

"Where did you find it?"

"In your truck."

"How did you get on with Don Héctor?"

"The police chief and the judge participated in the meeting. Such sordid people. May I inquire, sir—how did they entrap you?"

"What are the terms?"

"The chief wants two hundred thousand dollars."

"Less than I thought."

"That is merely the beginning. There are substantial payments to be made to the judge, to the director of the Matablancos prison, and to the director here. Plus lesser payments to various associates of the chief, various personnel of the Matablancos prison, and various personnel of this penitentiary. Don Héctor Acosta Casanova wants fifty thousand for his services as intermediary. The total exceeds five hundred thousand."

"Pay them."

"But, sir, if I may say so, surely there must be a more appropriate alternative procedure."

"If there is, I'll be dead before you find it."

From a pocket of his jeans Adrian took out a list. He had worked on it all day, adding and deleting names. The first name was Freddy's; the others had been less easy to decide. Initially he intended a list of six. He thought, Can I be that selfish? The list grew to thirty names, forty names, until with anguish he reduced it. Several drug addicts were near death, but he scratched out their names. He thought, They *chose* death. His final list was of twenty names,

Freddy and a few other crippled men, but mostly pathetic women with sick children.

He said, "I want these people released with me."

"Sir," said Ennis, glancing at the list, "it will cost a king's ransom."

"Go back to Don Héctor and negotiate a deal. Deliver half of the money at noon tomorrow, the other half when I telephone you in Downsville to tell you that we're all free. I want to walk out of here within forty-eight hours."

"This is, may I protest, most unbecoming."

Adrian felt the stirrings of a temper tantrum. "You bombastic little clerk. You and your master—in your own way—are as corrupt as these Mexicans."

"Mr. Burner could use his connections in Washington. Our ambassador to Mexico . . ."

"*No!* It would reach the *media!!* It would upset my *mother!!!* Do you have fifty dollars?"

Two days later, all of the prisoners on the list were liberated, so suddenly that even Freddy had no chance to bid Adrian farewell. This saddened Adrian: he would miss Freddy. Yet it seemed to him better and more beautiful that neither Freddy nor the others should know who their liberator was. Adrian was the last to be liberated. As he emerged into sunshine, the dusty plaza in front of the penitentiary was thronged with dirty, hungry children. He wondered, Does it matter—on which side of the wall they live?

23

From the prison Adrian took a bus to the center of Reynuestro, where he bought an antibiotic for his dysentery. He checked into a cheap hotel and called Mr. Ennis, waiting by the telephone for his order to release the rest of the ransom and full of entreaties that Adrian leave Mexico. "Of course," said Adrian, "when I find Lázaro and my pictures."

That night, his dysentery eased. At daylight, he boarded another bus and returned downriver to Matablancos. In confinement he had brooded about his search and concluded that Susana knew more about Lázaro than she had been willing to reveal. Why had Lázaro gone to Susana to show her the pictures? Why was her photograph on the wall of his hovel?

He reached the brothel at midday, approaching it with caution to be certain he would encounter no policemen. He found Susana in her cabaña, asleep. When she turned to him and lifted away the covers, he discovered that her arms and face bore the blue traces of recent beatings. "Why?" he demanded.

"Because of you," she said. "The *jefe* would not believe we weren't lovers. Poor Feo. He was harder on you."

She lifted his T-shirt, kissing the wounds on his torso. As she did so he glimpsed their bodies reflected in the glass that covered the primitive painting of Christ's hands, only His hands, gripping His cross. He asked, "Who painted that picture?"

He did not hear her answer because during his beatings his

eardrums had been damaged and lately at intervals the world resembled a silent film. Most of the time the actors talked, but then
only their lips moved in the silent film and he had to wait a little
before the sound came back and he heard them clearly. He asked,
"Who painted that picture?"

"Are you deaf, Feo? Lázaro did."

"How long have you known Lázaro?"

"Since childhood."

"Is he your lover?"

Susana's lips moved.

"¿*Cómo?* Your husband?"

"My brother."

"Mother of God."

"Well, my half-brother. We had different fathers. My mother
never . . ."

"¿*Cómo?*"

". . . never married."

"Why didn't you tell me?"

"I had to protect him."

"Where is he?"

"God knows. He said he missed fishing. I gave him some money
and he headed south, with that donkey."

"You must have an idea."

"Tampico, maybe? He used to fish there. Our village, maybe?
He goes back sometimes. It's so far."

"Your village?"

"San Antonio del Río, south of Tampico, so far. It's not on
any map."

"I'll find it."

" . . ."

"¿*Cómo?*"

" . . ."

"Darling Susana, why don't you come with me?"

"The *jefe* might come after me."

"To a fishing village?"

"You'll never find Lázaro. I miss . . ."

"¿*Cómo?*"

Adrian walked to the Old Market, where he bought clean linen and a cardboard suitcase. In the evening, Mr. Ennis met him at the bus station and gave him fifty thousand dollars in new bills. The midnight bus to Tampico was packed full, so Adrian slept in a chair at the station. He missed his wooden crate. At dawn he decided not to wait for the next bus and walked to National Highway 101. His toes still hurt, the walk was hard, and he did not prosper as a hitchhiker.

From a ladder against a muffler shop I watched him standing at the roadside as cars and trucks rushed by under the dusty sun. It seemed to me that with his beard and long hair, the wrinkles of pain around his eyes, he had a slightly wild look. Hours passed before a truck stopped. As he climbed to the cabin with his cardboard suitcase he gripped his ribs, and I wished to cry out to him, "You're growing far too fond of the glamour of the poor."

PART VII

Fish

24

In Tampico, Adrian met Christ.

Or rather, he could have met Him but declined the honor. He had been walking along the Río Pánuco, lined with the huts of fishermen, looking for Lázaro, when he crossed a bridge and saw a man in an empty lot, picking through a rubbish heap.

Startled, Adrian paused, gazing at him from across the road. The man was barefoot, wore only the briefest underwear, and was otherwise naked. He was tall, well made, his arms and legs had no holes that suggested drug addiction, and his eyes, brown hair, and beard evoked paintings by El Greco. Adrian said aloud, "Why, that's Christ!"

Finding nothing in the rubbish, Christ sat on top of it, doing nothing. His shorts were pink and flimsy, like a woman's panties, nor could they wholly conceal his crotch. Adrian hesitated. He wished to approach Christ, offer Him clothes.

Tampico was an ugly city full of oil refineries and blue buses that coughed black smoke, but if it was ugly it was also rich, and the shops overflowed with fine things. Adrian might well have led Christ from the rubbish heap up dusty stairways in the open air to shops on the sides of hills, but for cloudy motives he did not. He walked away, changed his mind, returned to the dump, but Christ had vanished. For the rest of the day Adrian abandoned his search for Lázaro, returned to his hotel, and wept that he had not clothed Christ.

25

He had traveled several hundred miles from the Rio Grande to Tampico on the Río Pánuco and the Gulf of Mexico. For days, he haunted the shores of the river, mingling with fishermen, looking for Lázaro. The fishermen lived with their women and teeming children amid high grass and reeds in junky houseboats and wooden shacks and abandoned cars, chugging in old motorboats onto the polluted river with poles and nets, seeking meager harvests of silver fish and brown shrimp.

In prison Adrian had lost not only his clothes and books but his snapshot of Lázaro. Wandering from boat to boat and shack to shack, he asked the fishermen, "Have you seen Lázaro Flores Faustino? Has crosses tattooed on his forehead and carries a Mickey Mouse watch? When he drinks he drops the watch into his beer? I owe him money."

Empty stares. A fisherman said, "I know the bum. Haven't seen him lately, but give me the money and I'll watch it for him." One afternoon by the river Adrian encountered a little old woman stumbling beneath a burden of sticks. He lifted the sticks from her back and carried them to her shack, and she said, "Yes, I saw him. I remember the tattoos."

"Did he have a donkey?"

"Donkey? I saw no donkey. He had an old rowboat. Went out fishing alone in the mornings. Always drunk in the afternoons, shouting nonsense, throwing bottles at the river and the fish. He lived down there, in the grass, but that was . . . weeks ago? Had a big bundle of something. He spoke to me once."

"Why?"

"He wanted money."

"To get drunk?"

"He said, 'To go home.' "

At the bus station, Adrian asked the girl in the information booth how to reach San Antonio del Río. She unfolded a map: "I can't find it. Here's the Río San Antonio, and there's a town, Acalutla —so far."

Adrian took a bus another several hundred miles south, along the sea through Tuxpan, Poza Rica, and Papantla. The deeper he journeyed, the more radically the landscape changed. Gently the utter flatness of the Rio Grande Valley had sloped upward as he moved farther and farther from it: now mountains of mauve and darker velvet beckoned from the interior of the land above the coastal road. In the dazzling sunshine the sea became an Antwerp blue; along the shore the anger of the sea and wind had created sandbars and behind them the translucent green of myriad lagoons. After changing buses and hitching rides, Adrian reached Acalutla and the Río San Antonio.

San Antonio del Río, it seemed, lay yonder many miles downriver at the head of a peninsula that thrust into the sea. It had rained recently, the roads were washed out, so Adrian hired an old man and a motorboat. As he wound downriver, he reflected, Are not these the ravishing tropics? The river snaked like a twisting gorge through silent jungle: silent save for exotic birds—brilliant, huge-billed toucans; immense bevies of ivory doves; iridescent hummingbirds humming with their wings. Great turtles and alligators emerged from shallow waters to the shores of the river as though thirsty for the sun.

He glided past neglected ruins, ancient Totonac temples vanishing under vegetation. In the center stood a high pyramid, so pocked with openings of perfect squares that it resembled a vast beehive, fashioned no doubt before the rapacity of Cortés in some forgotten golden period a millennium ago. Today the temples were inhabited by turkey vultures, but as Adrian lamented such lost civilizations he glided on. Toads perched on rocks; enormous frogs climbed trees. The trees were of lush variety, mingled with palms and frond, hung with curtains of liana so dense that the sun could not penetrate and from afar the forest inward seemed as dark as a moonless night.

In late afternoon, he reached the mouth of the river and San Antonio del Río. It was a village with a dusty little plaza, dwellings of adobe brick and wooden shacks, a constabulary, a few shops, and a single paved road. At one end of the road stood a white adobe church, its roof caved in, at the other end a white adobe tavern, the Bar 69. San Antonio had no hotel, and no electricity. The hum of a generator suggested that Bar 69 was special, so Adrian entered it seeking refreshment.

Inside, fluorescent lamps sputtered, but Bar 69 was a murky place. Chairs and tables crudely chopped from wood and painted blue stood on cement, but the room beyond had an earthen floor. Mounted above the bar were the license plates of (stolen?) cars from Texas, Oklahoma, and Wisconsin. In a corner two young men flipped the rods and figurines of *futbolito*. They wore T-shirts, SURF MORE and BEER IS HIGHLY NUTRITIOUS. Adrian sat down at a table. A dumpy woman, of fading youth, emerged from a back room with an older gentleman, then sat with him at the next table as he zipped up his fly, lit a cigarette, and cried out for beer. A rough man appeared behind the bar, popping open bottles of cold beer. All eyes fixed on Adrian, as though startled by his blondness. He ordered a bottle of Corona beer and a bag of tortilla chips. The bartender asked, "Why are you here?"

Adrian weighed the question. His instinct told him that if he mentioned Lázaro in such a sealed village, then Lázaro would be forewarned and he would never find him. Better to hunt his prey alone, or wait until he had made some friends. He answered, "To fish."

"..."

"*¿Cómo?*"

"..."

"I'm looking for a room."

". . . no rooms . . . ," the bartender said.

SURF MORE walked over to Adrian. He was tall, with a mustache and a pleasant manner; his T-shirt was spattered with the entrails of fish. "I'm Arcadio," he said. "You can stay with me."

"*Vamos,*" said Adrian.

With his cardboard suitcase he followed Arcadio down dusty paths, through alleys loud with barefoot children, to a grove of bamboo and coconut palm that overlooked the confluence of the river and the sea.

The grove was a compound, really, almost a hamlet to itself. The habitations were wooden shacks with earthen floors, thatched on top with woven palm leaves. Women and girls with twig brooms were sweeping the dirt yard. Frond grew savagely, filtering the dappled sun that fell gently on numerous children.

The yard and shacks were busy also with other traffic: chickens, pelicans, and ducks; flea-infested kittens; and pigs that wandered from the compound to the sea. Flies buzzed. The yard was piled with buckets of metal and yellow plastic. A striped cat and a fat duck quarreled over a fish. Parrots perched on bamboo branches, talking.

The shacks exuded the scent of fish, frying in oil. At the doors stood bombs of butane gas, and bicycles. Inside the shacks, votive candles burned before statues of the Holy Virgin and the Sacred Heart and enchanted mounds of sticks, stones, and chicken bones. A battery radio sang mariachi music. Arcadio lived in the compound with his mother, married brothers, younger brothers, nephews, nieces, married sisters, and maiden aunts. The shacks lacked running water, but in the yard was a cement well. With a rope and bucket, Arcadio drew water, inviting Adrian to taste it, cool and sweet.

Beneath a bower of fern, the outhouse was an architectural marvel. It leaned like the Tower of Pisa, jerry-built of tin, bamboo branches, sheets of plastic, propped up by the trunks of trees and rubber tires; the wet air near it oozed a horrid stench. In another corner of the yard stood a little shack with a dirt floor, a wooden bed, and a mattress made of palm thatch. "My grandmother's," said Arcadio. "She died last month. You can live here alone."

"How much should I pay you?" Adrian asked.

"Whatever you please."

"Fifty thousand pesos? By the week?" It was about twenty dollars. Beyond lay the beach, lush with palm, littered with coconuts, and beyond them the curling waves, the brilliant sun, and the blue sea.

"That's far too much," Arcadio said.

"Half that, then?"

"Gracias. No es de lujo." It's nothing fancy.

"It's perfect," Adrian said.

26

And yet, for time suspended, Adrian had no hope of hunting Lázaro. He fell ill, living between his shack and the outhouse as dysentery again attacked him. Now it was compounded by violent vomiting, nor did the penicillin, metronidazole, and other antibiotics he had bought in bulk at Tampico do any good. Nor was the infection from the food of Arcadio's kitchen, since he could not eat. In his languor he treated himself as he had treated so many others, sipping a clear solution of boiled water, sugar, and salt simply to prevent his dehydration. As he lay on his bed of thatch, he was certain that he heard worms nibbling at his bowels. Indeed, when he was finished in the outhouse he gazed into the pit, moaning, "Oh me, do I see the beasts?"

At Tampico, he had struggled to resume his push-ups and running, without success. His ribs ached, at night stabbing at him, as did the bones of his left wrist, but he knew anatomy and as he probed the bones with his right hand he decided that in the torture they had been cracked, not broken. They'll mend, he thought, but he did not know what to think about his feet. His toes seemed better, yet despite his ointments the wounds on his soles would not quite heal; mere walking meant more pain. And despite the *jefe*'s assurances that the cattle prod would leave no marks, a burn lingered on his scrotum.

On the wall of his shack was a jagged mirror, but he had a horror of it. Finally he looked at his reflection and said aloud, "Oh me,

my eyes are hollow. Oh me, my hair and beard are much too long."
With his scissors and razors from Tampico he cut and shaved them,
only to be more dismayed. His cheeks were hollow. He heard
Diana's voice as clearly as he had heard his own. "The churlish
crease below your mouth is much sharper. Your radiance has vanished." He answered her aloud, "Oh, Mother, I'm not the man I
was when I fell into the hands of the *jefe*."

He did not complain, but the women of the compound grew
alarmed and began to fuss over him. They insisted that he eat,
feeding him shrimp broth, chicken broth, and on the third day
boiled white fish. He threw them up. They began again. In a week
he could hold down morsels of white fish, and from fish he progressed to coconut milk and small mixtures of mashed pineapple
and banana. The women bicycled to the mountains, where they
consulted a *curandero,* whom sophisticated people might call a
quack but whom the women revered for his mastery of benign
witchcraft. The *curandero* gave them medicinal herbs, such as Indians ate before Cortés, and as his dysentery eased, Adrian fancied
that the herbs did him good. The women washed his feverish body
with the cool water of the well.

In a fortnight his bowels felt better, but he remained feeble. In
his bones and feet he felt constant pain. Antibiotics were one thing,
opiates quite another: no little fault for him. Better to endure the
pain. His worst agony was getting through the night, lying in darkness between sunset and dawn on his bed of thatch. Since he had
no books, he reverted to reading the thousands of pages in his head,
even to the accents and the punctuation. He wanted to scream
them out, but whispered so as not to wake the compound.

MEPHISTOPHELES
Fasse wacker meinen Zipfel!
Hier is so ein Mittelgipfel,
Wo man mit Erstaunen sieht,
Wie im Berg der Mammon glüht.

Grasp my coat and grip it tight!
Here we reach a giddy height,

Where the mountain shows to view
Fires of Mammon flaming through.

In the lucidity of dawn he knew that his starvation in the penitentiary had caused chemical changes in his brain. Those mutations in their turn had produced his mystical experience: he floated. Such pain as now deserved more floating. He raised his whispers almost to a shout.

FAUST

Wie seltsam glimmert durch die Gründe
Ein morgenrötlich trüber Schein!
Und selbst bis in die tiefen Schlünde
Des Abgrunds wittert er hinein.

Yon glimmers vale and precipice
In eerie dawn, whose deadly glow
Lies lurid on the black abyss
And lights the chasms far below. . . .

He did not float, and his pain sharpened. Eventually he dozed off. In his dream, all jellyfish dissolved and he floated alone above the planets, gazing down at the roof of Heaven, the color of byse.

He woke well before daylight. He heard Arcadio and his brothers rising from their beds, chattering, gathering their nets, pushing their boats down across the sand into the river and the sea. When he returned from the sea in daylight, Arcadio came to Adrian's shack with a green net slung over his shoulder. He said, "Don Adriano, you'll never get better if you stay in bed."

"Arcadio . . . ?"

"We're going out again. Do you want to fish?"

"Fish?"

He thought, The fish cannot make me worse. As he stumbled with Arcadio to the shore, the fisherman said, "Maybe you should go back. You're so weak."

"Is God still angry with me?"

Yet Adrian felt refreshed by the spray of salty water against his face as he sat in the prow of the motorboat and, with Arcadio and several of his younger brothers, headed from the estuary out to sea.

Arcadio sat aft, by the outboard motor, tending the tiller as the boys attended to the fish. They used rods and bait sparingly, making their big catches with nets of green nylon attached to bobbing cork buoys and unraveled to a length that seemed to reach the horizon. These fishermen rose each morning an hour before dawn, dressed by the light of kerosene lamps, and hastened to the sea to cast their nets. Thereafter throughout daylight they journeyed back and forth to shore and ocean, harvesting their catches and again casting their nets.

In the deep sea, they caught mostly striped yellow and orange fish and bigger silver and golden fish, calling them variously *ronco* and *sierra cason, mojara* and *guachinango,* names that Adrian wished he knew in English and never did. When they had drawn in their nets, piling them so high the boat seemed swathed in green mist, they attended to the catch, throwing back to the sea whatever fish were too small and eviscerating the fish they kept. The boys donned rubber aprons and worked swiftly at chopping blocks with cheerful skill. With sharp knives they slit open the bellies of the fish, and with their copper fingers they plucked out the pink entrails.

To Adrian the sun and salty air seemed therapeutic, diminishing his pain as he accompanied the fishermen to sea day after day and shared their work. The yellow fish waiting to be eviscerated had a death rattle, too eerily human, a loud macabre gurgling sound as they gasped through their gills and mouths and gave up life. Mistakenly at first when he cleaned fish Adrian chopped off their fins and heads. Arcadio rebuked him, but he learned quickly, and he could judge which fish to keep and which still belonged to the ocean. In the afternoons, Adrian packed fish into a great rubber sack, lifted the burden to his back with a sling around his forehead, and carried it barefoot miles along the beach to market. Arcadio insisted on paying him a wage, usually a dollar or two a day, according to the catch. Adrian felt immensely proud of those wages.

The fish market was a tin shed, where amid much shouting and confusion the fish were heaped on counters, weighed, packed in ice, and shipped to Mexico City to be eaten. Adrian hoped that in the market he would find Lázaro, for if Lázaro had come home to go fishing, would he not need to sell his fish? He did not see him. Adrian had bought binoculars in Tampico; now whenever he went seaward with Arcadio he scanned the other fishing boats for Lázaro's tattooed head. Along the shores of the Río San Antonio, men, women, and children stood hip-deep in high reeds and shallow waters dredging for shrimp and prawns and blue crabs, but Lázaro was never with them.

Adrian's dysentery returned, less harshly. In his distress he hurried to Arcadio's sisters, begging for herbs. They had no more, so that afternoon he borrowed Arcadio's bicycle and pedaled inland to the mountains, looking for the *curandero*.

The women called that master of white witchcraft Padre Pablo, though he was not a priest and never had been. "He studied for the priesthood," the women had explained, "but—he told us so —his flesh was weak. He left the seminary and took a wife." Adrian had trouble finding Padre Pablo's house. It was high on the side of a mountain, reachable only by dirt paths that the morning rains had turned to mud. Before his torture Adrian might easily have ascended the paths without getting off his bicycle, but today he did well to push the bicycle up the slope until near its summit he happened on a goatherd, who pointed to the Padre's house.

It was a large, rambling habitation on a jutting cliff, built variously of rotting wood and adobe blocks, surmounted by a thatched roof. Adrian penetrated a fence of sticks, crossed the muddy yard, and stuck his head through an open door, crying out, "*¡Hola!*"

Candles flickered; a ceremony seemed to be in progress. A young woman and her infant child knelt before a humming, mumbling old man, who in circles above their heads swung a smoking thurible of fragrant incense. Deeper in the dark room, an old woman put a finger to her lips, commanding Adrian to be silent, then beckoned him to enter.

The interior was bizarre, a mixture of bucolic domesticity and Baroque Spanish shrine. Near the door was a sort of altar, framed in a bedpost wrapped with red ribbon and corn husks. The altar was a table covered with linoleum and littered with votive candles, rocks, icons of the Virgin, bottles of liquid, bottles of herbs, and bunches of overripe bananas. Nearby stood a life-sized statue of St. Anthony of Padua in his brown Franciscan habit, holding the Infant Jesus. At the end of the room stood a white stove and a swinging bed; the walls were covered with pots and pans. Across the dirt floor, roosters and geese waddled in and out.

Padre Pablo was ancient, with skin of brown parchment, a brief white beard, and hair of bleached straw. He was robed in a black soutane, not a simple priest's but a bishop's soutane, with a shoulder cape and purple trimmings, threadbare, however, and out at the elbows. On his feet were a pair of green Adidas sneakers. Adrian imagined Cardinal Galsworthy in senile retirement. As Padre Pablo hummed and intoned his prayers, it became evident from his supplications that the young woman had a tumor in her stomach and her tiny daughter was sick with fever. Adrian hoped that Padre Pablo might do them good, for though Acalutla and San Antonio had public clinics, their shelves were bare because the bureaucrats and politicians stole the medicines and sold them for cash. The poor made do with witch doctors; indeed preferred them.

Swinging his blazing thurible higher and higher, Padre Pablo grew more fervent in his prayers. ". . . *y oración y ensalmo para susto . . .*" . . . and the prayer and incantation to cast out fright: woman of God, child of God, I heal you by invocation of the name of God, His Son, and the Holy Ghost. Three distinct Persons and one true God, by Saint Roque, by Saint Sebastian, and by all the virgins of Heaven, by Your most glorious Passion, Resurrection, and Ascension, deign to heal this woman and this child afflicted with whatever evil, fright, or fever by the intercession of Your holy Mysteries. "*Cuánto amante es Jesus, cuánto amante es Jesus, así sea, Amén.*" He added a psalm from the Latin Mass for the Sick: "*Miserere mihi, Domine . . .*" Have mercy upon me, O Lord, for I am afflicted: my eye is wrathful, and my soul, and my belly: my life is wasted in grief, my years in sighs: my strength ebbs in my poverty, and my bones ache. He concluded with his blessing, "*en el nombre del Padre, del Hijo, y del Espíritu Santo.*"

As the benediction wafted with the smoke of incense over the afflicted woman's head, Adrian knelt down in the backwash. He hoped that it might help to soothe his dysentery and his cracked bones, though he did not quite pray. He thought, At last, I am living in the eighteenth century.

Padre Pablo handed the woman a vial of herbs; she dropped some pesos into a jar and, bundling her child, went out, singing. The *curandero* sighed, and hummed. "Hmmm, hmmm, hmmm. Poor woman. She'll die soon. I never claimed I could cure cancer. But the herbs should help the child. Hmmm, hmmm, hmmm."

Adrian said, "Padre Pablo, I am—"

"I know who you are. Every woman from San Antonio talks of your golden head. You are Don Adriano."

"I'm afraid so."

"And your dysentery?"

"I need more of your herbs."

"Hmmm, hmmm, hmmm." He rummaged among the jars on his altar, extracting herbs and seeds. "Don't take too many," he cautioned, pinching the medicines into vials. "This sarsaparilla should help you, and isn't the orange annatto pretty? Hmmm, hmmm. Be stingy with this ipecac. Sprinkle the medicine on coconut milk, drink it before you go to bed, and come back to me next week. Here's a bit of belladonna lily, a little mangrove bark; use them prudently; small doses will do no harm. Hmmm, hmmm."

Adrian took out fifty thousand pesos.

"Too much," said Padre Pablo. "Ten thousand is plenty."

"May I use your outhouse?"

"You are most welcome. Hmmm, hmmm."

When he returned from the outhouse, Adrian asked impulsively, "Do you know Lázaro Flores Faustino?"

" . . ."

"*¿Cómo?*"

" . . ."

"*¿Cómo?*"

"*Madre de Dios,* so young, so fair, and going deaf. Have you been beaten?"

"Rather badly."

From the depths of the room, the old woman and two younger women approached Adrian and kissed his ears. "*La señora*," said Padre Pablo. "My wife. My daughters. Would you like some herbal tea?"

"My stomach's angry with me. Could we walk outside?"

It was late afternoon: the sun was a large apricot. From the high cliff, Adrian and Padre Pablo for a moment meditated together on the peaceful kingdom at their feet. The mountain was rich with myrtle and olive trees, rolling down to the flatness of the coast, sensuous with palm and green lagoons. Adrian could see the spires of Acalutla to the west, the devouring jungle north and south, the sinuous river, and at the river's mouth the boats, the sea, and the eternal gauzy blue where the ocean met the sky. Down there it was wet and hot; up here the air was benignly cool. At first Adrian felt refreshed, but suddenly he turned to a tree and vomited behind it, as Padre Pablo hummed. When Adrian was finished the old man said, "Strange that you should mention Lázaro. I dreamed of him recently."

"What was he doing in your dream?"

"Falling."

"Through space?"

"Into water and blood."

"Why, Padre, he *did*—at Matablancos."

"An evil place."

"How long have you known Lázaro?"

"Since his infancy. Hmmm, hmmm."

He led Adrian to lower ground; he shuffled a bit, suggesting rheumatic bones. They descended to a grove of olive trees with an adobe shrine, a tiny white chapel with a façade toothy at the top, an open arch, and little perforations in the walls to admit light. Inside were wooden benches, a lumpy plaster altar, and simple icons of the Virgin. "I am the guardian of this place," said Padre Pablo. "It used to be that we had a real priest, but there are so few priests now. He was a good priest, though he lived with a woman. His sons and grandchildren are all over this mountain, goatherds mostly. He died so long ago. My first wife died the year he did, so I married his widow. You just met her—*la señora*. Hmmm, hmmm."

Padre Pablo sat facing Adrian on a bench, but his voice was elsewhere, reliving abandoned time—as it used to be when the people had a real priest and in the dark nights they covered the slopes of the mountain with processions to the Virgin, hymns, fireworks, and flaming candles. They loved the prayers in Latin because they could not understand them. The people had a thirst for mystery, then and now. Sometimes as it used to be a peasant girl might think she saw the real Virgin, and who knows? perhaps she had. Today the real priests would rail against such silly superstition, and how sad! how sad! that so much in Holy Church had changed. "Hmmm, hmmm. Why, only the other day, the priest in Acalutla called me an old quack. So be it. It's better here, high on the mountain, and down there, in San Antonio, because we have no plumbing, no electricity, and no science. The people are happy. They thirst for mystery. Hmmm, hmmm."

He rose, walked to the chapel wall, and, as though seeking some-thing, traced it with his fingers. It seemed to Adrian that the old man might be going blind. The old man said, "Look here, Don Adriano, Lázaro's paintings." Indeed as Adrian looked closer he saw the outlines and faint colors of murals painted in a childish hand—heads of the Virgin and the saints, Stations of the Cross—crude but even in their faded state suggesting a bizarre talent. "I made the paints," Padre Pablo continued, "from plant dyes. Pity, I did not mix them properly. Look at them today, peeling, fading; in a year they'll be invisible. When he painted them, Lázaro was only ten. Such a lovely child . . . before he turned bad."

"When did he turn bad?"

"When his father abandoned his mother."

"I must find him, Padre Pablo."

"Why?"

"He stole some paintings from me. They may not be any good, but my soul is in them."

"Lázaro stole? Hmmm, hmmm. He may be bad, but he never was much of a thief."

"I wish him no harm, Padre. I want only my pictures. I've the feeling he is near."

"So do I. I dreamed that too. Where have you looked for him?"

"Everywhere in San Antonio—in the sea, the fish market, the shrimping fields . . ."

"Perhaps you have looked in the wrong places."

Adrian followed Padre Pablo up to his cliff. The old man said, "Look down there, at the river. I cannot, any longer, see quite so far. Inland, do you see a little tributary? That is the Río San Antonio Pequeño, but the common people call it the Río Diablo. It's not really a river, more of a swamp. People live there, but most fishermen are afraid of it. When his father abandoned his mother, Lázaro went there to weep, and fish."

"I'll find him."

"I didn't say he was in the swamp. My dreams . . ."

"I'll visit you soon. Until then, I beg you, Padre Pablo, dream. Dream and dream of Lázaro."

"Hmmm, hmmm, hmmm."

Next day, Adrian asked Arcadio to take him to the Río Diablo. Arcadio shuddered. "I'd do anything for you, Don Adriano," he said, "but not that. Not down the Río Diablo. That swamp is full of snakes, bats, and evil."

Near the fish market that afternoon, Adrian bought an old motorboat and—alone—embarked for the Río Diablo. As he penetrated inland along the Río San Antonio, he passed bleak, uninhabited little islands and verdant pasture of the mainland, where cows and horses grazed, but they were the last congenial creatures of his quest. Miles upriver, the waters forked. He glided southward into the narrow tributary.

Soon he was engulfed in a great moist silence and savage vegetation. The river dwindled, growing ever more narrow as it merged with swamp, ending altogether when the gnarled branches of mangrove trees thrust down into the water with such density that further passage was impossible. The trees seemed turned upside down, their roots suspended in the air and their branches aspiring not toward the sky but to the center of the earth, forming myriad new trunks. Adrian tethered his boat and stepped into the thicket.

The thicket had a terrifying beauty. As he stood on a branch, clinging to another to secure his balance, he marveled at the profusion of liana and moss; black orchids blossomed among the lichen even as he watched. Snakes hung from branches; a green iguana that with its tail of rings stretched six feet long stared at Adrian from a branch above his head. When Adrian moved, only very slightly, the iguana took fright and plunged into the swamp. His next movements seemed miraculous: he *walked* on the water, dashing across it upon his hind limbs, his body and his tail upright in the murky air, then vanished into caverns of mangrove.

Adrian ventured more deeply into the thicket, but his vigor had been sapped by his illness, and his progress was halting and slow. He needed a machete, but as he progressed from branch to branch he had only his bare hands to thrust aside the curtains of vine and frond; the deeper he penetrated, the less the sun shone through and the darker the thicket became. Yet he kept his head and carefully tied vines along his way into looping knots as markers lest he lose himself in that labyrinth.

Finally he heard voices. The thicket thinned; in less dense vegetation, houses on stilts teetered above the swamp, dwellings of bamboo and thatch huddling all together, with tiered openings of perfect squares that resembled beehives and crude Totonac temples. Old men, younger men, barefoot, clad in raglike shirts and short pants, hopped in and out of the squares like bees. In San Antonio, Adrian had heard vaguely of these marsh men, *caballeros del pantano*, knights of the swamp, vagabonds, criminals, romantics such as himself, who yearned somehow to cast off the modern world and regress to happier beginnings; living on jungle fruits and the flesh of savage animals; for pesos catching snakes for their skins, alligators for their hides, iguanas for their white, sweet, tender meat; and fishing for exotic eels.

Adrian hesitated. He wished to cry out, *Lázaro! Lázaro!*, but he feared the swamp men, imagining that they might kill him or at the least that they would hide his prey. He lingered on the edge of the colony as the skies darkened and rain began to fall. He knew that in the drenching rain the jungle became as black as night; dreading now the swamp men, now the darkness, he retreated through the jungle toward his boat.

As he groped toward the Río Diablo, the forest roared beneath the torrent. Light no longer touched even the ceiling of the thicket; vampire bats, as though thinking it was night, ceased to hang from branches, opened their wings, and fluttered past his head. In the darkness he lost his way, unable to find the knotted vines he had left as markers. Then he saw one, yet as he reached out it was not a vine but a dangling snake. In terror he flailed headlong through the thicket, desperate and exhausted, until at last by unknowing luck he happened on the Río Diablo, upstream. Painfully he made his way over mangrove branches until he found his boat, half full of water. He hastened home to San Antonio, uncertain of his next excursion down the Río Diablo.

During the next days, his courage was not tested. The rains grew so fierce, the waves so high, that all commerce stopped on the Río San Antonio, and fishermen were afraid to fish. Suddenly the clouds would clear and the sun shone brilliantly; as unpredictably, the skies blackened and the torrents resumed. Oddly, the dampness seemed to blend with Padre Pablo's herbs to improve Adrian's health; his dysentery subsided; he gained a little weight. The rains turned Arcadio's compound to a pudding of mud.

Unwilling any longer to wade through mud to his bed, Adrian decided to pave the earthen floor of his shack. He borrowed Arcadio's wheelbarrow and visited the little market in the village, returning with tools and bags of cement.

Cement. He had learned to lay pavement at Downsville, but not well. Struggling to remember the correct proportions, he mixed cement, sand, gravel, and water in the wheelbarrow and, with his trowels and hoes, laboriously laid the floor. The result was lumpy and took days to dry, but Arcadio's sisters were enchanted. They asked, "Will you do that for us?"

Cement. As he paved much of the compound, neighbors came

to watch. It occurred to him as he worked that wood or cement beneath his feet were givens of life he took for granted, yet the great multitude of the tropics lived in dirt. The neighbors asked, "Will you do that for us?"

Cement. Soon Adrian became a familiar figure in the village, buying bags of cement at market and pushing his wheelbarrow down muddy paths to shacks with earthen floors. Everyone told him, "We have our pride. We'll pay you."

"When?" asked Adrian, his ribs stabbing as he added wire-mesh barriers to doorways against scorpions, which bit children.

"Next month."

"Please don't forget! I need the money!"

Cement. In his bare feet and shabby clothes, his hair and beard growing long again, pushing his eternal wheelbarrow, Adrian became also a figure of fun. Padre Pablo—or, more probably, his señora—had told Arcadio's maiden aunts that Adrian was looking for Lázaro: within a day everyone in the village knew it. When inbred half-wit children saw him approaching with his wheelbarrow, they threw mud and stones at him, shouting, "Lazar-O! Lazar-O! Lazar-O!" Adrian reflected, Why do I remain here? I'll never find him. "Lazar-O! Lazar-O! Lazar-O!" Yet something held him, not least the demands for cement floors. The women of the village flocked to Adrian. Whenever he emerged from a hovel, he found women in the road, waiting to run their dark fingers through his fair hair, nor did he protest, since it gave them pleasure. At night, as compensation for his labors, young men invited him to the Bar 69.

He disliked bars. However, the nights were long, San Antonio had no true diversions, and from boredom he began to frequent Bar 69. Guillermo, the rough bartender, owned not only Bar 69 but half the village, since so many of his customers had no money and drank on credit. Weekends were worst, when the bar stayed open until daylight and the men drank beer and cheap brandy without stopping.

Once drunk, they seemed, if that was possible, even more uncouth than their compatriots in the bars of Matablancos. Not enough to squirt lemon juice into their beer; they spat on the floor. They talked ceaselessly of women, of their own reserves of semen, of aphrodisiacs from the sea. They engaged in howling quarrels over *ostiónes,* oysters, and whether eating *ostiónes* helped or hindered their ejaculations.

Ejaculations!

Everybody hated Guillermo, never more than now. Until recently he had provided not just cold beer but the refreshment of his back room, where the dumpy woman of dubious youth entertained gentlemen; but her mother fell ill in Tampico, and she deserted San Antonio. "Where's the new girl?" the young men roared. "She'll be here any day," Guillermo kept promising, but the days passed and the new girl did not appear. Curious about the back room, Adrian paid a visit during the interregnum; it had no bed, only a wooden chair, a dripping tap, and some dirty towels.

Adrian entered Bar 69 one evening amid considerable excitement. A pair of youths were in the corner, flipping the rods of *futbolito;* a fellow fed coins to the jukebox, which could play but one song, something about a single rose that grew on the far side of the moon, incessantly. Other youths swigged bottles of beer as they queued by the door of the back room, impatient for the services of the new girl. Finally all of the men were serviced, and the new girl emerged, walking across the earthen floor onto the cement beneath the fluorescent lamps and the American license plates. It was Susana. Adrian sipped his Corona beer and said, "I've never seen such a lovely dress."

27

Indeed her dress was lovely—of pastel cotton, soft blue and creamy white, with yellow tulips and pink butterflies printed on it. There were slight puffs at either shoulder, little bows above her bare elbows; the waist was tight, favoring her slim hips, but the skirt reached modestly beneath her knees, and the bodice demurely almost to her gracious neck. Susana sat down with Adrian and said, "Thank you, Feo. I bought it in Tuxpan."

She wore no make-up, nor did she need any, though her ears had tiny pearls. Her auburn hair wound languidly in tresses over her right shoulder nearly to her taut breasts. She smoked no marijuana; her green eyes were clearly focused on Adrian's blue ones, but her high color had a blemish, a thin bandage across her cheek. Adrian asked, "Why did you leave Matablancos?"

"The *jefe* beat me once too often. I spent two weeks in Tuxpan, recovering."

"And yet, thank God, you're home."

"I had to come home, Feo. I knew you'd be here."

"Darling Susana . . ."

As they conversed, new young men kept approaching the table, requesting her service. She asked them, "Will you buy me wine?" Protesting, they paid Guillermo three thousand pesos for each glass of sparkling wine, and in the middle of her sentences she broke off with Adrian to withdraw to the back room. As he waited, he tasted her sparkling wine, yellow soda water. She returned to Adrian and resumed conversing as though they had not suffered a moment's interruption. She stroked his hair and said, " . . . "

"*¿Cómo?*"

"Poor Feo, you're deaf. Are you still in pain?"

"Much of the time."

"It hasn't hurt your looks. In Matablancos, you were too fine. Here, I adore your hollow cheeks and your burning eyes. *Eres si bello, Feo.*" You're so beautiful, Ugly.

"Have you seen Lázaro?"

"No."

"And the *jefe*? He won't come after you?"

"He's bound to, eventually."

"God! What will he do?"

"Kill me."

Outside, the night ranted with rain and storm. Adrian waited until nearly daybreak, and as the rain subsided escorted Susana to her home. She lived, not near Bar 69, but down long dirt paths, much closer to the sea. Her home was tiny, a lonely wooden shack, perched on a mound of black sand beneath coconut palms overlooking the estuary. Inside, she lit a kerosene lantern and her votive candles. She had laid down thatch to hide her dirt floor, and her rude appointments were immaculate, not least her icons of the Virgin and Lázaro's painting of Christ's hands, only His hands, gripping His cross. As the sun rose, thrusting stabs of light through the little window, Adrian for the first time studied the painting.

Lázaro could hardly draw, knew little of anatomy, so his rendering of the hands was crude and childish. The colors were somber, yellowish wrists and long fingers grasping a thick fragment of wood of the deepest brown. Adrian was intrigued by the vitality of the fingers gripping the cross, a clinging—desperate—strength, and finally he had no doubt of the painting's remarkable raw power. He asked Susana, "Did Lázaro paint this before or after he went bad?"

"Long after," Susana said.

Thenceforth Adrian avoided Bar 69 and saw Susana in the afternoons at her shack or by the sea. He pretended to be blasé about her evening traffic in the bleak back room, but it saddened him, and she knew it from his eyes. From odd remarks he deciphered eventually her devotion to her craft. She loathed the life she led, but early in her adolescence, beneath moonlit palms there on San Antonio beach, she received the first jerk of warm, thick fluid into herself. The sensation lasted but an instant, yet with all the horrors of whoredom, she was driven to seek the instant endlessly. At the core of her she was a whore because—only for that instant—she enjoyed the work.

Otherwise she was constantly alone, seeming to have no friends save Adrian and wanting none. During the rains, sandbars by the estuary had nearly joined, forming a new lagoon; in late afternoon, wearing sandals and a denim skirt, a green nylon net slung over her shoulder, she went there to fish. As the sun set, through twilight until dusk, she stood in the water to her knees and cast her net. Of an evening, not finding her at home, Adrian walked out to the lagoon to help her fish.

Their catch was meager, but as darkness lowered, Adrian emptied the net into her plastic bucket, and they wandered back across the beach, laughing, holding hands like lovers. The sky was ablaze with stars. Soon they were in a grove of palm, lying together among fallen coconuts on a bed of fronds. As Adrian hovered over her, Susana placed her head against a coconut, opened his jeans, pulled them down, and kissed his stomach. He felt a tingling breeze blowing from the lagoon against his unclad buttocks, and as he began to float he remembered Rome.

He remembered rooms. He saw walls. He saw walls of red damask. He saw walls of green damask. He saw gilded armchairs and blazing chandeliers. He saw busts of Roman emperors and busts of Barberini cardinals and sculpted lions crouching on marble floors.

His hotel was the Hassler, where Mr. Burner III had arranged his lodgings in the regal suite, overlooking the church of Trinità dei Monti, the obelisk of Pius VI, and the Spanish Steps. Adrian was sixteen, on holiday from his school in Normandy; his father had been dead not quite a year. The season was winter, soon after Christmas, unusually cold.

Early on a brilliant morning, he hurried from the Hassler in a Savile Row overcoat, woven of tweed, trimmed with fur, past the obelisk of Pius VI (Pontifex Maximus) and down the Spanish Steps to an appointment with a friend. The distance was not short, but he loved the gusts of frigid wind against his face as he strode with his swift, boyish gait past the Palazzo Barberini through the Piazza della Repubblica to the Piazza dei Cinquecento and that immense palace of concrete and glass, Stazione Termini, the railroad station.

A crowd had gathered on the broad sidewalk before the Stazione, believing that a film was being shot because a man of patrician appearance, in flowing costume, paced back and forth, reading a breviary. In Rome, where cardinals were (nearly) as commonplace as altar boys, the sight of yet another would never in the course of things cause heads to turn, but this Eminence was singular. Tall and elegant, he disdained the broad-brimmed black hat favored by the common run of clergy and broadcast his cardinalhood by wearing his scarlet biretta upon his silver curls; against the cold he wore a long black cape, but in the wind it billowed and betrayed a lining that was crimson, the color of his socks above his archaic buckled shoes. Vagrants approached him, begging for money; when he handed them paper lire, they genuflected on the pavement and kissed his ring. From the periphery Adrian watched and thought, He got the money from my father.

Standing there, he caught Cardinal Galsworthy's eye. The Cardinal hastened to him, crying, "Adrian! Beloved child! At last. You look so well. Aah, I love your high color!"

"Less high than yours, Lord Cardinal." Adrian laughed, kissing his icy sapphire but not bothering to genuflect.

"Ha-ha! I asked you to meet me here because I've things to show you. Come along, dear child, and watch your purse. This is Rome's worst neighborhood, full of pickpockets."

Cardinal Galsworthy guided him down a teeming street alongside the Stazione into the Via Gioberti, heaving with old women hawking lottery tickets, espresso bars, cheap trattorias, fast-food counters, money changers, derelicts, vagabonds, kinky-haired North Africans, and, even at that hour, aging streetwalkers standing in doorways, shivering in the wind, wearing faces that were painted masks. They emerged suddenly into a sunny piazza, where without prompting from His Eminence Adrian recognized Fuga's balconied Baroque façade of St. Mary Major. As they entered the basilica the Cardinal whispered, "This is my titular church."

A choir chanted a melody of Palestrina's; on the high altar and at side chapels, several Masses were in progress. Nuns and porters rushed to their Titular, bowing, kneeling, grabbing for his ringed hand, but as patrician cardinals were wont to do, he barely glanced at them, mechanically extending his sapphire to be kissed and, without missing a step of his noble gait, walked on. He led Adrian to a chapel on the Epistle side, where as steep stairs descended he paused before a niche and a glass sarcophagus: it held the body of a dwarf.

"This is Saint Pius V," the Cardinal said. "Excommunicated Elizabeth of England." He suppressed a chuckle. "Condemned her to the flames of Hell."

Adrian gazed at the dwarf, vested as a pope in white, velvet, ermine, with crimson slippers on his tiny feet. He thought of his father, as gnomish on his deathbed, and half expected the dwarf to demand of him, "Scratch my foot." As the Cardinal crossed himself and knelt to pray, Adrian fled the basilica in terror.

On the street, the Cardinal asked, "Did I frighten you, dear child? What were you thinking?"

"Of my father," said Adrian.

"Your father." The Cardinal seemed as troubled, less willing to say why. He asked, "Do you remember, Adrian, that your father entrusted me with your education?"

"He did not mention it in his will, Your Eminence."

"Quite true—but you know it to be so, and I mean especially your moral education."

Yet he fell silent as they walked up the Via Merulana toward the Viale del Monte Oppio. Approaching a park with the ruins of ancient temples, they encountered Africans. The sidewalks swarmed with Africans, their faces blacker than ebony and slashed with tribal scars. Strewn endlessly on the sidewalks and the frozen grass were beads and trinkets and ebony figurines, all for sale, but

Adrian saw no buyers. The carvings were of pygmies with heads like Minotaurs, puffed-up bellies, conical navels that drooped to their knees. "Senegalese," said the Cardinal of the craftsmen, "Ethiopians, Somalis . . . they have nothing to eat."

"Nothing to *eat?*" Adrian marveled. "I've never known anyone with nothing to eat!"

The Cardinal led him from the boulevard down a side street, into a makeshift building of wood and tin and a small bare room where veiled nuns with ladles stood before steaming pots, serving soup to Africans. Scores of Africans squeezed in and out, crouching on linoleum in the corridors to eat oranges, loaves of bread, and bowls of lentil soup. Touched, Adrian asked, "Who pays for this?"

"You do," the Cardinal said.

They continued their stroll, down the Viale del Monte Oppio until they came to a park on the Colle Oppio, Opium Hill, overlooking in the cold sun the Colosseum and the Arch of Constantine. The Cardinal sat on a stone bench, Adrian beside him, tingling with excitement since civilization itself seemed to sit at his feet. He said, "I . . . I can't quite believe the beauty of this, Eminence. The Colosseum, where emperors fed Christians to the lions, and the Arch of Constantine, the first emperor to become a Christian. Thank you, Eminence, for bringing me here, *grazie, grazie, Eminenza, grazie tante!*"

"*Prego.*" The Cardinal smiled, rather sadly. He said, "You are a precocious youth. Sometimes, I fear, more precocious than Christian."

"Eminence?"

"You will recall, Adrian, it was I who recommended to your father that you be sent to the Benedictines in Normandy for your education. I have, recently, received a disturbing letter from Father Abbot."

"Eminence?"

"The abbot was puzzled you seem to have so few companions, and that on weekends you disappear from school—alone. He assigned a lay brother to follow you."

"And . . . to spy on me?"

"That was hardly his intention, beloved child. He was concerned for your safety. Now he is concerned—no more than I—for your soul."

As the Cardinal continued, Adrian sulked. "I know human nature," the Cardinal said, "and human needs, perhaps more intimately than you might expect. I might abide your consorting with prostitutes at Strasbourg Saint-Denis were you three or four years older. I would deplore it, wag my finger, but the sap of youth is painful to contain and secretly I would understand. But, Adrian, you are only sixteen! How old were you when you started?"

"Fourteen."

"Sweet Jesus."

"Nearly fifteen," Adrian protested.

"This stone bench is not a confessional. I cannot command your conscience or your will. I can warn you solemnly, and I shall. Vice, dear Adrian, especially in one so young, is not only dangerous but addictive. It not only coarsens but it kills. It will erode the finer parts of you, and it promises you a future of lonely desolation. That is merely for this life. As for the next . . ."

The Cardinal sighed, reluctant to go on. He said, "I have done my duty under God. We shall not speak of this again for two years. Will you . . . will you at least promise me to abstain from prostitutes till then?"

Adrian now saw not the Colosseum and the Arch of Constantine but the dark, squeezed streets of Straz-boor San-*nee,* where several evenings thence he had been intending to return to lie with a delicious girl, hardly older than himself, savoring her soft mounds and nooks languidly for several hours before he ejaculated. On the stone bench he turned to gaze at the Cardinal's head, all silver curls and crimson watered silk, nostrils flaring in the frigid wind, pale skin so tightly stretched across the cheekbones from a lifetime of self-denial, and he felt what in his childish heart he considered pity.

He answered, "No."

Early next day, by prearrangement, Cardinal Galsworthy came in full robes to Adrian's suite at the Hassler to conduct him in his limousine across the Tiber to the Apostolic Palace. However, he seemed uncertain and embarrassed. He said, "I have not slept. I passed the night in my chapel, praying, but I could not decide. Seeing you, beloved child, makes my decision obvious but no less hard. Forgive me, Adrian, but in the absence of your promise I cannot, in conscience, present you to His Holiness."

Adrian pretended to be indifferent. He stammered, "B-but the check . . ."

"Were it anyone else," the Cardinal continued, "I could have overlooked a private vice, yet I told the Holy Father that despite your extraordinary wealth you are a pure child. He is, believe me, my dearest friend. I will not deceive him."

"Won't he miss my check?"

In his scruples and frustration the Cardinal threw up his arms. Adrian, despite himself, began to play a game. He said, "I forget where I put it. In a drawer somewhere? Will Your Eminence help me look?"

What an odd chase ensued, as the Cardinal in his brilliant scarlet followed the adolescent Croesus in his blue double-breasted suit from room through gilded room, over Persian carpets and marble floors, past sculpted lions and busts of Roman emperors. "Not there . . . ," said Adrian pulling out drawers, ". . . nor there." By sleight of hand at last he found it, in a red damask salon, inside a Louis Quatorze table, beneath a Gobelin tapestry of Versailles in snow. He handed it to Cardinal Galsworthy.

"*Grazie, Adriano.*"

"*Prego, Eminenza.*"

The check was small by Northwood standards, two million dollars, payable to the Holy See, and cashed with dispatch. Before it was, Adrian flew out of Rome to Paris, where he repaired with haste to Straz-boor San-*nee*. He enjoyed his ejaculation . . . mildly. Thereafter until he finished his studies in Normandy he resented the Benedictines and as best he could avoided chapel, escaping to Paris whenever possible and the pleasures of Straz-boor San-*nee*. They were, he thought, pleasures still worth pursuit, but since his clash with Cardinal Galsworthy on the Colle Oppio somehow not the same.

In America, at The University, he continued to fornicate with miscellaneous slim-hipped sylphlike women, less often. The Cardinal's jeremiad haunted him. Vice, dear Adrian, is not only dangerous but addictive. It coarsens and it kills. It promises you a future of lonely desolation. Increasingly, he suffered postcoital sadness. Throughout his marriage, despite numerous temptations, he was loyal to Antonia. Now in an instant the Roman interlude in full detail flashed through him as he hovered above Susana on the bed of fronds and she kissed his stomach and he felt a tingling breeze blowing from the lagoon against his nakedness.

Again he craved the vast comfort, and again his dread of sadness in its wake, his mourning for his wife and son, his pride in his chastity as atonement, distant quaint notions of right and wrong, collided with his craving in the instant that came next. He craved also a vast detachment and ascended with his soul to another realm, floating above his flesh. Thus . . . no consummation: he watched his body roll violently across the fronds, away from Susana.

It astonished him that in that moment she turned away as well, languidly.

She cried to him across their bed of frond, "I couldn't because I love you, Feo."

He came to her shack next day pushing his wheelbarrow, loaded with cans of soup. He asked, "Darling Susana, what other little things of life might give you pleasure?"

She laughed and answered, "Will you pave my floor?"

Cement. He fetched his tools and cement. Susana helped him to move her sticks of furniture out of the shack, watched as he mixed the cement in his wheelbarrow and spread it on her earthen floor, but when evening came she went to her employment at Bar 69 and left Adrian alone to watch it dry.

Cement. Well after midnight, he moved the furniture onto the new floor and collapsed in exhaustion on Susana's bed. Lately his dysentery had bothered him again, and now his ribs and feet throbbed with such pain he wondered whether he might not best go north to seek medical treatment. On the table beside the kerosene lamp were some magazines he had ignored as he moved furniture; eager for distraction from his pain, he moved closer to the lamp and looked at them, all horror comics.

Puzzling. Susana never read anything, and he knew from her conversation that she hated horror films and horror comics. He turned the pages. Bats flapped human hands for wings; toads had the heads of choirboys; turtles grew the heads and breasts of beauty queens. A blonde sexpot hurled a lance through an oil portrait of the Devil, telling him to get out of her life. The Devil hopped out of the frame. Blonde: *"¡Regresa al infierno!"* The Devil: *"¡Maldita!"* He strangles her. Blonde: *"¡¡Aaaagghhhh!!"* The comics were really rather funny, not in the least frightening, but when Adrian heard a sound and glanced up at Susana's little window, his blood chilled. A face looked in—Lázaro's.

Adrian rose from Susana's bed, stumbling outside. Lázaro now stood at a distance from the shack, under a palm tree, poised to dash away, but seeing Adrian's painful gait, he lingered. Beyond the palms, just above the sea, appeared the glimmerings of dawn. Adrian paused to regard his prey. As ever, Lázaro was barefoot, wearing the black pants that drooped to his pubic hair; his tattooed torso was splashed with somber yellows and startling red. Adrian wondered, Has he been painting? Against the daylight, beneath the dying stars, taunting Adrian, leaping here, hopping there, Lázaro danced.

Ah, how he danced, as nimbly as Adrian had on the roof of the police brothel, swaying his hips, twirling, advancing, retreating, swinging side to side, rumba and tango and mariachi, singing nonsense and those lyrics about a single rose that grew on the far side of the moon. He opened his arms to Adrian as if inviting him to dance, howling *"¡Camiseta camiseta camiseta camiseta!"* T-shirt T-shirt T-shirt T-shirt! When Adrian approached him, he danced away, crying, "Come and catch me!" but Adrian tripped on a tree root and was too feeble for the chase.

Lázaro vanished through a palm thicket.

28

Susana returned presently to her shack and Adrian's bitter accusation that she had deceived him. "I didn't know Lázaro was about," she protested, "until last week. He begged me for some horror comics, so I went into Acalutla and bought them."

"Where is he hiding?" Adrian demanded.

"I'm . . . not sure." She pointed inland, over the tangle of trees. "Out there . . . in there . . . somewhere."

Adrian walked painfully to his motorboat, headed downriver toward the Río Diablo, gazing at the shores, the other craft, and the faces of fishermen. Near the confluence of the rivers he saw men in canoes headed toward the swamp and from a distance followed them, watching as they parted the curtains of liana and penetrated the jungle on little streams too narrow for his motorboat but navigable for canoes. On the morrow he returned with a canoe lashed to his motorboat, found a stream and paddled deep into the darkening thicket and found nothing but iguanas and snakes. Soon he ascended to the mountain and the refuge of Padre Pablo. "You have not found him?" the old man marveled. "I dreamed you did. I saw you, with your golden hair, standing in his little house, above the misty swamp. Did you go deep enough? Will it ever happen? Indeed it happened, in my dream. Hmmm, hmmm. Here are new herbs, to calm your bowels, and other herbs, to calm your soul."

"How may I thank you, Padre?"

"Will you pave my floor? Hmmm, hmmm."

Cement. The rains returned as Adrian paved the floors of Padre Pablo's rambling house. And as he worked, the old man followed him from room to room, telling all he knew of Lázaro. Adrian had heard other fragments from Susana, so between the humming witch doctor and the lovely whore he learned the history of his prey.

By now he could hardly learn too much of Lázaro, who fascinated him for reasons he had yet to fathom. Was Lázaro illumined by some hidden spark that Adrian envied because he could not see it? Was his quest of Lázaro propelled by some deep and unacknowledged wish to share his chaos?

29

Felipe Flores, Lázaro's father, was a policeman. He never married Lázaro's mother, Juana de Arco Faustino, but he lived with her for so long and sired so many of her children that to all appearances they were man and wife. Such irregular unions were common throughout Mexico; despite their admonishments, even the priests accepted them and baptized the issue. Indeed, before Felipe, Juana de Arco had borne other children by other men, but she had always coveted Felipe. Once she entered his bed, she became monogamous because she considered him her husband.

Felipe had no fortune, living from a pittance as a sergeant in San Antonio del Río's tiny constabulary and by such extortions from merchants and petty criminals as he could manage, but he did own a warren of muddy shacks off the little plaza. Felipe was a brawny man with the huge yellow teeth of a horse. Even before she knew him, Juana de Arco had begun to lose her teeth, but most of them were still rotting in her gums when their first child—Lázaro—was born.

Siblings followed at intervals rarely longer than a year; within some years the warren of shacks was overrun not only with Juana de Arco's children but with her sisters and brothers and sisters-in-law and brothers-in-law and their children also. They lived the kind of communism that only the early Christians practiced. All of their clothes they kept in a high cardboard box by the door that opened to the street. In going out, a child or an adult grabbed whatever garb he could; the first one up was the best dressed. Lázaro was beloved of that brood of siblings, above all by his mother, and no wonder: his nature seemed as lustrous as his raven eyes, his perfect teeth, his laughing smile, and the luxuriance of his curls. Such an angelic child!

No sooner could he talk, no sooner could he scrawl his name and read words in San Antonio's little school, than he showed his keen intelligence, outshining the other pupils and mastering books beyond his years. He was naturally religious, at bedtime reciting the Rosary with his mother, haunting the church to polish candlesticks and serve Mass in those days when San Antonio still had a priest. Then, because he adored his mother, and she needed money, when he was hardly eight or nine he found work with the village baker and started to sell bread.

Well before dawn, until hours later when he went to school, Lázaro would emerge from his shack, run barefoot beneath the stars along the dirt road to the other side of the plaza and the baker's ovens. Filling an old flour sack as big as he was, he lifted the burden to his back and wandered through the village and into the hills, crying "¡Pan! ¡Pan! ¡Pan!" climbing the muddy paths in rain or sunshine as day broke, knocking on rude doors, selling loaves of bread. By his bread he came to know everybody in the village, along the river, on the mountain, and the people loved him for his familiar hawking and merry smile.

At home, he had a gift for mimicry and making pictures. He mimicked this fishwife's walk, her husband's drunken ravings, to devilish perfection, sending his mother and Susana, his elder half-sister, into fits of laughter; yet his childish crayon pictures were special not for their fidelity to life but for their shocking blends of color and distortion. His houses were not ordinary dwellings; one wall sagged as the other soared, and he thatched the roofs with entangled blue snakes. Iguanas he colored orange, and turned their tails into burning candlesticks. His palm trees grew on icebergs.

On the mountain, Padre Pablo took a kindly interest in him, giving him herbs for his mother to soothe her toothaches and mixing paints from plant dyes to nourish his flair for pictures. The *curandero* led him down through groves of olive to the adobe shrine, where he watched as Lázaro, much like some Renaissance apprentice, painted his first Stations of the Cross. Padre Pablo was so pleased that he wrote to an acquaintance, Maestro Pío, who directed the little Academia del Arte at Tuxpan, near the sea many kilometers to the north.

Old Maestro Pío took his time, but within a year he visited the chapel and met Lázaro. He told Padre Pablo, "This child has no technique, he cannot draw, his taste for the bizarre invites disgust, but there is no question of his native talent." He turned to Lázaro, half his size: "Come to me in Tuxpan."

Within a fortnight Lázaro bought a bus ticket with his bread money and visited Maestro Pío at Tuxpan. The Academia del Arte was a ramshackle house on the blanched corniche, the boulevard that followed the wide river soon ending in the sea. The maestro took Lázaro to the roof; he wore a painter's smock, his white hair and beard were speckled like his palette, and he seemed wisdom itself. He said, "Look down there, child, at the water and the palms. That is the Mediterranean and the south of France . . . where I learned to paint. Could you love as I do the straight, neat palms, dividing the road with their whitewashed trunks? It is beautiful, but even better, it is orderly. That is what I shall teach you most: order. I have painted this scene so often. It is the south of France."

As he spoke the sun set, and in the rosy twilight the palm tops were invaded by flights of *tordos,* common black thrushes that perched on the branches and screeched in chorus, a sound so shrill that Maestro Pío shouted to be heard. "Imagine, Lázaro, one day you also will study in France. Imagine! You will love a pretty girl, she will break your heart, but your gift will console you and you will paint well. Imagine!" Lázaro was so happy that he hardly heard the maestro talk of money, but finally it was clear that beginning in the autumn, when he turned twelve, he would reside at the Academy for a tiny fee. "But, child, can you afford it?"

"I'll ask my father," Lázaro said.

However, when he returned to San Antonio, discussing tuition with his father proved to be untimely. Felipe had grown tired of

Juana de Arco, of her graying hair, her rolling fat, her rotting, toothless smile, and decided just then to abandon her for a younger, more svelte woman, with teeth. To his credit, Felipe's conduct in the matter was not wholly feckless. Before evicting Juana de Arco and her entire brood from his shacks off the little plaza, he troubled to find them a hovel of bamboo and thatch in a palm grove near the sea. The scene of the departure never left Lázaro.

Juana de Arco sat in the middle of the road, waving her arms, shaking with sobs, as her elder children haggled and fought with Felipe's sisters and brothers for possession of furniture, crockery, and clothes. The high cardboard box by the street door was ripped apart as children and adults tore at trousers and shoes, dresses and panties and T-shirts, Lázaro losing every shirt as his family kept little else. Too embarrassed to be present, Felipe in his policeman's uniform stood at the end of the road where it met the plaza, holding groceries with one arm, the other around the waist of Ester, his new woman. Lázaro raced down the road to spit on his boots and curse him, swearing oaths on God and the Devil that he would never forgive his father.

The village looked on as the banished woman and her children pushed a wooden cart with their bits of property down the dusty streets to the beach and their new, mean house. Juana de Arco crouched on the dirt floor, refusing food and drink and crying out "¡Felipe! ¡Felipe!" until, days later, her ducts ran dry and she had no more tears to shed.

Thereafter Felipe gave her nothing to feed the children; for months they ate whatever fish they caught, such coconuts as fell about the shack, and stale bread. For cash they relied on Lázaro's coins from the baker. Padre Pablo tried to help, giving Juana de Arco three goats and encouraging her to sell cheese. However, the yield was meager, customers were few, and the cheese business did not flourish. At dusk, Susana, only two years Lázaro's senior, drifted out of the shack and farther down the beach, where beneath other moonlit palms she fell into her commerce with men. Her mother, not stupid, knew soon enough why Susana began suddenly to bring home a few pesos, but even as she took the money, her daughter's debasement fed her grief.

It was not unusual for Lázaro—it might happen several times a day—to pass his father in the street. Though they never spoke, and Felipe tried to look away, with his eyes Lázaro burned the hair and flesh of his father's head. Within a year, Felipe's new woman gave birth to their first child, the occasion for another reproach. Whenever he encountered Ester carrying the child, Lázaro hissed. *Hssssssssss.* Walking backward, he preceded Ester down the street, hissing at her face in front of the village. *Hsssssssssssss.* He continued to go to school and sell bread, but after the abandonment he avoided the village church. More and more, whenever he could, he paddled a canoe down the Río San Antonio to the Río Diablo and the swamp, where for hour upon hour, for days when it was possible, he wept and fished for eels.

He loved the swamp because there he escaped and rejected forever the world as it was and inhabited the other world that had become, almost, his. Look down there, child. That swamp is the Mediterranean and the south of France. Imagine, Lázaro, one day you will study in France. Imagine! You will love a pretty girl in the south of France, and you will paint such beautiful pictures. Imagine! He was tempted to suicide, but distracted himself finally by building a tree house. It was a warped house, cradled by mangrove trunks, cobbled of leaves and driftwood, and deeper in the thicket than the dwellings of those other fugitives from life. Yet even that refuge could not console him only several months after he turned fifteen.

Suddenly, and not from any known disease, Juana de Arco died. When his mother entered her pinewood coffin, the child Lázaro died also and climbed into the coffin after her. He left his younger siblings to fend as they could under the care of aunts and drifted out of San Antonio, away from the river and the swamp, northward.

Upward through Papantla and Poza Rica he wandered, through Tampico and inland northwest to Xicoténcatl then south to San

Luis Potosí then northward again through Ciudad Victoria toward Monterrey. He lived by his wits, cadging meals, seeking menial jobs occasionally but compulsively moving on, stealing only to survive, aspiring vaguely ever northward. Unawares, he was joining those multitudes of Mexicans and peoples of the deeper south in their great migration toward the Rio Grande and (they were sure) a sweeter life. He was sixteen, nearly seventeen, when he reached the Rio Grande, the Río Bravo as Mexicans know it, at Reynuestro. Eventually he drifted downriver, almost to the sea, and stopped at Matablancos.

At once he was attracted to the railroad bridge, joining the legions of Mexican youths who have stolen into the United States above the barbed wire, suspended by their fingers from the high girders, swinging their bodies with the grace of monkeys and creeping inch by inch to the Promised Land. Before entering Paradise, high on the middle of the bridge, Lázaro always paused. At night, he was enchanted by the lights of Texas, by the neon glow of Amigoland, of K mart, Wal-Mart, Walgreens, of Boca Chica far beyond, and he loved the noise and spectacle of the human traffic beneath his feet, the trucks and automobiles bumping and honking across the bridge and the tides of naked men and boys beating on the other bank with their plastic bags. Lázaro haunted the highest girders of the bridge, thrust upward to those heights by some occult force when not busy down below with games of mischief. He became a river rat.

He began innocently, selling chewing gum and flowers on Gateway Bridge, but he fell among bad companions. Many of the youths and children who hung about the bridge sniffed glue. Lázaro enjoyed sniffing glue and paint from Coca-Cola cans because when he was dazed enough he forgot his hunger and soared above the mangrove branches of his tree house, above the girders of the railroad bridge, and his father never abandoned Juana de Arco and he never lost his T-shirts from the cardboard box and Susana never became a whore and his mother never died and in the rosy twilight the *tordos* screeched and with Maestro Pío he sailed for the south of France and he loved a pretty girl and became a famous painter.

Glue and paint punched holes the size of pins in the brains of many sniffers; they damaged the nerves, the membranes of the nose, the glands of the liver, depriving the mind of oxygen, turning the sniffers into twitching gnomes and rabbits who burrowed in the grass. Some addicts had better luck; over time, Lázaro's tissues developed a tolerance for the noxious toluene vapors, and they made him only moderately mad. Yet his eyes were red, the odor of his breath was foul, and he frightened off more ordinary people. His friends, such as they were, he met under bridges and in dismal bars, where he drank much beer.

Oh, those bars of Matablancos, throbbing with jobless youths, plagues of shoeshine boys, terrific heat and dense flies; yellowing posters of women's breasts and ceaseless yellow cheap Corona beer; soccer on the color television blaring from lumpy walls; men queuing in platoons to use the pissoirs and the stink of urine in the wet air; the violence of quarrels as night continued and finally flashing knives that dripped blood; and police with their drawn guns bursting in. For Lázaro it became a point of honor to clash with the police.

The police seemed as fond of Lázaro's company, arresting him often and confining him for brief periods or longer ones in the municipal prison off National Highway 101 or in the state penitentiary on Calle González. From his first exposure to prison life he was fascinated by the tattoos he saw on hardened criminals, and soon he was initiated into their cult. He became a votary of the Aztec Mass, submitting without murmur to the perforation of his flesh with fine and unclean needles, the rubbing in of inks of red and blue, resulting in grotesque displays. Over the years his torso became a panoply, hearts pierced with lances, the face of a toothless woman, a snake with a man's head wearing a visored cap, and intricate spiderwebs that laced his shoulders.

When not confined for brawling with the police or petty theft, often in the evenings Lázaro swam the river into Texas and hung out at Hope Park, where he got high on beer and glue with his chums of that place. Some companions lurked in bushes, leaping out with knives at other Mexicans or at hapless Central Americans emerging from the river, and occasionally Lázaro helped them rob. He stole reluctantly, only for food and pocket money, had pity for his victims, and at heart never considered himself a thief. He was loath to inflict violence, and never raped a woman or struck a child, lamenting that his chums lacked his scruples. On the Mexican side of the river, his chums vied with the police as thieves and rapists, but the police surpassed them.

The Mexican police and underworld so intersected that except for styles of dress they were the same. The police used such unfortunates as Lázaro as lookouts, pack animals, stool pigeons, releasing them from jail in exchange for future service and jailing them again at pleasure. At night, on the riverbank, they gave Lázaro a walkie-talkie; he spied on refugees creeping out of the brush, called in the police, then watched as they robbed the men, raped the women, and terrified the children. When the police ran marijuana or cocaine across the river, Lázaro was a mule. When they needed intelligence on drug trafficking they did not control, they sent him into the stinking bars and labyrinths he knew so well, with orders to sniff it out. Sometimes he free-lanced as a coyote, for humble fees leading refugees across the river to squalid motels in Downsville, displeasing the Mexican police. Smuggling bodies was another franchise they coveted for themselves and their allies in business: when Lázaro talked back to them and threw some punches, they returned him to the penitentiary.

In the penitentiary, Lázaro mingled with a cult of Satanists who had links to the police and who indeed claimed high officials of the police as votaries. Cocaine traffickers and thieves could hardly invoke God or His Virgin Mother for protection of their crimes, but they could invoke Satan, and they did. In the milling, sunny courtyard of the Center for Social Readaptation, Lázaro dabbled with paints occasionally; when the Satanists noticed his gift for the grotesque, they gave him a little money and commissioned some pictures.

Lucifer reigns over the universe of evil; he is the Privation of Good, the Deceiver of Mankind, the Prince of Chaos and of Darkness. He is the great Adversary, roving like a lion about the world, seeking souls to devour. However, he is not the only devil. Multitudes of lesser devils serve his cause. Like Satan, the lesser devils are fallen angels and distinct persons, each with his own character, tastes, and special odious tricks.

As in Heaven before they lost it, so in Hell the lesser devils are still divided strictly according to caste, having (as it were) their own commoners, knights, barons, counts, dukes, and royal dukes—retaining in the Inferno the same niches they held in the celestial hierarchy before the Fall. Thus in Hell the former angels and archangels are little devils, but the erstwhile Principalities and Powers, the Thrones and Dominations, are barons and counts, while the quondam Cherubim and Seraphim are dukes and royal dukes, wielding enormous force and ranking just below Prince Lucifer.

It was these myrmidons of Lucifer that the Satanists of the Center for Social Readaptation cultivated. They venerated especially the devils who personified the capital sins of Pride, Covetousness, Lust, Anger, Gluttony, Envy, and Sloth. They were madly fond of Mephisto of demonic legend, "a sort wandering in shadow, a mysterious kind of devil, dark through and through, malicious, restless, and stormy." Handing him their money, the Satanists told Lázaro to paint them pictures of demons they could worship.

Lázaro spent the money to buy glue; thus during the next days he was too absent from the world to do much work. He managed, as his trance receded, to paint the face of *Lujuria,* Lust. His Lust was not a conventional devil, only faintly anthropomorphic. Since he drew so haphazardly, his demon was not easily recognizable as the head of a horse, but it horrified enough. The eyes were green flames, and the beast's bridle of mottled eels tied chaotically together was bursting off. The nostrils were volcanic craters, spurting out not lava but a creamy fluid that resembled semen. The lips snarled, revealing teeth too big even for a horse, huge and yellow, inspired by his father's. The Satanists were enchanted.

So enchanted that they boasted about Lázaro, and when he was released from the penitentiary he was invited by strangers to a mysterious nocturnal ceremony at a luxurious ranch outside Reynuestro. He feared what he might see, but he was lured by the beauty of evil.

The ranch belonged, apparently, to a drug lord, boastfully rich. Jaguars and BMWs were parked in profusion outside the palatial house, its portico supported by Ionic columns the striped color of peppermint candy. Inside, the décor was as glossy, dominated, however, by enormous dark crucifixes and inverted crucifixes— cross, inverted cross; cross, inverted cross; cross, inverted cross. The bathrooms were half the size of soccer fields, paved with Siena marble and appointed with faucets of gold. During cocktails, police officials in blue uniforms embroidered with gold braid mingled with chic women, portly men in Hawaiian shirts, and youths with diamonds dangling from their pierced ears. Lázaro in his dirty jeans and T-shirt seemed out of place, but when his hosts handed him painting materials he understood. They wanted his artistic memorial of their ceremony, and encouraging him to be weird, they paid him with a chubby little packet of cocaine.

Immediately Lázaro withdrew to a marble bathroom and stuffed his nostrils with the demonic powder. Thus he was never wholly sure of what he witnessed or what he did during the hours that followed midnight. He would always vaguely recall a ceremony that seemed like a Mass. A fat man in a black chasuble and a black cowl stood before a black missal and burning black candles on a black marble altar, reading Latin prayers backward, never saying "good" but only "evil" and never "Christ" but only "Satan," interpolating elaborate blasphemies and curses. Eventually a young woman, naked but for the chains that bound her, writhed on the altar as the fat man threw off his vestments and ravished her. At Communion, the (stolen? consecrated?) hosts were liturgically white and unleavened, but the black chalice held wine the color and odor of urine.

Lázaro may not have painted his commissioned pictures, or he may have; as the other guests copulated on thick carpets and cold marble, men with women, women with women, men with the diamond-eared youths, Lázaro may not have torn off his own clothes and joined them, or he may have. It is certain he consumed much black-label whiskey and more cocaine, and that some hours after dawn he awoke in a ditch outside the locked gate of the ranch, rubbing his sore forehead. An abandoned truck stood there near the road, so he climbed into the cabin and looked at the mirror. He had been tattooed again, now—on either extremity of his forehead—with bright blue inverted crosses.

Lázaro felt ashamed and guilty. He had passed too many bedtime hours reciting the Rosary at Juana de Arco's knee, too many mornings polishing candlesticks and serving Mass in his village church, not to retain some reverence for the faith of his childhood. Branded on his face for the part he took in blasphemy, he saw at once in his misfortune the angry and vengeful hand of God. He sat at the roadside, possessed by remorse, sobbing. "O Jesus! O Holy Virgin of Guadalupe! O Mother of God! Mother of God!"

He stood up, swearing oaths to repent, to reform his ways, resolving that he would never return to the wickedness of his life in Matablancos.

On the road, trucks roared by. He stuck out his thumb. Finally a truck stopped. Lázaro headed south, toward San Antonio del Río.

In his village, a typhoon had destroyed the adobe church: the roof had fallen on the priest as he tried to save the Sacrament, and San Antonio had been without a padre ever since. Desperate to confess himself, Lázaro rushed to the mountain, praying that a make-believe priest might do.

When he saw Lázaro, Padre Pablo uttered a groan of shock. He asked, "Oh, Lázaro, where is the child? Where is the lovely child who painted the saints in my chapel? When you left us, you were an angel. You have returned to us a devil." From the swinging bed and the back rooms, *la señora* and Padre Pablo's daughters emerged, keening sorrow at the sight of the blue crosses upside-down on Lázaro's forehead and the spiderwebs that crept out of his T-shirt onto his arms. The daughters cried, "But he's so *ugly!*"

Lázaro knelt at Padre Pablo's feet, confessing all his iniquity and crimes, begging mercy and absolution.

"¡Ay perdone, padre, ay perdone!" Forgive me, Father, forgive me, for I have sinned!

The padre prayed over him for days, then used all his craft to remove Lázaro's inverted crosses.

For over a week he subjected him to crude bloodlettings, injections of herb and plant dyes, bleached saffron from safflowers especially, in his struggle to blanch out the brands on Lázaro's forehead. As he worked he said, "Hmmm, hmmm, hmmm," soothing Lázaro's troubled spirit and strengthening his resolve to lead a nobler life. The operations were not a complete success. The inverted crosses, though much fainter, remained permanently visible.

Lázaro embraced the padre, descended the mountain, and withdrew to the swamp. He enlarged his tree house, and—with chalks and plant dyes that Padre Pablo had given to him—painted new pictures of the saints. One day, on a visit to San Antonio to buy a few provisions, in a dusty road near the constabulary, he encountered his father.

Felipe, too, was different. He had lost much of his brawn, turned gray, shrunken. On the mountain, Lázaro had been told that Ester did to Felipe at sunset what Felipe had done to Juana de Arco at high noon. Piqued by his failing powers, one day Ester disappeared from San Antonio with all of their children. Now Felipe lived only with his sisters in his shacks.

Father and son faced each other across the road. Felipe opened his arms, not finding words to speak, and moved toward Lázaro. The son hesitated, as though trapped in a crucial instant of choice, the kind of instant not often given to unhappy souls yet enabling them to decide between love and lasting bitterness. Felipe smiled, just a bit, but enough to reveal his immense equine teeth. Lázaro said, "Hsssssssssssss."

He returned to Matablancos. He had missed the glow and the high girders of the railway bridge, but once back in the realm of the Rio Grande he did not wholly revert to wickedness. He sniffed less glue and drank more beer and cheap brandy. He worked occasionally, becoming a fair mechanic. He struggled to avoid his old chums among the river rats and the police, though he missed the thrills of that life if not the constant violent treachery. When he was drunk, ever more often, he resumed his brawls with the police, and the police resumed throwing him in jail. He became, for no reason he tried to fathom, fond of donkeys.

In the years that followed, he ventured back and forth, back and forth, between Matablancos and his distant village. At Matablancos according to his means he would buy or steal a donkey, ride it south a hundred miles to San Fernando or La Joya, then release it on a grassy field or give it to a stranger. At San Antonio del Río, he fished or shrimped alone from a canoe or paddled into the swamp to add levels to his tree house. The bridge, the village, and the swamp became his haunts. Eventually his half-sister Susana followed him from San Antonio to Matablancos, causing him new sorrow.

Deep in Lázaro, not only during his spasms of repentance, the leavings of goodness dwelt. In childhood, before Felipe abandoned Juana de Arco and before Susana entered adolescence, she and Lázaro had been close. They swam together, fished together, collected fallen coconuts together, kept house together, recited the Rosary together, attended Mass together, sang together, danced together, laughed together, wept together, bathed together, and chastely shared the same bed.

At Matablancos, Lázaro descended to his knees to implore Susana to stay out of the police brothel, but once she undertook the work he went there often to skulk about and shield her from harm. When she smoked marijuana, he was shocked! On another spree of repentance, yearning to set a good example, he reduced his drinking and found a job making windshield wipers.

Again, he came to nothing. He was consoled on the railway bridge, sitting high above the river on the girders, swinging his legs, drinking Corona beer, throwing his empty bottles at policemen, not minding when they drew their guns. Look down there, child. That is the Mediterranean . . . the south of France . . .

30

In finer weather, Adrian resumed paddling through the swamp, more deeply than before, without result. On the mountain, Padre Pablo decreed, "There is only one thing to be done. Lázaro is lost. We must ask Saint Anthony of Padua to find him."

Adrian knew St. Anthony as the heavenly tracer of lost objects, not of missing persons, but he was desperate. He said, "*Oremus.*"

"A simple prayer might fail," said the old man, twinkling. "I've noticed it never hurts to flatter a saint, or to storm Heaven in his name. We need something extra. Hmmm, hmmm, hmmm. A . . . procession!"

Adrian supposed that a few goatherds and their women might appear for the ceremony on the mountainside next evening, but he underestimated the cult of St. Anthony and his own charisma. By now everybody between the mountain and the sea knew of Adrian, and if none had paid him for paving their muddy floors, for tending their sick children, for giving them medicines and food, yet in their poverty they were moved and grateful. In the morning, *la señora* mentioned the ceremony to a few souls; by sunset, San Antonio del Río and the hamlets of the mountain emptied as the populace swarmed to Padre Pablo's adobe shrine.

The padre descended from his cliff vested as a bishop, not only in his soutane with the purple trimmings but wearing a tilting miter, a shabby cope, and gripping a wooden staff shaped like a corkscrew. He was attended by women and children with burning candles,

followed by men bearing on their shoulders flower-strewn plat-
forms with life-sized statues of the Virgin of Guadalupe and of St.
Anthony of Padua holding the Infant Child, followed by a choir
of forty boys singing hymns.

Señor, Señor, ten piedad,
  ten piedad de nosotros.
Señor, Señor, ten piedad,
  ten piedad de nosotros.

Lord, Lord, take pity,
  take pity on us.
Lord, Lord, take pity,
  take pity on us.

From the cliff, more boys sounded sour trumpets and ignited
noisy firecrackers. The white chapel was far too small to hold so
many; Padre Pablo climbed a wobbly ladder to the roof and
preached to the multitude.

". . . and we know, dear children, from the miracles of his life,
that if we beseech Saint Anthony and storm Heaven with a thousand prayers, ten thousand prayers, a million prayers, he will in-
tercede before the throne of God, uttering the names of Lázaro
and of our dear Don Adriano a thousand times, ten thousand times,
a million times, until at last it will be decided in the great and busy
heart of God that Lázaro—our own beloved Lázaro—will cease
to be lost and shall suddenly be found. How well you know Saint
Anthony, dear children, how deep and burning is your devotion.
How well you know his holy titles—Confessor of the Church, Ark
of the Testament, Hammer of Heretics! How well you know his
holy miracles—his sermon to the fish at Rimini; his mule that knelt
before the Blessed Sacrament; the Child Jesus cradled in his arms;
his recovery of his stolen Psalter by the pointing hand of God!
Hmmm, hmmm. Look, dear children, at Saint Anthony as he holds
the Infant Child. Pray, dear children, pray and weep. Pray, pray,
pray, to Saint Anthony of Padua, storm Heaven and Saint Anthony
of Padua, that Lázaro, our lost lamb Lázaro, shall suddenly be

found! Hmmm, hmmm, hmmm. Pray a thousand prayers, ten thousand prayers, a million prayers . . ."

By now night had descended, and the crowd had grown so fervent that it wept and swayed, unable to remain in a single place. En masse it moved higher, up the side of the mountain, toward the very top. Men and children took hold of Adrian, forcing him to stand on the moving platform beside St. Anthony, and he responded in their spirit by kissing the saint's face. The mountainside became a rising river of blazing candles as the sour trumpets blared, more firecrackers burst, and together the faithful and the choir sang.

Señor, Señor, ten piedad,
ten piedad de nosotros.
Señor, Señor, ten piedad,
ten piedad de nosotros.

Upward they groped through myrtle and olive groves, through sparser evergreen and through chill, until they reached the summit of the mountain. By then the people had forgotten Adrian as they released their own sorrows, begged their own favors, but he hardly cared. Below, he saw the lamps of San Antonio and Acalutla; above, the terrifying brilliance of the stars. As the people wept and shouted, knelt and waved their arms, he felt a palpable communion between earth and Heaven. A young man, whom he knew as a client of Susana's at Bar 69, hugged and hugged the life-sized statue of the Virgin as though she breathed, then bent and kissed her feet. The young man wept and shouted, "Hail Holy Queen, Mother of Mercy, our life, our sweetness, and our hope!"

"Our life, our sweetness, and our hope!" the people wept and responded. "To thee do we cry, poor banished children of Eve, to thee do we send up our sighs, mourning and weeping in this valley of tears!"

t dawn, Adrian returned to the Río Diablo. As he paddled in the tiny tributaries of the swamp through the barriers of vine and frond, a voice called down at him, "Lazar-O! Lazar-O! Lazar-O!" He glanced at the ceiling of trees: on a branch sat a child, whom he recognized from the village. The urchin screeched, "Lazar-O! Lazar-O! Lazar-O!" Adrian thought, Ah, those idiot children.

San Antonio del Río was full of them, the issue of inbred matings, of cousins coupling with first cousins and uncles with their nieces, inevitable in a village so remote from the rest of the common run. This urchin was one of many who had taunted Adrian behind his wheelbarrow in the road, hurling mud and stones, shouting "Lazar-O! Lazar-O! Lazar-O!" His body was misshapen and his face unfinished, with a left eye too close to his ear, the right ear almost an orifice of his neck. However, clad only in swimming trunks, he swung from his branch with the poise of a chimpanzee. It occurred to Adrian that in the swamp this child, also, had found a sanctuary. Adrian gazed up at the idiot and asked, "*¿Quién eres tu, niño?*" Who are you, child?

The child could not hear or he was largely mute, saving his gift of speech for his next outburst of "Lazar-O! Lazar-O! Lazar-O!" Suddenly, as much like a bird as a chimpanzee, he took off, flying from branch to branch, vine to vine, far above the swamp, pausing now and then to look back at Adrian. He took a reverse turn, down a canal so hidden behind drooping foliage that hitherto it had escaped Adrian's eye. In his canoe, Adrian kept paddling, following the child through obstacles of vegetation nearly to exhaustion, venturing deeper into the morass than he had ever done.

The idiot led him to a more open space, less dense with liana and plant, and, as the stream dwindled, less of a swamp. Adrian moored his canoe and walked over a floor of fallen logs toward a thicket of mangrove. At its edge, cradled between trunks, was a tree house.

A ladder woven of vines led up to it, but before climbing he looked about. Not a soul in sight, unless he counted the idiot child, not a child really but an eerie thrush, a dark angel silent now and flying high away into the thicket. Adrian mounted the ladder.

The house had several levels, but in his fatigue he stopped at the first, falling to the bamboo floor short of breath and gripping his painful ribs. The room was warped, with one wall higher than the other three, apparently a sort of bedchamber. How deeply—how enviously—Adrian admired Lázaro's frugal sense of life, an asceticism of the barest bones he had of late aspired to himself. Like his hovel in Matablancos, this space of Lázaro's was nearly empty, save for a sleeping mat of thatched leaves, a snapshot of Susana, and a neat pile of horror comics.

Adrian climbed the ladder to the next level, its driftwood walls loftier and more colorful. Was this Lázaro's *gallery*? Pinned everywhere on the walls were paintings. Here were several of Adrian's rustic pictures, his bridge pictures of the flower sellers, his railway children in boxcars with their bulging eyes, and several of his Stations of the Cross. He wondered, Where is my pearl, the head of St. Francis?

Beside each of Adrian's paintings hung a similar picture that Lázaro evidently had painted with his own hand. Adrian gazed at these, compounded from what he knew were the dyes of nature and applied on canvases that seemed to be of goatskin. All of the pictures clearly were traced from Adrian's originals, Lázaro's way of compensating for his lack of technique, of imposing on his own haphazard gift an unwonted order. Yet it was his choice of color that made the pictures different and gave them a new life.

From the dyes of swamp plants, the colored juices of fruits, berries, leaves, flowers, roots, and fish, from mixtures of iguana urine and mosslike lichens, Lázaro had transformed Adrian's paler creations. His tints of indigo, of Tyrian purple, of saffron and of crimson madder, he had juxtaposed in such a way as to make them startling but not grotesque. The desperation of his flower sellers and boxcar children, the tears running down the women of Jerusalem's cheeks, the agony of Simon of Cyrene lifting the burden of the Cross, were more poignant in Lázaro's pictures than in Adrian's. Instantly Adrian saw this, even as he was burned by such flames of innate talent so superior to his own.

He heard feet scuffling down a ladder from above: when he turned to look, there, crouching in the narrow door, smiling just a little, was Lázaro. He wore only his odious jeans; in the early light his torso with its tattoos and spatterings of paint shone brightly, and he crooked an arm around a bundle of canvases rolled up and neatly bound. He said, "I saw you coming."

"Your pictures are beautiful, Lázaro."

"I can't draw, Don Adriano."

"I wish I'd painted them."

" . . ."

"¿Cómo?"

"You look sick, Don Adriano."

"I've suffered, Lázaro, because of you."

"La camiseta."

"I'll give you a thousand T-shirts."

Adrian took off his own and held it out to Lázaro, who refused it with a sneer across his goateed ravaged face. Adrian continued, "I'll send you to an art academy. My head of Saint Francis may be as fine as your pictures. Give me my painting of the head, and blessings will follow."

"Want to see my studio?"

He motioned Adrian to climb the ladder of vine to the next level, but as he did, Lázaro beneath him leaped down in the other direction. The early sun had risen to the treetops, still not thirsty enough to drink the mist that lingered on the jungle floor. Dancing in mist that reached his knees, hugging his bundle of paintings, Lázaro withdrew into the mangrove labyrinth.

Adrian explored the rest of the tree house and left it bearing rolls of Lázaro's pictures—the only art, he thought, worth saving.

32

Sadly he climbed the mountain, but Padre Pablo was in no state to console him. The *curandero* lay ill with lumbago on the swinging bed, unable to heal himself, his señora and the daughters standing over him, banging pots and pans.

He said, "Oh, oh. I fear sleep. I have a terror of my sleep. I have told the señora and my daughters to bang their pots and pans and never to let me sleep. Oh, oh. I dream too much of Lázaro."

Adrian asked, "Where is he?"

"In water and blood? Does he drown, in water and blood? I do not wish to know. Has he left us? Did I see him bleeding on a white bed? I did! Indeed I hope I did not! Has he left us? Will he leave us? Oh, oh, oh. Should I ever have disturbed Saint Anthony of Padua? . . ."

In haste, Adrian decided to leave San Antonio del Río. As he threw his meager things into his cardboard suitcase, Arcadio and his brothers and sisters and the children and the maiden aunts assembled outside his shack, crying and begging him to stay. He stuffed much money into a flimsy envelope, passed it to the maiden aunts. He said, "For medicines. For any sick child between the mountain and the sea. It should last much time."

This was Saturday afternoon, and because on Saturdays she began her work early, he hurried next to Bar 69 to bid farewell to Susana, who was smoking marijuana and not quite lucid. She said,

". . . word yesterday from the *jefe* . . . not coming for me . . . coming for me? . . ."

Heedless of her fears, he asked, "Have you seen Lázaro?"

"Have you seen the *jefe*?"

"What did he say?"

"I'm . . . not sure."

"Ah. Has he gone back to Matablancos?"

"Has who?"

She had put away her lovely dress of pastel cotton, soft blue and creamy white, tulips and butterflies printed on it, and reverted to the dreary denim that she wore when she worked at the police brothel. Her auburn hair still fell in languid tresses across her shoulders, but her skin though ever smooth seemed more cynical at the mouth, while the drug made her green eyes swim. The drug did not appear to soothe her nerves. She acted like a nervous cat, touching everything in sight, knocking over glasses of her fake sparkling wine, running to the jukebox to play the song about the single rose that grew on the far side of the moon, tiring of it instantly and pulling out the plug. She returned to sit at Adrian's table and said, ". . . don't know . . . don't know what to do . . . silly me . . . silly you . . . you're so *deaf*, Feo . . . Will the *jefe* come? Maybe he won't come? Is it too late, Feo?"

The disjointed nature of their conversation was compounded by the frequent interruptions of impatient young men demanding to be serviced. In the middle of syllables Susana vanished from the table, then soon emerged from the back room to light another stub of marijuana and resume her recital of fear and nonsense. ". . . said he'd kill me . . . sure he'll kill me . . . loved his sunglasses? . . . oh, that sleeveless jacket? . . . he'll never show his face. Tell me it's a dream, Feo."

"A dream, Susana."

"Do I feel better?"

She got up, joined the youths flipping the rods and figurines of *futbolito*, played the record about the rose that blossomed on the moon, withdrew again to the back room, rejoined Adrian at his table. He said, "Darling Susana, leave this life."

"It's too late," she said.

"This instant," Adrian insisted. "Get out of here. Go to Tuxpan, or San Luis Potosí. You love beautiful icons and churches. Puebla is full of them. Go there? Go far away, to Baja California, where nobody knows you? No matter where, go. Do you want a dress shop? I'll buy you one. Do you want a restaurant? I'll buy you one. Do you want . . ."

"Poor Feo . . . filthy rich . . ."

"Dishonorably, disgracefully, blasphemously rich. My wealth is like the worms inside my bowels—the more I purge them, the more they breed. The more I spend, the more I have. The more . . ."

"What would I do with a restaurant?"

"Better, anyway, than you're doing now? I've still a lot of cash, here in my suitcase. You can have it."

"I can't take your money, Feo."

"Darling Susana, why?"

"You're not a client."

"Mother of God! A whore's honor?"

"A whore's choice. Isn't it all too late, Feo? . . . *jefe*'s coming . . . *jefe* coming? . . . wherever I go? He'll find me."

"I'll hide you. Smile, Susana, nod your head, and I shall see that it's done. I'll buy you a little house . . ."

" . . . "

"*¿Cómo?*"

" . . . "

An older gentleman—uglier and drunker than the rest—approached the table. Susana withdrew with him into the back room.

Adrian fled.

At the estuary he put his cardboard suitcase and the bundle of Lázaro's paintings into his motorboat and headed upriver. The news of his medical benefaction had spread instantly through San Antonio, and at the sight of him departing the people of the village rushed to the riverbank to wave him farewell and shed tears of loss. "*¡No vaya, Don Adriano, no vaya!*" Don't go! don't go! they cried out to him. Idiot children clustered beneath coconut palms, chanting, "Lazar-O! Lazar-O! Lazar-O!" He passed men, women, and children hip-deep in high reeds dredging for shrimp and blue crabs, passed the misty confluence of the Río San Antonio and the Río Diablo. His voyage became a film played backward as he glided by the Totonac ruins infested with turkey vultures and glanced at the cloudless sky and saw soaring formations of ivory doves. At Acalutla, he gave away his motorboat to the first fisherman he met.

At daylight, he boarded a bus for Matablancos. From experience he had faith in Padre Pablo's dreams and prophecies, and he believed that he would finally seize Lázaro in another pool of water and blood or wounded on a white bed. He hoped as well that somehow he would at last retrieve his head of St. Francis, divided vertically into halves, youthful, insouciant, shadowy, disenchanted, blue eyes gazing heavenward, childishness and wisdom, innocence and darkness side by side. Yet he wondered, was he as compelled now to possess the head of Francis as to pursue the chase of Lázaro for its own sake? After Tuxpan, the landscape became another film in reverse as gradually the green lagoons dissolved and the mountains of mauve and velvet vanished and the land grew utterly flat as it became the valley of the Rio Grande. On the bus, Adrian dozed and dreamed.

His jellyfish returned, dancing in slow motion with toads who had the heads of choirboys. In his sunglasses and sleeveless jacket, a knife in his hand, the *jefe* entered Bar 69, and the back room, looking for Susana, sighing. . . .

33

That evening, Adrian reached Matablancos. He left his suitcase and the rolls of Lázaro's paintings in a locker at the bus station and hurried by taxi to the railway bridge. As Lázaro had so often done, he surmounted the torn fence and broken barriers of barbed wire and climbed the girders to the top of the bridge.

The wind was cool. The lights of Amigoland not far away and of Boca Chica much beyond could hardly hold for him the same enchantment that it held for Lázaro and multitudes of other Mexicans, but for an instant Adrian was as dazzled and for half an instant he joined the cult and imagined that indeed God lived just across the Rio Grande. The wind was cool: hinting of a change of season and the beginning of the valley's brief winter. Just beneath him, the ceaseless boys were hanging by their fingers from the girders and with cries and grunts swinging their bodies into the United States. Deeper beneath him, another huge migration was in progress across the crooked stream, but tonight the naked men coughed and shivered in the chilling breeze. Several drunks and glue sniffers shared the summit of the bridge with Adrian, but not Lázaro.

Adrian persevered. During the next days he took a mean room in downtown Matablancos, but at night he rarely slept there, crouching instead in high grass near the railway bridge or climbing it again to look for Lázaro. He revisited Lázaro's old hovel on Calle Córdoba, but it was inhabited by hubcaps and smooth tires.

In the alleys off Calle Abasolo he trudged from bar to urine-stinking bar, asking questions. ". . . and has a Mickey Mouse watch? Drops the watch into his beer? I owe him money." A bartender: "He was here a few nights ago."

Still Lázaro eluded him. Adrian kept his faith in Padre Pablo's dreams and prophecies, but as he slept fitfully in the grass his own dreams blended with the prophet's in a sort of celestial pool. He saw the future more and more distinctly. The image of Lázaro's body, bleeding on a white bed, began to blot out all others.

Adrian knew that if Lázaro lay wounded and bleeding he might be brought to the notorious emergency room of the *Hospital General*. He thought, I'll add the hospital to my nightly rounds. Next evening, he walked along Avenida Canales onto the grounds of the hospital and to the door of the emergency ward. A guard told him, "You can't come in here."

The guard was young and good-looking, with thick hair and a thin mustache as trim as his black uniform. He bore no gun, but as Adrian persisted he reached into his trouser pocket, taking out a red lollipop.

"Ah," said Adrian, "you like lollipops."

"Love them."

"May I have one?"

"I've run out."

"What's your name?"

"Victor."

Adrian withdrew, trudging along Avenida Canales looking for a grocery, finding none, and finally happening on a pharmacy that sold lollipops. He bought several boxes and, laden with them, returned to the hospital and Victor's astonished smile. Victor said, "Pass."

For nights thereafter Adrian became a familiar presence in the emergency ward. It was a large, bright, white room with mats of black plastic and sheets of grayish white and metal beds with the yellow paint chipping off, run by interns and nurses who were mostly young women, oddly. A room so awash with blood might otherwise be the reserve of men, and this one resembled a butcher shop. The sirens of distant ambulances approaching provided a mood of permanent foreboding, a sort of contrapuntal music for the horrors already present. The patients were predominantly the human remnants of car wrecks, and young punks with knife and bullet wounds.

The punks were covered with tattoos: snakes, daggers, skulls, hearts, dragons, birds, women, and JESUS. They were dispatched not only from the bars and streets but from the penitentiary, which commonly furnished the hospital with young men whose faces had been mangled by jagged glass bottles. Ears and noses dangled from bloody heads; eyes were half gouged out; knife stabbings produced violent convulsions. Adrian helped the women to lift bodies from the stretchers to the beds, so often that eventually his clothes were caked with blood. An old cleaning woman made her constant rounds, but she had only a mop and bucket, paper towels and bars of brown soap, thus Adrian on subsequent evenings appeared with new mops and buckets, sponges and bottles of disinfectant, to help her scrub, looking forward to it.

The hospital was desperate for equipment, needing not only mops and disinfectants but antibiotics, beds, pillows, and even sheets. In the emergency room the sterilizer regularly broke down, and the women worked with unsanitary tools. At times they had to cope with such quantities of blood they dumped it in the wash-basin. Yet they coped valiantly, hooking the bodies to intravenous solutions, draining bullet and stab wounds of water and blood, bandaging them tenderly, soothing traumas, and saving many lives. During pauses in the carnage, they ate. From a local cafeteria everlasting boys in white shirts and black pants filed through the swinging doors bearing tin trays laden with tacos, enchiladas, soda pop, cakes with green frosting, and a local delicacy, *frijoles refritos,* refried beans. The women rarely had time to finish their feasts before the carnage resumed. They told Adrian, "You should see us on Saturday night."

Matablancos became a madhouse on Saturday night. Young men emerged from their grubby jobs eager to throw away their meager wages and thirsting for beer, sex, and violence. Adrian began the

evening by visiting the throbbing bars in the alleys off Calle Abasolo, enduring again the pestilential shoeshine boys and the putrid
air that stank of urine and Corona beer. From the bars he walked
to the railway bridge, troubled by a disturbance.

A dozen river rats were swinging from the girders, drinking beer
and hurling their empty cans and bottles at vehicles and pedestrians
below. The naval police screeched up in squad cars, stopping traffic
on the bridge; placing wooden barriers about, they drew their guns.
Among the vagrants on the girders was a shirtless, screaming man,
but the police kept people at a distance, and Adrian could not be
certain he had seen his prey. The police allowed little time for
obscenities and threats, firing at the vagrants almost at once. In
the disorder a pair of bodies fell directly to the pavement, but the
shirtless man sang and twirled and danced a little while atop the
girders before more shots rang out and he staggered and plunged
into the river.

Amid the cheers of other spectators and the contrapuntal wail
of approaching sirens, Adrian had no further doubt. All dreams
and prophecies were fulfilled. Without waiting for the ambulances,
he hurried to the hospital and the women in the emergency ward.
Soon the bodies were brought in. Two of them were dead, but
Lázaro was alive.

Adrian lifted him from his stretcher onto a metal bed. Lázaro
had received a bullet that entered through his upper stomach and
fled through his back. As the women removed the medics' bandages,
the holes seemed so small and clean that Adrian had hope. The
women were swift, hooking Lázaro to bottles and machines and
with little scissors cutting away his clotted black pants. A policeman
with a notebook entered.

Policeman (rather fat): "Who is he?"

Victor (prince of lollipops): "He has no papers."

Adrian (offering the bloody rags): "Do you want his pants?"

The policeman declined them and left. Lázaro writhed on the
white-gray sheets, whimpering with pain, conscious one moment,
comatose the next. He wore filthy white briefs, stained at the crotch

with blood. The women cut off the briefs and shaved his body. He
gazed at Adrian and smiled.

"Maestro . . ."

"Dear Lázaro . . ."

"Are you disappointed with me?"

"No, Lázaro, I loved the chase."

"Maestro . . ."

"Where is the head of Saint Francis?"

"I'll ask my father."

He regressed to his stupor, but as his body writhed Adrian marveled at the snakes and birds tattooed to his buttocks. The women
shaved away his pubic hair, revealing more tattoos around his
phallus—cross, inverted cross; cross, inverted cross; cross, inverted
cross. They retracted his prepuce, smearing away clotted blood and
covering the glans and the remainder of his genitalia with a liquid
the color of mustard. Then they eased a plastic tube up the canal
of his phallus until it stopped inside his viscera. Fresh blood pumped
out. They kept tossing away bloody plastic gloves onto the next
bed.

A surgeon walked in. He said, "I see cases like his every night.
I'll save him." Victor, sucking his lollipop, was not so sure. He
said, "*Problemático.*" As Lázaro was wheeled toward the operating
chamber, Adrian ran along the linoleum corridor, pleading with
the surgeon for admittance. "You haven't the proper clothes," the
surgeon said. "Danger of infection." Adrian returned to the emergency room, sitting in a wooden chair, dozing a little as the swinging
doors opened and the boys in black pants entered bearing their
cakes with green frosting and bowls of refried beans. He was only
half awake when the surgeon appeared from the operating chamber
and asked Victor for a lollipop.

"His intestines were like a battlefield," distantly he heard the
surgeon saying. "The liver and the kidneys were blown to bits. A
dum-dum bullet. *Se murió.* Thanks for the lollipop."

Se murió. In slow motion Adrian saw the dum-dum in its metal
jacket with the hollow point cleanly penetrating Lázaro's torso,

waiting patiently until it reached the center of his intestines, exploding, and as cleanly departing through his back. *Se murió.* He's dead. Adrian asked Victor, "Where have they put him?"

"In the coroner's laboratory," said Victor.

He led Adrian down long linoleum corridors to the cleanest room in that hospital, all cement and stainless steel. Lázaro was laid out on a cement block, wrapped in a shroud of blue plastic, neatly bound with white tape and a tag that said *"Desconocido"*—Unknown. His bare feet stuck out.

Adrian sighed. "I'll say some prayers. Will you join me, Victor?"

"I'm superstitious," Victor answered. "I'll wait in the corridor."

Alone with Lázaro, Adrian repeated fragments of his father's funeral Mass, reciting the old liturgy in Latin. *Sed libera nos a malo . . . a porta inferi.* Soon he was in his vaulted chapel, beneath the painting of St. Michael Archangel banishing Lucifer from Heaven. He saw Cardinal Galsworthy in his black chasuble, the bishops in their purple, the priests and monsignori with thuribles of burning incense and blazing candles. Mozart's *Requiem* grew so loud that when the choir and orchestra sang the Dies Irae he raised his hands to shield his ears. *Dies irae, dies illa, Solvet saeclum in favilla: Teste David cum Sibylla . . .* Too frightened to continue, he mumbled, *"Requiescat in pace,"* and ended the funeral. Leaning over, he kissed both of Lázaro's cold feet. Victor crept in, sucking his lollipop.

"Why did you kiss his feet?" Victor asked.

"He liked my pictures," Adrian said.

Well after midnight, Adrian walked from the hospital down Avenida Canales to Calle Uno and the bus station, where he retrieved his cardboard suitcase and Lázaro's paintings. He had left his linen and some T-shirts in his harsh hotel room not far away, but he was too tired to fetch them. He strode directly from the bus station up Calle Uno, through chilling gusts of wind across the Gateway Bridge, and into the United States.

PART VIII

Snow

34

And yet . . . Adrian John Northwood had not quite finished his passage through the Kingdom of the Poor.

He had spent so much time in Mexico absorbed by his futile quest that he seldom thought of his friends on the other side of the Rio Grande—or of his refuge, the Casa San Francisco. Do you remember only faintly the faces of his beloved?

Do you remember Dianita, his baby daughter, she of the chiseled features and noble head; Alejandro, the angelic adolescent, once a guerrilla in the mountains of El Salvador; Rodrigo, the robust and ungrammatical paladin of the Border Patrol; and Miss Rice, the semiliterate television starlet who yearned for Adrian's body and ended up helping in the cafeteria? You easily remember Mr. Ennis, Mr. Burner IV's servile emissary, hardly one of the beloved.

Collectively the beloved were shocked by Adrian's gaunt, shaggy appearance and his fitful deafness, but blithely he refused to reveal the causes. Dianita, much grown and beginning to crawl about, clung to Alejandro and Miss Rice, hardly recognizing her father, consenting to his hugs and kisses only after several days. The Casa San Francisco housed hundreds of refugees, as thronged as it ever had been.

In his barrack rooms, devotedly put in order by Alejandro, Adrian found an accumulation of letters from his mother. In a frenzy he tore them open, as eager for Diana's written word as other men craved wine.

■   ■   ■

... and as the weeks pass I am more and more desolate, bewildered by your silence and fearful that you have fallen into harm. Have you any *notion* of my suffering? Have you any *notion* of how often my hand has picked up the telephone, dialed your number, and at the last instant hung up, ever obedient to my vow that we shall the two of us remain children of past centuries and communicate only by the written word?

Given your unyielding silence and refusal to come home, I have fulfilled my previous warnings and dismissed four respectively of elderly domestic and equestrian staff, with adequate pensions drawn on our joint account No. 3. I shall continue this policy and each month dismiss two respectively of domestic and equestrian staff until you return to Northwood Hall.

Since declaring his bankruptcy, your brother Pius has moved out of his apartment on the East Side and into two squalid rooms in Queens. (I enclose his new address, not that you care.) He does not enjoy poverty and now advises me that he intends to return to Northwood Hall to live and to establish a brokerage business in his rooms. He has begged me for a loan to buy computers, "fax" (?) machines, and suchlike to install in his library, and I am inclined to oblige him. He will probably invite clients to pass weekends, since he believes that the surroundings will impress them. I think that Pius may have bested you at last, since not even you, dear Adrian, can refuse your impecunious little brother the refuge of Northwood Hall.

Maude, dear thing, is on the point of death. . . .

■   ■   ■

There was also a letter from Cardinal Galsworthy.

■   ■   ■

. . . and puzzled by your recent silence. I assume that you have been enmeshed in some adventure, and pray that you have explored its depths. Or are your *sublime* follies yet to come? At last I have a title for my meditation on St. Francis—*A Fool for Christ.* . . .

. . .

Adrian wrote at once to his mother, mentioning nothing of Mexico, assuring her of his safety, and forbidding her to discharge more servants from Northwood Hall. In his reply to Cardinal Galsworthy, he said much about Mexico, devoting plentiful detail to his mystical experience in the Hole at Reynuestro. He wrote also to the address in Queens.

> Brother,
>   This is sent on the condition that you conduct your business in New York City and not at Northwood Hall.
>   Toujours ton frère,
>
> ADRIAN
>
> Enclosure.

He wondered, Where is my checkbook? He opened the drawer of his table and found it straightaway, neatly placed by Alejandro above a packet of financial statements. He wrote a check to Pius for two million dollars, enclosed it with his note, then walked to the main post office in Downsville and mailed it along with his letters to Diana and Cardinal Galsworthy.

And do you remember Jody Corn, the screaming redneck—and Mrs. Sebastian Bean, the richest woman in Texas? Jody and his rough companions continued to spy on Casa San Francisco from their nearby tower and to harass the refuge with grass fires, which since Adrian's return proved harder to contain. Mrs. Bean's attorneys were outmaneuvering Mr. Burner IV's hired barristers in federal court, finally convincing a judge that the Casa San Francisco was not a true religious sanctuary and winning his edict to shut it down.

"Most regrettable," fussed Mr. Ennis, wiping his fashion eyeglasses. "Most unfortunate, most unforeseen, and—if I may say so, sir—I am personally quite sad."

"Won't Burner IV appeal?" Adrian demanded.

"He is by no means certain that an appeal would be practicable."

"He must do something!"

"Why, sir, he has already moved heaven and earth. Meanwhile—we have, lamentably, no doubt of this—the government will act."

That evening, Rodrigo visited Adrian and ruefully confided that his superiors in the Border Patrol had assigned him to lead a raid on the refuge, at dawn. Adrian protested, "Rodrigo, you can't."

"I got no choice." In his starched olive and polished boots, he was more muscular and splendid than he had ever seemed, a tribune of the state. "I'm a *federal officer,* Ay-jay."

"A higher calling than our friendship? If you do this, I'll drop you—your own words, Rodrigo—like a hot brick."

Next morning, Rodrigo at their head, a dozen Border Patrol agents drew up in rusty green vans, penetrated the ragged fence, crossed the neat lawns into the cafeteria, the dormitories, and the unfinished chapel of the Casa San Francisco. The operation was humane and mostly symbolic. Never drawing their guns, the agents swept through the refuge, politely asking for documents that no alien could produce. They arrested fifty Central Americans, all single adult men, leaving families whole. Lacking space in their detention rooms and camps, they seemed loath to arrest more. Rodrigo's face was grave, his demeanor, as ever when he was at work, detached and cool. He unhitched his walkie-talkie.

"Nine-sixty-six. Six-oh-six."

"Go ahead, six-oh-six."

"Fifty OTMs interrogated, Casa San Francisco. Documentation negative. Detained."

"Proceed with detainees to station for processing, six-oh-six."

"Proceeding as instructed, nine-sixty-six."

When the agents had locked the aliens inside the vans, Rodrigo walked back across the lawn toward Adrian.

"Ay-jay?"

"We ain't talkin', Rodrigo."

"I wanted to tell you somethin'." He seemed suddenly short of breath. "I'm—I'm shippin' out of Downsville." He offered his hand, but Adrian turned his back. Minutes later, when Adrian looked in that direction, the vans were filing down the boulevard and Rodrigo was gone.

Jody Corn had much increased his gang of rough companions. They gathered in ever-growing numbers in the next meadow, beneath his wooden tower, cursing, swilling beer from cans, and playing, on their huge stereo luggage, deafening country music. Some wore T-shirts—6-WHEEL ROLLERS, POPS OF PARK RIDGE, BORN IN THE USA!—but despite the cool breezes as many wore no shirts at all beneath their blue overalls or were naked to the waist save for suspenders that held up their pants or colorful tattoos that covered their arms and chests. Each day, more skinheads joined them.

These were ugly youths with acne-pocked faces and shaven heads and tattoos on their arms of American flags, skulls, bones, and swastikas. From pointed metal poles they waved Confederate flags and black-and-red flags with the Iron Cross and swastika and another banner, HITLER YOUTH. In the mornings, they marched in military drills to the edge of the shelter's lawns, raised their right arms stiffly, and shouted, "*Sig Heil!*" In the evenings, they encircled the shelter from the river to the boulevard, wearing steel-toed boots and waving torches.

One midnight, as the refuge slept, the Hitler Youth invaded the grounds with bullhorns, shouting, "Scum! Filth! Subversives!" Adrian rose from bed, ran to his window. The thugs marched down the gravel paths, brandishing beneath their blazing torches an armory of clubs, knives, and prickly chains. "Dogs! Lice! Communists!" In the wake of the storm troopers curious stragglers followed, rednecks in blue overalls, young men in T-shirts and suspenders, some wearing headphones, others sharing with the world the melodies that blared from their stereo boxes.

> It's only a river
> That's not so deep or wide
> A boy can throw a stone across
> And reach the other side.

"Whores! Cockroaches! Terrorists!" Several of the thugs carried jerry cans.

> It's just a muddy water
> Cuttin' through the land
> But a man can make a dream come true
> Just across the Rio Grande.

They sprinkled gasoline about, touched torches to it, and set fire to the wooden chapel.

> Sometimes it seems
> Like God must live
> Just across the Rio Grande.

In their stupidity the thugs forgot to cut the telephone lines, so in response to Adrian's call firemen and police came quickly. The chapel was largely consumed, but the rest of the refuge was spared. As the fire raged, young men of the shelter clashed with the thugs, the battle yielding a noisy mixture of blunt instruments, sharp instruments, entangled bodies, bloody heads and limbs, but no loss of life. No human life! Do you remember Prince, Adrian's beloved horse? The thugs invaded the stable and sliced his throat. In the morning, many of the aliens with children fled. Adrian remained, but he moved some of his possessions, and Dianita and Alejandro, to Motel 5½, miles away near Boca Chica boulevard.

The guards and police did as best they could, the Border Patrol tried to help, but at odd times during the days that followed, the Hitler Youth resumed their lightning raids in force. Within a fortnight, much of the Casa San Francisco—the dormitories, the cafeteria, the dispensary, Adrian's own barrack—was a smoking ruin. Many aliens dispersed to distant meadows and the gutters of the city to sleep, defecate, and beg. Adrian, happy that he owned Motel 5½, housed dozens of the refugees in its humble rooms. The Border Patrol harassed them, and soon most were arrested or they drifted away, aspiring northward.

———

In his room at Motel 5½, wishing to record the disaster, Adrian resumed the foolscap pages of his University Essay. The loss of his refuge was too painful, and he wrote but fragments. A recurrent phrase: "Another failure!"

"You haven't done too badly," I told him.

"Leave me alone," he mourned.

Adrian shifted in his chair, leaning to the floor to unroll and gaze at Lázaro's paintings. I said, "You had so many of your own. Where are they?"

"I let them burn."

"You told me once, 'There are victories beyond art.'"

"Did I ever really believe that?"

"Your deeds say so," I answered. "Amidst so much evil, you have practiced every corporal work of mercy. You've fed the hungry, refreshed the thirsty, clothed the naked, sheltered the homeless, tended the sick, visited the imprisoned, and—a bit too often!— buried the dead. You bought a lot of lollipops. You laid so much cement."

"All for myself."

"Who cares?"

"Don't you?" asked Adrian.

"That depends on your future. Your fortune . . ."

"I've thought constantly of that. I'll give away my fortune, but I can't give up Northwood Hall."

"But you can't have Northwood Hall unless you keep your fortune."

"That's my riddle."

"Somewhere I said—do you remember?—that if you covet the Kingdom of Heaven, then go, sell all you possess, give the money to the poor, and . . ."

"But I have Heaven—Northwood Hall."

"That's blasphemous."

"It's at least a colony of Heaven. Could I renounce my galleries? My gardens? My Greek statues? My woods? Could I give up my books?"

" 'And when the young man heard this word, he went away sad, for he had great possessions.' You're such a coward!"

"You're such a phantom!"

"What will you wager?"

"Are you the voice of God—or a madness inside my head?"

Adrian's dysentery waxed and waned. His ribs and feet still hurt. Miss Rice, tending him in bed, touched the wrinkles of pain around his eyes. When he got up, he shaved off his beard, had his hair cut, and thought, *I shall return to Northwood Hall.*

He had no mind to make the journey by himself. He knew that leaving the valley with baby Dianita and Alejandro would be difficult. Dianita had been born in Texas, but Adrian lacked proof. Alejandro had no papers and no rights. Adrian felt a debt as well toward several other aliens who had served him with devotion since the day he built his refuge by the river.

From his travels throughout the valley with Rodrigo, he knew every snare the government had put in place to entrap the undocumented. If he ventured with his aliens from Downsville to the Border Patrol's last checkpoint on the highway at Sarita, he would be recognized and the aliens would be seized. If he drove a car, it would be confiscated and he would risk imprisonment for transporting them. If he drove a truck, the agents would crawl through it with sniffing dogs seeking bodies in hidden nooks. If he tried to walk around the checkpoint with his charges, they might step on a ground sensor, and the results would be as harsh. The Patrol monitored all flights from Downsville Airport.

Multitudes of aliens had fled the valley by hopping trains. Many had been caught, but the Border Patrol was harassed and undermanned, and most escaped. The road to liberty, Adrian concluded, was by train. But how, by train? He could hardly subject his children to a sealed boxcar or ride with them beneath one, clinging to the iron bars.

He had heard recently of an unusual escape by rail that ended tragically. Some Mexican peasants were sealed inside a truck trailer being carried northward on a railway flatcar. Unhappily, the car was left to idle in the sun, the Mexicans could not break out, and they baked to death. Adrian thought, If I do it well, a trailer on a flatcar is our surest means of flight.

He assumed it would be expensive, and it saddened him that— so often when he had a problem—he bought his way out. Moreover, he was mildly unhappy to be breaking laws. He rationalized —summoning from eighteenth-century theology probabilist pretexts for dubious behavior, spinning in his mind neat little syllogisms that urged him to do as he intended. 1. We should resist unjust laws. 2. But, this law is unjust. 3. *Ergo,* we must break it. *Lex dubia non obligat!*

Do you remember the junkyard, the immense cemetery of wrecks and tires, rusty machinery, old cement mixers, TRASHED? Do you remember the junk dealer?

"*Chinga,*" the junk dealer asked, "what happen to you? You the same rich guy?"

"Lost a little weight," said Adrian.

"You oughta lay off drugs."

"Ha-ha! I need your help."

"Another truck?"

"A trailer."

"*Chinga.* It'll cost you."

In detail, Adrian explained his needs, paid the junk dealer much cash, and returned to Motel 5½ to prepare further for his journey. Miss Rice was there and made a scene. She said, "I'm coming with you, AJ."

Adrian was embarrassed. His mother would be cool enough to Alejandro and little Dianita; she would never welcome a half-educated media woman to Northwood Hall. As he groped for words, Miss Rice insisted. "You're my family," she said. "It would be horrid not seeing you, but I couldn't live without Dianita and Alejandro. You're my family." Amid her tears he promised, "I'll think about it."

On the afternoon of his departure, Adrian visited the environs of the river for the last time.

At Amigoland, as he paused in the parking lot watching bourgeois Mexicans and new Americans pour out of the shopping palaces heaped with Japanese gadgets and processed food, a cold drizzle began to fall. Hunching in his flimsy nylon jacket, he crossed the highway, over damp meadows past the radio tower, to the ruins of his Casa San Francisco. New refugees squatted beneath its charred beams, with their huddled bodies sheltering their children against the drizzle as they struggled to light campfires.

Adrian descended through the gray reeds to the river's edge. The drizzle turned to a lashing rain. Yet even in the rain, as ever several dauntless children swung from the girders of the railway bridge, crying out encouragements to each other as they groped toward Heaven. Adrian doubted he would pass this way again, but he knew with certainty that the inexorable darkness of the Rio Grande would flow through him always.

Could he ever forget the addicted child, FUNKY COLD? In the rain he looked about, his eye resting on the other shore where FUNKY COLD had cursed him and vanished into Mexico, then to the radio tower and the meadow where he escaped finally.

As Adrian had dozed on the bus between the south and Matablancos, FUNKY COLD had entered that dream: Adrian watched him die. He died just over there, across the river, in the Zona Zur near the police brothel, among the cement blocks and tilting wooden houses and other doomed glue children. His addiction had destroyed all feeling in his legs, one day he woke to find he could not walk, and it was thus that he expired, crawling about on his hands and stomach, in a phosphorescent trance of delight and starvation.

Again Adrian wondered of FUNKY COLD, as he did of Lázaro, What did I want from them? In seeking them did I crave a communion with their nothingness in order to achieve my own? Was it envy of them or just a new adventure? *Nothingness?* In the penitentiary yonder when I had to beg to eat, in the Hole at Reynuestro when I floated, didn't I come close to nothingness? Hmmm, hmmm, hmmm. He turned his back on the river and walked in the rain toward his motel, humming. The rain began to mix with snow.

"Hmmm, hmmm, hmmm. Hmmm, hmmm, hmmm. Hmmm, hmmm, hmmm."

At Motel 5½, as he packed his things, he decided to take only his linen, his papers, and Lázaro's paintings.

He fingered through the pictures now, humbled by the vagabond's talent and stabbed by mourning. The flower sellers and the boxcar children, the distraught women of Jerusalem, Simon of Cyrene grappling with the Cross, shone with a lyrical imagination conceived in centuries of unconscious time, honed in the suffering of a single man, and hurled at the eye in sensuous indigos and crimsons sucked from a Mexican swamp.

It was nearing dark, and time to leave. Adrian's traveling companions assembled in his room—to make a party of eight. In walked Alejandro holding Dianita; Baco, the Salvadoran guerrilla; Octavio, the Nicaraguan guerrilla; two Guatemalan women . . . and Miss Rice.

From the beginning Baco and Octavio had protected the refuge with their fists and clubs; both bore old bullet wounds that would not heal, and they had fought with ferocity against the Hitler Youth. The Guatemalan women, as penniless as the guerrillas, had long tended Dianita and scrubbed the dispensary on their hands and knees. The guerrillas would work in Northwood Stables, the women in the kitchen of the great house, replacing domestics whom Diana had pensioned.

Loyalty to devoted helpers was a hallowed Northwood law; upon that principle Adrian overcame his qualms and invited Miss Rice to join his adventure. The rain had washed off her make-up, reddened the acne on her cheekbones, and as she faced Adrian now she looked like a frightened child. Alejandro, his seraphic countenance made ruddy by the cold, his brown eyes on fire with excitement, struggled to be calm and pretended—as Baco and Octavio did—that their clandestine flight northward would be like any guerrilla operation. Dianita was special. She had to be drugged.

Wherever he had traveled in the world—walking through the

tunnels of the Paris Métro, up the Spanish Steps, down the tumid streets of Cairo—Adrian had noticed that women who begged carried sleeping infants. They needed the children to arouse pity, but they drugged them to keep them quiet. Sadly, Adrian did the same to Dianita, feeding her a glass of milk laced with phenobarbital and Valium. When her noble head slept, he wrapped her in blankets, and the party went out, shivering in their jackets, into the cold night.

Miss Rice drove Alejandro and Dianita in Adrian's junky car; Adrian followed in his rusty truck with Baco, Octavio, and the Guatemalan women, past the neon glare up Boca Chica boulevard until the junkyard, where the dealer waited. Adrian gave him back the car and truck, and—as snow fell—the party entered a long trailer from beneath, through a trapdoor.

Inside, the trailer was packed with crates of tomatoes consigned to Houston, but near the front, above the trapdoor, a space had been reserved for the secret passengers. The conveniences of the journey were Spartan—on the floor some plastic mats, a large flashlight, boxes of cookies, bottles of water, and a plastic portable toilet. Tiny ducts had been punched into the trapdoor to assure a supply of air.

From experience Adrian knew that the Border Patrol seldom penetrated a sealed boxcar or a trailer unless the agents saw something amiss, had some reason to suspect hidden aliens or drugs. The rear doors of the trailer had been shut on the outside and sealed with heavy chains secured by a padlock. Unless the agents heard a human sound, crept beneath the trailer with sniffing dogs and with flashlights detected the nearly invisible trapdoor, Adrian and his fugitives would be free.

He switched off his flashlight, reminding all to be silent whenever the train should slow down or stop. In total darkness the fugitives obeyed him as a truck pulled the trailer out of the junkyard and they bumped down Boca Chica toward the yards of the Southern Pacific railroad, farther west. There they waited at least an hour before they heard loud machinery lifting the trailer, and it came to rest upon a flatcar.

Another hour, a whistle sound, and the train pulled slowly out. Freight trains such as these normally numbered one hundred, two hundred cars, making thorough search impossible and increasing Adrian's confidence. The train sped north toward the great yards of Harlingen, thirty miles thence. At Harlingen, as it idled, Adrian heard a human tide, the shuffling of feet, the odd phrase in Spanish, the muffled cries of children, aliens rushing out of sheds and abandoned buildings he knew were there to jump aboard the train, clambering to the tops of boxcars and grain gondolas, forcing open doors, burrowing beneath the undersides of cars to ride on boards and metal bars between the wheels. Walkie-talkies followed them, radio static, the calm, unrelenting voices of Border Patrol agents communicating in English, spotting now this alien, now another, yanking them from their nooks and crannies, and the contrapuntal cries in Spanish of men and women pleading to be freed.

Amid the tumult dogs approached, sniffing no doubt for hidden bodies and causing the huddled bodies within the trailer to freeze with terror; Adrian cuddled Dianita, rejoicing that she slept on. The wind shrieked, possibly disorienting the senses of the dogs, and though barking now and then as they passed the trailer, they did not linger. Finally the dogs and voices drifted off. The train moved.

It gathered speed. Adrian turned on his flashlight, telling his companions to be cheerful, as he served them cookies. Wind buffeted the trailer ferociously; the breath of his companions became vapor in the flashlight's beam, and all trembled in the deepening cold. Adrian opened the trapdoor a crack; the snow beneath was dense, and flakes flew in. Another sixty miles or so, and they would reach Sarita, the valley's last checkpoint. If they passed that, they would roll on to Victoria, two hundred miles to the north, where as always the train would pause and they would descend through the trapdoor, free. Adrian thought of the past and the future.

He thought of Northwood Hall, as he did so rising from the cold and snow and floating above the rose-red castle of towers and chimneys, descending into courtyards, strolling through galleries, emerging into formal gardens garnished by urns and Greek statues and thence into woods thronged with brooks and singing birds . . . all his. He gamboled with Dianita on the lawns; the sky seemed as blue with byse as the color of his walls.

When Dianita grew, she like Alejandro would attend stern schools to learn languages, literature, and music. When she blossomed as a young woman, waltzes would waft across the lawns on summer evenings as she danced at balls with a young man who would break her heart. From a stairway or a balcony Adrian would watch her, if he lived that long.

He was not sure he would. Once Dianita was settled with a governess and Alejandro attended school, once physicians had healed Adrian's ribs and bowels and repaired his hearing, he would be leaving Northwood Hall again. How he loved his home, but on the river and in Mexico he had embraced a deeper passion. The poor were more interesting, more alluring, and thus more glamorous than the rich; he envied them as much as any vagabond could envy him; not even his mother could dissuade him from resuming his romance. Weren't multitudes starving in the dust of Africa; weren't famines and epidemics raging to the east and south; were not children perishing in Peru? His romance had barely begun.

Well after midnight, the train slowed as it approached the final checkpoint at Sarita. Adrian flicked off his flashlight, commanding silence.

Our mystical billionaire prayed silently, O Lord, unless you are a phantom, let us pass.

The train stopped. The wind roared, hammering the walls of the trailer and howling at the snow with such anger that flakes shot through the air ducts. From a distance a dog barked, and men speaking English ran along the tracks.

Soon enough the sounds of Spanish as more men and women were yanked from crannies between the wheels and they and children cried out for mercy from man and God. Some agents stood near Adrian's trailer, conversing by walkie-talkie: one of them leaped onto the flatcar. Dianita stirred, wetting her diapers, crying. With his cold hand, Adrian covered her tiny mouth; she writhed, and he feared he might smother her as he struggled to keep her silent. The agent spoke.

"Nine-sixty-six. Nine-sixty-six?"

"Nine-sixty-six."

"Six-oh-six."

"Go ahead, six-oh-six."

"Fifteen aliens detained, night train."

Adrian thought he recognized Rodrigo's voice, but in the wind he could not be sure. He ached to hug Rodrigo, to beg forgiveness for having turned his back on their uncommon friendship.

"Complete search, six-oh-six."

"It's so f——ing cold, nine-sixty-six."

"Proceed with detainees to station, six-oh-six."

"Proceeding as instructed, nine-sixty-six."

Adrian heard a pair of boots thump to the ground. The train crept forward, gathering speed at last, and when it was swift he flicked on his flashlight. Alejandro's eyes shimmered; Miss Rice giggled; Baco and Octavio sang a song of martial victory; the Guatemalan women wept with thanksgiving. Dianita fussed, whimpering as she had when Adrian drew her from the whore's womb.

Alejandro said, " . . ."

Miss Rice said, " . . ."

Adrian murmured, "Northwood Hall."

In Texas
In Mexico
In the North
1989–1992

ABOUT THE AUTHOR

Edward R. F. Sheehan has led a varied life as a journalist, diplomat, novelist, academic, and dramatist. He was a foreign correspondent for *The Boston Globe,* then press officer at the United States embassies in Cairo and Beirut. He has contributed to leading American and international publications, including *The New York Times* and *The New York Review of Books,* from Europe, Africa, the Middle East, and Central America. In 1973, he won the Overseas Press Club Award for distinguished interpretation of foreign affairs. As a Fellow at the Center for International Affairs at Harvard from 1974 to 1978, he founded and chaired the prestigious Middle East Seminar.

Mr. Sheehan's play *Kingdoms* was produced at the Kennedy Center in Washington and at the Cort Theatre on Broadway. The eminent critic Clive Barnes named it one of the Best Plays of 1981. In 1989, of Mr. Sheehan's *Agony in the Garden,* Jonathan Kirsch wrote in *The Los Angeles Times:* "A brilliant if eccentric book—truly I will never read another headline about Central America without recalling Mr. Sheehan's dreamlike images of beggar and whore, jungle fighter and revolutionary, torture chamber and cathedral."